CHRISTMAS AT THE LITTLE BOOKSHOP BY THE SEA

ELIZA J SCOTT

Storm

Ebook ISBN: 978-1-80508-737-3
Paperback ISBN: 978-1-80508-739-7

Cover design: Rose Cooper
Cover images: Shutterstock

Published by Storm Publishing.
For further information, visit:
www.stormpublishing.co

ALSO BY ELIZA J SCOTT

To my wonderful editor, Kate Gilby Smith, who sowed the seed for this book. Thank you so much, Kate xxx

ONE

SUNDAY 3RD DECEMBER

Dusk was creeping in over Micklewick Bay, slowly swallowing the crisp blue skies of earlier, the first stars twinkling in the evening sky. Frost sparkled in the glow of the vintage street-lamps that lined the stylish square of shops, adding to the festive atmosphere of the Victorian seaside town on the North Yorkshire Coast.

It had been a busy week at The Happy Hartes Bookshop, which was just how thirty-three-year-old Florrie Appleton liked it. It was the first Sunday in December, the bookshop was closed for the day, and she and her boyfriend and business partner Ed Harte had spent the bulk of that time decorating the shop while singing along to jaunty Christmas songs. Gerty, the resident black Labrador, had "assisted" by running off with the odd Christmas tree bauble when she thought no one was looking, secreting them in her bed to nibble on later. She'd perfected her "it wasn't me" expression, which made Florrie and Ed hoot with laughter.

Florrie climbed down from the ladder, pushed up her glasses and took a step back. A thrill rippled through her as she admired the luxurious garlands she'd spent the last couple of hours stringing above the bookcases along to the counter. Her arms ached with all the reaching and stretching, and her cheeks were flushed from exertion, but she didn't mind one jot. As far as she was concerned these garlands, trimmed with the most adorable miniature books and threaded with fairy lights, were totally worth the effort and the considerable expense. Florrie had fallen in love with them as soon as she'd set eyes on them, and had bought enough to decorate the little cottage she shared with Ed, too – whenever the couple had a spare minute to decorate their own home.

To say Florrie was in a festive mood would be an understatement. She loved Christmas and, in particular, she loved Christmas at The Happy Hartes Bookshop. She'd been a regular customer ever since she was a small child when the then owners, Mr and Mrs Harte – who were also Ed's grandparents – would dress the generously proportioned bow windows of the double-fronted shop with fake snow and plump snowmen. Mrs H never did things by half-measures, especially when it came to glitter; in those days, the whole shop had been doused in a liberal dusting, even Mr H himself, much to his amusement.

'All kiddies love twinkly, sparkly things, especially at Christmastime; makes it extra magical, lovey,' Mrs H had said to Florrie, in her first year as The Happy Hartes' Saturday girl, she remembered with a smile.

Florrie would never forget the thrill of peering in at the bookshop's window display as a child, her glasses on the end of her reddened nose, her brown eyes lit up with wonder. But the excitement hadn't stopped there. Once inside, the evocative smell of books would curl around her nose while she waited to see Father Christmas in his grotto at the back of the shop. She could remember her excitement building as she inched closer to the front, holding tightly onto her mum's hand, her little heart beating quickly in her chest. It had been utterly magical, and she'd treasured those memories to this day.

'Right, that's all done.' Ed's voice pulled her out of her reminiscences as he eased himself out of the window, dusting glitter off his hands, creating a sparkly cloud around him. Dressed in faded jeans and a grey slogan T-shirt that showed his muscular arms to their best advantage, he flashed Florrie a wide grin, making her heart leap. Gerty jumped up from her bed by the counter and trotted over, wagging her tail happily. Ed bent to ruffle the Labrador's ears. 'All right, Gerty-Girl?'

'Is it finished?' Florrie asked. Her insides were bubbling with excitement. No one had been allowed even the tiniest of peeks at his progress on the Christmas window displays; he'd kept his festive-themed creations hidden away behind strategically hung curtains. The secrecy had only served to increase Florrie's curiosity – and that of the bookshop's loyal clientele. It had even generated chatter on the town's social media pages, with guesses as to the theme ranging from snow scenes to a giant Father Christmas complete with reindeer, and everything Christmas-related in between. The speculation had amused the couple no end.

'Yep, it's all finished. And now,' Ed said in a dramatic stage voice, his grin growing wider as his navy-blue eyes crinkled, 'it's time for the moment of truth.'

His words sent a thrill cascading through Florrie as she made her way over the shop floor towards him. She felt like she was six years old all over again.

'Want to take a look?' He pushed his dark, floppy fringe off his face, revealing more than a little sprinkling of glitter.

She gave a happy smile. 'Are you kidding? I've been waiting for you to ask that all day!'

Brimming with anticipation, Florrie peered through the gap Ed had made in the curtain at the side of the first window. She gasped with delight as she took in the wintry woodland scene before her. 'Oh, Ed!' It could have been plucked straight from a Christmas fairy tale. She could almost smell the frosty air. Overwhelmed with emotion, Florrie felt her throat tighten. 'It's *beautiful*,' she said, her voice a whisper. She envisaged herself gazing upon it as a small girl, her imagination whisking her off on all sorts of adventures with the woodland animals that would come to life when no one else was looking.

'You like it?' Ed asked from the other side of the curtain, a hint of uncertainty in his tone, his North Yorkshire accent a softer version of Florrie's and the other locals of Micklewick Bay.

'I *love* it, Ed – it's perfect,' she said, her voice cracking. 'It's even better than your autumn displays, and I thought they'd take some beating.'

'You really think so?' Ed was his own worst critic and seemed oblivious to his talents. Florrie regularly reminded herself that it was no wonder he thought that way with such cold, distant and critical parents. They were the polar opposite of her own, who were warm-hearted and loving, keen to support in any way they could.

'I do. It's wonderful,' Florrie said, the threat of tears abating.

'I'm glad you like it,' he said, his voice lifting with happiness and more than a hint of relief.

'I defy anyone not to.'

'Ah, I nearly forgot. Stay where you are, one tick.' Ed reached behind him and a moment or two of shuffling ensued. 'Fingers crossed it works – I haven't tried it all out together yet.' He flicked a switch.

Florrie watched, a thrill dancing through her as the scene came to life. 'Oh, wow!' There was so much to look at. 'How on earth did you do all of this? It's *amazing*! Everyone's going to love it. In fact, there's no way I'm going to be able to get any more work done now, I just want to spend the rest of the day gazing at it.'

With an unimpressed sigh, Gerty ambled her way back to her bed where she flopped down and rested her head on her paws. Ed laughed at her distinct lack of interest. 'I'm not so sure Gerty would agree with you.'

Reluctantly, Florrie pulled herself away from the festive display. She turned to Ed who, at six-feet-four, towered above her petite five-feet-two. He was wearing a wide smile, his eyes shining happily. Florrie's heart squeezed with love for him. She stood on her tiptoes and pressed a kiss to his lips, delighting in the soft warmth she found there. 'How do you even *do* these things?'

'Ah, trade secrets.' He slipped his arms around her waist, pulling her close. 'Actually, the truth is, I used to help out with displays at an art gallery near to where I lived in London; picked up a few tips while I was there. Had no idea they'd come in handy later.'

'Well, I'm glad The Happy Hartes Bookshop is benefitting from your skills.' The couple had taken over the shop eighteen months before. Since then, Ed's creative window displays had become legendary, helping to increase the bookshop's once-flagging sales.

'Me too, though I'd hardly call them skills.'

'Stop selling yourself short, Ed,' Florrie said softly. 'And don't underestimate how much pleasure your window displays are going to give people this Christmas, and I don't just mean kids. Someone could be having a rough day, and when they walk by the bookshop's windows, I reckon their mood will be lifted in an instant by your handiwork.'

'That's a nice thought.' He gave a modest smile before bending and kissing her softly, triggering a fizz in her stomach.

Florrie tipped her head back, resting her hands on his solid chest. 'Now I understand why you kept disappearing to the shed. This must've taken you hours, and there must be glitter *everywhere*!' She made a split-second decision not to mention that she'd also noticed him sneaking up to the attic in their cottage when he thought she wasn't looking. Many of her favourite reads were stored up there, so she made frequent trips herself, but she'd not seen any evidence of what he'd been up to, except that some of his storage boxes had been disturbed. It had set her mind wondering, but she hadn't liked to ask what he was up to, or looking for, for fear of sounding like she was keeping tabs on him.

'I can't deny I've loved every minute. And you're not wrong about the glitter, the shed's sparkling at the moment, but don't worry, I'll clean it up.' Smiling down at her, he stole another quick kiss. 'Ready to see the second window?'

'Am I *ever*? Though I don't know how you're going to match the winter wonderland I've just seen.' She pushed thoughts of his trips to the attic out of her mind, telling herself now wasn't the time to dwell on them.

He laughed, releasing her from his embrace. 'Well, let's hope you won't be disappointed.'

'Are you kidding? I know I'm going to love it!' She followed him over to the other side of the shop, enjoying the view of his broad back, his muscles visible from beneath his T-shirt.

Reaching the window, Ed held the curtain back, allowing Florrie to peer in. She clapped her hands to her cheeks.

'Oh, wow! There's so much to take in!' She laughed with delight. 'It's just wonderful, Ed!'

'One second.' Again, he leant back and pressed a switch. 'There we are.'

Once more Florrie looked on in awe as Ed's handiwork came alive.

'Any good?' he asked. 'Please tell me everything's working.' There was uncertainty in his voice again.

'It's just... Oh my goodness! It's just *breathtaking*, Ed. We're going to have queues forming on the pavement outside so people can take a look.'

Ed laughed. 'As long as some of the folk from the queues pop in and do a spot of shopping, I won't be complaining.'

Several long minutes passed before Florrie was finally able to tear her eyes away from the display that featured a vintage-style sitting room dressed for Christmas. It oozed an air of nostalgia and cosiness. She eased herself out from behind the curtain and flung her arms around him. 'You're amazing!' she said, covering him with more kisses and making him laugh.

'I'm not sure about that, but I'll take as many of these delicious kisses as you're happy to give out.' His eyes were warm with affection as he enveloped her in his arms.

Gerty jumped to her feet and trotted across to the couple, nudging Ed's leg with her nose, her tail wagging hard.

'Now then, Gerty-Girl, you've been a patient lass, haven't you, just letting us get on with things?' Ed reached inside his pocket for a dog biscuit and offered it to the Labrador who took it gently before ambling back to her bed.

Ed unplugged the electrics while Florrie fastened the many ties at the side of the curtains, ensuring no customers could sneak a look before all was revealed tomorrow evening. Their friend, the nationally revered author, Jack Playforth, had been booked to perform the official unveiling, followed by a reading from his latest novel. Nibbles and mulled wine were included in the ticket for Jack's reading, which Florrie and Ed thought would be the perfect way to finish the evening.

'Right,' said Ed, glancing at his watch. 'We just need to vacuum the bits off the floor and get the storage boxes put away. That shouldn't take long. I can finish the reading room tomorrow; I'll have plenty of time to get the decorations up in time for Jack's event.' He pushed his fringe back off his face, oblivious to the flurry of glitter he'd sent into the air again. 'I'd quite like to grab what's left of the evening and spend a bit of time with my gorgeous girlfriend. We've both been that tied up with getting this place ready, feels like we've barely had chance for a proper conversation for ages.'

Florrie couldn't argue with that. They'd been working flat

out for weeks, making sure their festive plans for the bookshop were in order. 'Hmm. So who's this gorgeous girlfriend you're referring to?' she asked, feigning a coquettish smile. 'Not sure I know her.'

Ed pulled her towards him, nuzzling her nose. 'Mmm. Well, she's pretty special; beautiful on the inside as well as the outside, bright as a button, too. Oh, and did I mention she's one of the most kind-hearted people I've ever met?'

Florrie smiled up at him, happiness flooding her chest as her heart squeezed with love. 'You know what Jasmine would have to say if she caught you talking like that, Ed Harte?'

He laughed and gave her a knowing look. 'Oi, you two, give over with the mush before I see my dinner again!' he said, imitating Jasmine's blunt tone.

'You got it in one.' Florrie couldn't help but chuckle. Pixie-faced, flame-haired Jasmine was one of her best friends who professed not to have a romantic bone in her body. And she most definitely didn't do "mush", as she called it, nor did she like to witness it.

'Just as well she's not here then.' Ed pressed his lips to hers.

His kiss may have been gentle, but it was full of promise. It set butterflies dancing in her stomach as she felt the solid warmth of his chest pressed against her.

'I think cracking on so we can head home sounds like a very good plan,' she said, when they finally pulled apart.

'Mmm. Me too. And I'll look forward to sampling more of your kisses later.' He treated Florrie to a lopsided smile that made her heart dance.

'In that case, what are we waiting for?'

TWO

Florrie was giving the arrangement of children's festive books a final tweak when her phone pinged. She made her way over to the counter and scooped up her phone to see a message from her closest friend, Maggie Marsay. Florrie smiled as she swiped it open.

> Hiya Florrie, hope the festive decorating's going well. Can't wait to see it! The town's buzzing with chat about Ed's window displays!! Forgot to ask earlier but can you put that book on Landies away for me? Am pleased to say Bear doesn't have it! Another Christmas pressie sorted! Phew!!! I'll pop in and get it tomorrow. Thanks, flower! Don't work too late!! Mxx

She ended the message with a stream of cheery Christmas-themed emojis.

Florrie fired off a quick text back, pleased by Maggie's mention of Ed's window display; it really was generating a buzz of anticipation in the town.

> Hi Mags, don't worry, it's already tucked away
> under the counter. Didn't want to risk anyone
> else snapping it up in case I couldn't get
> another one in time for the big day! How're you
> feeling? Fxx

Maggie and Bear's first baby was due later that month and when Florrie had last seen Maggie at The Jolly Sailors, where their group of friends met every Friday evening, she'd complained vociferously about her baby bump. She declared it was so huge it was now making it difficult to sit at her worktable and reach her sewing machine where she made her exquisite keepsake teddy bears for her cottage business The Micklewick Bear Company. 'Honestly, I could do with adding an extra metre to my arms so I can reach the dratted thing,' she'd said, demonstrating and making the friends chortle.

Seconds later, a reply landed.

> Like a beached whale that looks as if it's got a
> serious case of trapped wind doesn't come
> anywhere near to how I'm feeling – or looking
> for that matter! I'm even more ENORMOUS
> than I was on Friday!!! How is that even
> possible? I need to have this baby
> SOON!!! Mxx

Florrie laughed out loud at the long line of whale, wind and outraged face emojis Maggie had added at the end of the text.

Maggie and her husband Bear had been trying to start a family for several years, their attempts peppered with false alarms and heart-breaking miscarriages. But this pregnancy had surprised and thrilled the couple whose greatest wish was to become parents. As far as they were concerned, the much-anticipated arrival of "Baby Marsay" couldn't come soon enough.

Bear was an ardent Land Rover fan – or a "Landie Anorak" as Maggie had recently taken to calling him on account of his growing interest in them. Teasing aside, she'd been thrilled when Florrie had told her they'd taken delivery of a much sought-after book dedicated solely to the iconic vehicles, knowing how much Bear would be delighted with it. Though Florrie had told her friend she'd probably better check their bookshelf and make sure he didn't already own a copy.

Florrie had just sent off a quick reply when Ed returned from putting the vacuum cleaner away in the store cupboard that doubled up as a small kitchen area in the room at the back of the shop.

'Phew! I'm not sorry that's done.'

She glanced up to see him walking towards her, a familiar easy smile on his face. 'I thought I was never going to see the end of those snowflakes – I was beginning to think they'd been breeding.' While Ed had been wielding the vacuum cleaner, Florrie had busied herself rearranging the baubles on the Christmas tree and making sure everything was shipshape with Santa's Grotto at the rear of the shop before moving on to the book displays at the front. She was a perfectionist and wasn't happy until everything looked just so.

She set her phone back down on the counter and laughed. 'I've got a feeling we're going to be finding them long after the Christmas displays have been dismantled.'

'I reckon you could be right.' He came to a halt beside her, throwing his arm around her shoulder.

The pair took a moment to survey their day's work. Along with the festive garlands strung above the bookshelves, there was a traditional-style Christmas tree beside the counter which Florrie had decorated with book-themed baubles, while a smaller one sat on the table in the central display. This one was made entirely from books, albeit fake, and both trees were trimmed with twinkling fairy lights.

A warm glow filled Florrie's chest. The shop was positively brimming with festive cheer. 'It looks amazing,' she said, giving a wistful sigh, thinking how thrilled Mr and Mrs H would have been to see it.

'It does,' said Ed, smiling down at her. The look in his eyes and subsequent squeeze of her shoulders told her he knew what she was thinking.

'It's all thanks to you, Ed.' Her eyes landed on the little grotto he'd constructed for last Christmas. It was enchanting, and looked every inch like the one in her childhood dreams.

'There's no way I'm taking all the credit – it's teamwork.' He beamed at her. 'We've done it together, you and me. Our combined efforts have come together to create the whole Christmassy effect, which I have to say does look pretty awesome.'

Teamwork. Florrie liked the sound of that, and what she liked even more was being part of a team with Ed. His recent secretive trips to the attic back home shot through her mind, momentarily discombobulating her. Not that she had any problems with him venturing up to the room, he had as much right as she did – when he'd moved in with her, Florrie had told him the cottage was his home now, too, that he should treat it as such, and she'd meant it – but the way he was going about it, sloping off when he thought she hadn't noticed, almost lent an air of sneakiness to it which had started to trouble her. But this evening, she didn't want any negative thoughts to spoil their happy moment and she chose not to let them linger.

Florrie locked the bookshop door, and the evocative scent of conifer, eucalyptus and rosemary drifted into her nose from the wreath she'd fixed there earlier that afternoon. She smiled at how pretty the decoration looked, with its fairy lights and berry-red bow, as she stowed the key away in her backpack while Ed clipped the lead onto Gerty's collar.

'Brrr! It's freezing!' She pushed her hands into her gloves, her words coming out in a cloud of condensation. The plummeting temperature contrasted sharply with the warmth they'd left inside, making her glad she'd worn her thick duffle coat and woolly bobble hat.

'It's a perfect night for snuggling in front of the fire,' said Ed, his breath floating out around his face. He was equally well wrapped up in his navy peacoat and checked scarf.

Florrie couldn't argue with that; it was one of the things she loved most about winter evenings, especially since Ed had moved in with her and they could snuggle up on the sofa together.

'Mmm, sounds good, especially if it's with a mug of ginger-bread hot chocolate topped with cream and marshmallows.' She slipped her arm through his and tucked her chin into her scarf as they set off down Victoria Square. Gerty trotted ahead at the end of the lead in her usual jaunty manner.

'Now you're talking.' Ed smiled down at Florrie. 'I think we're in for a few frosty evenings; according to the weather fore-casters, our part of North Yorkshire's going to be hit with a hard frost and snow's predicted for the end of the week.'

'Ooh! How exciting.' Florrie's eyes shone. She loved how snow transformed the town into a scene straight from a Victo-rian Christmas card. She glanced around her, happiness filling her chest. Victoria Square couldn't have looked more festive if it tried, even without a dusting of the white stuff. The store-keepers had gone to great efforts to make their businesses look ready for the season, with Christmas-themed displays in their windows and large wreaths hanging from their doors. Small Christmas trees were fixed above each doorway, laced with warm white lights that twinkled softly, while further lights were festooned from shop to shop. A long sandstone planter, filled with seasonal plants, ran down the centre of the square, dividing the road and ending at the bottom with a small round-about where a clock stood proudly, its face beaming out in the dark. While at the top end of the square, a tall, plush

Christmas tree stood, white lights twinkling from its great boughs.

Florrie found her gaze being drawn to Lark's Vintage Bazaar, a shop over on the other side of the square that was owned by another one of her best friends. 'Ooh, look! Lark's finished her display,' she said. 'Let's go and take a closer look. It's bound to be really special.'

'Looks good even from here,' said Ed. He clicked his tongue for Gerty as Florrie made to tug him across the road. 'Come on, Gerty-Girl, this way.'

Florrie's eyes swept over the scene before her, the glow from the hundreds of fairy lights illuminating her face. Lark had clearly let her creative side loose on her festive display. The window was framed with thick, frost-covered faux Christmas tree branches, trimmed with silver baubles, fir cones and large white feathers. Standing in the centre, to a backdrop of a night sky studded with a scattering of tiny blinking stars, was a mannequin wearing a vintage white maxi dress shot with strands of silver.

'It's stunning!' Florrie gasped.

'It is,' said Ed, sounding suitably impressed. 'It's going to give our displays a run for their money, no doubt about it. And don't you think the mannequin looks a bit like Lark herself, with its blonde hair and serene expression?'

'Ooh, yes, I see what you mean.' Florrie gave a warm smile at the thought of her sweet-natured friend. 'I bet you won't be the only person who says that. Actually, now I think about it, I can see Lark in that dress, too – it's very her.'

'Yep, me too. Maybe she'll sneak in the window and create a live display.'

'I wouldn't put it past her,' she said, chuckling. Florrie felt the fizz of excitement in her stomach as she turned and gazed around the square. Everyone seemed to be making more of an effort this year; even Cuthbert, Asquith & Co, the stuffy solicitors' firm, had a fully decorated Christmas tree in their window.

Ed followed her gaze. 'Yeah, there's only a couple of shops left to finish their window displays. Wait till tomorrow when we can share ours with everyone.'

'Ooh! I'm so excited for them all to see it.' Florrie beamed a smile at him. 'I know they're going to love it.' She shivered, suddenly aware of the cold that was nipping at her face and seeping up through her boots.

'Come on, you look nithered already,' Ed said, using a Yorkshire expression for being cold. He rubbed his hand briskly up and down her arm. 'Which way do you fancy heading back? The quick way through the streets and alleyways or along the top prom?'

'I know it's freezing, but I really fancy getting some fresh air. Are you okay with the top prom?'

'The top prom's cool with me, and I reckon Gerty wouldn't mind the extra leg-stretch. Best foot forward, that'll warm you up.' He held his arm out and she slipped hers through it.

Getting some fresh air wasn't Florrie's only reason for wanting to head back along the prom; she was eager to see the Christmas trees in the large windows of the Victorian houses that lined the road. Their occupants always went to town big time with the decorations, trying to outdo their neighbours. Festive wreaths were the latest thing that had become a focus of neighbourly competition – the bigger and more opulent, the better. Florrie wasn't disappointed by what she saw as they made their way along the broad sweep of the prom. More trees had gone up since the previous evening, shining out and joining the glow from the lights that had been strung between the vintage streetlamps. Florrie's heart lifted at the sight – it was as if the residents of the little seaside town couldn't wait to embrace Christmas. She caught Ed's eye, exchanging a smile with him. He squeezed her arm, making her smile grow wider.

They strode along, the salty air blowing in off the sea stinging her cheeks as they chatted away, only pausing for Gerty to have a quick sniff at whatever pungent aroma caught her interest. Florrie gazed up at the clear inky-blue sky. It was splashed with millions of tiny stars, in the middle of which sat a pale moon, quietly casting its luminescent glow. On the beach below, waves crashed against the line of pebbles on the shoreline, mingling with the odd cry from a solitary seagull. Out to sea, a solid wall of darkness was punctuated only by the clusters of lights from ships making their way along the busy shipping route to and from Teesside further up the coast.

They only encountered a handful of people on their way home, mostly dog walkers and the odd car driving by. At this time on a Sunday evening, everyone would no doubt be hunkering down in readiness for their favourite TV drama, kids doing last-minute homework.

As they walked on, Florrie wondered if her old boss was looking down, a fond twinkle in his eye, revelling in his role that had brought her and Ed together, and the resultant renaissance the bookshop was enjoying. She hoped he was.

THREE

By the time they arrived at the gate of Samphire Cottage, Florrie's hands and feet were numb with cold. She pushed open the front door, welcoming the warmth from the central heating as it wrapped itself around her. She kicked off her boots and unwound her scarf, the contrasting temperatures making her glasses steam up almost instantly, while her cold fingers started to tingle as she struggled to undo the toggles of her duffle coat.

Once Ed had freed Gerty from her lead, the Labrador trotted down the hallway to the kitchen on her usual quest for food.

'S'good to be home,' he said, hanging up his coat on the run of hooks by the door. 'I'll get the fire on in the living room straight away, then it'll be ready for when we get settled down.'

'And I'll stick the kettle on, just as soon as my glasses have cleared,' Florrie said with a laugh, as she attempted to peer through the misty lenses, molelike.

'Mmm. Sounds like a plan.' Ed smiled down at her, planting a kiss on the end of her nose. 'Ooh, that's seriously chilly.'

'You should feel my feet.' She wrapped her arms around his middle, snuggling close and savouring the warmth that emanated from him, the mist gradually clearing from her glasses. 'Let me steal some of your toastiness!'

'You're not expecting me to kiss those, are you?' he asked, feigning a look of alarm.

'What?' She tipped her head back, looking up at him quizzically.

'Your feet.'

'My feet?'

'Yep.' He nodded.

'Don't be so daft.' She giggled.

'Phew!' He grinned, delivering a kiss to her lips.

'Hey, you, they're not that bad!'

'I'll take your word for it.'

It was well after eight o'clock by the time they'd eaten their evening meal – a hearty home-made chicken stew they mopped up with thick wedges of crusty bread from the local deli – and washed up and tidied away. Tiredness crept up on Florrie, and at Ed's suggestion she went and changed into her fleecy pyjamas while he made a couple of gingerbread hot chocolates. 'Be generous with the marshmallows and grating of chocolate,' she said as she disappeared upstairs.

'Yes, your ladyship,' Ed said, chuckling.

Armed with their mugs, the aroma of gingerbread rising into the air, the couple padded their way along the hallway, with Gerty ambling behind them. Stepping into the small, neat living room, a feeling of relaxation spread through Florrie. A fire danced merrily in the grate while classical festive music murmured gently in the background. The heavy vintage curtains were drawn against the chilly night and a selection of carefully placed table lamps cast a soothing glow around the room, adding to the already cosy atmosphere created by the dusky-pink colour of the walls. Gerty stretched out in her usual place on the rug in front of the fire, ready to toast herself.

Florrie curled up on the sofa beside Ed, cradling her mug in her hands. She gave in to a wide yawn. 'Ooh, s'cuse me.' It was going to be a battle to keep her eyes open at this rate. Ed stretched his legs out in front of him, rubbing Gerty's tummy with his socked feet. The Labrador groaned happily, making them chuckle. It was a scene of utter contentment, such that you could almost hear the walls breathe out a blissful sigh.

Allowing the soft music to wash over her, Florrie rested her head on Ed's shoulder, as the reassuringly familiar scent of him floated under her nostrils: soap, mossy cologne and a hint of his "artisty" smell, as she often described it. He responded by wrapping his arm around her. She savoured moments like this, the two of them – and Gerty – unwinding together in their cosy home after a busy day at work.

Being with Ed had made Florrie happier than she'd ever dared dream possible – once she'd admitted to herself that she had feelings for him and allowed herself to open her heart, that is. He filled a void in her life she hadn't known existed until she found herself unexpectedly falling in love. But even she would be the first to admit they'd got off to a rocky start, particularly last year when he'd walked out of her life without so much as a backwards glance – or so she'd thought at the time. Much as she'd fought it, tried to tell herself she didn't care, that she didn't need him, the reality was that she'd been unable to imagine ever feeling whole again.

The anger she'd felt when he returned had quickly turned to relief once he'd explained that he'd needed some time away to clear his head and unravel his thoughts without the influence of his parents putting pressure on him to hand over the bookshop. And she'd been beyond thrilled when he'd told her there was no place he'd rather be than here in Micklewick Bay, with her. Since Ed had moved in with her at Samphire Cottage, they'd settled into a happy rhythm, her uncertainty a distant memory. Or so she'd thought, until he'd started disappearing into the attic, giving her the impression he was keeping a secret.

It had crossed Florrie's mind many times how different Ed was from his parents, for which she was thankful; there was no way she'd still be a joint owner of the bookshop if he'd been remotely like them. Her own relationship with her parents had always been tight, especially so since her mum was diagnosed with Stage 1B Hodgkins Lymphoma while Florrie was away at university. Though Paula had made a full recovery, Florrie lived in fear of the cruel disease returning. She hadn't realised it at the time, but it had caused her to focus all her emotional energy on her parents and very probably, to a lesser degree, Mr and Mrs H.

Even her year-long relationship with Graham – or "Mr Beige" as her friends had dubbed him – had fizzled out long before he'd cheated on her with a work colleague. She hadn't been as gutted as she'd expected when he'd told her they were finished. It didn't help that his kisses had felt like perfunctory displays of affection, clinical almost, whereas Ed's... Phew! Ed's kisses had the power to turn her insides into a molten mess. The first time his lips had touched hers, it had just about blown her socks off, despite the fact she'd only recently broken up with Graham and had decided to avoid relationships for the foreseeable future. And she loved that his kisses still had the power to make her feel that way.

Her mum's illness had also meant that Florrie, who was by nature a homebird anyway, hadn't wanted to stray too far from her hometown and her parents. She'd been more than happy to settle in Micklewick Bay – a place she loved – working in her beloved bookshop, with her posse of best friends close to hand.

It was these family-orientated traits that had, in part, drawn Ed to her, as well as her calm and gentle nature. Florrie offered the stability he'd always craved – albeit unknowingly. He told her often how she'd instilled a contentedness in him he hadn't imagined possible, and it warmed her heart.

Florrie's gaze was drawn to the fireplace, Gerty snoring gently beside it, as mesmerising flames reached up the chimney. She could feel the ache in her shoulders from today's earlier exertions at the bookshop gradually slipping away as slumber started to wrap itself around her.

Seconds later, her heart swooped and her eyes opened as thoughts of Ed's trips to the attic barged their way into her consciousness, throwing cold water over her comfortable drowsiness.

Florrie wasn't certain how to broach it, reluctant to take the edge off their lovely day and spoil the chilled tone of the evening. Things had been so crazy busy recently, making the time they had together, relaxing like this, all the more precious. But she couldn't shake the feeling Ed was keeping something back – it wouldn't be the first time – which worried her more than she cared to admit. But experience told her it was best not to push it; he'd talk about it when he was ready. It wasn't going to be easy; he was master of keeping things to himself. And, worse, of burying his head in the sand.

Florrie subconsciously drew in a deep breath, releasing it in a weary sigh.

'You okay?' Ed asked, dropping a kiss on the top of her head and giving her arm a squeeze.

'Mm-hm,' she said, hoping he wouldn't guess her thoughts. 'Just feeling cosy, that's all.' *That's all, my foot!*

But determined as she was to keep her anxiety at bay, she felt the floodgates of her mind open and a tidal wave of worries whoosh in.

FOUR

THREE A.M. MONDAY 4TH DECEMBER

Florrie wasn't sure how long the phone had been ringing. It had started off as a distant sound, slipping into her dream, before gradually filtering through to her consciousness. She became aware of Ed moving beside her, heard his voice, thick with sleep, as he answered the call. She stirred, slowly blinking herself awake, her slumber-fuzzy mind trying to make sense of what was happening. That the room was still swathed in darkness did little to help her confusion.

In the next moment, panic shot through her. Her eyes pinged open as adrenalin surged and thoughts crashed into her mind. She was wide awake. Ed was on the phone! In bed, right beside her. Someone had rung! Her insides started twisting, making her feel sick as her thoughts went straight to her mum. Threat of the dreaded lymphoma lurked at the back of her mind like a malicious spectre, a constant reminder of just how ill her mum had been, of how close they'd come to losing her.

Florrie sat bolt upright and flicked on the bedside light, watching Ed's face closely. His expression darkened, sending fear prickling over her body.

'Who is it?' she asked urgently, her heart thudding hard

against her ribs. Calls in the middle of the night only meant one thing: bad news. She sat poised, all her senses on high alert, ready to grab the phone, convinced the call was for her. It was all she could do to stop herself from tearing it out of his hand. Her breathing started coming in short bursts as her pulse whooshed noisily in her ears. She cursed herself for her bedtime habit of always turning her mobile phone off. She should have left it on, then whoever it was – her dad, the hospital – would have been able to reach her straight away rather than troubling Ed.

'Who is it?' she asked again, swallowing down the lump of anxiety that had lodged itself in her throat. *Oh God, please make Mum be okay. Please make Mum be okay. Please make Mum be okay.*

Ed pushed himself up and raked his fingers through his hair. 'My father.' He rolled his eyes and shook his head, the phone pressed against his ear.

'Oh.' Florrie flopped back on her pillows, relief washing over her. A tiny thought at the back of her mind told her that a call from Ed's father never brought anything good, but she would rather have that than bad news about her mum; that she'd been taken poorly in the night and been rushed to hospital. Florrie drew in a calming breath, feeling her heart rate settle. Nothing could take priority over her concern for her mum – or her dad, for that matter, but he regularly described himself as being "as fit as a lop", and had no health issues. *Touch wood.* But the relief that there was no need for Florrie to worry about her mum was immeasurable. For tonight, at least.

She closed her eyes and released a shaky sigh, nausea draining away. Would there ever be a time when she didn't have a worry about her mum at the back of her mind? she wondered. A time when she didn't live in fear that the cruel disease had come back to wreak more havoc and heartache? She doubted it, but at least she managed her worries on a daily basis, kept them contained. Well, until they were woken up by phone calls in the middle of the night and her default worry kicked in with a vengeance.

She felt Ed wrap his hand around her fingers, giving them a reassuring squeeze. She glanced across at him. 'Sorry,' he mouthed the word, mustering up an apologetic smile. He'd evidently guessed what had been going through her mind.

'S'okay,' she whispered, squeezing his hand back and returning his smile. The final traces of panic slowly released its grip only to be replaced by a feeling of concern for Ed, who was clearly on the receiving end of an ear-bashing from his father. *Who would do that at this hour?* Peter Harte, that's who, she thought. Florrie considered him a selfish bully who only ever got in touch when he wanted something, which she assumed was the reason behind this phone call. She wondered what time it was in Antigua where Ed's parents currently lived. How typical that Peter wouldn't stop to think of the time difference, that he was calling at an antisocial hour. And even if he had, from what Florrie knew of him, she very much doubted he'd care.

'So you keep telling me, Dad.' Ed puffed out his cheeks. She could hear his father's disembodied voice ranting away in the background, its familiar jabbing, angry tone. As she pulled the duvet up around her, Florrie's ears pricked up. She could have sworn she'd heard mention of Jean Davenport's name in amongst the torrent of words. She couldn't even begin to imagine what reason Peter Harte would have to drag mild-mannered Jean into one of his grievances. And, much as she didn't like to feel that she was eavesdropping, Florrie couldn't help but listen out in case her friend's name cropped up again.

Jean Davenport had been a trusted and loyal friend of Ed's grandparents, and now regularly helped out at the bookshop. She was inoffensive and kind-hearted, and Florrie felt a stab of alarm that she should feature in one of Peter Harte's verbal attacks.

A few moments later, Ed barged headlong into his father's diatribe. 'Look, Dad, I'll call you later when I'm more awake; it's just gone three in the morning here which is hardly the best time to have this kind of conversation.' His jaw tightened as his father continued regardless.

'I don't understa—' Ed threw up his free hand as more angry gabbling quashed his words.

Florrie threw him a sympathetic smile.

'I am listening, Dad, but all I'm hearing is you yelling at me without actually telling me anything I can make sense of.' He rolled his eyes in exasperation. 'I don't know what's so urgent, surely this can wait until mor—' Ed held the phone out in front of him, frowning at the screen. 'Ugh! Infuriating man! Accused me of not listening then hung up.' Ed fell back onto his pillows and dragged his hand down his face.

'Is everything okay?' As soon as she'd asked, Florrie realised it was a stupid question. Clearly, if someone feels the need to call you in the middle of the night, everything wasn't okay. 'I mean, are *you* okay?' She didn't like to say she'd heard his dad shouting.

He turned to her, an air of defeat about him. 'It would seem my parents have a bee in their bonnet,' he said flatly. 'Again.'

Florrie's heart sank. 'You mean about the bookshop?' She thought – *hoped* – they'd moved on from that, accepted the way things were, albeit begrudgingly. Indeed, they'd hadn't heard a peep out of them regarding it over this last year. She dreaded to think why they should think to resurrect their grievances now.

Ed turned to her and sighed wearily. ''Fraid so. Said he and my mother knew it would lead to trouble, us having the bookshop.'

'Trouble? What kind of trouble? What does that even mean?' she asked, scrunching up her nose.

'That's the thing, I haven't a clue.' He scratched his head in puzzlement. 'None of his ranting made any sense, he kept saying Grandad had been irresponsible, had created a can of worms. And he mentioned something about... well... it was hard to make sense of what he was saying to be honest.' The lengthy pause and his troubled expression set a feeling of unease squirming in her stomach. She wondered if it was linked to his father mentioning Jean Davenport. Much as she was tempted to ask, she thought better of it. Something told her Ed would have brought it up if he'd wanted her to know. Why he wouldn't want to share it was a mystery, but it was the middle of the night, she told herself, things would make more sense in the morning. And besides, it wouldn't be the first time he'd kept his worries to himself. Hopefully, he'd share them when he was ready.

'Unfortunately, my father doesn't know how to have a conversation with me without getting full of hell,' Ed continued. 'It's as if it's the only way he knows how to communicate – with me, at least. I daresay my mother's been winding him up like she usually does.' He glanced over at Florrie, a look of regret on his face. 'I'm sorry this has all blown up again.'

'Hey, you've got nothing to be sorry about,' she said. The concern etched on Ed's face tugged at her heart, overriding her own worries. She shuffled across and snuggled into him, resting her head on his chest and wrapping her arm around him. 'I'm sure everything'll be all right. If it's about us handing over the bookshop, we just need to stick together and stand firm. Hope-fully, they'll get the message.'

'I'm not so sure it'll be as easy as that.' He absently smoothed his fingers over Florrie's arm, pressing a kiss to the top of her head. 'He sounded pretty het-up just then. And some-thing tells me there's more to it than them wanting the bookshop.'

Florrie swallowed, the feeling that Ed was holding back on

her growing, and the reason behind it taking on a deeper sense of gravity. 'I know what you said about your dad not knowing how to talk to you, but do you think it might be an idea to hear what he has to say? Maybe you could call him back when he's had a chance to simmer down, at a time that's good for both of you, in private?' She peered up at him, hoping her words would offer some reassurance.

'You have no idea how unappealing that idea is. All that man does is rant.'

'I get that, but do you think it might appease him a little if you call him back, at a more reasonable time, hear him out? At least that way, you might get an idea of what's bugging him now, whether or not it's us having the bookshop.' She hoped she wasn't overstepping the mark; she knew how tetchy Ed could be about contacting his parents.

He blew out a noisy breath. 'I really don't want to waste any more time dwelling on them and their latest drama. And whatever has got him rankled—' He pinched his lips together, slicing his words off. 'Anyway, it's late and all I want to do right now is cuddle up with you and try to get back to sleep.' With that, he turned his phone off and slid it in the drawer of his bedside cabinet, closing it firmly.

Taking his cue, Florrie reached across and flicked the light off with a snap. But much as she savoured the feel of his arms closing around her, it didn't stop her mind from going into overdrive. She'd always suspected his parents' grievances over Mr H's will and the bookshop would resurface. It made her wonder at the timing of their latest objection, not to mention where Jean fitted in with it all.

As the night wore on, it was apparent from the heavy sighs emanating from Ed that the call had pushed sleep out of his reach, just as it had for her. The implications of his father's call tormented their thoughts, creating an air of unease in the bedroom. It was deeply unsettling for both of them.

Florrie's stomach clenched for the umpteenth time since she'd heard Peter Harte's harsh voice barking out of Ed's phone.

Though Mr Cuthbert from Cuthbert, Asquith & Co Solicitors had done all he could to reassure Ed and Florrie that Mr H's will was absolutely watertight, she still struggled to shake the feeling of guilt that being bequeathed something so generous as a half share in a business had created, even if that business hadn't been doing so well at the time – Mr H, consumed by his grief at losing his beloved wife, had lost interest in the bookshop and the profits had plummeted accordingly.

But now, a year-and-a-half later, Florrie and Ed had breathed new life into the bookshop and were reaping its rewards. Between them, they'd brought the business up to date, giving its social media pages an overhaul, having a website designed for them where customers could subscribe to a newsletter, tempted by various special offers and early tip-offs of the author readings and book signings that had become a regular feature. There was also a loyalty card which had proved very popular with the Happy Hartes' customers. And though these improvements had been implemented, there was one thing the couple had been determined wouldn't change, and that was the family values and old-fashioned service the well-loved shop was renowned for. In fact, it made them all the more determined to reinforce these qualities, hence the loyalty card.

It gladdened Florrie's heart to see that Ed finally had his fear of books under control, which was an added bonus. It was something that had come about in no small way thanks to her patience and support, putting the knowledge she'd gained from her time offering home-tutoring in English, something she'd done up until a few years ago. One of her students had been dyslexic and Florrie still had a selection of the resources she'd used in their lessons. As well as the tinted overlays (for both laptop screen and paper), Ed had been amazed when Florrie had told him about a laptop with specially colour-coded keys to help people who had dyslexia. He'd snapped one up, as well as a reading and scanning digital pen. His relief at just how much these things helped him had made Florrie's heart squeeze.

When he'd first arrived in Micklewick Bay Ed had been at a crossroads in his life and was ready for a change of direction. The timing couldn't have been better and his new role as joint owner of The Happy Hartes Bookshop had been just what he'd needed – even if he hadn't realised it at first. And now he was revelling in creating his much talked about window displays as well as taking photographs and designing images for the bookshop's social media pages, which had grown enormously since the summer thanks to his artistic flair.

It would be unbearable if Ed's parents were resurrecting their grievances once more – if indeed that was what the phone call was about. Florrie could picture them both, sitting on their perches like a pair of greedy vultures, waiting for the perfect moment to swoop in and snatch the bookshop out of their hands.

But something was gnawing at the back of Florrie's mind, telling her that there was more to the call than Ed was letting on.

FIVE

MONDAY 4TH DECEMBER

'Looking forward to this evening?' Ed asked as they were clearing away their breakfast dishes later that morning.

Florrie had been excited about the Christmas window reveal since they'd first planned it, especially with Jack Playforth agreeing to give a reading. It had created a great buzz amongst the bookshop's clientele. But the phone call had tarnished her excitement slightly, not to mention it had made her feel tired thanks to the hours of lying awake that had followed.

'I so am.' She turned and smiled at him, noting the air of tiredness that lingered in his expression, though she held back on commenting. 'I think your gorgeous window displays are going to generate a lot of excitement.'

'Thanks.' He smiled, kissing her cheek. 'I just hope everything works properly. We don't want it to fall flat and be a massive anti-climax when Jack flicks the switches. Imagine that. Jack goes, "Ta-da!" and... absolutely nothing happens,' he said, chuckling.

Florrie laughed, too. 'Even without all the bits that move, it's still pretty special – it could never be an anti-climax. And, anyway, Jack will handle it well if the electrics decide not to play ball. He's brilliant at making light of a situation and ad-libbing.'

'True, he's a down-to-earth bloke.'

'And Jean's so thrilled he's doing it – the opening, I mean.' Florrie smiled fondly as she thought of her friend. Jean Davenport, who was in her seventies, was Jack's birth mother whom he'd found when he'd come to the town searching for his long-lost family. She'd also been an old and very dear friend of Mr and Mrs H as well as being a loyal customer of The Happy Hartes Bookshop for many years. In the time she'd worked there, Florrie had grown very fond of Jean, and had got to know her well, particularly her taste in books – romance with a hint of mystery. She took great pleasure in recommending new authors to Jean, as she did with all her regular customers.

'Yeah, I'll bet she is,' Ed said flatly.

Florrie was instantly alerted to his change of tone. She stole a look at him. 'You okay?'

He turned to her. There was no doubting the troubled look that had drifted into his eyes. 'Yeah, s'just…'

She waited a moment for him to elaborate. When he didn't, she said, 'It's just what?' Though she didn't really need to ask, she knew exactly which path his thoughts had taken.

Ed pushed his lips together as if deliberating what to say. Just when Florrie was beginning to think he was never going to answer, he said, 'S'just, I was thinking about the call from my dad, that's all.' His voice tailed off, as if he regretted saying anything.

'Oh, right.' Florrie's heart plummeted. She hoped merely mentioning Jean's name hadn't acted as a reminder of the call. 'Have you heard any more from him?' She'd spotted him fish his phone out of his bedside table as he was getting out of bed earlier, and turn it on.

Ed sucked in a deep breath, his chest expanding. 'He's

texted a couple of times. I haven't had time to call him back. Can't say I'm looking forward to it, actually.'

Florrie couldn't blame Ed for that. All the same, she felt to avoid his father's calls and texts would only serve to prolong the agony. It hadn't escaped her attention that, once they'd landed downstairs, he'd turned his phone off and pushed it into the drawer in the kitchen dresser. She still couldn't shake the feeling that Peter Harte had something new to grumble about, but she hadn't managed to fathom out what it could be.

'Do you think getting it over and done with would help?' she asked cautiously, aware she'd already suggested this. 'You know, grasp the nettle, get the call out of the way. Then you could maybe get it off your mind. And you never know, what-ever it is that's rattled your dad might be nowhere near as bad as what you're expecting.' *Who are you trying to kid?*

'Or it could be a whole lot worse,' Ed said darkly. 'Anyway' – he injected a brighter tone into his voice – 'what were we talking about before?' His not-so-subtle change of subject was difficult to ignore, but for the sake of harmony, Florrie took his lead.

'We were just saying how we're raring to go for the Christmas countdown.' She flashed him a wide smile, the change of topic instantly boosting her mood. 'I can't wait for our customers to see it all!'

Ed couldn't help but laugh. 'If you're this excited for Christmas at the age of thirty-three, I can't even imagine what you were like when you were a child.'

Relief washed over Florrie; they were back on track.

'I think I drove my parents potty.' She giggled. 'Having said that, the pair of them are pretty Christmas crazy, too, so maybe I get it from them.' She released a happy sigh. 'I can remember the first Christmas they decorated the Wendy house Dad had built for me in the back garden. I was seven years old. They really went to town: a wreath on the door, Christmas tree in the window, fairy lights hung from the roof, and a host of festive decorations inside. They even included a little electric stove. It was awesome, so Christmassy.' She chuckled. 'They told me Santa's elves had decorated it as a reward for me being a good girl all year – I'd been given a few awards for my reading and writing and Mum and Dad said they were very proud of me, plus I'd been made a librarian of the junior school library – got a badge to prove it, too.' She gave a feigned superior expression.

'That, I can believe.' He grinned at her. 'Sounds like an awesome memory,' he said softly.

'Oh, it is.' Her eyes shone as she was transported back to the day, the twinkling lights, the smell of woodsmoke and frosty air vividly coming to life in her mind. It suddenly struck her that Ed never talked about things he'd done as a child; fun days with his parents. From what she could gather, such things had been few and far between. In fact, he'd told her very little about his childhood. The only thing she'd managed to glean was a sense of loneliness and self-sufficiency. But surely he must have had some fond memories of Christmas.

'How about you? Did you get giddy with excitement waiting for the big man to drop down the chimney?' she asked, tucking her hair behind her ear.

'No, not really. Christmas was never a big deal with my parents.' He gave a shrug. 'Wasn't that much different to every other day, apart from that the row they had was invariably bigger and more explosive than their everyday variety, no doubt thanks to the extra booze they'd consumed. I usually spent it in my bedroom, keeping myself below the radar, if you like, out of the firing line.'

'Oh, Ed.' Florrie felt a great pang of sympathy land with a thud in her chest. What child spends Christmas day on their own in their bedroom? And what parent lets that happen? 'That's so sad, I'm really sorry to hear that.'

'I didn't tell you that to get your sympathy, it's just how it was. I never felt sorry for myself. I've always been okay in my own company.' He gave a shrug. 'And I certainly didn't want anyone feeling sorry for me.'

Florrie felt a swell of emotion. How could his parents be so selfish? So wrapped up in their own self-centred lives? Wasn't it innate to want to nurture your children? Make their days happy. Get joy from seeing them laugh and have fun. That was how her parents had been. Her friends' parents, too. Stella's mum had brought her up on her own and had worked her fingers to the bone to ensure her daughter didn't go without. And Jasmine, a single mum too, she juggled three jobs so Zak and Chloe had the same as their friends. It was all borne out of love. She recalled her mum telling her that it filled her heart with happiness to see Florrie enjoying herself, that it was the best feeling in the world.

'You'll understand that when you have kiddies of your own, sweetheart. It's the same for your dad, too. We both want the best for you and we both want you to be happy. We'd do anything for you – I'd lay down my life for you.' Her mum's words regularly came back to her.

'Oh, don't say that, Mum.'

'Well, it's true, lovey. Mind, I'm not sure we could get your dad to give up his eighties music night, so you'd probably best not ask him to do that. I reckon it'd be a step too far,' Paula had said with a giggle.

Back in the moment, Florrie bit down on the tears that threatened. She rushed over to Ed, throwing her arms around him, burying her face into his neck.

'Hey, what's this all about?' he asked, pushing himself up and hugging her back.

'I hate the fact that you've got no happy Christmas memories from your childhood. Everyone should have some – it's not right that you don't.'

He laughed. 'It's really no big deal.'

'Well, I think it is. And I've decided that's all about to change,' she said, an idea rushing into her mind.

'It is?' he said, his voice muffled by her hair.

'It is. Your festive memory bank is seriously in deficit and I intend to remedy that. From now on I'm going to make sure you have loads of happy festive memories to choose from. A whole selection of them.' She squeezed him tight, inhaling his warm familiar scent that was guaranteed to make her heart leap. 'I'm about to embark on "The Happy Christmas Memories Project". I suggest you prepare yourself for a festive onslaught,' she said, making a mental note to text her friends as soon as possible; it would be great if they could be involved, too.

Smiling tenderly, he took her face in his hands and looked deep into her eyes, setting butterflies loose in her stomach. 'Florrie Appleton, I don't know what the heck I've done to deserve you, but I thank the day you decided you could put up with me and my quirks.'

His words melted her heart. She gave a mock weary sigh and rolled her eyes. 'Admittedly, it's pretty tough, but I suppose it helps that you're kind of easy on the eye.'

Ed let out a hoot of laughter. 'I'm not so sure about that. And I never had you down as shallow, Miss Appleton.' He pressed a kiss to her lips, his stubble brushing against her skin and sending her pulse rate soaring.

Gerty, determined not to be left out of things, heaved herself up and pushed her solid body between them, her tail thudding against the floor, amber eyes peering up at them.

Ed's gaze switched from Florrie to Gerty. 'Now then, Gerty-Girl, I'm not saying you're a passion-killer, but I'll have you know your timing could only be described as pants right now – you've just interrupted a five-star kiss.'

Gerty wagged her tail some more, making Florrie giggle. 'Ahh, bless, she thinks you're saying lovely things to her.'

'I know.' Ed's gaze softened. 'But we do still think you're

very special, pants timing or no pants timing.' He smiled down at the Labrador and tickled her under the chin.

'We sure do,' said Florrie, ruffling Gerty's velvety ears.

'Getting back to what we were talking about before you tempted me off topic with your kisses... What I was going to say was that I've already got some great Christmas memories. Our first Christmas together last year. Your mum and dad made me feel so welcome. I can't ever remember being so happy on a Christmas Day. As for the Christmas dinner!' Ed rubbed his stomach. 'Your mum certainly delivers the most amazing York-shire portions. I don't think I've ever eaten so much delicious food in one day. And her roast potatoes... oh, *wow!*' He smiled, his eyes crinkling at the corners. 'Yeah, that was an awesome day.'

'You can *still* say that even though you witnessed my dad's dancing?'

'Especially cos I witnessed your dad's dancing. I've never seen anyone put so much enthusiasm into bustin' some shapes.' He gave a hearty chuckle.

Bustin' some shapes. Florrie couldn't help but laugh at the description of her dad's energetic attempts at dancing to the eighties playlist he'd blasted out that Christmas Day, fuelled by a glass or two of wine – well, every Christmas Day as far back as she could remember, actually. She'd share Ed's "bustin' some shapes" comment with her mum later so they could enjoy a chuckle together. Everything Charlie Appleton did, he did with great enthusiasm and his dancing was no exception.

'He's a great bloke, your dad. Your mum, too.'

'What? Are you putting my mum in the same bonkers cate-gory as my dad's dancing? She'd be mortified!'

Ed chuckled some more. 'No, definitely not. I think your dad's dancing is in its own unique category there.'

'You're not wrong.' Florrie giggled.

'I think what I'm trying to say but going right around the houses to say it, is that I can see why you're the person you are.'

'See why I'm...? Ugh! Now my brain's beginning to hurt. I haven't a clue what you're trying to tell me.' Though Florrie frowned, she had a hint of mischief in her eyes.

'You're wonderful because of your parents – how they've been with you, brought you up. They're really decent folk and have passed on their good values to you. But you're also wonderful just...' He gave a shrug. 'Just because you're you.'

'And what do you reckon Jasmine would have to say about that, I wonder?' asked Florrie, feeling the heat of a blush his words had triggered.

'I don't think what Jazz would have to say could be repeated in the presence of such sensitive ears.' Ed nodded in Gerty's direction.

'I think you're right.' Florrie giggled.

'Anyway, if I'm not mistaken, I think we have some kisses to catch up on.' Ed's eyes twinkled at her.

'I do believe you're right.' Florrie felt a flutter in her stomach.

'Well then, what are we waiting for?' he asked, before getting to his feet and scooping her into his arms, brushing his lips against hers.

SIX

The walk along the top prom to the bookshop that morning could only be described as bracing. Stretched out above the town was a vast expanse of cornflower-blue sky, white clouds scudding along on the brisk breeze. Seagulls called as they dipped and dived, skimming over the waves. Florrie and Ed strode forth at a vigorous pace, Gerty trotting along in her familiar jaunty way, tail swishing, nose twitching as it was assaulted by myriad interesting smells. They nodded at the familiar faces they encountered, dog walkers, people making their way to work, all wrapped up well against the wintry weather. Cyclists whizzed along the cycle lane in a whir of wheels. A particularly vocal herring gull was perched on the chimney pot of one of the imposing Victorian houses that enjoyed spectacular views of the bay, screeching for all it was worth, its cries carried off by the wind. The sea to the left looked bitterly cold, the frothy white breakers crashing on the shoreline sending foam splashing into the air. The usual group of surfers was loitering by the pier, bobbing in and out of the water, their shiny black wetsuits giving the appearance of a pod of seals.

Florrie and Ed followed the curve of the road, bringing the commanding line of cliffs on the opposite side of town into view. Standing proud was the mighty Thorncliffe, its vast hulk a powerful presence on the coastline. From here it was easy to make out the quaint, whitewashed Clifftop Cottage that was home to Maggie and Bear. It sat within the curtilage of Thorncliffe Farm, to which the cliff had given its name, and its patchwork sprawl of fields sparkled with frost. Nestled below was the cluster of characterful cottages where Micklewick Bay had its origins. The higgledy-piggledy houses clung onto the cliffside like a cluster of limpets, their red-pantile rooftops glowing in the pale, winter sun. Here the meandering network of alleyways and snickets had a collection of names that tickled the tourists, amongst which was Micklemackle Yard, Herring Lass Row, Gabblewickgate and Blatherin Alley.

Standing before these cobbled streets was The Jolly Sailors pub facing bravely out to sea where it hunkered down against the elements. It had sat there stoically for several centuries, withstanding all that the salt-laden sea air and brooding high spring tides could throw at it. The hostelry was a favourite haunt of Florrie and her close group of friends, particularly so on a Friday evening. It had been their meeting place for years, where they'd indulge in the landlady Mandy's famously hearty portions of fish and chips and a good old catch-up, sharing what had gone on in their week, offering words of comfort and support where needed over a bottle or two of wine and a good old belly laugh.

Gerty paused at a wooden bench, its pale wood and shiny brass plaque betraying its newness. The Labrador looked up at them with enquiring amber eyes – she'd already picked up on their new routine.

'Good lass.' Ed patted her head and she wagged her tail.

Florrie's eyes scanned over the newly inscribed plaque that was fixed to the backrest of the seat, her heart squeezing.

Dedicated to the memory of Dinah and Bernard Harte of The Happy Hartes Bookshop, who loved this view.

It still stung that they'd both gone, but Florrie and Ed had agreed that funding a bench here on the prom, looking out to sea, would be the perfect way to commemorate them.

No words were exchanged as Florrie and Ed sat down, lost in their own thoughts, his leg pressing against hers as they gazed out at the view. A couple of ro-ro ferries in the distance punctuated the undulating dark blue of the North Sea, gulls dipping and diving and skimming over the waves. An unforgiving wind was blowing in off the sea, whipping around the couple and nipping at their cheeks. It was only a matter of minutes before the cold of the bench started seeping through Florrie's duffle coat. She tucked her chin deeper into her scarf and hugged her arms around herself.

Ed gave a sigh. 'I could never tire of looking out at this.'

'Yeah, me neither. I still get a thrill every time I look at it – it's different every day.'

'I can see why my grandparents loved it so much.'

Florrie inhaled slowly, the chilly air filling her chest. 'Me too.' She felt a wave of sadness rise up through her as she recalled how Mr H used to push his wife along the prom in her wheelchair, stopping here so they could take a moment and sip tea from a flask while they savoured the view. Mrs H had suffered a stroke a couple of years before Mr H had died. It had affected her mobility, but her husband had been determined that nothing was going to stop her from enjoying her daily venture along the top prom and glimpse of her beloved Thorncliffe. Florrie and Ed had thought it fitting to fund a bench here in their memory and, since its installation, they'd taken to stopping at it for a few minutes each morning.

'Here's where I feel closest to my grandad,' Ed said, pushing his wind-tousled hair off his face before wrapping his arm around Florrie. 'I know the bookshop would be the most likely place, but it's here, with this amazing panorama that he used to enthuse about all the time, where I really feel he's near.'

'I get that.'

'We've picked the perfect spot for a bench in his memory – my grandmother's, too.'

Florrie nodded, resting her head on his shoulder. 'You're right. They'd both be thrilled with it. This view really touched him, he used to say it was almost a part of him, spoke about it all the time.' She cast her gaze along the vista that stretched out before her, the silhouettes of industry looming way along to the left of the coastline, sweeping along the broad stretch of golden sand, all the way up to the cliffs. It really was breathtaking and easy to see why it had been so popular with wealthy Victorian holidaymakers, and why so many had built their grand homes in the town. In fact, the "new" part of town on this side of Skitey Bank was built on the money generated by the very industry that still powered ahead further up the coast. 'I feel your grandad's presence here, too.' The happy thought prompted a smile. Her old boss had made a huge impact on her life in so many positive ways, as had his wife. If it hadn't been for him, she'd never have got to meet Ed; she'd never have found out how a *proper,* all-encompassing love felt, which was nothing like the lukewarm version she'd had with Graham. She glanced upwards, her smile widening. *Thank you, Mr H.*

Ed clapped his hands on his knees, pulling her back into the moment. 'Right, I don't know about you but I'm in danger of freezing to the spot here. I reckon we need to get cracking so we get warmed through by the time the bookshop opens.' He got to his feet, pulling up the collar of his coat, then held out his hand to Florrie.

'I'm not going to argue with that.' She grinned up at him, slipping her gloved hand into his. The biting wind had started to make her eyes water and she could barely feel her fingers.

The thought of wrapping them around a steaming mug of tea when they got to the bookshop was most appealing.

'Come on, best foot forward,' Ed said, slipping her arm through his, setting the pace as he strode ahead.

Before long they reached the top of Skitey Bank that twisted and turned its way down to the bottom prom and the beach. Taking advantage of a gap in the traffic, they hurried across to the other side, passing the derelict shell of the once magnificent Micklewick Majestic Hotel that occupied the end of a block with views out to sea. It had been on the market for a considerable amount of time, with rumours aplenty as to why it hadn't sold, who was in the bidding for it and tales of what had become of its previous owner. In that time, it had fallen further into disrepair and Mother Nature had taken over, weeds self-seeding with abandon here, there and everywhere. The guttering was hanging off in places, water cascading down the former hotel's walls when it rained. Florrie dreaded to think what another winter would do to the building.

Soon, she was unlocking the door of the bookshop, the mouth-watering aroma of freshly baked Christmas cakes wafting up from the bakery two doors down. As soon as she stepped into the warmth her nose started tingling and her glasses steamed up.

'First things first,' she said, removing her glasses and wiping them with a tissue she'd fished from her pocket, 'I'm going to stick the kettle on. I won't be able lift a finger – literally, they're frozen! – until I have a hot mug of tea inside me and I've properly thawed out.'

Ed looked at her and laughed. 'You usually can't lift a finger unless you've had a hot mug of tea inside you whether they're frozen or not.'

'Fair point.' Florrie giggled as she popped her glasses back on and began unwinding her scarf.

Satisfied that Ed was busying himself at the front of the

shop, Florrie ensconced herself in the small kitchen. She hurriedly filled the kettle, then fished her phone from her bag. She fired off a quick text to her friends, sharing her idea for The Happy Christmas Memory Project, saying how she'd love them to be involved and that any suggestions would be gratefully received.

It was Lark who replied first.

> Ooh! Love it!! Very happy to be involved. I'll get my thinking cap on! xxx

Maggie's text arrived hot on her heels.

> Count us in – Baby Marsay's arrival permitting! How about ice skating over at Middleton-le-Moors? I can eat cake & spectate while you lot fall on your backsides!! Mxx

Florrie chuckled at that, but Maggie's suggestion had set her thinking. For the last couple of years, at the start of December, a temporary ice rink had been set up in the car park at the front of The Golden Fleece pub. It wasn't very big, but it had proved a popular attraction. She doubted very much that Ed had ever been ice skating; it was something she'd only done a couple of times herself, but the rink at Middleton sounded fun, especially if they could nip into the pub afterwards. It was definitely a contender, especially with the stylishly characterful market town decked out in its festive finery. A frisson of excitement ran through her. It hadn't taken long to get her Happy Christmas Memory Project underway.

Stella's reply landed just as Florrie was filling the teapot with hot water.

> Brilliant idea! Danskelfe Castle has lots of Christmas events. Sure I saw mention of sleigh rides. Think you have to book in advance. Count me in on anything! Sx

'Hmm. Sleigh rides?' Florrie tapped her finger against her mouth. Danskelfe Castle was in a stunning location, perched on a precipitous crag over on the moors and set in extensive grounds. Stella's mum Alice had paid it a visit a couple of months ago with her partner Rhys. The pair had returned singing its praises.

Florrie's imagination started running wild, picturing herself and Ed hurtling around the castle's beautiful grounds in a sleigh pulled by reindeer. She chuckled at herself for getting carried away. 'It's hardly likely to be reindeer, Florrie!' she said softly as she hurriedly tapped "Danskelfe Castle" into the search bar on her phone. But reindeer or not, it sounded like an ideal contender for The Happy Christmas Memory Project and she was keen to learn more.

Her heart lifted as the website filled the screen; it looked glossy and professional. She clicked on the "Christmas" tab, her eyes dancing over the array of events and experiences on offer, including the sleigh rides Stella had mentioned – pulled by three horses. Florrie zoomed in on the details. Each "sleigh"– which was a festively decorated open carriage complete with roof, and an achingly nostalgic Christmas air – had seating for twelve people and ran at multiple intervals throughout the day starting from ten a.m. 'Oh, wow!' With excitement rushing through her, thoughts started blooming in her mind. Would their group of friends be interested in joining them? she wondered. There were enough of them to just about fill a whole sleigh ride, and their presence would make the experience even more memorable for Ed, of that she was sure. For all of them, too, for that matter.

She hurriedly scanned the available dates, one eye on the door, willing Ed not to venture down there, curious as to what she was up to. Her heart began to sink as she scrolled through the slots, the words "Fully booked", "Fully booked", "Fully booked" appearing as if on a loop. 'Oh, no!' She could feel her excitement slowly ebb away. She'd left it too late. Of course she had! Sleigh rides at Danskelfe Castle were bound to be a popular attraction.

Despondently, she continued to scroll, the odd single space showing up here and there. She'd almost lost hope when... 'Oh!' She stopped, doing a double-take as her eyes alighted on a completely empty sleigh for Sunday the seventeenth of December at three fifteen p.m., the final slot of the day. She blinked, checking it again to make sure she'd read right. Her heart gave a happy leap. She had! There was a whole sleigh completely empty! 'Talk about lucky,' she said, her insides dancing – she could hear Lark's voice in her mind, telling her it was meant to be.

With each sleigh ride taking approximately half an hour, the timing couldn't be better; the level of light would be perfect – not too dark, but sufficiently dusk and cosy for them to appreciate the twinkly lights shown in the website's photos that lit the way to and from the castle's courtyard. Her pulse started galloping. This was perfect for inclusion in The Happy Christmas Memory Project, but she needed to make a decision quickly before the seats were snapped up by someone else, which they invariably would be if she left it too long.

'Right, no time like the present.' Florrie seized the moment, and another round of hastily tapped out texts to her friends followed. Last on the list was Jasmine. Florrie's fingers paused over her number as she pondered over the wording of the message. She was reluctant to put her friend under any extra financial pressure; there was no getting away from it, the sleigh rides were expensive, though not extortionate like some she'd heard of. She knew Jasmine struggled to afford any extras at this time of year and she didn't want to make her feel awkward, or that she'd have to miss out on something the rest of them were all taking part in. She also knew the suggestion of her covering the cost of her friend's ticket ran the risk of hurting Jasmine's pride, which was the last thing Florrie wanted. She needed to handle this carefully.

Florrie's mind moved quickly, searching for a solution that would mean she wouldn't have to put Jasmine on the spot. She desperately wanted Jazz to be a part of the experience (the thought of her missing out for financial reasons didn't feel right) – and there was enough room for the kids, which though it was even better, added to the dilemma. In the next second, an idea lit up in her mind. The group of friends clubbed together to buy one another Christmas presents each year, and they hadn't organised Jasmine's yet as they'd been struggling to agree on what to get her – she was the trickiest of the friends to buy for, not being one for the usual toiletries and perfume. A ticket for the sleigh ride would be perfect! On top of that, getting tickets for Zak and Chloe would solve the problem of what to get them for Christmas, too; she'd be happy to cover the cost of those if the others had already organised their gifts for the kids.

A wave of relief and happiness washed over Florrie simultaneously and she tapped out a text to Jasmine, simply asking her to keep the date free for herself and the kids, saying she'd explain later. As an afterthought, she added that they should all wear Christmas jumpers. She knew her friends well enough to know she didn't need to run it by them before booking the tickets; they'd be of the same mind as her and more than happy to go with her suggestion.

While she'd been dithering over what to do about Jasmine, the others had responded with an assortment of enthusiastic texts and celebratory festive emojis. All were eager to come, asking for partners to be included – Nate was apparently keen to join as Lark's "friend". It made Florrie chuckle. She wondered if poor old Nate was ever going to escape from the "friend zone". In the next moment a text pinged from Jasmine.

Have put it on the calendar! Most mysterious!!
Jxx

Buzzing with happiness, and with no time to lose, Florrie fished in her bag for her purse, hoping with all her might that no one else had snapped up the places in the meantime. She couldn't tap in her details quick enough, her pulse jumping as the order went through. Tucking her purse away before Ed spotted it and wondered what she was up to, she fired off a quick text to Maggie, Stella and Lark, explaining briefly how she'd got Jasmine and the kids' Christmas presents sorted but asking them to keep it under wraps for now.

Florrie quickly poured the tea then picked up the mugs and headed out of the kitchen, her heart pounding with happiness. It was impossible to stop the smile that was spreading across her face as she made her way back to the front of the shop. The Happy Christmas Memory Project was underway! It was going to take some willpower to keep this surprise to herself till the moment was right.

She found Ed leaning over his laptop at the counter, deep in concentration, his fringe flopping forward. The creak of the floorboards alerted him to Florrie's return. He looked up, brushing his hair off his face. 'I was just about to send a search party out.' His eyebrows quirked as he spotted her expression, a grin hitching up the corners of his mouth. 'You're looking rather pleased with yourself.'

'Just got sidetracked with a few texts from the lasses.' She beamed at him, doing all she could to rein in the excitement that was currently fizzing away inside her. Much as she couldn't wait to tell him about the sleigh ride, she wanted to print off the tickets, tuck them into a Christmas card and present them to him that way.

'Well, from the way you're smiling, it looks as though they've been entertaining.'

'Just a bit.' She chuckled, setting the mugs down on the counter.

Oh, if only you knew!

SEVEN

Florrie was adding more copies of *The Night Before Christmas* to the display of children's festive books by the door. It was one of her favourite childhood Christmas stories. She had fond memories of her mum reading it to her at bedtime as they snuggled up together, Florrie delighting in the rich illustrations. She still had the book slotted safely in one of the bookcases in the attic at Samphire Cottage, keeping company with the many other treasured books from her childhood. All the same, she couldn't resist a quick flick through right now.

Leah, the bookshop's young assistant, was serving a customer at the counter, chatting away in her usual friendly manner. She reminded Florrie of herself at that age; a hint of shyness about her, her love of books shining through. In a recent conversation, Florrie and Ed had discussed showing their appreciation for the young girl's hard work and dedication by adding a generous bonus to her Christmas wages. Leah was an asset to the bookshop and fondly thought of by their customers.

Florrie checked her watch, her heart giving a little leap. There was just an hour to go before the "grand reveal". She caught Leah's eye, and they shared a smile that told of excitement and anticipation.

Just then, the bell above the door jangled merrily, a blast of chilly air rushing in. Florrie turned to see Maggie easing herself in and hurriedly closing the door behind her.

'Ooh, it's lovely and toasty in here after being out there – it's bloomin' freezing. There's definitely snow on the way.' She gave a shiver before spotting her friend. 'Now then, Florrie,' she said, smiling broadly as she waddled over to her.

'Hi, Mags.' Florrie beamed at her. Maggie was a colourful sight in her berry-red boiled wool coat, stretched over her enormous baby bump, set off by a multi-coloured stripy scarf and lime-green velvet cloche pulled down over the dark waves of her hair. Her cheeks were flushed, and her nose was glowing red from the cold. 'So, how's things?'

'Good, thanks, despite being the size of a very large hippo.' Maggie patted her bump. 'Not to mention being rushed off my feet with Christmas orders, not that I'm complaining. Mind, I haven't a clue what I'd have done without Jean – she's been a real star and her work is amazing. I just hope she doesn't get fed up of making bears when Baby Marsay here makes his or her appearance.' A cloud briefly crossed her face. Jean Davenport not only helped out at the bookshop, but she also worked for Maggie, assisting with her hand-crafted bears.

'I'm sure that's not going to happen, Mags. Only the other day she was in here saying how much she loves it, and she enjoys working with you,' said Florrie, keen to allay her friend's concerns which she knew had been troubling her the closer she got to the baby's arrival. 'I've never seen her looking so happy. What with Jack coming into her life, and her keeping busy here at the bookshop and up at Clifftop Cottage with you, it's all made a real, positive impact on her life. I thought she was never going to get over the loss of Mr H. Now she says she's glad she hasn't got time to dwell on it.'

'Well, that's good to hear – seems we're helping each other out.' Maggie's expression brightened. 'Anyroad, you haven't half got it looking wonderful in here.' She glanced around the shop, her eyes shining. 'Ooh, and I love the garlands. Are they the ones you were telling me about, with the little books on them?' She went to take a closer look, her footsteps soft over the carpet. She gave a gasp of delight. 'Oh, they're *gorgeous*.'

'Thanks, we're really chuffed with them.' Florrie added the last book to the display and made her way over to her friend.

'Oh, wow! That's the Christmas tree made of books you were telling me and the lasses about. It's adorable!'

'Isn't it?' said Florrie, the smell of frosty air that clung to Maggie's clothes floating under her nose.

The bell above the door rang out again as another couple of customers arrived. Florrie glanced across to see mother and daughter Susie and Sophie Frampton who were regular faces at the bookshop. Both looked around, beaming broadly as they took in the decorations. Florrie greeted them with a warm smile. 'Hello there.'

'Hello,' Susie said cheerily. 'Thought we'd get here early, take a look at the books before it gets too busy.'

'Good plan. We've just taken delivery of Jenna Johnstone's latest book and it's selling like hot cakes. I know you're a fan of hers,' said Florrie.

'Ooh, thanks for the tip off. I've been waiting for it to come in. Sophie's come to look for some book ideas for her Christmas list to Santa, haven't you, Soph?' she asked her six-year-old daughter.

Sophie, who was wearing a woolly hat with a huge pom-pom on the top, smiled shyly and nodded, setting the pom-pom bouncing.

'My mum used to bring me here to do that, too, when I was little.' Florrie smiled kindly at Sophie. 'I used to get very excited about it, especially Santa's grotto. And do you know what? I think his elves must've paid us a visit through the night because when Ed and I got here this morning, it was all set up at the back of the shop.'

The little girl's eyes grew wide. 'Really?'

'Yes. It's all sparkly and pretty. Would you like to take a peek?' Florrie asked.

'Ooh, that would be lovely, wouldn't it, Soph?' Susie said.

'Yes,' Sophie said with an adorable lisp, excitement dancing across her face as she slipped her mittened hand into her mum's. The gap in her wide smile revealed she'd had a recent visit from the tooth fairy. 'Is Santa in the grotto?'

'He's not here at the moment, but he sent us a message saying he'll be here on Fridays and Saturdays.'

'We'll have to book a slot for that, Soph,' Susie said, before heading towards Santa's grotto.

'So, flower, are you all set for "the great reveal"?' Maggie asked, making jazz hands.

'Yep, everything's ready. This is the calm before the storm.' Florrie felt excitement flutter in her chest.

Maggie chuckled. 'From what I can gather, it's generated a lot of interest. People were talking about it in the street just now. I can't wait to see what Ed's come up with this time, especially after that amazing autumn one – that was *so* cosy, got me feeling all snuggly. It's going to take some beating.'

'He let me have a look at the display last night, and I can tell you it's absolutely gorgeous – I reckon it's the best yet.' A thrill rippled through her as the images filled her mind. 'He's just adding the final Christmas decorations to the reading room. My mum and Jean are in there with him, setting out the nibbles.'

'Great stuff. I had to come into town to catch the Post Office before it closed – I had a load of orders to send out. Bear dropped me off while he nipped to the decorators and said he'd meet me here. Thought I might as well pick up that book on Landies we were talking about while he's otherwise occupied.'

'Ooh, good idea. It's in a bag under the counter. I'll get it for you once Leah's finished serving Mrs Bakeford.'

With Mrs Bakeford heading out of the shop with her purchases, Maggie made her way over to Leah who reached under the counter and retrieved the book. 'There you go,' she said, handing it to Maggie.

'Thanks, flower,' she said, waiting while Leah stamped her loyalty card and took payment.

'Right, is there anything I can do while I'm waiting for Bear to land? Knowing what he's like, he could be a while in the DIY store.' Maggie rolled her eyes affectionately as she slipped the book into her roomy bag. 'He seems to find such places fascinating.'

'I can't think of anything right now, Mags, everything seems under control and, anyway, shouldn't you be taking things easy?' Florrie asked.

'Pfft! Have you been talking to Bear? He's stuck on repeat at the moment, always telling me to sit down and put my feet up.' Maggie chuckled. 'And I keep telling him I'm pregnant, not ill! Honestly, I'd get nothing done if it was up to him.'

It hadn't escaped Florrie and Ed's attention how Bear had been fussing around his wife like the proverbial mother hen, always checking she was okay, making her cups of tea and keeping her well-supplied with her favourite lemon sherbets that she'd developed an insatiable craving for. 'Tell you what, it's been a while since we've had a cuppa. You could always stick the kettle on, if you like?' Florrie checked her watch. 'And since it's not long before everything kicks off with the window reveal, you and Bear are welcome to hang around for that.'

'Sounds good to me. I'll go and get that kettle on.' Maggie rubbed her hands together as if she meant business. 'Tea okay for you, Leah?'

'Perfect, thanks, Maggie. Milk and one sugar, please,' Leah said politely, flashing her a smile just as another customer arrived.

'Ooh, I knew I had something to tell you,' said Leah, watching as the customer headed over to the Sci-Fi section, her smile suddenly exchanged for a frown.

'Oh?' Florrie headed over to her, no clue as what it could be.

'I don't want to worry you, especially today of all days,' Leah said, lowering her voice.

Her words immediately set alarm bells ringing in Florrie's ears. She had a feeling she wasn't going to like what she was about to hear. 'But...'

Leah shot her an apologetic look. 'That creepy guy, Dodgy Dick, has been sniffing around again. Don't worry, he didn't come inside.' She raised her hands on seeing Florrie's eyes widen with alarm. 'It was earlier this morning. Wendy was with him. They'd parked up in front of the shop and he spent ages looking at all the other window displays while she strutted off somewhere, done up to the nines as usual. He was on his phone most of the time, sneering in that horrible way he has, but he kept glancing over at the bookshop. Mind, I made sure he knew I was watching him. He's so *slimy*.' Leah gave a shudder as if to emphasise the point. 'I meant to tell you earlier but with us being so busy I haven't had a chance until now.'

What? No! The mere mention of Dodgy Dick was enough to set panic loose in Florrie's stomach. He was the local frontman for an out-of-town company whose practices were decidedly shady. His reputation had become so bad recently, some people had even started to refer to him as a gangster. And from the way he swanned around town in his top-of-the-range four-wheel drive, his glammed-up wife, Wendy, at his side, an ever-increasing air of intimidation about him, it was a role he seemed to relish. But what had got Florrie in such a spin was his involvement with Ed's parents when they'd been trying to get her and Ed to sell the bookshop. Dodgy Dick had been part of the reason Ed had hot-footed it out of town, with his relentless campaign to get his hands on the business. What had started off as pushy had become intimidating to the point of being sinister. Disappearing was the only way Ed could think of to get him and his parents to back off. The tactic had worked at the time, but Florrie felt her concern building as to the reason behind Dodgy Dick hanging around outside the bookshop today. Something told her he hadn't been simply killing time.

By Ed ignoring his father's calls and texts, had he unwittingly forced his parents to crank their plans up to the next level and involve Dodgy Dick once more? she wondered. She sincerely hoped not.

Florrie swallowed down the lump of concern that had risen up into her throat, conscious of her galloping heart rate. She mustered up a smile, adopting a breezy tone. 'Thanks for letting me know, Leah. He was probably just killing time while he waited for Wendy. Unfortunately, his unsavoury manner has a habit of making us suspicious of every little thing he does, even going to buy a newspaper from what I've heard.' She gave a small laugh, hoping the young assistant hadn't picked up on her concern. 'I wouldn't give it another thought. Mind, I think it's probably best you don't mention anything to Ed. I don't want the likes of Dodgy Dick to take the edge off all his hard work – he's been looking forward to this evening. It would be a shame for anything to spoil it.'

'No probs.' Leah beamed at her, apparently convinced. 'Dodgy Dick *so* isn't worth that.'

Though nausea had started swirling in Florrie's stomach at the implications of the unscrupulous businessman's interest, there was no way she was going to let what she'd just learnt spoil this evening. Mustering all her strength, she pushed Dodgy Dick and Ed's parents out of her mind with a hefty nudge and turned her thoughts to the magical window displays Ed had put so much effort into getting perfect. Nothing was going to detract from the event they'd been working so hard towards. They all deserved to enjoy it.

EIGHT

Thanks to the posts Florrie had added to the bookshop's social media pages, as well as those of Micklewick Bay's, a great crowd had gathered outside The Happy Hartes Bookshop in time for the unveiling of the window displays. Though it was muted by the glass, the upbeat conversation was filtering into the shop. Florrie was astonished at the number of people who'd turned up. She'd spotted the first few loitering at around four thirty, apparently bagging themselves a prime spot. It had surprised her since the unveiling wasn't due for another hour, not to mention how bitterly cold it was – the wind had a habit of blasting up through the square straight off the sea.

And now the number had grown from half a dozen to a great swell of people. She'd guessed it would be busy, but neither she nor Ed had anticipated anything like this.

She was standing at the front of the bookshop with Ed, her parents, Leah, Maggie – who'd been joined by her husband, Bear – and Jean Davenport. Jack Playforth had just nipped to the bathroom before they opened the doors and the fun began.

'Bloomin' 'eck, have you seen how many folk are out there?' said Charlie, chuckling as he peered through the glass in the door. 'The pavement's packed and cars are struggling to get by on the road.' Even from this side of the door, the buzz of antici-pation that filled the air was palpable.

'Oh, my goodness, looks like there's hundreds!' said Jean Davenport, her eyes shining. 'Where've they all come from?'

'It's a mixture of your Jack officiating and folk being keen to see our Ed's display,' Paula said, peering around her husband to get a view. It gladdened Florrie's heart that her parents had started to refer to her boyfriend as "our Ed".

'Blimey, there's a photographer and what looks to be a tele-vision camera!' Paula's voice rose with excitement. 'Charlie, you've got better eyesight than me – I'm right, aren't I? That's a telly camera, over there, just by the streetlight and next to the fella with the daft hat, the one that's got a massive feather in it.'

'What? The camera's got a massive feather in it?' Charlie asked, his face a picture of puzzlement. 'Why would a camera have a feather in it?'

'I don't mean the camera, you daft apeth.' Paula gave his arm a reproving nudge. 'I mean the fella beside it is wearing a hat with a huge feather in it. You can't miss it, it's like something from a pantomime.'

'Some folk'll wear owt.' Charlie pulled a face. 'But then again, I suppose it is pantomime season. Anyroad, where are you pointing?' He squinted through the glass and let out a throaty laugh. 'By 'eck, you're right, love, it is a daft bloomin' hat and the feather's just poked the woman standing next to him right up the nose. She doesn't look too chuffed about it at all.' His shoulders shook with mirth. 'Ey up, she's giving him a right earful now. That'll teach him to wear summat as daft as that hat.' He chuckled some more, making his face flush.

Florrie bit down on a laugh, not daring to make eye contact with Ed.

Paula turned to the others and rolled her eyes good-naturedly. 'Never mind the fella with the hat, Charlie, can you see a telly camera? That's what we're interested in.'

'Oh, aye, yep, I can see a telly camera as well. Blimey, it's a right big 'un.'

'I wonder who told the telly folk?' said Jean, craning her neck to see it.

Florrie and Ed exchanged glances, each giving the other a shrug. 'Not me,' said Florrie. She'd informed the local newspaper, but hadn't contacted the TV station; she hadn't thought to.

'Me neither. I would've mentioned it if I had.' Ed looked as puzzled as she felt.

As Florrie was racking her brains as to who it could be, Jack returned from the bathroom. She wondered if Jack had contacted the TV station on the quiet. He was always keen to promote the bookshop, it would be so like him to do it.

'Right,' he said, clapping his hands together, 'I think it's time to put the good folk of Micklewick Bay out of their suspense. We all know it's Ed's window displays they're itching to see – it's got nowt to do with wanting to hear me prattling on. Come on, Ed, lad, get that door open.' Jack grinned broadly, his eyes crinkling at the corners.

The excitement inside the shop was nothing compared to the level on the street. The square was bouncing! Ed opened the door wide, and a great roar of applause went up as Jack stepped out. A chorus of whoops and cheers quickly followed. Florrie glanced at Ed in disbelief, the smile on her face growing wider.

Jack stood, waiting for the applause to die down, his stern resting face belying his good-natured personality. He'd been much maligned in the press in his early days of fame thanks to his dour looks, regularly being described as curmudgeonly, but the description didn't match the man Florrie had come to know. And tonight his face was wreathed in smiles.

Since his arrival in the town, he'd become a much-loved

local celebrity, embraced as if he'd been a resident all his life. It was something that had made his mother Jean incredibly proud.

Jack lifted his hands in a gesture for the crowd to quieten down, but it had little effect.

Florrie gazed out at the vast throng of people, all wrapped up against the cold, hardly able to believe what she was seeing. It was heartwarming to see so many people. Amongst them she spotted Jasmine with Zak and Chloe, the two children chatting away excitedly. Stella was there, too – she wasn't hard to miss being so tall and no doubt in a pair of her vertiginous heels. She was with Alex, her boyfriend of the last few months; the pair made for an attractive couple. They were standing next to Lark and her friend Nate who ran an upcycling store in town. Seeing the two of them together, so easy in one another's company, brought a smile to Florrie's face. It was no secret that Nate would like to be much more than Lark's friend but thus far she'd resisted taking their relationship down that route, arguing that the seven years between their respective ages meant she felt he was too young for her.

Jean grabbed onto Florrie's arm. 'That's my lad they're all cheering.' Her eyes were shining with pride. Florrie reached for her hand, giving it a squeeze.

'You must be so proud, Jean.'

'Oh, I am, lovey, so very proud.'

The thought that Mr and Mrs H would have been in their element right now flitted through Florrie's mind, followed by a quick squeeze of her heart, making her wish they were here to see it.

'Thank you very much for turning out when it's so bloomin' freezing, folks,' Jack said in his rich North Yorkshire accent, instantly lifting Florrie's spirits. 'I know I can speak on behalf of Florrie and Ed when I say that your support of The Happy Hartes Bookshop is very much appreciated – it warms our happy hearts, so to speak.' He tapped his hand to his chest.

'Here, here,' said Florrie, as another round of applause burst out.

Jack turned and flashed her a quick smile. 'And I promise not to witter on for too long. I know you're all dying to see what magic Ed's created behind these curtains and we don't want any of you to freeze to the spot with me boring you to tears.' He chuckled.

'You could never bore anyone, Jack!' a female voice called out.

'Aye, too right,' said another. 'You can whisper sweet nothings in my lugs any time you like.'

A ripple of laughter ran around the gathering.

'Thank you very much, I might take you up on that offer,' he said dryly, a smile tugging the corners of his mouth. 'Anyroad, before we go any further, so none of the little kiddiewinkles miss out on seeing the unveiling, I think it'd be nice if we could have them at the front, so if we could just have a bit of a reshuffle before I press the magic button.'

Jack waited patiently while the crowd rearranged itself and a line of excited children stood before him. 'Ready?' he asked.

The crowd roared its reply, children jumping up and down.

'Okay, prepare yourselves to be utterly captivated by the magical Christmas display of The Happy Hartes Bookshop. Five! Four! Three...' The crowd counted down with him, their voices filling the square.

On the count of one, Jack pressed a button on the remote he held in his hand, and the curtain on the winter wonderland scene slowly glided open.

Set to a backdrop of a starry night sky, the space had been decorated as if it were a snow-covered clearing in a wood – albeit on a smaller scale. A cluster of faux conifers stood in one corner, their branches drooping under the weight of fake snow, while fir cones were scattered over the ground. In the centre was a small wooden sleigh upon which sat a sack in sumptuous red velvet complete with a thick cord tie in a rich shade of gold. The sack was bulging with books, some of which had spilled out around it, while a group of woodland creatures looked on. Though everything was fake, it looked remarkably realistic. It was spellbinding.

Behind the scenes, Ed flicked the switch that controlled the display.

A collective gasp of awe went up as the scene came to life, all twinkling lights and sparkling snow. The children were utterly enthralled. They ceased their jumping about and all stood gazing at it, mouths open, eyes shining as a pale half-moon was suddenly illuminated with a soft glow and stars began twinkling in the velvety night sky. In the next moment, a bushy-tailed squirrel scampered up a tree, while faux snowflakes began tumbling gently from above. The whole effect was magical, and another rousing cheer went up.

Florrie looked at Ed who feigned wiping sweat from his brow. 'Fingers crossed all goes smoothly for the second window,' he said.

'I'm sure it will.' She wrapped her arms around his middle and gave him a squeeze.

'Are you ready for the next one?' Jack asked, a laugh in his voice as the crowd cheered their reply. 'Wonderful! Come on, you can count down with me again. Five, four...'

Jack pressed the button and the curtain in the second window began to move before grinding to a halt. Everyone watched in silence as Jack tried the remote once more. Again, nothing happened. 'Ey up, looks like we're going for a little added dramatic effect.' Jack chuckled, glancing back, his eyes searching for Ed.

'Bugger,' Ed said under his breath, his smile falling. 'It worked perfectly when I set it up.'

Florrie glanced at him. 'What can we do?' she asked worriedly.

He hurried round to the front of the display, slipped inside the curtain and did a spot of tweaking. Moments later he said to Jack, 'Give it another go, see if that's fixed it.'

Jack nodded. 'Right then, folks, let's see if Ed's worked his magic.'

Florrie and Ed looked on, holding their breath as Jack pressed the button. This time the curtain began to move. Florrie caught Ed's eye, relief washing over the pair of them.

'Looks like he's fettled it.' Jack beamed out at the sea of faces as another chorus of delighted 'Ahhs' rose up followed by an appreciative round of applause.

Like the first display, everything was created in miniature, but this one had been designed to replicate a cosy living room decorated for Christmas in a vintage style. It had stirred warm feelings of nostalgia inside Florrie when she'd first set eyes on it.

A squishy chair with a thick, woollen throw over its back sat before an open fireplace that had the remnants of a fire in its grate. Beside the chair was a small table upon which an open book had been left, cover side up, next to an antique lamp. Bookcases were tucked into the spaces either side of the fireplace, their shelves bulging with an array of winter-themed reads. Opposite the chair was a sideboard set with yet more books and a tray bearing a crystal glass containing the dregs of "brandy", a slice of half-eaten Christmas cake and a plump carrot complete with a bite taken out. In the corner was a Christmas tree, decorated with tiny baubles and topped with a star, a pile of presents stacked beneath. A black Labrador, bearing an uncanny resemblance to Gerty, was sitting beside the chair. It was wearing a surprised expression as it gazed in the direction of the fireplace where a pair of snow-covered black boots, trimmed with white faux fur, appeared to be disappearing up the chimney. As if that wasn't enough, snowy footprints, sparkling with frost, led from the hearth and across the rug to the sideboard. There were garlands swagged along the wall and a pair of embroidered Christmas stockings hanging from the fireplace, with yet more books peeking from the tops. Like the first display, Ed's attention to detail was impeccable, and although this window couldn't have been more different to the first, it was no less magical for it. Indeed, Florrie had wished she could climb right in and snuggle down into the armchair as she watched Santa climb up the chimney when Ed had first shown her the display.

Ed reached down and flicked another switch. In an instant, the embers in the grate suddenly began to flicker, while over on the sideboard, the table lamp emitted a warm glow. The multi-coloured fairy lights on the Christmas tree twinkled enchantingly, and Father Christmas's boots started bobbing up and down the chimney, while the Labrador's head cocked to one side, its ears lifting as it looked on. The children at the front gave a gasp of joy as a tiny toy mouse scurried over the floor.

Yet more cheers and applause follow, echoing around the square.

'Everyone loves it, Ed.' Florrie beamed up at him. 'Just as I knew they would.'

He glanced down at her, smiling. 'Does this qualify for inclusion in The Happy Christmas Memories Project?'

'It most certainly does.' She nodded, taking in the joy shining in his eyes.

NINE

Half an hour later, after Florrie and Ed had given a quick interview to the press and TV reporter, the shop was bustling with customers and a queue was forming at the counter where Florrie and Leah were busily serving people. The pair quickly fell into a system with one bagging up the purchases while the other took payment. It seemed to be working efficiently as Florrie kept one eye on the clock; she didn't want to overrun into Jack's time.

They'd decided to keep the shop open for the hour between the window reveal and Jack's reading in order to maximise on any potential sales it might generate. It had been Ed's suggestion. 'It's an ideal opportunity, so we'd be mad not to take advantage of it,' he'd said. Florrie couldn't argue. She loved how his enthusiasm for the bookshop had grown since they'd first taken the helm.

She stole a quick glance around the room. Things had tailed off from the initial rush, but there were still a number of customers browsing the aisles or admiring the Christmas decorations. The excitement of earlier still hung in the air, though now it was more of a jolly burble rather than the exuberant roars and cheers. She spotted Jean and Paula over by the door to the reading room, greeting people warmly, taking tickets and guiding them to their seats. Both women looked to be enjoying themselves enormously which gladdened Florrie's heart.

Her gaze next landed on Stella, head and shoulders above the rest and looking uber-smart as always. She was describing something animatedly to Jasmine, Maggie and Lark, her long, blonde hair pulled back into neat ponytail. Jasmine's vibrant red pixie crop stood in stark contrast, as did Lark's flaxen blonde waves, woven with fine plaits and threaded with silver beads. They'd all been best friends since primary school, with the exception of Maggie whom Florrie had met when they'd been students at university in York. Though she'd known her the least amount of time, Maggie was the friend Florrie was closest to.

With the line of customers at the till finally dying down, Florrie left Leah in charge and headed towards her friends where she was greeted with happy smiles.

'Hey, Florrie, the windows are amazing.' Stella squeezed the top of Florrie's arm. Judging by her long, dark coat and black trouser suit she'd clearly come straight from her chambers in York where she was based as a criminal barrister.

'Thanks, Stells, and thanks for coming. I'm so glad you could make it, though I thought you were tied up in a trial.'

'I managed to wangle an early finish with the judge. Used my cunning powers of persuasion to get him to agree that we'd reached a good point to adjourn for the day.' She flashed a wide grin, the star-shaped diamond studs she always wore glinting under the lights.

'Didn't think you'd be able to use your style of "cunning powers of persuasion" in court, Stells.' Jasmine gave her an impish smile. She looked toasty in her padded jacket, its deep shade of green emphasising the colour of her hair. 'Thought that kind of behaviour would mean you'd end up in court on the wrong side of the law as it were.' She gave a throaty giggle, setting the others off.

Before Stella had met Alex, she'd been resolutely single, refusing to be tied down to a relationship and was well known amongst her friends for her colourful love life. But those days were apparently well behind her now, and she freely admitted she'd fallen for Alex hook, line and sinker. She pulled a face at Jasmine though she couldn't help but laugh. 'Very funny, Jazz.' A smile played over her mouth. 'I can assure you, the powers of persuasion to which you allude were kept under wraps – as they always are when I'm in court. And if you saw what a crusty old sourpuss His Honour Judge Mitchem is, you'd understand why. The simple fact is it actually made sense to finish at that point. He could see it, too, hence I'm here on time. And besides, I'm a one-man woman now, as you know.'

'Aye, so you are,' said Jasmine. 'And it's taking some getting used to it.' She shot Stella a cheeky grin.

'You're not wrong, not that I'm grumbling.' Stella smiled back.

'Aye, I know, we didn't see that one coming, did we, lasses?' Maggie chuckled.

'Sure didn't.' Florrie observed her friend. There was no getting away from the fact that being in love suited Stella; she was glowing with happiness.

'Ah, that's because Cupid waited for the right man to come along before he took aim and fired his arrow.' Lark's pale green eyes twinkled. She was looking every inch the boho hippy chick, wrapped in a flowing velvet coat in a rich shade of amethyst, her feet encased in a pair of cosy looking slouchy boots.

'You reckon?' Stella chuckled. 'Anyroad, when d'you think he's going to take aim at you? Poor old Nate deserves an award for his patience.' Her words triggered a ripple of giggles from the others.

They were stopped from saying anything further by

Jasmine's children who rushed over on a wave of excitement. They had been allowed to spend their pocket money on some of the new trendy stationery items the bookshop had just taken delivery of. Leah had advised on what would appeal to a younger target market, and it would seem she was right.

Zak and Chloe were quickly followed by Jasmine's mum, Heather, who was taking the children back home so Jasmine could stay for Jack's reading.

'Time we headed off, lovey.' Heather gave a warm smile. She and Jasmine shared the same red hair and luminescent skin.

Jasmine returned her smile. 'Okay, Mum, thanks for this. I really appreciate it. I'll head back as soon as it's finished here – shouldn't be too late.'

'No need to rush, flower. Your dad's watching some sport on the telly, so it's not as if I'd be getting much sense out of him for the rest of the evening. Once these two have gone to bed, I'll be quite happy snuggled up in your living room, reading my book.' She tapped her recent purchase that was tucked under her arm.

'You're a star.' Jasmine beamed at her mum before turning to Zak and Chloe whose freckled faces were wearing matching mischievous expressions. 'Be good for Grandma, you two little monsters, okay?' Jasmine said affectionately, ruffling Zak's dark red hair before giving Chloe's strawberry-blonde pigtails a gentle tug. They both nodded enthusiastically.

Just then, Leah bounded over, her cheeks flushed from the warmth of the room. 'Have you seen the time, Florrie?'

'Ooh, no.' Florrie glanced up at the clock. 'Thanks for letting me know, Leah, that last ten minutes has flown by.' She turned to her friends. 'I think we should probably head to the reading room now, lasses.' Her dark eyebrows drew together as she scanned the room, ticket-wielding customers filing past her on the way to where Jean and Paula were awaiting their collection. 'I don't know where Ed's got to, or Jack for that matter.'

'Last I saw they were having a natter in the kitchen with

Bear and Alex. Nate's there, too – looked deep and meaningful. I'll go see if they're still there and chivvy them along if they are.' Maggie smiled before heading down to the back of the shop.

Something deep and meaningful. The words sent a momentary shard of anxiety shooting through Florrie, piercing her bubble of happiness. Thoughts of the recent phone call from Ed's father rushed into her mind, quickly followed by what Leah had told her about Dodgy Dick hanging around. Was Ed talking to the men about his latest concerns for the bookshop? she wondered. Maybe asking their advice? Or was it to do with the reason he'd been disappearing into the attic, rooting amongst his stuff? Were the two connected? That thought made Florrie's stomach churn and she felt her buoyant mood begin to ebb away.

Don't think about that now! Just concentrate on the reading and what an awesome night this is. She plastered a smile on her face and made a determined effort to focus on positive thoughts, but not before her worries had been picked up by the everperceptive Lark.

'You okay, flower?' she asked, her armful of silver bracelets jangling as she reached out and squeezed Florrie's hand.

'I'm fine, thanks.' Florrie pushed her smile up higher. 'Something's happened, but I'll tell you about it later.'

'Okay.' Lark nodded, smiling gently. 'We're all here for you if you need us.'

'Thank you.' Florrie returned her smile.

'What's up?' asked Maggie, picking up on the conversation. 'The fellas are just coming, by the way.'

'Has something happened?' asked Jasmine, whose smile had been replaced by a frown.

'Please tell me buggerlugs is behaving himself.' Stella's face had turned serious. 'I've already warned him if he messes you about, I'll relieve him of his testicles and feed them to the seagulls. And that's just for starters.' It was easy to see how she'd make for an intimidating opponent in court.

Kev Poppleton, a regular at Jack's readings who was walking by on his way to the reading room, winced at the comment, and upped his speed, making Maggie giggle.

Florrie's gaze swept over the four concerned faces looking back at her, her heart instantly warmed by their love and loyalty. They were all fiercely protective of one another, ready to offer words of support and comfort at the drop of a hat. If any one of the group was feeling down or having a hard time, no matter the reason, the others would rally and do all they could to help make things better. Florrie had been so glad of their friendship when Mr H had passed away, and through the ensuing drama with Ed's parents and the bookshop. They'd been a tower of strength, bolstering her, encouraging her to face the day even though all she'd wanted to do was hide under her duvet and forget what was happening with the rest of the world.

She mustered up a reassuring smile. 'Everything's fine, there just seems to be...' She paused, smiling a *hello* at an excited-looking customer who was walking by, ticket in hand. 'I can't really say too much now, but I'll just tell you quickly that his dad rang the other night, though I'm not really sure of the reason.' It didn't feel right to mention that she was sure he'd bandied Jean's name about.

'Oh, Florrie.' Lark pressed a hand to her chest, her many bracelets sliding down her arm.

'And we all know Peter Harte never gets in touch with good news,' said Jasmine.

'Please tell me you're joking.' Stella's face was as dark as thunder. 'I thought they'd gone quiet.'

'They had.'

'But I thought they'd accepted how things are,' said Maggie.

'I thought so, too, but something about this feels different. I'm not a hundred per cent sure it's about the bookshop. And what's worse, Leah told me Dodgy Dick was hanging around outside the shop for ages this morning.' Florrie drew in a deep breath, her heart feeling heavy at the reminder. 'Anyway, I daresay I'll know more by our get-together on Friday. I'll share it all then. In the meantime, we'd best get through to where the action is.'

Jack's reading proved to be the perfect distraction for Florrie. He held the audience, including her, in his thrall as he read from his latest novel, tension hanging in the air. It was set in and around Micklewick Bay in the seventeenth century and based on infamous landowner Benjamin Fitzgilbert who'd lived a double life as a wealthy and highly respected gentleman by day and a prolific smuggler under the darkness of night. Jack's writing was so evocative Florrie had almost been able to smell the damp of the tunnel, hear the sails of the ships flapping in the wind and see the clouds rushing across the moon. Gasps were exhaled as he described how gunshots were fired into the dark- ness, a woman's blood-curdling scream, the sound of someone falling...

'And that' – he closed his book and looked up at the capti- vated sea of faces – 'concludes this evening's reading, folks. I'm afraid if you want to know what happens to Brave Lass Bess, you're going to have to read the book yourselves. And for those of you who haven't already got a copy, I'm very pleased to say, you can buy one here and I'd be happy to sign it for anyone who's interested.' He gave a roguish smile and the audience erupted into raucous applause, cheers bouncing around the room. Jack's readings always went down a storm and tonight's was no exception. In fact, Florrie thought it was his most popular yet, no doubt helped by the fact that he'd based this novel on local history.

Florrie looked up at Ed who was standing next to her at the

back of the room, behind the audience, clapping his hands with great gusto, a delighted smile on his face. He caught her eye and gave her a wink. There was no trace of the concern clouding his features the way it had after his father had rung. She told herself he could have been talking to Jack and the other men about anything in the kitchen – it didn't have to be his father's latest phone call, or Dodgy Dick, or the reason he kept disappearing into the attic.

Ed leant towards her. 'That was fantastic! I'd say it counts as a happy Christmas memory. What do you reckon?'

She beamed a smile up at him, joy surging through her. 'Oh, absolutely!'

He dipped his head and placed a gentle kiss on her lips, sending her heart into a frenzy. *Oh my days!* Despite what was going on in the background, she loved this man with an intensity that burnt fiercely inside her.

Florrie turned back to face the room, clapping hard along with the rest of the audience, a huge smile on her face.

TEN

As the last customer finally left the bookshop, Florrie locked the door and pulled the blind down, the spicy aroma of mulled wine they'd served with the nibbles lingering in the air. Her body was still buzzing with a high from Jack's book reading.

'I think that went okay. What d'you reckon?' Jack asked in his usual understated way. He was looking happy and relaxed as he stood alongside the others by the counter, his now-familiar post-event-glow shimmering around him. No one would ever guess at his growing status as a national treasure and Florrie regularly found she had to pinch herself that she could actually consider him a friend.

She turned to him, eyes incredulous. '*Okay?* It went more than okay, Jack. It went amazingly well. And your reading... it was just *spellbinding*. You captured the atmosphere so perfectly. In fact, you could actually hear the audience holding its breath.'

'You *so* could. It was fantastic, Jack,' said Jasmine, oozing enthusiasm.

'Aye, it was that.' Nate nodded heartily. 'I could've listened to you for hours. Think I'm going to invest in the audiobook so I can dive back into the story while I'm working.'

'Ooh, good plan,' Lark enthused.

'Thank you so much for agreeing to do it for us, Jack,' said Florrie. 'We're really grateful for all of your support for the bookshop.'

'Yes, thank you, Jack,' said Ed, beaming at him. 'And I agree with everyone, the reading was amazing, I'd say it's your best yet. I reckon the audience thought so, too, as we've sold every single copy of your book, and we'd bought loads in. We've had to take orders as well.'

'Hey, no need for thanks. I enjoyed myself. There's nowt like locking folk in a room so they have no choice but to listen to you while you prattle on.' He gave a throaty chuckle. 'And let's not forget, I benefit from every book sale, so it's me who should be thanking you and Florrie for having me here and flogging my books.'

'They were hardly locked in, Jack,' Alex said, chuckling. 'They all looked perfectly happy to be here, which is hardly surprising.'

'We had to turn folk away, didn't we, Jean?' said Paula.

'We did.' Jean nodded emphatically.

'Aye, well.' Jack looked momentarily bashful. 'I reckon it must've been the promise of tasty scran and glass of mulled wine that tempted them.'

'I don't think so.' Maggie giggled, rubbing the small of her back as she succumbed to a frown.

It was always a given that Jack's author events would be sold out within minutes of being announced on the bookshop's social media pages. The shop would be swooped on by customers, all clamouring to get their hands on a ticket – Florrie and Ed always made sure to hold some back for family and friends. 'Aye, well, I suppose it gives folk summat to do of an evening when there's nowt on the telly,' Jack regularly said, in his self-deprecating way whenever he was told of the interest his appearances generated. Since his first event last year, he'd become a regular fixture at The Happy Hartes Bookshop, with his readings and book signings, which he seemed more than content with. It was something Florrie and Ed would be eternally grateful for; his involvement had helped with their plans to give the bookshop a new lease of life.

'I'm so proud of you, lovey.' Jean dashed a tear away from her cheek, gazing affectionately at her son.

'I'm not surprised, Jean. I can't tell you how glad I am that I managed to get here to witness Jack's reading. It was breathtaking.' Stella smiled at her. 'I'm itching to read the book for myself now.' She patted her designer handbag where she'd slipped a copy.

'The whole event's been amazing,' said Bear, in his deep voice. 'From the window reveals to the atmosphere in the shop, to Jack's reading. It's been a totally brilliant evening.'

'It *so* has,' said Leah, beaming at the author.

'And it ain't over yet if I can tempt you lot to a drink at The Cellar. I warned Bill and Pim we might be popping in.' Jack cast a hopeful look around the group of friends.

Florrie had been looking forward to spending the rest of the evening curled up on the sofa at home with Ed. She'd nipped out to the gift shop in her lunchbreak and picked up a little token which she'd been looking forward to presenting him with. But the temptation to continue the wonderful time she was having with her friends found her looking at him hopefully.

'I'm game,' he said, giving an easy shrug.

'Me too.' She smiled, thinking it didn't make any difference what time she gave him the little gift; it was only a bit of fun after all.

'How about you, missus?' Bear glanced down at Maggie. 'Are you up to it, or are you ready for home?'

'Hey, don't let this bump fool you! I'm definitely up to it,' Maggie said wholeheartedly.

'Right, Jack, mate, sounds like you can count me and Mags in,' said Bear, grinning.

'Aye, me too,' said Nate, his eyes shifting to Lark.

'I'm in court in the morning, and I've driven down here so I'll just have the one tipple,' said Stella. She turned to Alex. 'Don't feel you have to come away early with me, though. I'll understand if you want to hang back. I would if I didn't have some work to do.'

'I'll probably head back with you. I've got some plans I need to look over before I meet with a client in the morning.' Alex was an architect with a busy practice. He and Stella had apartments opposite one another in the newly converted, and highly desirable Fitzgilbert's Landing that had once been a large warehouse on the top prom at the other end of town. Alex had actually drawn up the plans for the mystery buyer who'd snapped up the derelict building.

'I'll have to take a raincheck on that, I need to head home,' Leah said disappointedly. 'I promised I'd help Tilly with her English homework, which she's left to the last minute, as usual. I'll already get back later than I promised.'

'That's a shame.' Florrie gave her a sympathetic smile. She knew Leah was regularly called upon by her family to help out with her younger sister's homework. 'But don't worry, there'll be plenty of other times when you can join us.'

'True.' Leah mustered up a smile and nodded.

'I know it's a school night, but I reckon it won't do any harm to sneak in a cheeky bottle of beer, seeing as though it's for a special occasion,' said Jasmine, making the most of the opportunity to have some "me time" with her friends. 'After all, my mum did say I didn't need to rush back.'

Jack turned to Jean, a mischievous twinkle in his eye. 'You'll be on a pint of Micklewick Magic with Jaeger Bomb chasers again, will you, Mum?'

Jean giggled. 'Give over, son. It'll be a small sherry for me, as you well know.'

Florrie watched as he gave his mother an affectionate hug, topping it off with a peck on the cheek. It gladdened her heart to see how the bond between the pair had grown. Finding her son had given Jean a new purpose in life as well as giving Jack a place to anchor himself to after the death of his adoptive parents.

The group walked briskly down the square in a bubble of enthusiastic chatter, peals of laughter rising up into the night as they passed the cheerfully decorated shop windows. Frost sparkled under the streetlamps and the Christmas lights that were festooned from shop to shop. They turned the corner at the end of the row and hurried along Endeavour Road to The Cellar. Florrie had linked Maggie's arm, listening as her friend told her all about the latest orders that had flooded in for The Micklewick Bear Company. By all accounts, she was doing a roaring trade. Ed strode along with Gerty on the end of her lead. He was chatting to Bear and Jack, with Nate and Alex walking closely behind. From what she could gather, their conversation looked serious, making Florrie wonder again if they were discussing Ed's father's phone call. She tried to ignore the clutch of worries that started squirming in her stomach, the image of Dodgy Dick flashing through her mind.

Before long, the group tumbled into the stylish bar and were greeted with a warm smile by Brooke, one of the regular bartenders. She was walking by with a perfectly balanced tray of drinks in her hand. 'Hi there,' she said in a cheery voice, her dark ponytail swishing. She was wearing black skinny jeans, the micro-brewery's signature tweed waistcoat over a crisp white shirt, and a long apron, tied around her waist, emblazoned with The Cellar's logo.

A chorus of hellos followed as the welcoming atmosphere enveloped them.

'Ooh, it's lovely and warm in here,' said Jasmine, unzipping her jacket, her cheeks glowing where the frost had nipped.

'Mm. It is.' Florrie's glasses had steamed up as usual. She took them off, squinting at the chalkboard at the side of the bar.

The room was illuminated in a warm amber glow cast by the stylish lighting, emphasised by the candles in lanterns set out on the tables. Her glasses back on, Florrie's eye was caught by the bushy Christmas tree at the back of the room. It was decorated with a selection of quirky baubles and decked with hundreds of fairy lights, and topped with a bold, angular star. Further festive decorations were provided in the form of chrome stags' heads that were hung on the walls, baubles dangling from their antlers, while sumptuous garlands were fixed to the beams and studded with yet more richly coloured baubles.

The group headed towards the polished oak bar where a line of gleaming beer pumps sat, selling The Cellar's famous local beers. Bill, who was pulling a pint, turned and smiled. 'Evening, all,' he said. He was always immaculately turned out, with his neatly clipped beard and tidy crop of hair.

'Hi there,' said Pim in his melodic Dutch accent. He was Bill's husband and business partner, and had recently discovered that he was Stella's half-brother. As a consequence, the half-siblings had been doing all they could to get to know one another better. He was extremely tall, towering over Bill, and had a mop of glossy chin-length blond hair and eyes the same shade of blue as Stella's. Though he and Bill wore the same uniform as their staff, their waistcoats were in a slightly different weave of tweed. Pim's gaze swept over the group. 'Why don't I give you a few drinks menus? You can find yourselves a table and I'll send Brooke over to take your order.' He flashed a friendly smile at them.

'Sounds like a plan. Thanks, Pim.' Jack took the proffered menus and passed them round. 'Here you go, folks.'

'There's a spot free over there that should fit us all in.' Ed nodded in the direction of a semi-circular booth covered in tastefully aged leather. They all headed over to it, their feet clipping over the wooden floorboards.

Once their drinks had arrived, Jack cleared his throat. 'So, I've had something on my mind that I'd like to air with you all,' he said, glancing around at them, his expression suddenly serious. He paused, nibbling on his bottom lip, as if gathering his thoughts.

A frown crumpled Florrie's brow, wondering what it could be. She took in his serious expression, hoping he wasn't about to share bad news. She caught Ed's eye; he looked as puzzled as she felt. Her gaze moved to Jean who was wearing a small smile. *Oh*. It took Florrie aback a little. Did Jean know what her son was going to say? Florrie wondered. She quickly reminded herself that Jack's dour resting face often belied what he was thinking. And if Jean's smile was anything to go by, maybe she'd been too hasty in heading down the bad news route. Florrie certainly hoped so. And besides, she could hardly imagine he'd announce something that would put the dampeners on the wonderful evening they'd just had. He wasn't that kind of person.

Everyone was poised, all eyes on Jack, as they waited to hear what he had to say.

He ran his hand up and down his pint of beer, smoothing away the beads of condensation. 'Thing is, I've been approached by my publishers about writing my autobiography – heaven knows why they think anyone would be interested in reading about a boring old fart like me.' He pulled a "can you believe it?" face.

Stella, who was sitting next to Florrie, sat up straight. Her interest was clearly piqued, while Jasmine's eyebrows shot up.

'You see, they know about me coming here to Micklewick Bay in search of my family connection, and how I ended up finding my wonderful birth mother right here in the town.' He reached for Jean's hand, giving it a squeeze. She smiled back at him, her eyes glowing with affection.

'Oh, Jack, that sounds so lovely,' said Florrie. It hadn't escaped her attention that Ed had gone quiet. In fact, she could have sworn she'd felt him tense beside her.

'And it would make a brilliant story,' said Maggie.

'Aye, it would,' agreed Bear.

'Especially with the way you'd tell it,' Paula added. She'd been a huge fan of Jack's for years, and her bookcase was bulging with everything he'd had published.

'So would you use it as inspiration for a novel?' asked Alex. 'Or would it be a straightforward autobiography, with you actually telling *your* story?'

'Aye, well, see, that's the reason I'm bringing it up now. They want an autobiography, for me to tell *my* story, warts and all.' His eyes dropped to his pint; having a modest nature, he was clearly embarrassed by this. 'Which would mean I'd have to mention Florrie and Ed, and The Happy Hartes Bookshop.' He took a moment, his eyes flicking between the couple. 'I didn't know how you'd feel about that, kind of being pushed into the spotlight, as it were – if anyone was interested enough in buying a book where I blether on about myself, that is. As my agent pointed out, it's not as if I've kept my background a secret. Folk know I was adopted, and I'd come to Micklewick Bay in search of my birth family. The autobiography would obviously go into greater detail, clear up any rumours or duff information that's floating around. And it's common knowledge I do readings at the bookshop, so folk know of that connection. But if you'd rather I didn't, then I'd respect your wishes.'

Florrie didn't miss a beat. 'As far as I'm concerned, Jack, I think yours and Jean's story is such a special one, it really should be shared. I don't doubt for a second your fans would love to read about it – *I'd* love to read about it from your perspective,' she said. 'And I'd be absolutely fine with you mentioning me and the bookshop. Wouldn't you, Ed?' She glanced up at him, expecting to see him smiling, but instead she found an expression that she could swear bordered on hesitant, anxious, even.

'Oh, me too,' said Paula, who clearly hadn't picked up on Ed's reaction.

'Yeah, same here,' said Leah. 'I reckon they'd be clamouring for it.'

Hoping Jack hadn't detected Ed's sudden change in demeanour, Florrie injected her voice with a generous dash of enthusiasm and said, 'Ooh, Jack, how wonderful would it be if you could do a reading of your autobiography for the bookshop? If you wouldn't mind, that is?'

Jack's face broke out into a broad smile, and he gave one of his trademark throaty laughs, apparently oblivious to whatever was troubling Ed. 'It'd be my pleasure, lass.' He raised his pint to her. 'Cheers to that.'

'Aye, and cheers to a bloomin' brilliant night, and another one to look forward to by all accounts,' said Nate, raising his pint of Micklewick Mellow. They all followed suit – including Ed, who, much to Florrie's relief, had resurrected his smile – a chorus of "cheers" ringing out.

It was while Jack was elaborating on his autobiography that the reason for Ed's sudden change of mood dawned on Florrie: Jean Davenport. She couldn't shake the feeling it had something to do with his father mentioning her friend's name in the phone call. Whatever it was, she was determined to find out, though it wasn't going to be easy with Ed's habit of clamming up. She only hoped Jean wouldn't end up hurt as a result.

ELEVEN

TUESDAY 5TH DECEMBER

Florrie and Ed, together with Lark and Nate, were the last of their group still lingering at The Cellar. The others had been keen to take Bear up on his offer of a lift to their respective homes in the Land Rover, especially since the north easterly wind had upped the ante, adding a biting edge to the cold.

Florrie had been glad of the time to unwind after the hectic build-up to the unveiling of the windows and Jack's reading and, tired as she was, she wasn't in a rush to head off. There'd still be time to give Ed the little gift she'd got him when they got back home. Sitting beside him in the booth, she relaxed into him, his arm stretched out on the back of the bench behind her. He appeared to have put his odd reaction to Jack's proposed autobiography behind him, but it had loitered at the back of Florrie's mind, nudging her to follow it up. Despite that, she still managed to enjoy the rest of the evening, Lark and Nate being laid-back, easy company.

They'd been listening with interest as Nate described some of the fascinating items he'd encountered in his job upcycling and restoring furniture. He had a good eye and the ability to see potential in even the most dilapidated piece of furniture, sourcing new stock from a variety of places. On top of that, his prices were reasonable, ensuring turnover was quick. Thanks to this winning combination, his business was beginning to outgrow the little shop he occupied on Endeavour Street. Indeed, Florrie had sourced many of the items that furnished Samphire Cottage from Nate, including the vintage pine dresser in her kitchen and the small console table that sat below the window in the living room, not to mention a variety of book-shelves.

From the conversation that had followed once Florrie and Ed were relaxing in the kitchen at home, Nate had evidently set Ed's mind whirring.

Ed took a slow sip of his tea, before carefully setting his mug down on the kitchen table. The pair were looking shattered after their hectic day with the window reveal and Jack's read-ing. He glanced over at Florrie. 'So, I've been thinking about the future of the bookshop.'

Uh-oh. Florrie's heart nose-dived all the way down to her fluffy slippers as her heart simultaneously lurched up to her throat. Disconcertingly, his response to Jack's autobiography flashed through her mind. 'What do you mean?' She searched his face, hoping to find a clue in his expression, relieved so see a pair of happy eyes looking back at her. It clearly didn't involve anything horrendous, like handing it over to his parents or selling it to Dodgy Dick.

'Well...' A smile was hitching up the corners of his mouth. 'I've been thinking of a way around it for a while, but tonight's conversation with Nate provided what could be the perfect solution.'

'The perfect solution to what?' She couldn't help but smile back as puzzled thoughts started capering around her mind.

'So, you know he mentioned how he'd recently bought a staircase, the one that had been salvaged from Walker's at the bottom of the square?'

'Yes,' she said slowly; she couldn't even begin to imagine where the heck this was going.

'It got me thinking...' He grinned at her.

'Thinking what?' Her heart lifted at the happiness shining in his eyes.

He took another slow sip of his tea.

'Argh! This is torture! You've got to tell me! The suspense is too much,' Florrie said. Despite her protestations, she found herself giggling.

Ed laughed, his blue eyes crinkling in the way that made her heart flutter. 'You know how you said your dream was to have a tearoom at the bookshop but didn't know how we could get it to work with the layout and space we've got?'

Oh my days! This is exciting! 'Yes, but how come the conversation with Nate got you thinking about that?'

'That's where the staircase comes in.'

'Okay. I'm afraid you're going to have to elaborate on that. We can't have folk sipping tea on an old staircase, if that's what you're thinking.'

Ed threw his head back and let rip with a booming laugh, making Gerty jump up from her bed. 'I promise you, that's not what I had planned.'

'Thank goodness for that.'

When his laughter had subsided, he said, 'Okay, hear me out on this, but I haven't been able to stop thinking about it ever since Nate mentioned it, and if the staircase fits like I'm hoping it will, it could be the perfect solution.'

'I'm all ears.' Florrie leant forward, resting her chin on her hands. This was wonderful news, and not just because it involved her tearoom dream – it meant Ed was still invested in the bookshop's future, and that made her happier than she could ever imagine. She'd wait until a more suitable moment to ask why Jack's biography had bothered him, not wanting to pour cold water over his plans.

'So, you know how the flat above the bookshop is empty at the moment, and we were going to ask Bear to redecorate it for us before advertising for a new tenant?'

'Yes.' She listened with interest as Ed went on to explain how talk of the staircase had given him the idea of converting the upstairs flat into a spacious, book-themed tearoom. He went on to say how they could use some of the other rooms for different events and even extend the bookshop upstairs, giving more space to the second-hand and collectable out-of-print books they had. He suggested they could also stock more book-themed accessories, particularly those that were popular with their younger clientele. Florrie couldn't argue with any of it; his ideas were utterly compelling.

'Do you really think we could do it?'

'Of course!' He nodded vigorously. 'I wouldn't mention it if I didn't think it was possible. A couple who used to exhibit my work in London – Morwenna and Jay – did the self-same thing with their art gallery; they created a stylish coffee shop upstairs. It was a massive success, great for business. Said they wished they'd done it sooner. We could see if Alex would be happy to draw up the plans for the conversion and ask your dad if he'll do all the necessary building work – we'll pay them both, naturally. I don't expect freebies.' He looked at her, his expression bright with anticipation as he awaited her response.

It was great to see Ed so fired up. His enthusiasm was infectious, and Florrie could feel excitement bubbling up inside her. 'Wow! That would be so fantastic! I'm sure my dad would be more than happy to do the work for us and he could maybe get Bear to help. An extra pair of hands would speed up the process and reduce the disruption. I daresay he'd squeeze us in, too.'

Charlie Appleton ran his own small building company, with Paula dealing with the admin side of things. He'd taken care of the necessary building jobs when Florrie had bought Samphire Cottage, of which there were many. The property's knock-down price had reflected that it was a "doer-upper" and in need of a generous dose of TLC.

'That sounds great. I know Bear's not a trained builder, but he can turn his hand to anything. He and Maggie did a fantastic job of renovating Clifftop Cottage.' As well as working at Thorncliffe Farm – which was owned by his parents, as was the land where his home with Maggie was situated – Bear was a much-in-demand local odd-job man.

'They did. Dad and Bear sound like the perfect team, and we know from what Alex has done at Stella's apartment building, his designs are amazing.'

'If you fancy, I could have a word with Nate in the morning. I'm sure he wouldn't mind us popping down to take a look at the staircase,' said Ed. 'Then we could ask Alex to have a look, see where he thinks it would work best. Don't know about you, but I reckon at the back right-hand side of the shop. Should fit perfectly up against the wall there.'

The last time Florrie had seen Ed this animated was when he'd told her he wanted to be here in Micklewick Bay, with her, the two of them working at the bookshop. It had made Florrie's heart sing, and today it was having the same effect.

'I mean, I know there's already the staircase to the flat at the back of the shop, but it's a poky, functional affair and tucked right out of the way. It's hardly inspiring. We could make a real feature of the one Nate's got. And the separate access from the exterior door at the front wouldn't work, but a feature staircase within the actual bookshop would be fantastic.' He paused, his eyes shining brightly as he searched Florrie's face. 'What do you think?'

In the next moment, she jumped up and rushed over to him, wrapping her arms around his neck and covering him in kisses. 'I love it! I love it! I love it! It's such a wonderful idea! And it sounds perfect for the bookshop. Oh, my goodness, I really hope it'll fit!'

'Shall I take that as a yes, then?' Ed said, laughing as she continued with her delivery of noisy kisses.

With the excitement of Ed's idea still sinking in, Florrie said, 'Actually, don't move, I've just remembered something.'

'You have?' Ed shot her a puzzled look.

'Won't be a tick,' she called over her shoulder as she rushed off to retrieve her backpack from where she'd hooked it over the banister when they first got home.

'I got you this,' she said, returning a couple of minutes later with a festive gift bag swinging on her finger.

'Isn't it a bit early for Christmas presents?' Ed asked when she'd set it on the table in front of him.

'This one's best opened before Christmas, so you've got plenty of time to enjoy it.' She grinned at him, slipping into her seat and nudging the gift bag closer to him. 'I should warn you it's a bit fragile.'

'Very cryptic.' He returned her smile as he reached beneath the tissue paper and carefully eased out the item beneath. 'Oh, wow! It's a snow globe!' His smile grew wider as his gaze ran over the miniature woodland scene, a cosy-looking thatched cottage at the centre. He gave the globe a quick shake, chuckling delightedly as he watched the "snow" flurry around. 'My first ever snow globe. I love it!'

'I guessed you probably hadn't had one before,' she said, thrilled at his reaction. 'It's just a bit of tat, but I thought it might be another contender for The Happy Christmas Memory Project.'

'Oh, without a doubt it's going on the list! And it's not tat, it's fun! I'll keep it in my box of treasures and bring it out every Christmas.' He reached across the table, taking her hand and pressing his lips against it. 'Thank you, Florrie.'

'You're welcome. It's just a small gesture.'

'The thought behind it is anything but.'

TWELVE

TUESDAY 5TH DECEMBER

Business was brisk at The Happy Hartes Bookshop, and the first couple of hours since they'd opened that morning had whizzed by. Florrie and Leah had been kept busy serving customers and restocking shelves, with Florrie dealing with the orders that had been placed after Jack's reading, whenever time would allow. She'd been delighted with the positive feedback they'd been deluged with about their evening, and a buzz of excitement lingered in the shop. Ed's window displays continued to garner much interest on the pavement outside, "oohs" and "aahs" filtering through the glass. Several of the people who'd stopped to admire his handiwork had been tempted inside the shop, eager to take a look at the festive decorations and, in most cases, make a purchase. The tills had rung merrily, much to Florrie's delight.

As busy as she'd been, Florrie had regularly found her thoughts venturing down the path to Ed's suggestion. The prospect of them opening a tearoom upstairs sent a thrill rushing through her each time. It had toyed with her concentration, making it difficult to give the task in hand her full attention; she wished he'd hurry up and get himself back from Nate's upcycling shop where he'd arranged to meet her dad and Bear. And, as luck would have it, Alex had agreed to call in en route to his appointment with a client. She was desperate to hear whether their plans had legs. They'd decided not to share any of this with Leah just yet, thinking it was best to keep it to themselves until they knew whether the idea was feasible, but it had been a struggle to keep the smile from her face.

'Someone's happy this morning,' Leah had said when she'd caught Florrie grinning inanely to herself.

'Oh... um, it's just because last night was such a resounding success,' she'd replied, thinking quickly.

Florrie had surprised herself at how passionate she'd become about Ed's suggestion; she'd be bitterly disappointed if Alex advised them it was a no-go.

She glanced over at the clock above the counter, feeling a rush of anticipation. Surely Ed would be back soon. It had been over an hour since he'd popped out. *They must have decided whether using the staircase was doable by now!* She consoled herself that at least they'd set the ball rolling, rather than sitting around and pondering the idea. She'd hoped to have joined Ed to take a look at the staircase, but it wouldn't have been fair to leave Leah on her own. Paula – who had started doing the odd shift at the bookshop since business had increased at the store – hadn't been able to step in and help since she had a hair appointment and couldn't rearrange at such short notice. Oh, how Florrie wished she could be a fly on the wall as they discussed the logistics. Her heart had leapt every time the bell above the door went, expecting it to be Ed returning with news.

She was deep in conversation with Jean Davenport, going through the itinerary for next week's Christmas-themed visit by a group of children and their teachers from the local junior school, when Ed landed back with Gerty. Florrie's stomach looped-the-loop, and not just because he looked out-of-the-way attractive, with his dark hair all tousled and windswept, his complexion fresh. He scanned the shop, breaking into a wide smile as his eyes locked on hers, making her heart flutter. *Oh my days! Please tell me it's good news!*

'Hi,' he said, bending to kiss her once he'd released Gerty from her lead and had exchanged hellos with Jean. Florrie was relieved to see there was no evidence of the odd mood that had plagued Ed yesterday evening when Jack had mentioned his autobiography.

'Hi.' His cheeks felt chilly against hers, and cool, salt-laden air clung to his clothes. 'How did it go?' Florrie asked, as her heart rate upped its pace.

'Went well. Sounds very optimistic.' His smile reached all the way to his eyes.

Jean gave them a puzzled glance before saying, 'Listen, why don't I stay here and give Leah a hand while you two go and have a chat? The reading room's nice and quiet at the moment. We can manage.'

Florrie met Ed's gaze, attempting to read his thoughts. She glanced over at Leah who was chatting to Jessie Evans at the counter. 'There's no need for you to shoot off, Jean, we're happy for you to hear our exciting plans for the bookshop,' Florrie said, keeping her voice low, hoping Ed would agree. She beamed happily at the older woman. Jean was the soul of discretion and someone who Florrie would trust with her deepest secrets.

'Exciting plans? Ooh, now that does sound intriguing.' Jean smiled.

'Oh, Jean, it's all I can think about at the minute!' said Florrie, unable to keep the excitement from her voice.

Jean's eyes twinkled as Florrie and Ed gave her a quick rundown of their fledgling ideas for the tearoom. She clasped her hands together happily. 'Well, I think that sounds wonderful! It's just what the town needs, somewhere to go for a decent cup of tea and a slice of cake. The coffee shop on Skellergate isn't what it used to be, and I can't think of anywhere better than having a tearoom in a bookshop – and this bookshop, in particular. It's the perfect combination! Dinah and Bernard would be overjoyed to hear it, my loves.'

'I'm so pleased you like it, Jean, it means a lot,' said Florrie, a tug in her heart at the mention of Mr and Mrs H. In truth, she knew Mr H wouldn't have been that taken with the idea if he was still here; in his later years, especially after his wife had passed away, he'd been deeply averse to change. It had been a battle getting him to agree to stock a range of stationery that had become hugely popular thanks to Jenna Johnstone, a popular romance author, one of whose books had been made into a television series, and who they'd booked to do a reading at the bookshop. Jenna had collaborated with a small North Yorkshire artist who had a range of stationery emblazoned with images of her designs, the notebooks of which had become particularly popular. Jenna, who declared she used a fresh notebook for each new manuscript, had plastered images of the artist's collection across all her social media pages. It had created a huge amount of hype and Florrie had thought stocking a selection of the stationery was too good an opportunity to miss. Unfortunately, Mr H had shown he had a stubborn streak to rival the donkeys that traipsed the beach over the summer months, but Florrie's persistence had eventually paid off and they'd struggled to keep up with the demand.

'Yes, me too,' Ed said, quietly, before turning to Florrie. 'You'll have to head down to Nate's and take a look at the staircase. Honestly, Florrie, it's *amazing*. It's in great condition and the patina on the banister's just incredible. It'll be perfect for here.'

'So it's definitely doable, then?' Florrie's heart started pumping with anticipation.

'Alex thinks so. He'll need to get measurements, of course, but he seems to think the dimensions of the properties on the square will be pretty similar. Mind, he did say there'd be a load of building regs to comply with, but he didn't think it would involve anything insurmountable.'

'That's brilliant news!' Florrie could barely prevent herself squealing with delight.

'And Bear said he'd be happy to give your dad a hand, too, so it's all good.' Ed smiled down at her.

Florrie beamed back, her chest filling with joy as her mind started swirling with book-themed tearoom ideas.

'Actually, I've just remembered I need to tell Jack he doesn't need to pick up my order from the bakery,' said Jean, breaking into Florrie's thoughts.

She blinked, turning to Jean, her eyebrows arched in question. 'Oh?'

'He's popping in for his tea tonight and I asked him if he could collect my order on his way for me but since I'm here, I can get it myself. I'd best give him a call before it slips my mind. Won't be a minute, lovey.' She patted Florrie's arm. 'But your tearoom idea really is most exciting! And I promise I won't breathe a word.'

With Jean heading off in the direction of the kitchen to retrieve her phone from her handbag, Florrie turned to Ed, grinning broadly. 'So, do you reckon we can add this tearoom/staircase idea to The Happy Christmas Memory Project?'

'You know,' he said thoughtfully, rubbing his hand across his chin, 'I reckon we can. It doesn't matter that it won't get started until well after the festive period, but it'll definitely go down as a happy Christmas memory because of all the excitement it'll generate right now.'

'I like that.' Florrie smiled up at him. The couple weren't ones for public displays of affection, but at this very moment in time, she'd like nothing more than to wrap her arms around Ed and squeeze him tight. If he was to throw in one of his delicious kisses, then that would be an added bonus. She cast her gaze over to Leah at the counter where a queue was forming. It looked as though Florrie would have to wait until tonight to enjoy the feeling of Ed's arms around her, his lips soft against hers. The thought prompted an inward shiver of delight.

She was pulled out of her musings by the sound of Ed's phone ringing. He heaved a sigh, his face falling as he eased the offending object from the back pocket of his jeans.

'You've got to be kidding me!' He clapped his hand to his forehead, their happy mood of only moments ago crashing into hundreds of tiny pieces on the floor around them.

Florrie didn't need to ask as to the identity of the caller, Ed's reaction told her everything she needed to know.

He silenced the phone and pushed it back into his pocket. Florrie looked on with concern, words evading her. He was going to have to speak to his dad before all hell blew up. A few moments later, a ping, heralding a voicemail, sounded from Ed's back pocket. He raked his hands impatiently through his hair, catching her eye before quickly looking away. Now evidently wasn't the time to pursue the matter; she got the feeling it wouldn't go down well.

She was distracted by a flurry of activity over at the counter where Leah had been inundated with yet more customers. The young girl threw a concerned glance Florrie's way. 'I'd best go and help Leah,' she said to Ed.

'Yeah, 'course,' he said, forcing a smile.

THIRTEEN

Since the inception of The Happy Christmas Memory Project, Florrie had utilised any spare moments she had searching for festive ideas. She'd covertly booked tickets for an ice-skating session over at Middleton-le-Moors for the following afternoon and was looking forward to sharing the surprise with Ed. She wasn't sure how her news would be received, but she was content in the knowledge that he'd be happy about the table reservation she'd made at The Golden Fleece for afterwards. The pub was serving hearty Christmas dinners and there was nothing Ed liked more than to get stuck into a roast with all the trimmings. It would no doubt be appreciated all the more if they needed warming up after their stint on the ice.

Florrie was grateful to her mum for enabling her to put her plans in action; Paula had been even more thrilled to cover for her when she'd shared the reason behind it.

Maggie and Bear had popped into the bookshop briefly the previous day on account of Bear wanting to work out how they'd get the new staircase into the shop. They'd declared themselves unable to attend, which hadn't come as a surprise owing to Maggie's condition, and with Bear reluctant to stray too far from his wife just in case she went into labour. In any event, the couple had a prior commitment with Maggie's sister Sophia and her husband, and their brood of lively children. Bear, who was tall, built like a barn door, and bore more than a passing resemblance to a Viking with his bushy beard and unruly mop of jaw-length hair, hadn't hidden his relief at having the perfect excuse not to put his lack of ability on the ice to the test. 'I'm not exactly co-ordinated and light on my feet, or built for doing pirouettes,' he'd joked. Maggie had followed up with, 'Aye, but you attempting one would be so worth seeing.' The four of them had laughed heartily at that.

As for sharing news of the sleigh ride at Danskelfe Castle with Jasmine, Florrie had spoken to the others and they'd all agreed not to mention the details to their friend until they were en route to the castle itself. 'She's got the day blocked out which is the main thing,' Stella had said. Lark had followed up with, 'You know what Jazz is like, she'll fret about the cost or being treated like a "charity case" if she knows about it beforehand, even if it is a Christmas present. We really don't want to take the joy out of it for her.' They'd all agreed wholeheartedly with that.

Though Florrie had made a start with The Happy Christmas Memory Project, once Ed had mentioned the staircase and the tearoom, their thoughts seemed to have been filled with that. Even so, she made a mental note not to let progress on the project slide, which was why she'd also signed herself and Ed up for the annual Boxing Day Dip that took place in the sea in front of The Jolly Sailors. She'd placed a sponsorship form on the counter in the bookshop the previous day and they'd already managed to accrue an impressive number of sponsors, with customers promising to donate generously. The participants were to wear fancy dress, this year's theme being "Pantomime Dame", with the money raised going to the local community garden.

Ed had pulled a horrified face when Florrie had first announced it to him over breakfast. 'Won't it be freezing? I mean, the North Sea isn't exactly known for its balmy temperature,' he'd said, before taking a bite out of his toast and chewing hard. 'Makes me shiver just thinking about it.'

Florrie had giggled. 'Of course it'll be freezing! But the idea isn't to spend long in the water. You just make a quick dash for it, get yourself soaked, then run as fast as you can back to the Jolly where you can get changed and have a glass of brandy to help warm you through.' It had been a few years since Florrie and her friends had participated in the Boxing Day Dip, and if her memory served her correctly, the water had been so cold it actually hurt. Not that she was going to share that with Ed.

'I thought the idea was for *happy* memories. Not *hypothermia* memories.' Ed had eyed her, taking another bite out of his toast, apparently unconvinced by her suggestion. It had made Florrie giggle some more.

'You wuss! You're just going to have to get into the spirit of it. Trust me, you'll be laughing about it afterwards.'

He'd hurriedly swallowed his mouthful. 'Yeah, *years* afterwards when the biting cold has been erased from my mind and the blood has defrosted in my veins and started pumping round my body again.'

'Plus, I can't wait to see you dressed up like a pantomime dame!'

'You might look all sweet on the outside, but you have a wicked streak, Florrie Appleton.' Though Ed had shaken his head, he hadn't been able to help but laugh.

Florrie had taken the opportunity to pop into Nate's upcycling shop in her lunchbreak the previous day and had been enthralled by the staircase that he'd kept propped up in his storeroom at the back of his shop. It was a great sweeping affair, which boasted a gentle curve and ornately carved wooden spindles. Since then, she hadn't been able to get it out of her mind. And she'd had to agree with Ed, the perfect place for it would be the wall at the back right-hand side of the bookshop. It would make for a striking feature as it wound its way elegantly up to the first floor.

The next step was to arrange for Alex, who was also a qualified structural engineer, to call round at the bookshop with Charlie and Bear in attendance, too. It would give the three of them the opportunity to measure up and for Alex to gather all the information he needed to draw up his plans and prepare the planning application.

It was almost closing time. Florrie had let Leah head home early; the young girl had been buzzing with excitement at the prospect of a night out with her group of friends. She'd told Florrie they'd planned a trip to the cinema before finishing up at a pizza restaurant. The name Marty had featured regularly, a blush tinting Leah's cheeks each time. Reading between the lines, Florrie guessed Marty was as keen on Leah as she was on him. The thought warmed her heart.

Ed had been upstairs for the last half hour or so, looking around the flat, scribbling down ideas for the layout; though Florrie loved the idea of a tearoom upstairs, she struggled to envisage the logistics of it because she couldn't see beyond the current layout. 'My brain just doesn't work that way!' she'd said by way of explanation. Ed, however, told her he could see it as clear as day in his mind's eye, and from the exciting ideas he'd described, Florrie was more than happy to leave it to him to prepare the brief for Alex.

The shop was empty but for Florrie and Jilly Spencer, the customer she was serving, when the door opened, setting the bell jangling noisily. An icy blast of air whooshed into the shop

as the door was held wide. Startled, Florrie and Jilly Spencer
glanced across to see they'd been joined by Dodgy Dick. He
wasted no time strutting about, his chest puffed out in his
familiar self-important pose. His wife Wendy followed behind
him in a cloud of cloying perfume, teetering on a pair of
diamanté encrusted patent black heels. A feeling of unease
spread through Florrie, while Gerty sat up in her bed, mistrust
in her eyes.

'Ugh! Not that infamous pair,' Jilly Spencer muttered
under her breath, pushing her purchases into her shopping bag
and bidding Florrie a hasty goodbye. It would seem Dodgy Dick
was growing more notorious by the day.

The businessman met Florrie's eyes as he and Wendy swag-
gered towards the Christmas tree made of books. 'Ooh, how
very *novel*,' Wendy said mockingly, before breaking out into a
shrieking cackle that put Florrie in mind of nails down a blackboard. 'Did you hear that, Dick? I made a joke. "*Novel*"! Hah!
D'you get it? *Novel!*' She let rip with another round of her harsh
laughter. Florrie winced.

'Aye, very clever, love.' He smirked at Florrie. 'See, that's the
thing with my good lady wife, she's been blessed with beauty as
well as brains and a quick wit. Very sharp, she is, got a brilliant
business one of these.' He tapped his head. 'It's why we make
such a formidable team.'

And that's not the only reason. Florrie looked on, her
discomfort growing.

'Wendy here reckons this place would make a fantastic
beauty salon. Isn't that right, Wend?' He picked up a book from
the table, turning it over in his hand, throwing it down care-
lessly. Florrie felt herself bristle.

'It is, Dick. I've been saying for a while this shabby little
town needs bringing up to date. And I don't mean to be funny,
love, but this property is wasted as a bookshop. I mean, nobody's
interested in books or bookshops anymore. The smelly things

are outdated, full of dusty, boring books. Who even bothers to read them? Folk are keen to move with the times. Books belong in the Dark Ages, if you ask me.'

The snort Florrie gave was as much a result of what she'd just heard as it was the older woman's perfume. From the over-powering cloud that was filling the shop like a mist that had rolled in from the sea, Wendy had evidently sprayed with a heavy hand. Florrie was rewarded with a piercing stare from the businessman's wife, who was apparently undeterred.

'By my reckoning, this place is in the perfect location, being central, like. We could have a classy hair salon down here,' she said, sweeping her arm around in an exaggerated gesture, 'with upstairs being converted into a beauty spa and treatment rooms offering an array of exclusive cosmetic services. Dick and I have an extensive list of contacts who'd be glad to snatch our hands off to work here.' She went to give a supercilious smile at Florrie but all her heavily Botoxed face would allow was an alarming-looking gurn.

Florrie listened, her heart hammering in her chest. She willed with all her might for Ed to hurry up and get himself down here, as Wendy and Dick continued to strut about the bookshop, sharing their increasingly loud appraisal.

The pair made for an arresting sight, with their matching heavily dyed black hair – Wendy's was coiffured into a huge, bouffant affair, while Dick had recently favoured a slicked back look, which only added to his unsavoury persona – and both were draped in expensively cut black clothing. Jasmine regu-larly joked that they resembled a pair of carrion crows, poised and ready to pounce. And from the look of her plumped-up trout pout, Wendy was no stranger to the "exclusive cosmetic services" she'd referred to, and applied her make-up with a hand equally as heavy as the one she'd used for her perfume. To complete the look, she was bedecked in so much glittering jewellery, anyone would be forgiven for thinking she'd been decorated for the festive season, not unlike the Christmas tree at the top of the square. *She'd definitely give that a run for its money!*

'We watched your little moment on the local news last night, didn't we, Wend?' Dodgy Dick pulled out a book from the romance shelf, fanning the pages.

'We did.' Wendy gave an exaggerated guffaw. 'All I can say is, they must've been bloomin' desperate for news.'

'All looked a bit desperate full stop to me, trying to create a big fuss over a little, piddly place like this, making out it's summat special, just cos you've shoved some clockwork animals in the windows and covered it with fake snow. We felt sorry for you, having to go to such lengths to get some attention.'

'The fact the local news station was here had nothing to do with us – we didn't contact them. We don't know who did. But I'm pleased to say, it's generated a lot of positive interest in the bookshop.' Florrie felt her face flame with annoyance at his dismissive and wildly inaccurate description of Ed's hard work.

Florrie and Ed had watched Jack's unveiling and the subsequent interview with the report on the local news the previous evening. They'd both cringed with embarrassment at seeing themselves on the television screen, but, from what customers had said, it had proved a popular news article in the town.

Wendy glared at her.

'Hmm.' Dodgy Dick pushed the book back in its place. 'A little dicky bird tells me you and that daft lad of Peter Harte's still haven't come to your senses about selling this place. Shame. Especially when I have it in my power to make you a very tempting offer.'

Can't imagine who that little dicky bird is.

He slowly ran his finger along a bookshelf, "accidentally" knocking a book to the floor. 'Oh dear, how did that happen?' He fixed Florrie with a smile that was more akin to a snarl. She watched, her discomfort rising, as he moved on, stepping onto the book and grinding his heel into it as he went.

The thoughtless gesture sent a stab of anger through Florrie who did all she could to bite down on her outrage. It wasn't easy, but there was no way she was going to play into his hands and give him the satisfaction of knowing he'd riled her.

Wendy eyed her gleefully, a spiteful gleam in her eyes.

Though her heart was beating violently in her chest, Florrie stood firm. 'Ed and I don't need to "come to our senses".'

'That right?' He ran his tongue over his teeth, making her stomach twist. 'Some folk could do with knowing it's not always the most sensible option to dig their heels in, especially when they're holding the town back with their daft notions of family loyalty or other such tripe.'

'Entreshed, that's what I call it, isn't it, Dick?' said Wendy, puffing up her hair with her vivid red talons. 'Stuck in the past, no thought of looking to the future.'

'Aye, love, you do. And I reckon you've got a point.'

'Entrenched,' said Florrie, unable to help herself.

'That's what I said.' Wendy shot her a filthy look. Dick followed suit.

Choosing to disregard the spike of fear that shot through her, Florrie said, 'And some folk could do with knowing when to take no for an answer.' *What are you doing, Florrie? Oh my God! Have you lost your marbles? You're speaking to a mean and nasty man with dodgy connections and no scruples!* She drew in a fortifying breath, using every ounce of her strength in a bid to keep her voice steady. 'It's just as well Ed and I have turned the bookshop around and made it into a success, then.'

Another mocking shriek of a laugh escaped Wendy's red-painted lips. '*Success!* Did you hear that, Dick? She reckons this place is a success.'

Undeterred, Florrie continued, 'It is a success. And we have big plans for the future.' She regretted her last sentence as soon as the words had left her mouth. *What on earth possessed you to say that?*

Dodgy Dick spun round on his heels, pinning her with an icy stare, his eyes narrowing. 'And what "big plans" would they be then?' It hadn't escaped Florrie's attention his words had developed a slightly menacing tone. Her heart started pumping harder.

'They're in the early stages, so I couldn't possible share them at the moment.' She hoped he didn't detect the shake in her voice.

'Oh, I think it would be a good time to share them, before you make any silly mistakes. I'm very interested to hear what they involve, as I'm sure my colleagues would be, too.' He started to walk slowly towards her, a threatening air emanating from him, Wendy by his side. If they weren't so intimidating they'd be comical.

Gerty got to her feet, growling, her hackles raised.

'No one's going to be sharing any plans with either of you.'

The couple turned to see Ed making his way across the shop floor, his expression as hard as stone. Relief rushed through Florrie.

'Ah, look who the cat's dragged in,' said Dodgy Dick, pulling himself up to his full height of five-feet-six and puffing out his chest further. He put Florrie in mind of a little bantam cock bird, strutting about, fluffing up his feathers in a display of machismo.

Ignoring his comment, Ed said, 'I'm guessing you're here on account of my parents. Again.' His eyes were full of an anger Florrie had never witnessed before. 'So let me take this opportunity to make this perfectly clear. That way, you won't have to trouble yourselves again.'

Dodgy Dick turned to Wendy and smirked. 'This should be good, lass.'

Ed didn't flinch. 'Florrie and I will not be selling the bookshop. Not now, not ever. Okay? It was my grandfather's greatest wish that we run it together, and that's exactly what we're going to do. And we're going to make it a business he'd be proud of.'

'Pfft! You foolish young pup! You've no idea what a stupid mistake you're making,' Wendy said scornfully.

'I doubt that very much,' said Ed, as Gerty's growl reverberated around the shop.

Dodgy Dick looked up at Ed, his mouth twisting meanly. 'Leave it, Wend. Some folk don't know what's good for 'em.'

'It's just as well we do, then, isn't it?' Ed said.

'You'll learn,' Dodgy Dick said, his eyes flashing with silent fury that sent a shiver running up Florrie's spine.

'Now, it's gone five o'clock, so I think it's time you left… unless you'd like to buy something?' Ed held eye contact with him.

'I have no intention of buying owt from this dump, but I will take one of these for the grandkids. It's the least I deserve after that free advice I've just given you.' Dodgy Dick turned, pinning them with his shark-like stare. 'Don't let anyone say I'm not a reasonable man. I'll give you until the New Year to come to your senses about this place. I reckon by then you'll be keen for me to take it off your hands.' With that, he snatched up a copy of *It was The Night Before Christmas* and followed his wife as she sashayed out of the shop, leaving an air of displeasure in their wake.

Florrie waited until they were well away from the bookshop before rushing over and locking the door, quickly pulling down the blind. 'Oh my God! That was so awful!' She clasped her hands to her chest. 'I'm shaking like a leaf. I was literally willing you to come downstairs.'

Ed pulled her close, wrapping his arms around her. 'Well, it worked, I'd got this overwhelming feeling that something wasn't right.' He gently kissed the top of her head, squeezing her tight. 'I'm so sorry you had to experience that on your own.'

'What do you think they meant by saying we didn't know what a mistake we were making and how we'll be keen for him to take the bookshop off our hands?' Her mind was racing, Dodgy Dick's menacing eyes taking centre stage.

Ed pulled back, resting his hands on her shoulders, dipping his chin to look into her eyes. 'Don't take any notice, they're just idle threats. He's a bully, full of big talk and hot air, that's all. And his wife's no better.' His expression darkened.

Though his words went some way to reassure her, Florrie wasn't completely convinced.

FOURTEEN

THURSDAY 7TH DECEMBER

The following morning, Florrie and Ed arrived at the bookshop early to discover the Christmas tree from above the shop door had been ripped down and thrown into the tiled entrance of the doorway, the lights that had decorated it hanging down and swaying in the breeze.

'Oh my God!' A dart of panic shot through Florrie as she stood staring at the sight in disbelief.

'What the—?' Ed came to a halt, tugging Gerty back on her lead as the Labrador went to investigate. 'Is that egg running down the windows?'

'Looks like it. Who would even think to do something like this?' Her eyes brimmed with tears as she also took in the mangled wreath that had been ripped from the door and dumped on top of the Christmas tree. 'It's mindless and destructive.'

Ed's gaze swept around the square. 'From what I can see, we're the only shop that's been targeted.' He heaved a sigh, his breath hanging in a cloud of condensation.

'Why us, Ed? Why the bookshop...' Her voice tailed off as

realisation dawned. 'Dodgy Dick! He's who's behind this. I'd put money on it, it has all his hallmarks.' She could feel her cheeks burn with anger.

'Me too, though he won't have got his own hands dirty, he'll have paid someone to do it on his behalf. It's all part of his plan to intimidate us into selling the bookshop.' He put his arm around Florrie, squeezing her shoulder. 'But we'll show them we won't be beaten. We'll get this cleared up quickly, and the Christmas tree back in place before the shop's due to open, and before Leah gets here. We don't want her feeling she's getting dragged into it.'

'I agree,' said Florrie determinedly, rooting around in her backpack for the shop keys. 'Let's put on a united front, get this cleaned up and carry on as if it hasn't happened.' She made a silent promise that she was going to direct her focus on planning The Happy Christmas Memories Project. There was no way Dodgy Dick or Ed's parents' behaviour was going to dominate that by generating horrible Christmas memories instead. She'd make sure to get something in place this weekend.

All the same, it still didn't stop a background hum of anxiety from murmuring away, making it difficult for her to settle. From the stories that had been circulating since he'd been rumoured to be in the employ of a corrupt firm, Dodgy Dick now had no scruples in doing whatever it took in order to get what he and his bosses wanted. She didn't like to give too much thought to what he next had in mind for them and the bookshop.

'I hope Leah and my mum will be okay.' Florrie turned to Ed, a frown knitting her brows together. It had just gone two p.m. and they were heading out of Micklewick Bay on the way to Middleton-le-Moors for the hour of ice skating she'd booked as part of The Happy Christmas Memory Project. It rankled with her that she was feeling so distracted when they were supposed to be making special memories for Ed. After Dodgy

Dick's visit yesterday, she'd been having serious misgivings about leaving her mum and Leah in charge of the shop. She'd feel terrible if they had to deal with that man. The mess they'd found that morning had only added to her concerns. 'I can't help but feel guilty. What if Dodgy Dick and Wendy turn up while we're out? What if the creep starts with his threats and sinister questions?' Florrie's stomach was tying itself up in knots.

Ed turned to her, offering a reassuring smile. 'Try to put it out of your mind. I'd be very surprised if they showed up again so soon. Like we said before, the Christmas tree in the doorway, the wreath and eggs down the window is all down to him – he'll think he's done enough to rattle us for today. He'd be attracting attention if he rocked up at the shop again so soon, and though he's not the sharpest knife in the drawer, he's not that daft. He won't want to do that.' He indicated left, following the signpost for Middleton-le-Moors. 'Remember what he was like last time? It was me he focused his attention on – he won't want other people to know what he's up to. You know how keen he is to pass himself off as a "respectable businessman".' Ed emphasised the words mockingly. 'He's totally oblivious he's fooling no one. The word sneaky doesn't do justice to his methods.'

How could she forget what he'd been like? His campaign of intimidation had sent Ed fleeing in search of respite and headspace. The memory sent a shudder through her as she recalled Ed describing how menacing Dodgy Dick had been. She quickly pushed it out of her mind; she didn't want to head down the route of worrying about what else he might have planned for them.

'Don't let him dominate your thoughts and taint today. Our trip is meant to create happy Christmas memories which don't in any way, shape or form, include Dodgy Dick and his wife,' Ed said, the easy tone in his voice easing the wriggle of anxiety in Florrie's stomach. He reached across and gave her hand a squeeze.

'You're right.' She turned to him, pushing her mouth into a smile.

'I am. So, try to stop worrying – Leah and your mum'll be fine. There's no point in fretting about something that's not likely to happen, especially when we've got something fun to look forward to.' Taking in his broad smile, Florrie made a conscious effort to tuck her worries out of the way and focus instead on enjoying herself with Ed.

'And don't forget, your dad's not far away. He'll be there like a shot if your mum needs him, and Nate's just down the road, too. He's twice the size of Dodgy Dick, so I very much doubt the slimeball will want to take him on.'

Florrie giggled at the mental image Ed's words had triggered. 'Yeah, I doubt it, too.'

The further they drove from the seaside and out of the clutches of the salty air, the more the snow lingered on the footpaths and verges. Ed slowed his speed, driving steadily. She eased out a relieved sigh as tension ebbed away and her shoulders relaxed, Ed's voice of reason and upbeat tone offering the reassurance she needed. She glanced out of the window, surprised to see daylight was already succumbing to the dusk that was nibbling away at the pale blue edges of sky.

As they drew closer to Middleton-le-Moors, it became evident that winter had a tighter grip here, where the altitude was higher. The road to the town skirted the perimeter of the North Yorkshire Moors whose stark, wintry bleakness stretched out for miles in the distance. Frost sparkled on the roadside while snow dusted the naked branches of the trees and hedges that lined the route, glittering under the diluted rays of the sun.

'Blimey, look at the sky over there.' Ed nodded to the left of them.

'Ooh, looks full of trouble, doesn't it?' Florrie had already noted the foreboding clouds that had gathered over the moors, ready to release vast amounts of snow at any moment. She knew the moorland weather could be capricious, with sunny skies one minute and thunderstorms the next. As for the snowfall, she'd heard horrendous stories of people finding themselves stranded high up on the rigg roads, their cars getting buried in snowdrifts – the worst she'd been told was of a heavily pregnant woman giving birth in the back of a Land Rover, assisted by a local farmer and his girlfriend. Florrie couldn't even begin to imagine how terrifying that must've been. Much as she loved snow, she hoped it would hold back until they'd got their ice-skating session out of the way and were safely parked up in Micklewick Bay.

'Don't worry, I'm sure it won't affect us. I checked the forecast, and the moors are set to get a substantial covering, but it'll be much lighter here and back home. The roads have been gritted, too, so we'll be fine.'

'That's good.' Their eyes met, happiness dancing between them as they beamed at one another. Florrie had surprised herself at just how much she was looking forward to tackling this next item on the list of The Happy Christmas Memory Project, especially given Ed's sense of fun. He'd been in raptures when she'd presented him with the tickets the previous day. She'd booked them last minute, after checking her mum and Leah could cover for them, and had been excited to share the details with him.

'Oh, wow! I've always wanted to have a go at ice skating! This is awesome! Thank you!'

'Thought you'd be chuffed.' She'd been thrilled by his response.

'Will I need shin pads and a helmet?' he'd chuckled.

'Don't be so daft! It's not ice hockey! You're hardly going to be charging across the rink, chasing a puck and wielding a hockey stick,' she'd said, giggling.

'Hey, you never know. I might surprise everyone and have a natural affinity for it.'

'Much as I hate to burst your bubble, I very much doubt it. I reckon we'll both be spending most of the time gripping onto the side for dear life, which is pretty much how I remember my last attempts when I went with Jasmine and Stella. It was donkey's years ago, mind, but we still had a great laugh. Poor Jazz had bruises on her bum that lasted for weeks.'

'Er, remind me again why we're doing this,' Ed had said dryly, making Florrie giggle some more.

'I promise you, this festive experience will deserve its place in The Happy Christmas Memory Project. You'll look back on your time on the ice – whether it's on your bum or your feet – with a whole load of happy memories, I promise you.'

'Hmm. I'll take your word for it,' Ed had said, his wide smile betraying the fact that he shared her excitement. 'It's actually the thought of a meal at the pub afterwards that's keeping me going.'

Florrie had chuckled, shaking her head. 'Honestly, I reckon if you were an animal, you'd be a Labrador... you think as much about your belly as Gerty thinks about hers.'

'I hold my hands up to that one, and I'm more than happy to be in such good company.' He'd bent to ruffle Gerty's ears and been rewarded with a lick on the end of his nose.

As it turned out, Ed proved to be quite the natural on ice skates, but not before he'd provided a few laugh-out-loud moments where he'd pushed himself off from the side, waving his arms around windmill-like before ending up unceremoniously on his backside. He'd hooted with laughter, dusted himself off and tried again, getting the knack far more quickly than he and Florrie were expecting. Once he'd mastered the art of staying upright, he skated gently round the rink, Florrie's hand in his, the pair of them grinning from ear to ear as festive music rang out from the pub's speakers.

By the time their session was up, they were tired and hungry.

'That was the *best* fun!' Ed was glowing with happiness, his hand around a pint of alcohol-free beer. They were sitting in the warmth of The Golden Fleece, Christmas carols playing cheerily in the background, a roaring fire in the hearth, and a heavily bedecked Christmas tree twinkling away in the corner.

'Told you you'd enjoy it,' Florrie said, laughing at the joy shining in his eyes. They were both rosy-cheeked thanks to the heat kicked out by the blazing fire at the far end of the room, and the frost that had nipped at their skin whilst they were ice skating. 'And it's great to have another item ticked off the list.' She took a sip of her mulled wine, savouring the warmth and evocative aroma of festive spices that swirled under her nose. The chill from her wet trousers was becoming less noticeable by the minute. 'Mind you, I reckon we could be a bit achy tomorrow after the tumbles we took. The left cheek of my bottom's throbbing. It's going to be colourful tomorrow.'

Ed chuckled. 'Yeah, and I know I've used muscles I didn't even know I had just trying to stay upright.' He reached across the table and took her hand in his, a serious expression suddenly replacing his smile. He rubbed his thumb across her knuckles. 'I hope you know how much I appreciate what you're doing, Florrie.'

'Hey, it's not about you being appreciative, it's about you having some awesome experiences to add to your festive memory bank,' she said brightly. 'And besides, I'm hardly having a dreadful time, am I? It's great fun for both of us, doing things like this together. It's good to be able to have a bit of a break, to be honest. Much as I love the bookshop, we've been working flat out recently – we've needed this bit of down time. I didn't realise that till now.'

Ed nodded, looking thoughtful. 'You're not wrong there. Business has really taken off over this last year.'

Mention of the bookshop sent Florrie's thoughts skittering back to Dodgy Dick. Her mind had headed down that route several times since they'd arrived in the town though she'd made a conscious effort to focus on the good time she was having with Ed. She'd surreptitiously checked her phone to make sure there'd been no concerned messages from her mum or Leah, thankful there had been none.

Before long, two large plates piled high with Christmas dinner and all the trimmings arrived, together with an extra plate of vegetables and a jug of gravy. Florrie's tastebuds started dancing at the delicious aromas that were swirling around their table.

'Oh, wow! This looks amazing.' Ed wasted no time, dropping his napkin into his lap and diving straight in.

'Mmm. Those roasties!' Florrie popped one into her mouth and gave an appreciative eyeroll as the crisp skin gave way to buttery softness.

'It was great to see Maggie's Christmas teddy bears featuring so prominently in the Campion's window. Must've given her a huge thrill when she and Bear popped over to see them the other day.' Ed sliced into a large ball of sage and onion stuffing.

'It was wonderful to see them. I'm so happy for her, especially after all the trouble she had in the summer with that cousin of hers. Despite that, it's turned out to be a good year for her and Bear.'

Before their ice-skating session, Florrie and Ed had enjoyed a mooch around the shops that lined the Georgian market square, stopping to gaze into the tasteful window display of Campion's of York. It was the flagship store of the company that had recently been sold to a mystery buyer who had plans to invest in the flagging shops and restore its previous reputation as the place to buy exclusive and luxurious items. Adding to this, the new owner was keen to support local companies and cottage industries and was eager to stock the stores with goods that met his exacting standards. The shop in Middleton-le-Moors was benefitting from an extensive refurbishment programme, the scaffolding that had obscured the frontage for several months being dismantled just days before the town was decorated for Christmas. The shabby exterior woodwork had been given a fresh lick of eggshell paint, and a hand-painted sign, which included the logo Maggie had designed for the company, had been hung above the wide oak door. The window display was decorated in a suitably festive theme, including a luxurious Christmas tree, showcasing Maggie's limited edition handmade Christmas bears that were exclusive to Campion's. The sumptuous styling was a testament to the artistic skills of the visual merchandiser the store now employed.

Over their delicious meal, Florrie and Ed had excitedly discussed their plans for the tearoom in the bookshop, Ed doing all he could to help Florrie visualise his ideas. 'It'll be easier to picture when Alex has something drawn up,' he'd said.

Cautious by nature, the only part of the project that cast any doubts in her mind was the cost. The staircase itself was almost a thousand pounds, and that was with a great chunk of money knocked off the asking price thanks to the mates' rates Nate had generously given them. But, from what Ed was saying, the tearoom would occupy the two rooms at the front of the first floor, which meant the flat's kitchen would have to be moved – they couldn't have the wait staff lugging trays of tea and cakes along the hallway that led off to rooms that would be taken up with books and stationery. Plus, they wouldn't simply be able to use the kitchen and equipment they already had, there'd be rules and regulations to comply with; they'd no doubt have to kit the room out with a professional-standard kitchen. Then there was the matter of washrooms; they'd have to provide at least one, potentially two, since she doubted the outdated one in situ would suffice. And then there was furniture for the tearoom itself to think about. Her dad had offered to do the structural work for free, but neither she nor Ed would hear of that. Their project would take a huge chunk out of Charlie's building schedule and there was no way they wanted him to be out of pocket.

She didn't want to burst Ed's bubble, especially when he seemed so enthusiastic about the idea, but she didn't know how they would be able to afford to pay for it all. Granted, the book-shop had generated a decent profit over this last year in particu-lar, but it wouldn't go anywhere near covering the cost of Ed's plans. She supposed they could apply for a business loan, though that held little appeal with interest rates being what they were. There was no two ways about it, they were really going to have to give this some serious thought, get their ducks in a row if they were to approach a bank.

Oh my days! Florrie's mind was in a whirl, excitement being the overriding emotion.

By the time they'd left The Golden Fleece, buttoned up tightly against the cold, darkness had properly set in. The square looked even more magical than when they'd first arrived. Florrie cast her gaze around at the nostalgic scene of Christmas card perfection. It could have come straight from the pages of a Dick-ensian novel. Festive lights were festooned from each of the Georgian buildings, with glittering displays filling their windows, while a large Christmas tree dominated the centre. The sweet aroma of roasting chestnuts from the stall in the far corner of the square mingled with the smell of woodsmoke that curled up into the dark sky from the chimney pots. This was the only town, other than Micklewick Bay, where she could imagine herself living.

As they headed along the moor road towards home, feather-like snowflakes started tumbling from the sky, slowly at first, the flurry getting denser as they bypassed the moors. A gritter rumbled by on the opposite side of the road, showering rock salt over the car as it passed. Ed upped the speed of the windscreen wipers, snowflakes covering the glass as soon as one lot was swiped away. Though it appeared to be settling on the roadside and verges, Florrie was relieved to see the roads themselves were clear thanks to the endeavours of the gritter. She retrieved her phone from her backpack, texting her mum to say they were on their way home, and asking how things had gone at the book-shop. It didn't take long for a reply to land.

> Glad to hear you've both enjoyed yourselves, lovey. All went fine at the bookshop, just very busy! Gerty's been a good lass. Take it steady on your way back. Snow's been forecast. See you soon Love you! xxx

Her mum signed off in her usual way with a series of hearts and kissing face emojis. Relief rushed through Florrie. She puffed out a sigh, causing Ed to steal a quick glance at her.

'What's up?' he asked. From his tone, she could tell he was thinking the worst, that Dodgy Dick had shown his face at the bookshop, spreading his menacing air like a suffocating fog.

'Don't worry, everything's fine.' She was keen to quash his concerns. 'Looks like the bookshop had no unwelcome visitors, thank goodness. Mum says they've been busy, though.'

'That's good news, I mean Dodgy Dick not showing his face.'

'It is.' Hearing that had put her mind at rest more than she'd been expecting. 'And she says Gerty's been a good lass.' Her heart filled with warmth at the thought of the Labrador.

'Gerty's always a good lass,' Ed said affectionately.

'She is, she's a star.' She smiled at the thought of how much the Labrador would be enjoying being spoilt by her parents that evening. 'Mum also said heavy snow's been forecast for the moors so we should take it steady.'

'Don't worry, the car's got winter tyres on, we'll get home safely.'

Pulling up outside Florrie's parents' house, Ed stilled the engine and twisted his body towards her, light from the streetlamp spilling into the car, highlighting the gentle look in his eyes. 'Thanks for organising this afternoon, Florrie. I've had more fun than I could ever have imagined, and have loved every minute of it, even when I ended up on my backside.'

'Yeah, me too.' She smiled at him.

'What? You're saying you enjoyed seeing me end up on my backside?' His expression of mock hurt made her giggle.

'Well, now you come to mention it, it was pretty entertaining.'

Ed laughed. 'Seriously, though, I haven't had so much fun for ages.'

Joy bloomed in her chest. She'd had a brilliant time, too, despite how tricky it had been to keep upright at times, and her face had ached from laughing so hard. 'Which was exactly the object of the exercise, to create some happy Christmas memories.'

'Well, it definitely did that.' He reached his hand out, touching the side of her face before leaning in and brushing his lips gently across hers.

'Mmm.' Florrie felt her heart melt.

Seconds later, their moment was interrupted as the front door of the house was flung open and a blaze of bright light flooded the footpath, Charlie's silhouette appearing in the door frame. Gerty pushed her way past him and came bounding down the path, giving an enthusiastic bark as she stopped beside the car.

'To be continued when we get home,' Ed said, kissing the tip of Florrie's nose.

'Can't wait,' she said, a wave of happiness rising through her.

FIFTEEN

FRIDAY 8TH DECEMBER

'So how are the plans going for the tearoom?' Jean Davenport asked, her voice low. She and Florrie were in the reading room, preparing for a school visit later that afternoon. Leah was at the front of the shop, looking after customers.

'Oh, my goodness, Jean, it's so exciting but there's such a lot to think about.' Florrie beamed, adding another chair to the semi-circle she was setting out. 'Ouch!' She winced, the muscles in her back giving a painful twinge.

'Ooh, are you okay, lovey?'

'Mm.' Florrie nodded, massaging the protesting muscles and mustering up a smile. 'I'm fine, thanks, Jean. It's nothing serious, just my body reminding me about our ice-skating escapades yesterday. Ed and I are both suffering for it.'

'Ah, I see.' Jean chuckled. 'Well, you take it easy, no point in aggravating things.'

'You're not wrong.' Despite her nagging muscles, Florrie was eager to continue the tearoom conversation with her friend. 'Ed and I have been chatting loads about the tearoom, and I've been jotting down all our ideas and what we need to do. Honestly, I've never had so many lists!' She laughed. Florrie was an ardent list-maker and always had at least one on the go at any given time.

'Ooh, now that I can believe,' Jean said knowingly. 'And it's great to hear that young Edward is so enthusiastic about it.'

'I've honestly never seen him so fired up and excited about anything. I mean, he's absolutely brilliant with everything he does with the window displays and the creative side of things for the bookshop, but this new venture has really got a grip of him.'

'Ah, I'm absolutely thrilled for you, lovey.'

'Hmm.' Florrie's face clouded.

'Whatever's the matter?'

Florrie paused for a moment, wrestling with the idea of vocalising something that had been preying on her mind. 'It's just, as much as I love the idea of the tearoom and am totally on board with having one upstairs, I'm worried about the cost.' She pulled a regretful face. 'I really don't want to put the dampeners on Ed's enthusiasm, but I'd hate for us to get into financial difficulties and find ourselves in a position where we have to end up selling the bookshop.'

Jean looked thoughtful for a moment. 'You're wise to be cautious, lovey, but do you really think creating a tearoom upstairs would be so costly, especially with your dad and Bear doing the building work?'

Florrie drew in a deep breath. 'There's a chance it could. We haven't got as far as getting quotes, but there's the kitchen to consider.' She went on to explain about the type of kitchen and equipment they'd need, and the added expense of suitable washrooms, not to mention cutlery and crockery. 'And not forgetting there's Alex's fee to add on to that, though he did say he'd get us mates' rates, too, which is really kind of him. Even so, I'm just scared there's potential for it all to get out of hand and for the costs to spiral out of control. And I daren't even start thinking about how we'd manage to pay suppliers and staff.'

Florrie puffed out a deep breath; she felt suddenly over-whelmed by it all.

What she'd kept to herself was the phone call from Peter Harte and how Ed appeared to be searching for something in the attic. The more she thought about it, the more she couldn't help but think the two things must be connected in some way. It wasn't helped by the fact that Ed had surreptitiously sloped off when they'd gone to bed last night. She hadn't been asleep long when she'd been woken by the sound of boxes being dragged around above her, cupboard doors clicking shut, Ed muttering to himself. Whatever was going on had resurrected her misgiv-ings. Florrie would love nothing more than to share her worries with Jean, get her wise friend's take on things, but since she'd heard Ed's father mention her name down the phone, she had a horrible feeling Jean was connected in some way. Though she couldn't for the life of her think how. What she didn't want to happen was for her and Ed to put themselves in a financially precarious position, and for him to decide the bookshop was no longer for him. The mere thought sent nausea churning around her stomach.

Jean, who'd been listening intently while Florrie spoke, gave a sympathetic smile. 'I completely understand where you're coming from. Bernard and Dinah would be very pleased to hear you were being sensible about it, of that I have no doubt. But if you want my opinion, I'd find out how much everything is going to cost, as close to the actual price as you can get it, and then put serious thought into whether it's a viable option for you and Ed. After all, it wouldn't be the end of the world if you had to do it in stages, or put it off for a while, would it?'

Florrie hadn't thought of that. 'Hmm. I s'pose not.' Since Mr H had passed away, it had always felt good to run things by Jean, particularly matters relating to the bookshop. Her friend often provided ideas or solutions that Florrie hadn't even stopped to consider. 'And at least we'd already have the perfect staircase,' she said, brightening. They could afford to buy that, and she was sure Nate would keep it in storage for them if necessary.

'You see, no need to worry, lovey, problem solved. I often find if you look hard enough you can find a solution. I'm sure I don't have to remind you it was something Bernard and Dinah always used to say when faced with a problem.' Jean smiled kindly at her. 'I've held those words close since I first heard them as a young lass.'

Florrie's heart pinched at the mention of Ed's grandparents, and the reason they'd had to use those words in context with Jean. But now she thought about it, Jean was right, and so were Mr and Mrs H. She would put her misgivings about Ed to one side and focus on their tearoom plans.

Florrie had relayed the conversation she'd had with Jean to Ed as they were stacking the chairs, lining them up against the wall, after the visit by the school children – doing that made it easier to vacuum the carpet which was invariably messy after an event. Gerty was curled up by the radiator, glossy black head on paws, watching as they worked. It didn't escape Florrie's notice that Ed had looked disappointed when she'd suggested the option of putting the tearoom idea on hold or even doing it in stages if they thought it was going to stretch them financially. She'd felt like a total killjoy.

'I'd be as gutted as you if we had to do that,' Florrie said, meaning it. 'But I've been brought up to be careful with money and not to bite off more than I can chew. Even though Samphire Cottage was a bargain, it needed a lot of work doing to it, and I thought long and hard about whether I could afford it.'

Ed stacked the last of the chairs, turning to face her. Closing the gap between them, he rested his hands on her shoulders and dipped his head to meet her gaze. 'I totally get where you're coming from with the financial implications, I wouldn't want us to end up in a mess either, but it doesn't mean to say we can't consider it at least.'

Relief pushed a smile onto Florrie's face, though she still felt torn. The way her mind was working, it felt like his words were contradicting his actions. She wished he could let go of his habit of keeping worries to himself. It was all so confusing.

'How about we get the figures sorted, then take it from there?' he said, smiling back, his eyebrows raised in question.

'I like that idea.' Florrie pushed her doubts away; she was glad he didn't think she was being a killjoy. She wanted him to know she was as keen as him on the tearoom idea. She stood on her tiptoes and kissed him, the soft feel of his lips against hers sending any lingering doubts scurrying away. His arms slid around her, pulling her close. She took a moment to savour the comforting warmth of his body, wishing she could feel this way all the time.

SIXTEEN

'There you go but mind out, it's hot.' Ed carefully handed Florrie a mug of tea in her new festive mug. She'd bought one for each of them from the gift shop at the same time she'd picked up the snow globe for Ed.

'Thanks.' She took it, blowing across the surface before taking a sip. 'Mmm. I'm ready for this.'

'I can run you down to the Jolly, if you like? It's freezing out there tonight and it was threatening to snow when I stuck my head out the door a minute ago.'

It was just gone half past six on Friday evening. It had been another busy day at the bookshop after a frantically busy week, the window reveal and Jack's reading having set the pace. They hadn't been home long from work and had flopped at the table in the little kitchen of Samphire Cottage as soon as they'd burst through the door, with Ed only dragging himself out of his seat to make a pot of tea. Gerty had wasted no time in curling up in her bed by the radiator and was now snoring contentedly.

Throughout the course of the day, Florrie had made a determined effort to keep Dodgy Dick and his antics out of her thoughts. It would seem Ed was of the same mind – or at least that's what Florrie told herself – since whenever she'd mentioned the Christmas tree in the doorway incident, he'd batted it away, telling her not to dwell on it. His response had been similar when she'd tiptoed gently into asking if he'd spoken to his father. But there was no denying he'd been distracted by both matters, just as she had. On several occasions during the day, she'd caught him wearing a troubled expression. It had sent a jolt of alarm spiralling through her. He'd shaken it off as soon as he'd sensed her gaze on him, fixing a smile to his face and striking up a breezy conversation. On top of that, there'd been multiple times when he'd disappeared to take a call or deal with a text message, returning with a distant look in his eyes. Something told her it had nothing to do with their plans for converting the flat. He might be trying to protect her from whatever was going on, but he didn't seem to realise his lack of communication was frustrating her and only amplified her concerns.

It was beginning to feel like they were veering back and forth between laughing and having fun, and making plans for the future, to fretting about what his parents were up to or what Dodgy Dick would do next. It was difficult to keep up with, and emotionally draining.

That aside, Florrie was relieved they hadn't been troubled by any other unpleasantness after the outdoor Christmas tree had been ripped down, and she'd tried to convince herself it had been nothing to do with the roguish businessman, and was simply some random act carried out by a reveller who'd had too much to drink during the festive season. But her sense of reasoning told a different story, reinforced by Ed's old habit of clamming up.

She was also relieved that their conversation about the tearoom and the cost implications hadn't dampened his mood about the project. In fact, it appeared to have done the opposite and stoked his enthusiasm further, with him researching the type of kitchen they'd need and the cost it would involve. He'd told her he planned to spend the time she was out doing more research, digging further.

'I might take you up on that offer of a lift to the Jolly, if you don't mind, that is.' Florrie pulled her thoughts back to the present. 'Especially with how much I ache after our escapades on the ice yesterday, and I still feel like I've had a kick up the backside.' She rubbed the offending area. The inky bruise was the size of a large grapefruit, covering a generous proportion of her right buttock.

Ed chuckled. 'I know what you mean. And besides, I wouldn't offer if I minded. Can't have you hobbling down to the seafront, eating into your time with the lasses.' Smiling dark-blue eyes peered over his mug at her. 'It's been a full-on day, and the walk back home was bitterly cold, so it'll be even worse the closer you get to the bottom prom. And from what Bear said earlier, I gather he's happy to drop everyone off in the Landie when you're done tonight. Seems only fair I do the outbound run.'

Friday night was Florrie's night out with her friends. They'd been meeting at the Jolly for years and it was strictly girls only, though Ed had managed to wangle a pass one night. It was safe to say that had been a one-off. As a rule, Florrie walked to the pub, scooping up Jasmine on her way. Stella, whose stylish new apartment was further along the seafront and not on their route made her own way there, as did Maggie who came from the opposite side of Micklewick Bay, while Lark lived a stone's throw away from the Jolly at Seashell Cottage on Smugglers Row. All the same, Bear never minded dropping everyone off if the weather was inclement.

'That way, you'll have more time to chill before you set off.' Ed smiled at her, his eyes shining in the soft light.

'Sounds good,' she said, smiling back. 'It'd save me a good half hour, and it'd be quite nice not to have to rush around before I head out, not that I could do much rushing if I wanted to with my aching legs.'

'Tell me about it!' Ed laughed. 'We can pick Jazz up en route, Stella too, if she fancies.'

'Yeah, I'd better send them a quick text, let them know they can chill a bit. Jazz'll be especially pleased about that – she's always chasing her tail, poor lass.'

By the time they were ready to set off, the snow that had been forecast for Micklewick Bay had started to fall in tiny flakes, dancing frenetically in the car's headlights. 'It's watery stuff this, I very much doubt it'll settle,' said Ed, as he flicked the windscreen wipers on and put the car into gear.

'Good. Much as I love snow, I hope it doesn't, not just yet at least. We're expecting too many deliveries and there's Jenna Johnstone's author reading coming up next Wednesday. If it could just wait until the night before Christmas Eve, then it can do its worst.'

Ed chuckled as he negotiated the junction at the bottom of the road. 'I doubt the local kids will be keen to wait that long. They'll be itching to have snowball fights, go sledging and build snowmen.'

His words triggered a flood of memories. Florrie and her pals had been ecstatic one winter when the school's central heating boiler had broken down and they'd been sent home. They'd all trooped down to the gardens in their wellies and padded waterproofs and had spent their days sledging and having a whale of a time. They'd built giant snowmen, rolling huge balls of snow that grew bigger and bigger until they'd formed the shape of a head and a body, hunting around for anything suitable they could find to make a nose, eyes and a smile. At the end of the day, they'd gone home wet through, shattered and frozen to the core, but she wouldn't have changed it for the world.

The thought of these happy memories gave her a little prompt: The Happy Christmas Memories Project! She needed to focus her attention on planning for that instead of worrying about Ed's dad and Dodgy Dick. She turned to Ed. 'So did you love building snowmen and going sledging when you were a little lad, then?'

'Much as I hate to sound pathetic, I'm afraid I have to say I've never built a snowman in my life, I've never been sledging, and I have no memories of having a snowball fight.' The sleet was now driving at the windscreen and he increased the speed of the wipers.

Florrie could hardly believe what she was hearing. 'You're honestly telling me you've got to the age of thirty-five and you've never built a snowman or gone sledging?'

He stole a look at her and shrugged his shoulders, pressing his lips into a smile, the glow of streetlights reaching into the car. ''Fraid not. It's cos we were often in sunnier climes over winter, what with my parents' love of travel, so the opportunity never presented itself.'

'What? No way!' Florrie said. 'But building snowmen, sledging and snowball fights are a rite of passage round here – all kids have to do it.'

Ed chuckled. 'Well, I'm not strictly from round here, so I suppose that gives me a bit of an excuse.'

'Not in my book, it doesn't, Edward Harte, and it's one I intend to rectify as soon as we get a decent covering.' She gave his arm a determined prod, making him chuckle. 'Maybe I should wish for more snow instead of less, then on Sunday when we're off, we'd get the chance to put that right.'

'You sound pretty determined.' She could hear the smile in his voice.

'You'd better believe it. All we need is a couple of inches of the white stuff and we're in business, and if the forecasts are anything to go by, we won't be disappointed. You'd better watch out, my snowball throwing skills might be a tad rusty but being small always used to mean I could sneak in and catch my opponents when they were least expecting it.'

'Sounds to me like you're throwing down the gauntlet, Florrie Appleton.'

'That, Edward Harte, is because I am.'

'In that case, let's hope our ice skating-induced aches and pains have disappeared by then, or neither of us will be able to move very fast.'

'Pfft! There's no way I'm going to let a pulled muscle get in the way of whooping your ass at a snowball fight.'

'Challenge accepted!'

'Mwahaha! You've no idea what you're letting yourself in for.' She gave a theatrical chuckle, rubbing her hands together.

Ed let out a hoot of laughter. 'I can't wait!'

SEVENTEEN

By the time they pulled up in The Jolly Sailors' car park, they were ten minutes late thanks to Jasmine's babysitter.

'I can't bloomin' believe it. The one night I'm actually ready on time and not covered from head to toe in edible glitter and icing sugar, the flippin' babysitter can't get her backside into gear and get here on time,' she'd said when Florrie had knocked on her door. 'And it's not as if I could ask my mum to cover for her now she's come down with a stomach bug.'

As well as working part-time at Seaside Bakery and as a cleaner for Stella's mum's cleaning company, Jasmine had a side hustle making celebration cakes which had taken off beyond her wildest expectations, and she was now inundated with orders. Her dream was to give up her other jobs and focus solely on her cakes but thus far, being a single mum had meant she'd been too afraid to risk giving up her regular employment.

'Anyroad, are you going to tell me why I've had to book out the seventeenth for me and the kids?' Jasmine had asked as she buckled her seat belt in the back of the car. 'I haven't mentioned owt to the monsters or they'd be hounding the living daylights out of me to find out about it. But I have to say, I'm dying to know myself.'

'Nope, 'fraid I'm not in a position to share just yet,' Florrie had said, giving a mysterious smile.

'Really?'

'Yep, really.'

'Spoilsport!' Jasmine had reached forward and prodded Florrie in the shoulder, making her giggle. 'Don't suppose I can tempt you to share, can I, Stells?' she'd asked, turning to Stella who Florrie and Ed had scooped up before calling for Jasmine.

'Nope,' Stella had said with a smile.

'Well, as long as it doesn't involve taking a dip with the Goosebump Gals, I won't mind what the surprise is.' The Goosebump Gals were a group of women who went sea swimming each weekend, with Stella's mum Alice being a recent recruit. 'Gives me goosebumps just thinking about it.' Jasmine had chuckled.

When they'd arrived in Old Micklewick, Ed had taken a detour, heading down Smugglers Row where Lark's tiny home, Seashell Cottage, was tucked away in amongst the rows of higgledy-piggledy dwellings. He'd stopped the car on the road outside and beeped the horn. Seconds later, Lark had hurried out, her long, blonde locks covered by a brightly coloured trapper hat. She'd quickly jumped into the back alongside Jasmine. 'Thanks for this, Ed. I usually love the snow, but not when I'm heading for a night out with the lasses. I don't fancy having my clothes steaming away while I'm sitting by the fire.'

'I can see why that wouldn't appeal.' Ed had chuckled.

'Have fun, ladies,' he said as he pulled up in the Jolly's car park. The four of them scrambled out of the car, calling goodbyes over their shoulders and scurried off, hoods pulled up and heads bowed against the driving sleet. To Florrie, it felt like hundreds of icy needles were driving relentlessly at her skin.

They hurried along the snow-covered path, waves crashing

angrily against the shore in the background. Jasmine let out an ear-splitting yelp as she almost came a cropper, her feet sliding every which way. Luckily for her, Lark and Stella had acted quickly, catching her just in time. 'Blimey, thanks, lasses! I knew I shouldn't have worn these bloomin' boots, they're lethal.'

Her glasses dappled with snow, Florrie couldn't help but giggle at the sight of Jasmine being frogmarched by their friends. 'Come on, Jazz, let's get you in here where you won't run the risk of ending up on your bum.' Stella's voice was whipped from her mouth by the wind that was blasting in from the sea.

Florrie opened the pub door and was instantly met by a welcome rush of warmth. It was quickly followed by a burst of chatter and a lively blast of fiddle music. The four of them tumbled inside, Florrie battling with the wind as she pushed the door firmly closed behind them, her aching muscles grumbling. She was glad to leave the wintry night behind her for the next few hours while she relaxed and had a catch up with her friends. It felt like an age since last Friday when they'd had a proper chance to put the world and Micklewick Bay to rights. She savoured her nights at the Jolly with her pals. Despite their very different personalities, they all shared the same values and they were all women's women through and through, their friendship growing stronger over the years, the experiences they'd lived through and shared galvanising their bond. After one of their catch-ups, Florrie's spirits always felt thoroughly restored, her worries put into perspective. It was a feeling echoed by each of them. It took something serious for one of them to miss their Friday night get-together.

Florrie gave a quick scan of the cosy bar area as she pushed the hood of her duffle coat down. She was pleased to see the change in the weather hadn't deterred the regulars from turning out for their Friday night session. But then again, Mother Nature could do her worst, and the Jolly would still be packed to the rafters. There was something about its old, wonky walls that tempted folk back. The room was looking suitably festive, a Christmas tree, trimmed with copious bushy lengths of tinsel, stood against the back wall, Christmas cards were stuck to the stout, dark oak beams and a miniature blackboard sat on the bar advertising glasses of warm mulled wine or spiced cider.

'Flippin' 'eck, I'm nithered and we were only out there a few minutes.' Jasmine rubbed her hands vigorously together, sleet glistening in the tuft of vibrant red fringe that was peeking from the edge of her woolly hat.

'Tell me about it,' said Lark, giving a shiver as she unwound her scarf.

'A glass of vino'll soon fettle that, lasses.' Stella gave a smile, pushing back the hood of her olive-green sheepskin maxicoat. No matter what the weather, she always managed to look effort-lessly stylish.

'Ooh, Mags is already here.' Florrie stuffed her gloves into the pockets of her coat as she headed across the bar to their usual table that landlady, Mandy, reserved for them every Friday evening. She was pleased to see a fire blazing beside it in the dog grate of the huge inglenook fireplace.

Maggie looked up as the four women approached, her face breaking out into a smile. 'Now then, lasses. You finally made it.' She was wearing a fluffy jumper in a cheerful shade of tangerine that stretched snugly over her baby bump, a contrasting navy-blue scarf tied around her neck, while her dark waves hung loose around her shoulders. 'Ooh, and I see you've all been decorated with a dusting of snowflakes. Must be getting worse out there.'

'Yep, the snow's definitely got a bit heavier,' said Lark as a flurry of apologies for their lateness followed.

'It's my fault, as ever,' said Jasmine, sliding onto the settle next to Maggie. 'Well, that's not strictly true. I was ready but the babysitter was late. How typical is that?'

'Not to worry, Jazz, you're here now, and I haven't been here long myself. But, ooh, blimey, brrr! I can feel the cold air hanging on you.' Maggie gave a mock shiver.

'That's cos it's bloomin' freezing out there.' Jasmine grinned at her, chattering her teeth as if to demonstrate.

'Nutter,' said Maggie, giggling.

'You're looking positively radiant, Mags,' Florrie said, as she shuffled up the settle opposite her, taking in her friend's glowing skin and glossy mane of hair. Lark slipped in beside her while Stella took the seat at the head of the table.

Maggie beamed. 'Thanks. You don't look so bad yourself, flower.'

'Thanks for getting the wine in, Mags,' Stella said, lifting the bottle out of the chiller and filling the four empty glasses. She'd folded her coat over the back of her seat and was looking casually chic in a pair of skinny black jeans and a beige turtleneck sweater. Her hair was fastened into a loose bun at the back of her head, blonde tendrils falling gently around her face. 'You okay with your lemonade or are you ready for a top up?' She hitched an enquiring eyebrow at Maggie.

'I'm fine, thanks. I'm having to watch my liquid consumption since Baby Marsay here has decided to perch him or herself right on top of my bladder. I've been running to the loo every five minutes. I tell you, my step count is off the scale – or should I say, my "waddle count"?' Maggie chortled.

'Oh, blimey.' Stella pulled an amused face that teetered on the edge of concern. 'In that case, please do watch how much you guzzle. I don't fancy mopping up any puddles, especially *that* sort.'

'Stells, since when have you ever mopped up puddles of any sort?' Jasmine gave a hearty laugh. 'In fact, I'd be amazed if you even knew what a mop looked like.' The others joined in with her laughter, including Stella herself. She would be the first to admit to her lack of domestic prowess.

'Jazz does have a point, Stells.' Maggie grinned. 'Mind, you flourishing a mop wouldn't half be a sight worth seeing. I reckon some folk would pay good money to get a glimpse of that.'

'I'll have you know, I think there's a mop in my apartment,' Stella said, adopting a faux offended air.

'Note the use of the word "*think*",' said Jasmine, making them all laugh some more.

Stella responded by poking her tongue out at her friend before succumbing to giggles herself.

Florrie sat back, releasing a relaxed sigh. She loved this part of the week, getting together with her best friends, loved how the light-hearted banter bounced around them seamlessly. How they could rib one another mercilessly without the risk of anyone taking offence.

Beside her, Lark pulled off her hat and unbuttoned her coat, wriggling out of it. 'Ooh, that's better,' she said, flicking her long, golden waves, woven with tiny plaits, over her shoulders and making her armful of bracelets play a jangly tune.

Florrie took a sip of her wine, her eyes roving around the room, soaking up the atmosphere. The old pub oozed character with its low, heavily beamed ceiling and thick, uneven walls, imbued with centuries of history and hints of intrigue thanks to its smuggling heritage – something Jack had used to great effect in his novel. Heavy curtains were pulled across the stout mullioned windows, keeping the wintry night at bay, while repurposed hurricane lamps and wrought iron wall lights cast a warm glow, creating an achingly cosy air. An old ship's bell, hung above the chunky oak bar, gleamed alongside the highly polished beer pumps. While at the far end stood a salvaged ship's figurehead in the form of a bare-breasted woman. It had been washed up on the beach in front of the pub several years ago, and the landlord then had reclaimed it, declaring it would make a good talking point for the hostelry. He hadn't been wrong; it had proved to be the source of many conversations, with local fisherman, grizzle-faced Lobster Harry, hanging his mariner's cap from one of its nipples to indicate his presence in the pub.

'So,' said Jasmine, setting her glass down and sweeping her gaze around the group. 'What's the goss, lasses?' Her jade-green jumper emphasised her vibrant red hair and bright green eyes, the crop of freckles that danced across her nose and the apples of her cheeks lending her a youthful air. 'What have you all been up to since I last saw you?'

All eyes swung round to Florrie.

EIGHTEEN

'I think our Florrie – AKA our new *local celebrity* – has had the most going on this week, what with the window reveal, book readings and signings, and interview with the local news channel. Have things settled down after the bookshop was on the telly? Oh, and can we have your autograph?' Maggie flashed a wide beam Florrie's way. She'd sent her a text straight after she'd seen the news article on the television, raining praise and congratulations down on her and Ed. As had all of her friends. It had all felt slightly surreal to Florrie.

'Ooh, yeah! The kids and me watched that,' said Jasmine. 'You can imagine how excited they were when they caught sight of themselves in the background.'

'Aww, they looked so cute.' A gentle smile lit up Lark's pale-green eyes. 'And you and Ed did a brilliant job of promoting the bookshop – it looked *amazing.*'

'You did.' Stella nodded, Maggie and Jasmine following suit.

'Thanks, lasses. We've just about got over the embarrassment of seeing ourselves on the screen.' Florrie scrunched up her nose and gave a self-conscious laugh. *Did her voice really sound like that?* She had no idea her accent was quite so broad, all flat Yorkshire vowels, while her voice had sounded almost little-girl-like to her ears. She took a sip of her wine, hiding behind the glass for a moment, waiting for her internal cringe to subside.

'Any idea yet as to who contacted the news station?' asked Lark. She even managed to have an ethereal air about her in her winter clothes of a loosely knitted pixie dress in fading shades of purple. It was shot with sparkly thread and trimmed with shiny beads that glittered in the firelight. Florrie thought it lent her friend a fairy-like quality.

'Nope, none. No one's owned up to it yet.' She set her glass on the table. She'd trawled her mind several times, going through everyone she considered likely to do such a thing, each time drawing a blank.

'And much as I hate to drag the tone down, dare I ask, how's the situation with Ed's parents? Has he heard any more?' asked Maggie. Florrie had sent her friends a text earlier in the week briefly telling them about the phone call from Peter Harte, saying that she'd elaborate further when they were all together on Friday.

'Yeah, what's happening with them?' asked Stella, tapping her foot in time to the jaunty tune the band had struck up.

Florrie puffed out her cheeks and blew out a slow breath as the feelings generated by the phone call resurfaced. 'Well – I've already told Mags briefly about this, so forgive me for repeating myself, Maggie – Ed's dad rang in the early hours of Monday morning and launched straight into a rant – no surprises there, I know. Anyroad, I couldn't make out everything that was being said, but his tone sounded really aggressive.' Her stomach churned at the memory. 'He's *such* an angry man. I've no idea where he gets it from, he's nothing like Mr and Mrs H. And I don't know why he thinks it's okay to talk to Ed that way.'

'He's a bully,' said Jasmine, blunt as ever. 'Plain and simple.'

'I have to agree,' said Stella. 'So, what's the miserable old toad wanting from Ed this time?'

'The weird thing is, I'm not really sure. From the little Ed's told me, I actually don't think he's any the wiser himself – his Dad just seemed to get tied up in knots with his anger.' Much as she trusted her friends to be discreet, she didn't feel it was right to share that she'd heard Peter Harte mention Jean Davenport's name. 'But what I do know, is that Ed's reluctant to speak to him to see if he can get to the bottom of it, said it's just how his dad gets sometimes. It's beginning to feel like he's adopting his old attitude of "if I ignore it, it'll go away".'

'Which isn't remotely helpful,' said Stella.

'Tell me about it,' Florrie said, despondently.

'Has his dad called since?' asked Lark, her eyes gentle with sympathy.

Florrie nodded. 'Yeah, but Ed ignores him, then turns his phone off once we're at home.' She hesitated for a moment, deliberating whether to mention Ed's sudden interest in the attic. She was conscious of not wanting to taint their view of him, or appear to be painting him in a bad light. Telling herself they were decent women who knew her well and wouldn't think either of those things, she said, 'He's been rooting around the attic, too.'

'What d'you mean, rooting around?' asked Jasmine, her top lip hitched in puzzlement.

'It's as if he's very keen to find something, but acts all inno-cent when I ask if I can help.'

'And you think it's linked to his dad's phone call?' said Stella.

'I honestly don't know.' Florrie glanced between them, taking in their perplexed expressions. Expressing it out loud made her suspicions sound small and, dare she say, petty? 'Hey, listen, I'm sure it's nothing, it's probably just me overthinking as usual. Ignore me. He keeps all his art stuff up there along with a load of other paraphernalia.'

'I'm sure it's nothing, flower. It's easy to start heading off down a rabbit hole of worries once you start paying stuff like that too much attention. It's probably just the call from his dad that's unsettled you, made you start thinking something's wrong when it's not,' said Maggie.

'I agree,' said Lark.

'Yeah, you're right.' Florrie smiled, their words offering the reassurance she needed.

'On a different subject,' said Jasmine, before taking a quick sip of her wine, 'has anyone noticed how Dodgy Dick seems to have increased his presence in town, floating around like he owns the place?'

Lark nodded. 'He was loitering around Nate's shop the other day.'

'And we had Dodgy Dick and his equally dodgy wife, Wendy, sniffing round the bookshop the other night,' said Florrie, wondering why the shifty duo would be showing an interest in Nate's property.

'No way?' said Jasmine.

Florrie nodded. ''Fraid so. In fact, Wendy has designs on turning the bookshop into a hair and beauty salon, offering "exclusive" services.' The reminder sent panic rushing through her.

Maggie's brow furrowed. 'Why the heck would she want to do that? I mean, it's not as if the town doesn't have enough hair salons already, not to mention beauticians. She must've been winding you up – surely she wasn't serious?'

Florrie gave a weary shrug. 'I'm not sure. The whole encounter with them was weird. They created a really horrible atmosphere, I couldn't wait for them to leave. I reckon it was part of a renewed attempt at intimidation and, much as I hate to admit it, they did a pretty good job. Luckily, Ed came downstairs and told them in no uncertain terms we weren't selling, and that we had plans for the bookshop's future.' That she needed to share Ed's tearoom idea with her friends fleeted through her mind. No doubt Lark would already know with Nate having the staircase, but Lark was the soul of discretion and Florrie doubted she'd have shared it with the others.

'And how did that go down?' asked Stella, her tone suggesting she already had a good idea.

'Not great, as I expect you can imagine. In fact, he said he'd give us until the New Year to think about it.'

'And then what?' asked Lark, looking alarmed.

'I don't know, but I think he left us a warning.' She paused, drawing in a deep breath before telling them about the trashing of the outdoor Christmas tree and wreath, and how the shop windows had been egged.

'*What?*' Stella's eyebrows shot up.

'No!' Maggie's hand flew to her mouth, while Lark gasped.

'What a hideous man!' said Jasmine.

'Do you really think he was behind it?' asked Maggie.

'Much as I hate to admit it to myself, I can't think of any other explanation. We were the only shop targeted in such a way. It's too much of a coincidence.'

'Sounds like classic Dodgy Dick.' Maggie pulled a regretful face.

'I'm afraid it does, flower.' Jasmine reached over and squeezed Florrie's hand.

'Has anything else happened?' asked Stella, her tone serious.

Florrie shook her head. 'No, thank goodness.'

'Oh, Florrie, I'm so sorry this has started up again for you,' Lark said gently, her bracelets jangling as she rubbed her hand up and down Florrie's arm.

'Me too. Just don't forget you're not on your own, you've got us lot here to stick up for you, if that puffed-up little weasel starts giving you any hassle. We're just a phone call away. We'll see Dodgy Dick and his equally dodgy wife off for you,' Jasmine said fiercely, raising a smile from Florrie.

'And he really doesn't want to mess with our Jazz,' Maggie said with a giggle, setting them all off. 'Remember when she tore a strip off that lad who'd been two-timing Lark?'

'Ouch! How could we forget?' Stella winced. 'I reckon his lugs'll still be ringing with it. What was that final insult you hurled at him, Jazz? A pathetic little knobhead—'

'—with a penis the size of a hamster's,' the others chorused, before collapsing into a fit of raucous laughter.

'Oh my days! He was ten times the size of Jazz. His face was a picture, looking down at her!' Maggie could barely speak for laughing.

Stella wiped tears of mirth from her eyes. 'On a serious note, and like Jasmine said, don't forget you can call on us anytime you need help. Day or night, we're here for you, Florrie.'

'Too right we are,' said Lark, nodding vigorously.

'Aww, thanks, lasses. You're the best.' Florrie glanced around to see four earnest faces looking back at her. Her heart filled with love for them. Not for the first time did she feel blessed to be a part of such a loyal and supportive group of friends. 'I just wanted to let you know what was going on, but I've taken up enough of the evening and I didn't intend to bring the mood down. Though remind me to tell you all about the exciting plans we have for the bookshop later on, but I'm not going to utter another word about myself until you've all had a chance to share what you've been up to.'

'Sounds intriguing. And you haven't brought the mood down at all.' Stella smiled at her. 'You've been there for us when we needed you, my recent situation with my errant father being a prime example.'

'And for me with that horrendous cousin of mine, and all

the hassle she brought with her.' Maggie shook her head disdainfully at the memory. Her cousin Robyn had turned up out of the blue and managed to wangle her way into their lives. It hadn't taken long for her to put a huge strain on Maggie and Bear's marriage, with her manipulative and deceitful ways. At one point, they thought she'd never leave. When she eventually did, she'd left a cloud of drama in her wake that had almost broken Maggie.

'So, how's the trial going, Stells?' Florrie asked, keen to direct the focus on someone else. 'Sounds like you were having a right scrap with that defence barrister you were against.' Stella was a well-respected barrister who specialised in serious crime. When the friends were at The Cellar earlier in the week, she'd mentioned that she was prosecuting a particularly vicious assault trial against counsel who believed every client he defended was innocent, no matter how heinous the crime they were charged with. He'd gained a reputation at the bar for relentlessly attempting to wear his opponents down in the hope they'd accept a lesser plea. Stella never backed down which frustrated him – and all her opposing counsel – no end.

Stella reached for the bottle of wine, topping up all but Maggie's glass. 'As far as Rory Sinclair is concerned, he fights his corner. I respect him for that. Though he wasn't very happy when the jury came back with a guilty verdict for his client. The fact that it was unanimous on all counts made the victory extra sweet. That, and the knowledge a dangerous criminal has been locked up and the streets are safer for it.'

'Well done, Stells,' said Florrie. She admired her friend for how she could tackle such horrific cases and pack them away, not letting them intrude on her personal life. It took a strong person to be able to do that, she thought.

'And has he got over his disappointment at you being all loved up with Alex?' asked Jasmine, flashing her a cheeky grin.

'Not so sure disappointment's the right word, but he's given up asking me out for dinner.' Stella smiled back at her.

Stella had been resolutely single and had never been in love until she'd met Alex Bainbridge earlier in the year. Before then, Stella's approach to dating had meant for some entertaining stories of a Friday evening, as she'd shared details of her latest dalliances. But Florrie and the others had always thought there'd be someone who'd capture Stella's heart when she least expected it. Which is exactly what had happened.

Just then, the pub door opened and an icy breeze whooshed in. The friends turned to see Ando Taylor holding it open as if waiting for someone to come through. Whoever it was evidently wasn't in a hurry.

'Brrr! Bloomin' 'eck, get that door shut!' Jasmine shivered.

'Jeez, it's freezing.' Lark frowned, rubbing her hands up and down her arms.

'Why would you keep the door open like that?' Florrie asked.

'I think common sense has clearly escaped him this evening,' said Stella as a round of complaints went up from the other customers. Still, Ando seemed oblivious.

Eventually craggy-faced local fisherman Lobster Harry rolled in wearing a gap-toothed smile and a light dusting of snow on his well-worn mariner's hat.

'Take your time, why don't you, Harry?' Maggie rolled her eyes as the door slammed shut and the pair ambled their way over to the bar.

Jasmine had just started telling them about the latest problems with her ex-in-laws, who appeared to take great pleasure in making life difficult for her, when Ando appeared by their table. Florrie was relieved to see he wasn't worse for drink as he often was by this time of the evening, having propped up the bar for several hours.

'All right, lasses?' he asked, resting his hand on the back of

Stella's chair. She gave a small lift of her eyebrow. In his mid-forties, he had a weather-beaten face that belied his usual youthful garb of battered leather jacket, slashed jeans and a baseball cap worn back-to-front, covering his straggly bleach-blond ponytail.

'Aren't you freezing in those jeans?' Jasmine asked, frowning. 'Surely they won't be any use at keeping the cold out. I feel nithered just looking at them.'

'I don't feel the cold, like,' he said, with a hint of a swagger.

Florrie expected him to break into a smile, or a laugh to show he was joking, and was surprised when he didn't.

'Just as well.' Jasmine didn't appear to be impressed.

'Aye, it is.' He flicked his limp ponytail over his shoulder. 'Anyroad, I thought I should warn you it's snowing out there so it might be a good idea to keep an eye on the weather.'

'Thanks, Ando, that's kind of you to let us know.' Lark smiled up at him.

'It is, thanks, Ando.' Florrie smiled, too. He may be a bit of an overgrown daft lad sometimes, but he had a good heart.

'You doing all right, Maggie?' he asked, shuffling from foot to foot.

'I'm fine and dandy, thanks, Ando.' She smiled. He'd made a habit of checking she was okay since he'd witnessed a car accident she'd been in during the early stages of her pregnancy. He'd acted quickly, calling for an ambulance and contacting Florrie and Ed. The friends' respect for him had grown considerably since that time, despite his tendency to act the goon when he'd had a few pints of Micklewick Magic.

'Cool.' He gave her a bashful smile.

Just then Immy, one of the waitresses, hurried over and threw a couple of logs onto the fire, sending sparks dancing up the chimney and the sweet smell of woodsmoke into the air. She turned, treating Jasmine to a knowing smile, before heading back towards the bar.

'Aye, well, no probs.' Ando loitered a moment longer as if toying with the idea of saying something else. The friends all regarded him with interest. 'I was just gonna say, Jazz, that if you need walking home, I'd be happy to take you back, like. Thought we could maybe share a bottle of wine at your place, if you know what I mean?' He waggled his eyebrows suggestively. 'I've got one going spare back home, won it in a raffle. S'only cheap plonk, but I reckon it'll be better than my home brew – you have no idea what that did to my guts last Friday.' He gave a throaty laugh.

Jasmine listened, an array of horrified emotions crossing her face. Florrie daren't make eye contact with the others for fear of bursting out laughing.

'Erm, Ando, I—'

Jasmine was cut off by her admirer. 'We could stop off at my place and pick it up. I got a massive bag of crisps, an' all – a couple of weeks past their sell-by date, but the booze should mask the stale taste. And I've got half a jar of pickled eggs that need eating up, which I opened last Christmas. It'd be a shame for 'em to go to waste.'

Hearing Maggie stifle a snort, Florrie pressed her lips together, keeping her eyes firmly fixed on Jasmine, whose expression had morphed to one of utter mortification at mention of the eggs.

'Er, much as I appreciate your offer, Ando, I think I'll pass, thanks.' Jasmine forced a smile. Every week Ando propositioned her for a date and every week she turned him down.

'Aye, right, well. Fair enough.' He went to walk away but clearly had second thoughts. He turned and said, 'I'll just be at the bar if you change your mind. I reckon it'll be the best offer you get tonight.' With that he gave her a wink and sauntered his way back to the bar.

'Did I just hear right?' Jasmine glanced around at her friends who all collapsed into a fit of the giggles. 'How does he know I won't get a better offer, cheeky so-and-so? I can't imagine anything worse than spending an evening with him and his cheap bottle of plonk that's no doubt been doing the rounds with all the local raffles. It'll be one that no one wants and keeps getting donated over and over again, more like vinegar than wine.'

'It'll go well with the pickled eggs, then, Jazz.' Maggie could barely speak for laughing.

'Don't forget the stale crisps,' said Stella.

'Good point, and there's his home brew,' added Florrie.

'Ugh! Don't go there.' Jasmine shook her head, her top lip curling in distaste. 'And, please, no one mention what he said it did to his guts. I don't even want to think about that!'

'Yep, he sure knows how to treat a lady,' Stella said, dryly.

'Ahh, bless him,' said Lark, tender-hearted as ever. 'He means well, we shouldn't laugh at him.'

'You're right, he does,' agreed Maggie. 'But someone should have a word about his approach. Maybe Alex could give him a few tips, Stells?' She chuckled.

'Where would he start?' said Stella.

'Why, though?' Jasmine raised her palms in question, her eyes sweeping around the table. 'Why me? What is it about me that says my idea of a date with a bloke is a night in, stuffing my face with past-their-best pickled eggs and swigging the remnants of his home brew, which if I remember rightly, he calls "Gut Rot". *Please*, one of you tell me, I'm dying to know.' She looked at them imploringly, before joining in with their laughter. 'And I'm not having a pop at Ando here, I'm just trying to get my head around why he thinks I'd find that appealing.'

'To be honest, Jazz, I don't think he appreciates how awful his offer sounds. I get the impression he just says the first thing that comes into his head, hoping that it'll tempt you or that his persistence will eventually wear you down. He gets full marks for trying.'

'Aye, well, I wish he flippin' wouldn't keep trying. I don't have the time or the inclination for a fella in my life. The kids are my priority.' Jasmine sighed and rolled her eyes. 'Do you think he's ever going to get the message?'

'Doesn't look like it'll be any time soon, flower,' said Florrie.

'Anyroad, it's not that long since he had the hots for you. How come he's moved on to me?'

'He seemed to switch his affections once Ed arrived,' Florrie said, with a shrug. It was true, he'd regularly propositioned her – though, thankfully, not with the culinary horrors he was using to tempt Jasmine – asking her out on dates. But as soon as Ed had arrived on the scene and they'd become an item, Ando had backed off.

'Pfft.' Jasmine puffed out a frustrated sigh. 'Well, there's no way I'm going to hook up with a bloke just to put Ando off the scent. I'll just keep turning him down and hope he finally gets the message.'

'I feel sorry for him. He has a good heart if you look through all the bravado and the daft things he comes out with when he's had a drink,' Lark said kindly.

'I hope you're not trying to suggest I take him up on his offer, Lark!' Jasmine shot her a horrified look.

'Oh, no, not at all! That's not what I meant. I just think if he had someone to love him, he'd behave differently, that's all.'

'From what I can gather, he's never seemed keen on getting tied down,' said Maggie.

'Maybe he hasn't found the right woman, yet. I'm sure there's somebody out there who's perfect for him,' said Lark, her gaze drifting off into the middle distance.

'Aye, well, don't look at me,' said Jasmine, chuckling.

'On that note, I reckon we should get our food ordered,' said Maggie.

'Good plan,' said Jasmine, wearing an expression of relief.

'In that case, I'll go and place our order at the bar, and grab us another bottle of wine while I'm there. Snow or no snow, I intend to enjoy myself tonight. It's been a full-on week.' Stella pushed herself up and strode over to the bar in a waft of crisp perfume. She made for a striking image with her long legs and high-heeled boots, exuding an air of confidence, turning heads as she went.

NINETEEN

The jolly-faced group of musicians had struck up a lively round of traditional Christmas folk songs which had proved to be a popular choice. The group of friends joined the other regulars and enjoyed a raucous sing-along with much tapping of feet and fists thudding on tables in time to the beat.

'That was fab!' said Jasmine.

'Shame the same can't be said about your caterwauling,' Stella said dryly.

'Cheek!' said Jasmine, before giving in to a giggle. 'Mind, I take your point, I was giving it some welly just then.'

'We'd noticed,' said Maggie, chuckling.

'Hey, you can't beat a good vocal clear-out.'

'Those of us in earshot would beg to differ,' Stella added.

'Whoa, this looks great,' said Lark as Immy and Tara arrived at their table, each armed with two plates piled high with fish and chips. Soon the delicious aroma of their food filled the air around them, a tang of vinegar adding to the mix as Maggie doused her plate with a generous dash.

'Yours is on its way, Stella.' Immy gave her a friendly smile. 'As is the gravy and the mushy peas.'

'Fabulous!' said Jasmine. 'I'm absolutely ravenous, feel like I've been running around like a loon all day. I've only had an apple since breakfast.'

'An apple's not going to keep you going, Jazz, especially with all the racing around you do. I'd be keeling over.' Florrie shot her a concerned look.

'I'm fine. Didn't feel hungry till I got a waft of this grub.' She flashed Florrie a smile that said, 'Don't fuss.'

With the arrival of Stella's plate, the friends were soon tucking in with great gusto. Florrie took the opportunity to share the tearoom at the bookshop idea with her friends. She was thrilled when they all responded so positively. 'At least it proves Ed's sticking around and should send a strong message to his parents that he's not going to be getting rid of the bookshop,' Stella had said, echoing Florrie's thoughts. And they'd all agreed that Jean's suggestion of taking things at a pace they could afford rather than risking themselves coming financially unstuck was a good one, especially in the current climate. That they all thought along the same lines was reassuring.

'Oh, man, this is *so* good.' Jasmine rolled her eyes in ecstasy. 'Makes a nice change from the rest of the week when I've been having to wolf my food down and rush off to take the kids somewhere, or get back to ice the latest cake I've got on the go.'

'I'll bet,' said Lark, slicing into the crisp, golden batter of her fish. 'Just savour it, Jazz. This is your "me time", no need to rush off for anything.'

Jasmine smiled over at her, her eyes shining. 'Ooh, I don't half like the sound of a bit of "me time". With the exception of Jack's reading and our Friday nights, it's been in short supply recently, and tomorrow's looking like a stinker of a day. I don't even want to think about what I'm going to do with the kids now my mum's not well and can't look after them. I could do with there being two of me.'

'Heaven forbid!' joked Maggie.

'You'd be able to give the other one of you to Ando.' Stella gave a wicked chuckle. She was rewarded with a stern look and a swift kick under the table from Jasmine.

Joking aside, Florrie's heart went out to her friend who never seemed to have a moment to sit down and catch her breath. She was in awe of Jasmine, of how she kept track of everything, and of how she kept on top of it all; though Jazz joked about her life being chaotic, she was the most organised person Florrie knew. She'd been a single mum for over six years since the death of her partner, Bart, when she was pregnant with Chloe, losing her home not long after, but you rarely heard her grumbling about all she had to do, even if at times it seemed she was being pulled in a million different directions. She was a brilliant mum – everyone said so – with seemingly boundless energy, though Florrie did occasionally detect a whiff of tiredness about her. In fact, as she looked more closely at her friend right now, she picked up on the dark shadows that hung beneath her eyes, despite Jasmine's evident attempts to hide them with concealer. And there was a general undertone of weariness about her that wasn't usually there. *Poor Jazz.* Florrie pulled herself up with a start; the last thing Jasmine would want was her sympathy. Anyone Jasmine suspected of feeling sorry for her was in danger of finding themselves on the receiving end of a verbal savaging. Florrie winced inwardly at the thought.

'So, how's The Happy Christmas Memory Project going, Florrie?' Jasmine asked, pushing a gravy-dunked chip into her mouth and chewing enthusiastically.

'The ice skating yesterday was brilliant fun – thanks for suggesting it, Mags. Mind, we're both suffering a bit for it today. I've got a massive bruise on my bum.' Florrie chuckled.

'Don't worry, we won't ask you to show us.' Jasmine grinned at her.

'I hope whatever's going on with Ed's dad and Dodgy Dick haven't been too much of a distraction,' said Stella. 'You mustn't

let them spoil something as thoughtful as The Happy
Christmas Memories Project. And don't forget to holler if you
need help with anything, or for us to join in.'

'It's been a welcome distraction, actually.' Speaking of
distractions, something Jasmine had said earlier had set an idea
brewing in her mind. And it was one Florrie couldn't wait to set
in motion.

TWENTY

Once she'd finished her food, Florrie used the excuse of a trip to the loo to send a quick text to Ed – he'd told her earlier he'd keep his phone on while she was out in case her Friday night plans changed and she needed a lift back. An idea that involved helping Jasmine out of her childcare predicament the following day had been growing in her mind and she'd been itching to set the ball rolling. That it would kill two birds with one stone had only added to the thrill. She just needed to check that Ed would be up for it. As an added bonus, it was something that could be included in The Happy Christmas Memory Project.

> How does sledging & snowman building with Zak & Chloe sound for tomorrow if I can get cover for the bookshop? Fxx

A wide smile lit up her face when he replied immediately.

> Sounds great! Count me in!

'Yay!' Florrie did a little dance on the spot and fired off a speedy reply.

Fab! Thank you! Fxx

Next, she texted her mum to see if she'd mind covering for her in the bookshop the following day. Though Paula had already helped out so they could go ice skating, she knew her mother wouldn't mind doing another shift, especially if it got Jasmine out of a difficult situation. Paula had known Jasmine since she was a small girl and thought fondly of her and her children.

Like Ed, her mum replied quickly saying she was only too happy to help, especially once she'd heard the reason behind it.

On the way back to the table Florrie took a quick detour, peeking through the door to check on the weather. She was thrilled to see the snow had continued to fall since they'd arrived and now everywhere was covered in a blanket of the stuff. It wasn't sufficient to worry about them getting home – Bear had the Land Rover, after all – but it was enough to boost her hopes that her plans for tomorrow would be put into action.

'You okay there, Florrie?' asked Maggie as Lark eased out of the settle and let Florrie slip back in. 'That's a massive smile you've got on your fizzog.'

'You're right, it is,' said Jasmine, observing her with interest. 'I thought you'd just popped to the loo, but you look like you've been up to mischief. Think I might have a quick trip there, see if I come back smiling like that.' She cackled.

'I think I'll join you before a queue starts forming,' Stella said, dryly, her mouth twitching with a smile.

Florrie couldn't help but laugh. 'Hey, you shouldn't be talking like that, young lady, especially since you're all loved up with Alex.'

'Clearly old habits die hard,' quipped Jasmine, earning herself a mock dirty look from Stella.

Florrie pushed her glasses up her nose, willing her friend to agree with what she was about to put to her. 'So, I have a suggestion to make, Jazz.'

'Ey up, that sounds ominous,' said Jasmine.

'Well' – Florrie met her friend's gaze – 'as you now know, Ed has never built a snowman before, never had a snowball fight, and has never been sledging so I wondered if it'd be okay if we borrow the kids tomorrow? I mean, who better to show him how to do those things than Zak and Chloe? I've already checked, and my mum says she's happy to stand in for me at the bookshop, so that wouldn't be a problem.' Florrie was keeping her fingers crossed Jasmine wouldn't think the offer came out of pity for her childcare headache. 'I've run it by Ed, and he loves the sound of it. And if there isn't enough snow, then our plan B is to go to the cinema and see the latest Christmas film instead – seeing a Christmas film at the cinema's something else he's never done and is a contender for The Happy Christmas Memory Project. We'd finish off with a pizza. I should add, we're both already buzzing with excitement for the idea and would be massively disappointed if the answer's no. What do you think?' she finished with a hopeful smile.

All eyes turned to Jasmine.

She took a moment, clearly mulling it over. Florrie watched her friend's face for clues that might reveal how her suggestion had been received. 'Are you sure about this?' Jasmine asked, sounding half-convinced. 'I mean, having my two little horrors for the day? Much as I love them to bits, they can be a handful, and they're wound up like tops at the minute, what with Christmas on the horizon. You do realise you'll be completely knackered by the end of the day, don't you? And what about all your aches and pains from ice skating? How will you manage with that?'

Florrie laughed. 'We'll be fine – moving about actually helps. And we won't care if we're knackered. We'll have had a great time, it'll be so worth it, and besides, we'll have Sunday to recover.'

'Well, if you're sure... I know the kids won't need asking twice... I'd love you to take them snowman building, sledging and all the rest of it. Thanks, Florrie, you've just made tomorrow a whole load easier for me.' A huge grin spread across Jasmine's face, unmistakable relief in her eyes.

'Fantastic!' Florrie's smile mirrored Jasmine's. 'And it's me who should be thanking you. We'll have loads more fun with Zak and Chloe being involved. I so can't wait.' She rubbed her hands together gleefully. Much as she'd been dreading the disruption heavy snow could cause for their expected deliveries and scheduled reading with Jenna Johnstone, Florrie had decided it would be best to park that concern for now and deal with it if and when the problem arose. Instead, she'd focus on something positive for Ed and helping out her friend. Hopefully, with the salty air, any snow would be gone by early in the week – provided they didn't get any more, of course.

Before they knew it, landlady Mandy was ringing the ship's bell above the bar, signalling the end of the evening. 'Time, folks,' she said, her cockney accent floating over the burble of chatter. The friends made a move to leave.

'Flaming 'eck, that surely can't be the time, can it?' Lobster Harry was leaning against the bar, his bleary eyes betraying that he was on the wrong side of several pints of Old Micklewick Magic. He turned his attention to his half-drunk pint of beer, downing it in one. 'I'll have another couple if you don't mind, Mandy, love,' he said, as he wiped the froth from his mouth with the back of his hand before releasing a belch that ricocheted around the room.

'Charming.' Stella's top lip curled in disgust as she fastened the toggles of her sheepskin coat, making the others giggle.

'Good old Harry,' said Lark.

Outside, Florrie gasped as she was hit by a wall of bitingly cold air, her eyes taking in the crisp covering of snow that was sparkling in the glow of the pale winter moon suspended in a star-strewn sky. Woodsmoke from the pub's fire drifted out of the chimney, reaching upwards. A thrill started dancing in her stomach. The snow wasn't deep enough to cause problems, but there was enough to put her plans into action the following day, provided a thaw didn't set in, of course. She felt her excitement building. *Looks like we'll be sledging and building snowmen tomorrow!*

She spotted Bear's Land Rover parked up by the side of the pub, steam billowing from its exhaust, the odd snowflake swirling in the beam of its headlights.

'Blimey, it's raw out here,' said Jasmine, her breath curling out in front of her as she headed away from the Jolly. In the next moment she let out an ear-piercing screech as she lost her footing and landed on her bottom with a muffled *thwump*. 'Wargh!'

The friends all looked on, alarmed.

Florrie clutched her hand to her chest. 'Jazz! Are you okay?'

'Oh my God. These flaming boots!' She threw her head back and let out a loud hoot of laughter. Seeing she was unhurt, her friends followed suit, their giggles hanging in the frosty air.

Florrie and Stella helped her to her feet, almost losing their footing in the process which only added to their hilarity.

'What are you like, Jazz?' said Maggie, as she dusted snow from the back of Jasmine's padded jacket.

'Hopeless, I'd say! I've got a soaking wet bum and it's flippin' freezing – I wouldn't be surprised if I got frostbite on my butt cheeks.'

'Need a hand, Jash?' said a voice behind them.

The friends turned to see Ando Taylor swaying precariously under the light of the pub's sign.

'The offer'sh shtill open, if you're intereshted.' He gave an exaggerated wink followed by a leery smile.

'Jeez, when's he going to get the message?' Jasmine said, sotto voce, rolling her eyes. 'And it's still a no, Ando.' She turned away from him.

'Shuit yourshelf,' he said, before staggering his way back into the pub.

'You all right there, Jazz?' Bear leapt out of the Land Rover, laughing as he went to open the heavy rear door.

'I will be once I'm in the Landie and not risking my life walking across this death-trap of a path.' She grinned as Florrie hooked her under one arm and Stella the other, her feet slip-sliding over the snow as they made their way towards him, leaving the Jolly in the same way she arrived.

The living room at Samphire Cottage was toasty warm after the chill of outside. A lively fire was dancing in the grate and the soft lighting cast a cosy glow around the room. Florrie was curled up beside Ed on the sofa, sipping a hot chocolate and listening to their classical music playlist. A wave of contentment washed over her and she leant into him, resting her head on his shoulder, his head touching hers. He'd just finished sharing the details of the research he'd carried out for the tearoom that evening. He'd evidently covered a lot of ground in the time she'd been out. She loved how enthusiastic he was for it, that he was so clearly invested in the bookshop's future. It went some way to over-riding the doubts that had arisen since his father's phone call.

Gerty groaned from where she'd been snoring on the rug in front of the fire. She heaved herself up, wandered over to the sofa and flopped at Ed's feet with a *harumph*.

'Looking forward to tomorrow?' Florrie asked.

'Very much.' She could hear the smile in his voice. 'I think it's a brilliant idea having Zak and Chloe join us. We'll have a great time with them. I don't think I've ever met two more enthusiastic kids.' He gave a chuckle as he started to rub Gerty's tummy with his feet. The Labrador stretched out, luxuriating in the attention.

'Oh, they're that all right.' Florrie laughed, too.

'I meant to ask earlier, but have you got a sledge, or do we need to buy one in town?'

'Mum and Dad have still got a couple from when I was a kid, they're in their shed. My dad used to love sledging, too. He said he'd dig them out and drop them off in the morning when he brought Mum to pick up the keys for the bookshop.'

Florrie had just got her words out when Ed's phone started ringing from the coffee table, slicing through the relaxed atmosphere and making her jump. Ed tipped his head back and gave an exasperated sigh. 'Not at this time of night.' Gerty jumped up and put her head in his lap, sensing his change in mood.

They both knew the call could only be from his father. Florrie held back from asking him if he was going to answer it. She wondered how long it would take for him to realise the sooner he spoke to his dad, the sooner this bombardment would stop. And the sooner she'd feel more settled, knowing what had prompted this latest round of phone calls, not to mention what Jean Davenport had to do with it.

Ed let the call ring out, but it wasn't long until his phone pinged announcing the arrival of a voicemail message.

He glanced at Florrie and rolled his eyes. 'I'm turning that dratted thing off until after we've been sledging with Zak and Chloe.' With that, he snatched up his phone and did just that. 'I'm not going to let anything spoil tomorrow, especially when there are kids involved.'

'Ed, don't you think it might be—'

'I just want to focus on us having a good time with Zak and Chloe, then I'll think about talking to him, okay?'

'Okay.' Florrie smiled and pressed a kiss to his cheek. *Progress!* 'I promise, we're going to have a great time tomorrow.'

'That's what's important right now,' he said, his shoulders relaxing. 'I'm way more excited about going sledging than a bloke my age should own up to.' He gave her a heart-melting smile.

'Oh, you've clearly never heard my dad on the subject,' she said.

'Remind me to bring it up next time I'm having a pint with him at the Jolly.' They both chuckled at that, the mood lifting instantly.

TWENTY-ONE

SATURDAY 9TH DECEMBER

Florrie slid her glasses onto her nose and peered out of the bedroom curtains, taking in the wintry scene before her. At just gone seven thirty, darkness still lingered. In the soft light of the streetlamps, it was as if a vast white eiderdown had been thrown over everything and settled gently. Her heart gave a happy leap.

'How's it looking?' Ed asked from the bed. His mouth stretched into a yawn as he ran his fingers through his sleep-tousled hair.

'Perfect!' Florrie couldn't help but smile. 'Looks like a couple more inches have fallen overnight. Everywhere looks so pretty.' Her gaze travelled over the row of houses opposite. They seemed to sparkle in the half-light.

'Fantastic. Sounds like sledging and snowman building is on the agenda for today, then.' He beamed at her as he threw the duvet back and climbed out of bed.

'Zak and Chloe are going to be so excited.'

'They're not the only ones,' Ed said with a deep chuckle.

A moment later he was standing behind her, slipping his arms around her waist, the warmth of his body reassuring. He peered out over the top of her head. 'Looks so picture-perfect out there.'

'It does.' She turned to face him, looking up as he pressed his lips to hers, his kiss warm and inviting. She reached up, wrapping her arms around his neck, and he pulled her to him.

'I really appreciate you organising this, Florrie.' He gazed down at her, his expression soft.

'Hey, I'm looking forward to it myself.' She stood on her tiptoes and kissed him again.

Their kiss was deepening, Florrie losing herself in the moment, when the ping of a mobile phone bounced around the room. Their eyes flashed open and they froze, hardly daring to breathe, as if awaiting something to happen.

Florrie's stomach clenched, all feelings of passion leeching away. Ed took a step back and pushed his fringe off his face, anxiety clouding his features.

How easily a sound could affect a mood.

It took several moments for it to dawn on Florrie that the sound came from *her* mobile phone and not Ed's. He'd thrown his into one of the drawers in the kitchen the previous evening before they'd gone to bed. 'Out of sight, out of mind,' he'd said, shutting the drawer firmly. 'And that's where it's staying until we get back from sledging tomorrow. I'm not going to allow my parents to spoil our time with Zak and Chloe.' Florrie hadn't been sorry to hear that.

Relief flooded her, her heart rate steadying. 'It's mine, not yours. It'll be my mum or Jasmine.' She gave him a reassuring smile. He visibly relaxed as she headed over to her bedside table and scooped up her phone. She knew he'd have been thinking exactly the same as her, that the day's onslaught of texts and calls from his dad had started early.

She tapped her phone, its light illuminating the room as her eyes scanned the screen. 'It's Jazz. Oh, heck.' She laughed as she read the text that was peppered with a variety of worried face, crying and laughing emojis. Then she read it out to Ed.

> Hi Florrie, just checking plans are still on for today? Little monsters were awake when I got home last night & in my wisdom I told them all about it. They've been up since six bombarding me with questions!!! Over & over again!!! Argh! In case you haven't guessed, they're VERY excited!!! Thought I should warn you. Oh, and you're not the only one with a massive bruise on your bum, I've got one where I fell. Looks like a map of Australia!!! Jxxx

Ed chuckled. 'I dread to think what it must be like at Jasmine's house right now with all that excitement bouncing around the place. I'll bet her ears are ringing with the kids' chatter.'

'Ooh, and some.' Florrie chuckled. Zak, in particular, was lively especially when he was excited about something. He put her in mind of Jasmine when she was his age. He was bubbly, full of bounce and enthusiasm, and had a well-developed sense of mischief. And, just like his mum, you'd often hear him coming before he came into view. His effusive personality had got him into trouble on more than one occasion, especially at school, just as it had done with Jasmine, but he seemed to take it all in his stride. He'd inherited his mum's quick temper, too, especially if he thought an injustice had been done, his anger flaring like touch paper. And just like hers, it subsided quickly; neither were the sort to bear a grudge.

Chloe, in contrast, was a quieter, more diluted version of her mum and sibling. Even at such a young age, she was given to thinking deeply, though it was fair to say she shared their zest for life and was easily scooped up and carried along by her brother's ebullience. Unlike Zak, she'd inherited Jasmine's artistic streak and wasn't averse to sitting quietly and drawing or colouring when the mood took her. Where her beautiful singing voice had come from, however, remained a mystery.

Not one given to boasting, Jasmine's pride and love for her children was undeniable. 'I love them so much it hurts right here,' she'd said on more than one occasion, patting her chest where her heart lay, her eyes burning fiercely. 'I'd lay down my life for them.' Florrie didn't doubt that for a second. She was full of admiration for her friend who worked hard to give Zak and Chloe a secure and loving home.

'Jazz said she was cleaning a holiday cottage for Stella's mum today and needs to be there for ten o'clock so she's dropping Zak and Chloe off here at half nine. And my mum's calling in for the bookshop key and to drop the sledges off at half past eight,' Florrie said.

'In that case...' Ed took her hand and led her to the bed, its sheets still warm and ruffled from their sleep. 'I think we've got time to pick up where we left off with those tempting kisses of yours.'

Bang on the dot at half past nine, there was an enthusiastic pounding on the door of Samphire Cottage, accompanied by a babble of eager voices.

Smiling, Florrie opened the door to see Zak and Chloe beaming up at her, while behind them, the freshly fallen snow of the path was peppered with their footprints. 'Morning,' she said as Gerty pushed her nose through, her tail wagging hard.

'When can we go sledging, Florrie? Can we go now?' asked Zak, excitedly, his freckly face wreathed in smiles. 'Can Gerty come, too? She can ride on my sledge with me. It's gonna be *so* cool!'

'Yay! I want Gerty to come as well!' said Chloe. She was looking adorable in a powder-blue snow suit covered in pink flowers, a woolly hat with a huge pink pom-pom pulled down over her ears. Her blue eyes were shining happily. 'We've been awake for *ages*! I wanted to put my snow suit on as soon as I got out of bed, but Mummy said it was too early. And I've got some new wellies – look.' The little girl stuck out her foot, showing off a bright pink, fur-lined wellington boot.

Florrie inhaled the familiar smell of fresh washing she'd come to associate with Jasmine's children. They were always spotlessly clean and neatly dressed.

'Calm down, you two, give Florrie a chance to open the door,' Jasmine said, laughing, and giving an affectionate roll of her eyes. 'Morning, Florrie. You still sure about this?'

'Of course I'm still sure about it, we're looking forward to it. Come on in.' Florrie turned to Chloe. 'And I *love* your new wellies, Chlo. Do you think they do them in my size?' She smiled down at the little girl.

'I don't think so, these are just for little girls, but we can go shopping together and I can help you find some, if you like?' she said in her trill voice.

'Ooh, I'd love that. Shopping for shoes is one of my favourite things.'

'Morning.' Ed wandered down the hall from the kitchen as Jasmine and the kids tumbled in.

'Hiya, Ed. Can I race you at sledging?' Zak asked, grinning at him.

'I'm up for that.' Ed laughed. 'But I don't think I'll be much competition.'

'That's all right, I'll give you a head start,' Zak said generously.

'Thanks, Zak, I think I'll need it.'

'I'm going to build the biggest snowman. He's going to be as big as this house,' said Chloe, demonstrating with her hands, her eyes wide.

'Wow! He sounds fabulous. Can I help you do that?' Florrie asked.

'Yes, you can.' Chloe nodded enthusiastically.

'Morning, Ed,' said Jasmine before turning to her children. 'Wellies off at the door, kids.'

'Did I just hear right? Chloe's taking Florrie shopping for shoes? I didn't realise a girl's love for footwear started so young,' Ed said, smiling.

'You have a lot to learn then, Ed.' Jasmine shot him a knowing look. 'Chloe *loves* shoes, the pinker, and the more sparkly, the better.'

'Ah, I see. Just like Florrie then.' He chuckled, exchanging a look with Florrie who was laughing, too.

'Ed! Ed! Ed! I've asked Santa for some pink glittery tap shoes for Christmas,' Chloe said, tugging on his shirt sleeve and peering up at him from beneath long dark lashes.

'Have you? They sound wonderful.'

Chloe nodded. 'Oh, they are, they're the bestest.'

'Right, come on monsters, we're letting the cold air in standing here like this.' Jasmine stamped the snow off her wellies, the children following suit, before she ushered them onto the doormat.

Once they'd removed their footwear, Jasmine bustled them along the hallway. She handed Florrie a couple of backpacks, one pink and sparkly, the other covered in a variety of superheroes. 'There's a change of clothes for each of them – they're bound to get soaked or mucky, or both. And here's some money if you have a change of plan and take them to the cinema and pizza afterwards.'

Florrie stepped back. 'I'm happy to take the change of clothes, but there's no way I'm taking any money. It's our treat today,' she said with a smile. She watched Jasmine's expression change. She was clearly wrestling with her thoughts. The last thing Florrie wanted to do was hurt her friend's pride, but equally, she didn't want to take any money from her, especially when things were tight so close to Christmas.

When Jasmine went to protest, Florrie said, 'Don't forget, it's you who's doing us the favour, Jazz. This was my suggestion and both Ed and I are looking forward to it. It's a treat for us as much as the kids, and that it's another thing to add to the Happy Christmas Memories Project is perfect.'

'Well, if you're sure?' There was still a hesitant look in Jasmine's eyes.

'I'm positive.' Though Florrie's tone was friendly, she spoke firmly, hoping to convey that she wasn't open to any further argument.

'Okay, then,' Jasmine said, a note of reluctance in her voice. 'I'd best get off to work – it's changeover day at the holiday cottage so there's loads to do. I should be done by half past two, so just let me know when you want to drop the kids off or for me to come and get them.' She glanced into the kitchen where Zak and Chloe were fussing Gerty. The Labrador was in raptures, lying on her back, her legs in the air while the pair tickled her tummy. 'See you, kids, be good for Florrie and Ed.' She turned to Florrie, chuckling. 'Doesn't look like I'm going to be missed much today.'

'Bye, Mummy,' said Chloe. 'Love you.'

'See ya, Mum,' said Zak.

'Love you both, too. Don't forget to keep them ears covered when you're out in the cold, Chlo.'

'Okay, Mummy.' Chloe had suffered from an ear infection a few weeks earlier and had needed a couple of rounds of antibiotics before it finally cleared up.

'I'll make sure she does,' said Florrie reassuringly. She knew from what Jasmine had told her it was the little girl's Achilles heel, and that she was keen to ensure Chloe didn't succumb to another infection and risk spoiling her enjoyment of Christmas Day.

'Bye, Ed, have fun.' Jasmine grinned at him, with a look in

her eye that said, "Have you any idea what you've let yourself in for?"

'See you, Jazz. I'm sure we will.' Ed grinned back.

At the door, Jasmine turned to Florrie. 'Thanks for this, I really appreciate it. The kids have been so excited, they love you and Ed, you're like extended family to them – and me.'

Florrie felt a tug in her heart. She knew it hurt Jasmine that Bart's parents showed no interest in their grandchildren. 'Hey, we love you all, too. And I was going to say you're welcome to join us for a meal this evening. Nothing fancy. Ed's been saying he's got a taste for pizza, so we've got loads in the freezer – there'll be plenty to go round.'

Jasmine's face fell. 'I'd love to, and I don't mean to sound like I'm being awkward, but I've got a cake to finish icing. It's getting collected first thing tomorrow morning and some of the decorations are quite fiddly.'

'Well, just join us when you're done then. We can always stick an extra pizza in when you get here.'

'Are you sure?' Jasmine's frown lifted.

''Course I'm sure.'

Jasmine flung her arms around Florrie in an uncharacteristic display of affection. 'You're a star. Honestly, you've no idea what a help you're being. I hate fobbing the kids off when I'm busy with a cake, telling them to entertain themselves, but I know they'll love being here.'

'You could never be accused of fobbing your kids off.' Florrie felt her throat squeeze with emotion. 'You're a great mum, Jazz, the kids are testament to that. Stop beating yourself up, okay?'

Jasmine released her and nodded, her eyes glistening. 'Okay.' She sniffed. 'I'd best dash or I'll be late getting started.'

. . .

Half an hour later, Florrie and Ed set off with a high-spirited Zak and Chloe eager to get out into the snow. Gerty trotted along on the end of her lead, watching the children with interest.

Florrie slipped her gloved hand into Ed's as they made their way down the road, Zak and Chloe running ahead, trailing their sledges behind them. Her heart swelled with happiness. It was one of those perfect winter days, a pale sun shining down from a cornflower-blue sky, making everywhere sparkle, while the air was crisp and fresh, making her cheeks and nose tingle.

The two children soon got bored of pulling their sledges, complaining that it made it hard for them to run around in the snow and throw snowballs. 'Here, I'll take them,' said Florrie. Zak and Chloe didn't need telling twice, dumping their sledges and running off excitedly, their shrieks echoing around the street. Florrie stacked theirs on top of hers and Ed's, making it easier for her to pull them all along.

She'd just finished when Zak hurled a snowball in Ed's direction. It landed at his feet with a splat.

'Oh, it's like that, is it, big fella?' Laughing, Ed didn't waste a moment. He scooped up a load of snow, made it into a ball as best he could while holding Gerty's lead and threw it at Zak.

'Wargh!' Zak tried to dodge it, but it brushed by his arm, making Chloe squeal with delight.

'I reckon that's one-nil to me, don't you, Zaky Boy?' Ed grinned as he handed Gerty's lead to Florrie and placed his hands on his hips.

Gerty gave a happy bark, her tail swishing in the air, her eyes bright. She was eager to join in the fun.

'See, Gerty agrees,' said Ed. He bent to ruffle the Labrador's ears when a snowball exploded on the back of his neck. 'Argh!! That's *freezing*!' he said, gasping. 'You little rascal, Zak Ingilby!'

Florrie hooted with laughter as Ed fished bits of snow from

the depths of his scarf. 'That's what you get for crowing too soon.'

'Yeah, remind me never to do that again.' Ed pulled a face as he retrieved a large lump of the snowball that had worked its way down the collar of his jacket.

He'd just finished removing the last of the snow when Chloe gave an ear-splitting shriek of delight. He looked up to see another snowball hurtling towards him, this time landing squarely on his thigh, Zak chortling gleefully as he dusted snow from his gloves.

'Right, you're going to pay for that, you little squirt.' Laughing, Ed brushed the snow away and went to chase after Zak who ran off, whooping with laughter at the top of his voice.

Chloe was hot on her brother's heels. 'Zak! Zak! Wait for me! Zak! Wait!'

Florrie looked on, her cheeks aching from laughing so hard. She was thrilled that they'd already created another wonderful experience to add to The Happy Christmas Memories Project.

Soon, they were on the top prom, biting air whooshing in from the sea. Seagulls wheeled overhead, their plaintive cries carried on the salty breeze. The road was clear of snow thanks to the work of the gritter earlier that morning, and now cars drove along unhindered, their tyres making short work of the lingering slush. The broad pavement of the prom was a different matter, however, and was covered in a good five inches of snow. It made progress slow as they crunched their way along, not that it bothered Zak and Chloe, who were plodding back and forth, rosy-cheeked, their laughter and squeals of delight filling the air. Gerty watched them, her tail wagging, her ears cocked.

'Look! There's snow on the beach!' Zak pointed towards it.

'Wow! That's so cool,' said Chloe, tramping over to the wooden railings and peering down.

The cover of snow on the bank of pebbles and the sand,

stretching halfway to the sea, made for an unusual sight. It wouldn't last long in the salt laden sea air.

'Thorncliffe looks stunning.' Florrie's gaze roved over the top of the cliff that was covered in a vast blanket of white. Smoke was curling from the chimney at Clifftop Cottage, just as it was a little further along at Thorncliffe Farm. The Jolly and Old Micklewick came into view. It looked Christmas card pretty with its little wonky cottages, their rooftops dusted with snow.

As usual, Gerty stopped at Mr and Mrs H's bench, looking up at Florrie and Ed. They paused only briefly, taking in the view, mindful of Zak and Chloe's eagerness to get sledging.

'Morning, Grandad and Grandma.' Ed's words floated out in a cloud of steam as he gazed out at the panorama.

Florrie stole a look at him, wondering what was going through his mind, hoping he was managing to keep his thoughts clear of his parents for now.

He breathed out a sigh and looked down at her. 'Best make tracks, we've got some serious sledging to do.'

'You're not wrong there.' She smiled up at him, pleased when he smiled back.

They skirted round The Micklewick Majestic Hotel, the derelict building appearing less forlorn and neglected beneath a covering of snow.

Before long, the four of them and an excited Gerty had joined a gaggle of early morning sledgers at the top of Woodcutter's Hill. It looked magical, the branches of the surrounding trees bent under the weight of the snow, sunlight sparkling all around them. They found a clear area and positioned their sledges at the top of the hill.

'Right then, Zak, I reckon it would be a good idea if you and Chloe show us how it's done,' said Ed. 'Then I can have a go after that. What do you say?'

Zak seemed to grow a couple of inches in the wake of

such responsibility. He pushed his hands onto his hips. 'Yep, I think that's the best idea. Me and Chloe are skilled at sledging, especially me.' His confident tone and manner made Florrie want to smile, Ed too, she noted, from the way his mouth was twitching. 'Come on, Chlo, let's show Ed how it's done.'

'Okay.' Chloe went to stand beside her brother, her smile lighting up her pretty face.

The pair manoeuvred their sledges into the perfect position and sat down on them, wriggling about until they were comfortable. Zak turned, looking up at Ed and said, 'You take the rope in your hands, like this, see? And then, when you're ready, you push yourself off with your feet. Oh, and don't head for a tree or you'll crash into it and it'll really hurt.'

'Sound advice.' Ed nodded.

'Think you can do that?' Zak asked, regarding his pupil.

Florrie stifled a smile at Zak's grown-up tone. Much as she was desperate to, she daren't make eye contact with Ed.

'Yep, I think so, especially after your sound instructions.' Ed nodded, keeping his expression impassive.

'Good.' Zak turned to his sister. 'Right, Chlo, are you ready?'

'Ready.' She nodded, her smile stretching further across her face.

'Okay, then. One, two, three. Go!'

A second later the pair were zooming down the hill, Zak letting rip with a long, drawn-out roar of pleasure while Chloe's squeals filled the air, her pigtails flying out behind her. Gerty barked with delight as she looked on.

The siblings slowed to a halt at the bottom where the land evened out, Chloe's sledge spinning around in a final flourish.

'That looked like great fun,' said Ed, laughing heartily.

'I thought you'd like it.' Florrie watched as the two children pulled themselves to their feet, the pair of them laughing hard.

'Come on, Ed! It's your turn now!' Zak's voice travelled up the hill to them.

Ed didn't need telling twice. 'On my way!' He dropped onto his sledge and pushed himself off. 'Woohoo!' he yelled, as Zak and Chloe cheered him on.

He shot down the hill at an alarming speed, whizzing by the two children and crashing to a halt in a cluster of bushes, snow tumbling from their branches and covering him. His exaggerated cries of anguish were drowned out by Zak and Chloe's peals of laughter.

Florrie was still laughing by the time he'd climbed the hill and was standing beside her. 'That was so funny!' Her sides were aching, she'd been laughing so hard. 'Are you okay?' She couldn't stop the splutter of laughter that followed.

Ed feigned a hurt look. 'Good to know you find me so entertaining.'

'Ed's mint! He's just dead funny!' Zak beamed. He was clearly having a whale of a time.

'Ed, can I go on the sledge with you?' Chloe was jumping up and down excitedly. 'I want to crash into the bushes, too.'

Ed glanced over at Florrie, seeking her opinion. 'It didn't hurt, made for a soft landing. Bit snowy, though.' He grinned at her.

'In that case, I don't see why not,' she said, grinning back.

'Mint! Does that mean you'll come on mine with me?' Zak looked eagerly at Florrie.

'I'd love to. Come on, Zak, let's show Ed how it's done.' Florrie slipped off the backpack she'd been wearing – she'd come equipped with a flask of hot chocolate and a packet of Christmas-themed biscuits, anticipating they'd be a welcome blast of warmth and sugar as the cold started to set in.

Moments later the two sledges were lined up, ready for Zak to give the word.

'One, two, three... Go!' they all cried in unison before

pushing themselves off the top of the hill. Gerty charged down with them, barking as she went.

Zak's loud roar made Florrie's ears ring as they zoomed their way down, flying over the bumps in the ground, her heart hammering with exhilaration as wind rushed over her face. They were neck and neck until Florrie and Zak's sledge hit a large bump that sent them careering round in circles.

'Waaarrrggghhh!' Zak yelled at the top of his lungs.

Florrie let out a squeal before they ground to a halt, landing in a wall of snow with a soft *thwump*. She lay there, unable to stop laughing.

Somewhere in the distance she could hear cries of victory from Chloe and Ed. She pushed herself up and looked over to see them punching the air, Gerty jumping around them giddily. A wave of warmth spread through her at seeing this carefree version of Ed. He may have had a lonely childhood which, in turn, had led to him being reserved as far as friendships were concerned, but he'd taken to her group of friends – and they him – as if they'd known one another for years longer than they had, which was no mean feat, especially with how protective her pals were of one another. And now here he was, having the best time with Zak and Chloe, the three of them wearing expressions of unadulterated joy. Gerty barked, jolting Florrie out of her musings. She looked to see the Labrador rolling about in the snow in pure joy, her legs sending clumps of the stuff flying everywhere. 'Make that *four* of them wearing expressions of unadulterated joy,' she said under her breath.

'Right, I reckon it's hot chocolate time,' said Florrie, reaching for her backpack and pulling out a flask.

They were standing at the top of the hill, ruddy-cheeked and panting, their breath curling out in the chilly air around them. Florrie was convinced the already low temperature had dropped even further. They'd been sledging for over an hour and a half and the cold was beginning to set in, not helped by their wet clothes. Even Gerty had joined in with the fun. Much to their amusement, the Labrador hadn't been able to get enough of sharing a sledge and whizzing down the hill, her velvet ears flapping in the breeze. When they'd reached the bottom, she'd entertained them with more rolling around in the snow. The children had been in raptures at her antics.

'When we've had this, how do you fancy building a snow-man?' asked Ed, steam rising from the plastic mug of hot choco-late he had in his hand.

'Yay!' said Chloe, spraying a mouthful of biscuit crumbs everywhere.

'Cool!' Zak beamed. 'This has been the *best* day.'

Florrie and Ed exchanged meaningful glances. It *had* been the best day. She knew they'd have fun with the kids, but she hadn't anticipated just how much they'd enjoy themselves in the process. That it was helping Jasmine made it all the more perfect.

With the snowman finished – Frosty Freddy, as they'd named him, cut an imposing figure and was almost as tall as Ed, with a huge nose fashioned from a piece of scrunched-up foil Florrie had found in her backpack – they were making their way, home-ward bound, back up the path to the road when Florrie heard her mobile ping. She unhooked her backpack and reached inside for her phone. With gloved fingers she tapped on the screen to see it was a text from Maggie.

> Hiya Florrie, hope you're all having a fab time.
> How's the sledging going? Mxx

'It's Mags, asking about the sledging,' she said before typing out a reply, made difficult with fingers made numb by the cold.

> Hi Mags, it's been brilliant! We've all had a great
> time, even Gerty! Just heading home now. It's
> so cold!! Brrr!! How are the bear orders going?
> And how's the bump? Fxx

She finished with a selection of snow and cold-themed emojis.

Just as she was about to put her phone back in her backpack another text came through.

> Orders going well, thanks. Bump's still sitting
> on my bladder! Bear's heading into town to pick
> up some paint & wonders if you'd like a lift
> home? Mxx

The offer was undeniably appealing, as long as it wasn't putting Bear out. 'Maggie says Bear's heading into town and has offered to give us a lift home. What do you think?' she asked the others, hoping they'd like the sound of it, too.

Much to her relief, the reply was a resounding yes! The cold really was biting now and on top of that, the children looked shattered. Florrie tapped out a reply to which Maggie responded straight away, saying Bear would be parked in his Land Rover at the end of the path that led to Woodcutter's Cottage within the next ten minutes.

As they trudged their way up the path – the snow now worn smooth by the many feet that had trampled across it that day – Florrie gradually became aware of the low rumble of the Land Rover as it approached. It was a more than welcome sound.

'Thanks for this, Bear, I hope we aren't putting you out,' Florrie said, climbing into the back, followed by Gerty and Ed. Zak and Chloe sat in the front beside Bear. The warmth inside, as it wrapped around her, was bliss, especially now the breeze had picked up and had taken on a spiteful edge as it nipped at their faces.

'Cor! This is *so cool*! We're dead high up,' said Zak, looking around him. 'I'm gonna have a Landie like this when I grow up, Bear.'

Bear gave a deep chuckle. 'I'll let you have a drive of this when you're old enough, Zaky. How d'you fancy that?'

'Oh, man, that'd be mint!'

'Can I have a go, too, Bear?' asked Chloe.

''Course you can, sweetheart.' Bear beamed down at her indulgently.

Before long, they were pulling up in the snowy street that was home to Samphire Cottage.

'Thanks, Bear, I can't tell you how much I appreciate this. We were getting that cold, I think we'd have been in danger of becoming snowmen ourselves,' Florrie said, as he yanked the hand brake on. 'You're welcome to come in for a cuppa, if you've got time?'

'Thanks very much for the offer, but I'd best get back. I promised my dad I'd help him with some jobs on the farm this afternoon. The sooner I get there, the sooner they get done.'

'Fair enough.' She smiled at him. 'Well, thanks again.'

'Yeah, thanks, mate, much appreciated. I think I'd have totally lost the feeling in my toes if we'd had to walk back. I owe you a pint of Old Micklewick Magic.' Ed reached forward and clapped Bear on the shoulder.

'I'll hold you to that.' Bear laughed as they all piled out.

TWENTY-TWO

After taking it in turns to have a quick, warming shower, the four of them had gathered in the kitchen where Ed was heating a pan of hearty vegetable soup. It filled the cottage with its delicious aroma. Florrie was busy buttering chunky slices of bread, while the children sat at the small table, chatting away nineteen to the dozen, recounting their sledging antics with great hilarity. Gerty was watching from her bed, hopeful for any stray crumbs, drool beginning to form at the corners of her mouth. Their saturated sledging clothes were hung on a clothes airer next to the radiator; Florrie expected they'd take a while to dry out.

Once lunch was devoured, the table was cleared and she brought out a selection of board games – some she'd had since childhood – which was met with Zak and Chloe's usual burst of enthusiasm. After a quick deliberation, they all agreed to start with a game of Snakes and Ladders, with Zak putting in a request for Operation afterwards, declaring it looked "mint".

By the time Jasmine arrived, the four of them were cosied up in the living room watching a festive film, Chloe sucking her thumb as she cuddled into Florrie, Zak stretched out on the rug in front of the fire, stroking Gerty.

'Ooh, fabulous work, looks like you've worn the little monsters out. Shouldn't be any problems getting the pair of them to bed tonight.' Jasmine giggled.

'Honestly, Jazz, they're not the only ones who're worn out. I've felt my eyes growing heavy several times while we've been comfy on the sofa. The heat of the fire hasn't helped, mind.' Florrie stifled a yawn. 'See what I mean!'

It was when they were all tucking into pizza back in the kitchen that Chloe told Florrie and Ed about her Christmas nativity play. 'I'm an angel,' she said earnestly, brushing her hair off her face. 'And I'm singing a solo. I'm a bit scared but Mummy said it'll be fine, didn't you, Mummy?' She took a bite out of her pizza and chewed vigorously.

'I did, Chlo, and you'll be amazing.' Jasmine smiled gently at her daughter.

Florrie's heart melted into a puddle at the little girl's expression. 'I agree with your mummy – you'll be brilliant.'

'You so will, Chlo,' said Ed.

'I'm the donkey with Joshua Walton,' Zak said, matter-of-factly, pulling a long string of mozzarella from his pizza and stretching it out as far as it would go.

'Zak's the donkey's bottom!' Chloe covered her mouth as she burst into a fit of the giggles.

Florrie tried her hardest not to smile at her reaction.

'You'll be a brilliant bum, won't you, son?' Jasmine gave Zak an affectionate smile, ruffling his hair. 'I keep telling him he was made for the role.' Jasmine chuckled.

'I'm gonna be the best donkey's butt they've ever had. I'm gonna take my fart machine and make farting sounds the whole time, except for when Chlo's singing. It's gonna be *so cool*.' He cackled with laughter, mischief dancing in his eyes.

Ed burst out laughing. 'Well, that'll put a slightly different slant on things.'

'Won't it just?' said Jasmine.

'Mrs Gibbin will be *so* cross with you, Zak,' Chloe said, her giggles intensifying.

'Hmm. I think you'll find if you let loose with the fart machine, you'll be on shoe cleaning duty for a fortnight, young man, and all your games consoles will be confiscated.' Though Jasmine shot him a pointed look, it was clear to Florrie her friend was struggling to keep a straight face.

'I was only joking, Mum,' Zak said. His smile had fallen, but there was still an impish look hovering in his eyes.

'The expression, "a chip off the old block" springs to mind, Jazz.' Florrie hitched her eyebrows at her friend who responded with a look that feigned, "I don't know what you mean!"

'What's a chip off the block?' Zak looked between the two friends, puzzled.

'I think Florrie's saying you don't just look like your mum, but your personality reminds her of your mum, too,' said Ed.

Zak gave Jasmine a wide grin. 'Does that mean you were a farting donkey in your school plays, Mum?' He followed up by blowing a raucous round of raspberries. 'Does it run in the family? It'll be your turn next, Chlo.' He fell back in his seat, hooting with laughter while his little sister was giggling so hard, her face had gone bright pink. Ed snorted a laugh but tried, unsuccessfully, to disguise it as a cough, while Florrie's shoulders were shaking hard with mirth.

Jasmine pursed her lips together and did her best to give her son a stern look. 'No, I was never such a thing. I'd have been given detention for a week if I pulled a stunt like that.' She turned to Ed. 'Bet you weren't expecting such highbrow conversations when you agreed to have these two.'

'It's been brilliant,' he said, doing all he could to keep the laughter out of his voice. 'We've had the best day, haven't we, Florrie?'

'We so have,' she said, finally getting her giggles under control. 'They're awesome kids, a real credit to you.'

Chloe beamed happily at her mum as she took a bite of her pizza, basking in the praise.

'That right?' Jasmine asked, reaching out and touching the tip of her daughter's nose, pride glittering in her eyes.

'You guys are awesome, too,' said Zak. 'And Gerty as well. And guess what, Mum? Gerty sledges! Can you believe that? She was *so* mint.'

'She's clearly a Labrador of many talents,' said Jasmine, looking suitably impressed.

As the banter flowed, Florrie caught Ed's eye, and they exchanged happy smiles. It had been an amazing day. Florrie never doubted they'd have a great time, but it had gone way beyond her expectations. They'd both thrown themselves wholeheartedly into having fun with the kids. Florrie had even found herself daring to wonder if children would feature in her future with Ed, the thought crossing her mind that he'd make a wonderful father.

The same thought caught up with Florrie as she was in bed that night. Exhausted as she was, her mind couldn't resist the pull of reliving the events of the day, Zak and Chloe's infectious laughter echoing around her head. Their unbridled enthusiasm and unadulterated happiness brought a smile to her face once more, Gerty's upbeat antics joining them. The pure joy of it all. And how Ed had added to that. He'd been amazing with the kids, a natural. And it had been clear to see he'd enjoyed spending time with Zak and Chloe as much as they had with him. There hadn't been a single negative moment or a time when he'd looked like he'd had enough. As far as she was aware, he hadn't interacted much with children before now, but that hadn't mattered at all. Not for the first time did he remind her of his grandfather. Mr H had a gift for conversing with young-sters without making them feel they were being patronised, but that he was genuinely interested in what they had to say, that their opinions mattered. He'd been the same with her while she was growing up. It was something else that appeared to have skipped a generation if his parents were anything to go by.

Beside her, Ed's breathing deepened, and the beat of his heart slowed as he succumbed to sleep. She snuggled into him, making him stir. He absently pulled her closer and kissed the top of her head. There was no doubting she felt loved by him.

They'd been together for almost eighteen months and had never spoken about their long-term future, other than in reference to the bookshop and their plans for it. She had to admit, it spoke volumes that it was something she hadn't seriously considered until now. There was no getting away from the fact that she loved him deeply and had never been happier since he'd moved in with her. But, for some reason – one she hadn't even thought to question until recently, which, if she was honest, startled her – she'd never actually considered where their relationship would lead. Was that odd? she wondered. No, she told herself, it wasn't. There were reasons she hadn't, the biggest one being the bookshop and the fact that it had taken up pretty much every second of their waking hours.

Though Florrie knew that if she was completely honest with herself, she wouldn't have to dig too deep before she unearthed the reason she'd subconsciously held back from daydreaming about her long-term future with Ed. She still hadn't shaken her doubts from when he'd hot-footed it out of town not long after they'd inherited the bookshop. Just when she'd thought they were getting close, he'd seemingly turned his back on everything in Micklewick Bay – including her – with no prior warning, leaving nothing more than a flimsy explanation. Florrie had been in a state of confusion, and not a little panic, about what would happen to the bookshop, fearing she'd end up in business with Dodgy Dick.

Evidently it had affected her more deeply than she'd first

thought, leaving her with the fear it could happen again. The fear that he was flaky and might not stay the course.

Oh, Florrie! Don't go overthinking this. It's the road to ruin! He's done nothing to make you doubt him since he came back. He told you then he wanted to be with you here in Micklewick Bay, working at the bookshop. Nothing's changed. Stop putting yourself through it! If he clams up, doesn't share his worries, it's just his way. It doesn't mean he doesn't want to be with you anymore.

She exhaled softly. That was all well and good, but it didn't explain why he was being so secretive about his trips to the attic.

But she had to admit today, after the fun they'd had with Zak and Chloe, she'd dipped her toe in the water and allowed herself a moment to consider how it would be to have a family with Ed. Was that on the cards for them? she wondered. Would she like that? Her heart gave an unexpected happy leap. Yes, she rather thought she would.

Her thoughts finally exhausted, Florrie gave herself up to the tiredness that had been waiting in the wings. She closed her eyes and let sleep wash over her.

TWENTY-THREE
WEDNESDAY 13TH DECEMBER

A buzz of excitement was thrumming around the bookshop, partly thanks to Leah's unbridled enthusiasm as she anticipated author Jenna Johnstone's arrival for her reading that evening.

'Oh, my gosh! I can't believe you're actually real-life friends with Jenna Johnstone!' Leah was bouncing up and down on the spot, clapping her hands together, her dangly festive earrings bobbing back and forth wildly. 'I mean, she's so *cool*! And she's an actual *celebrity*! All my friends totally love her books, especially *And Now You Tell Me!*.' The successful book had been made even more popular when it had been optioned for television and had aired as a series in the summer. It had been the perfect showcase for Jenna's already popular novel. And whereas readers often complained that some TV adaptations bore slim resemblance to the book upon which they were based, *And Now You Tell Me!* had stayed true to the story, capturing the essence of Jenna's characters, her delicious Geordie sense of humour threaded throughout, making for some truly hilarious scenes.

Florrie chuckled. 'Yeah, it's one of my favourites, too. And, much as I would love to, I don't think I can say she's my friend, but she's definitely a friend to The Happy Hartes Bookshop. I couldn't believe it when she said she'd do a reading for us, and that's in no small way down to Jack.'

Jean was walking towards them with a tray of freshly made tea and smiled at mention of her son. 'Ooh, I almost forgot to tell you, my Jack says he was talking to Jenna on the phone last night and she said she was thinking of setting off early today. Said she didn't want to have to cancel if the weather got too bad, what with her travelling from yon side of Newcastle, out in the sticks somewhere.' Jenna and Jack were signed to the same publishing house and had met at their publisher's annual summer party in London. It was this connection that had encouraged Jenna to agree to an author reading at the bookshop.

'That's very decent of her.' Florrie had been so distracted making sure the bookshop looked perfect, she'd forgotten about the imminent threat of more snow. She could only imagine the disappointment it would generate if Jenna was unable to get there.

'Aye, it is. She's a lovely lass, by all accounts. Very down-to-earth, Jack says.' Jean set the tray down on the counter before bending to give Gerty a pat and a dog biscuit, both of which were received with the Labrador's usual enthusiasm.

Florrie hurried over to the door, hoping to find no signs of fresh snow. 'Ooh, goodness!' The chilly air took her breath away as she pressed down on the handle and peered out at the weather. Snow still hung around at the edges of the pavements and on the road where the grit hadn't reached. And from the spiteful nip in the wind, she guessed the temperature hadn't risen above freezing. People walking by wore pinched expressions and looked frozen to the core. She directed her gaze upwards to see thick clouds were now smothering the blue skies of earlier. They bore a faint purple tint that usually meant snow was on its way.

'Come in where it's warm, lovey, and get your cup of tea while you've got the chance.' Jean smiled kindly over at her.

'I'm not going to argue with that, it's freezing out there.' As Florrie went to close the door, her gaze snagged on the wreath she'd bought to replace the one that had been so mindlessly ripped to shreds the previous week. Dodgy Dick's arrogant, smirking face loomed in her mind, triggering a momentary feeling of dread, not least because of the latest incident that had happened earlier in the week.

They'd been sorting through the post when they'd come across a blank, padded envelope.

'Wonder what this could be?' Ed had said as he opened it, his face falling as he tipped out the contents onto the small table in the kitchen.

'What is it?' Florrie had asked, peering over at it. 'Oh—' Her face had fallen as her brain registered what she was looking at. It was the remnants of a snow globe, the glass smashed into tiny, jagged pieces. But what had made her blood run cold was that it was identical to the one she'd given Ed.

'I hate to say this, but the envelope's dry which suggests the globe had been deliberately destroyed before being placed inside,' Ed had said in disbelief.

'This is seriously creepy,' she'd said, her eyes roving over the shards of glass and miniature cottage, her pulse racing. 'There were loads of other designs to choose from in the gift shop. Makes me feel like I was being watched when I bought yours.' She'd given an involuntary shudder.

'I don't get it... who'd do such a thing?' Ed had said, his gaze meeting Florrie's.

'Dodgy Dick,' they'd both said in unison.

Once they'd recovered from their initial alarm, they'd agreed not to mention the unscrupulous businessman's latest deed. They'd continue as if nothing untoward had happened, since they weren't willing to give him the tiniest sliver of satisfaction. Ed had tucked the envelope safely out of harm's way, keeping it as potential evidence in case the situation escalated. He'd done all he could to assuage Florrie's concerns, describing it as nothing more than a "mindless and petty" act of intimidation. 'It's pathetic, when you think about it, laughable, almost.' She'd eventually found herself agreeing with him. But it did little to stop the anxiety that now gripped her each morning as she and Ed turned onto Victoria Square, wondering if any further unpleasantness awaited them. Unfortunately, this anticipation appeared to have created an air of calm before the storm. It lingered silently, seeping into Florrie's mind at any opportunity. It wasn't what they needed for Jenna Johnstone's reading. She just hoped Dodgy Dick wouldn't make his presence felt.

Ed, accompanied by Gerty, was adding the finishing touches to the reading room in anticipation of that evening's author reading, while Florrie was on the shop floor with Leah and Jean.

The bell above the door jangled cheerfully, making the three women look up. Leah clapped her hands to her mouth as she gave a giddy squeal, making Florrie and Jean jump.

'Hiya, guys.' Jenna Johnstone's lilting Geordie tones sent a pulse of excitement bouncing through Florrie. 'Eee, I can't tell you how glad I am to be here at last.' The author was wearing her signature deep-pink lipstick. Glossy chestnut-coloured hair, threaded with caramel highlights, was visible from beneath a boiled-wool cloche, while large, hazel eyes flecked with gold reflected the owner's cheerful disposition. She had a bulging overnight bag on her shoulder.

'Jenna! And we're so glad that you are.' Florrie beamed happily at the author. 'Thank you so much for taking the trouble to get here, what with the weather and everything. How was your journey? Did you drive down or come on the train?'

Stop gabbling, Florrie! Give the poor woman a chance to catch her breath! Usually calm and collected, Florrie felt suddenly nervous at coming face to face with one of her favourite authors. And when she got nervous, Florrie gabbled. She took a steadying breath, rounded up her nerves and went over to Jenna, holding out her hand, giving a friendly smile. 'Hi, I'm Florrie, by the way.'

'Hiya, Florrie, s'good to put a face to the name at last.' Ignoring Florrie's proffered hand, Jenna dumped her overnight bag on the floor and pulled her into a hug, engulfing Florrie in a mix of the fresh air that lingered on the author's clothes and her subtle floral perfume. Much to Leah and Jean's delight, she did the same with them.

'Oh, man! Wait till I tell my friends about this,' said Leah, grinning from ear to ear.

'Aww, bless you, you're such a sweetheart.' Jenna smiled warmly and wrapped her arms around the young girl once more, sending Leah's levels of joy off the scale.

'Can I get you a cup of tea, lovey? There's plenty in the pot, it's freshly made,' Jean asked. Florrie noted her friend was looking almost as excited as Leah at meeting the author. 'And we've got some lovely Belgian chocolate biscuits specially for your visit.'

'Oh, wow! They sound delicious. I'm a real sucker for a choccie biccie or two, as my curvy booty will testify.' Jenna gave one of her trademark throaty chuckles, delivering a playful tap to her bottom. The author's upbeat, sing-song accent only added to her friendly persona.

'Give over, you've got a lovely figure,' said Jean.

'You so do,' said Leah. 'You're an awesome role model for my generation. My friends and me all love your social media, and your podcasts are *amazing*, they're so positive.'

'Thank you so much, flower, that means a heck of a lot.'

'Milk and sugar, Jenna?' Jean asked, making the most of the opportunity to get a word in.

'Splash of milk, one sugar, thanks very much, Jean, pet.'

Florrie turned to Jean. 'I'll take Jenna through to the reading room.' She was keen for the author to see where she'd be holding her event, make sure she was happy with how they'd set it out. And she also wanted to introduce her to Ed.

'Okay, lovey, I'll bring the tea there.'

As soon as they stepped into the room, Gerty leapt to her feet and trotted over to Jenna, wagging her tail in an enthusiastic welcome. She plonked herself in front of the author and pressed a paw to her leg.

'Aww, aren't you just a little darlin'?' Jenna didn't hesitate to ruffle the Labrador's ears. 'And what's your name, then?'

'Jenna, meet the bookshop's resident Labrador, Gerty Harte.' Jenna had shot even higher in Florrie's estimation now she'd revealed herself as a dog lover.

'Well, hello there, gorgeous Gerty. And how wonderful that the bookshop's got a resident pooch, I love that!'

Florrie and Ed exchanged delighted smiles.

With Gerty's greeting out of the way, Jenna pulled herself upright. 'Oh, wow! What an enchanting space! I love the atmosphere you've created!' Her gaze travelled around the room, taking in the décor that had been given a facelift to suit the cosy romcom style of her books. The festive decorations had been joined by a large display featuring the author's latest publicity imagery – she'd emailed the relevant information to Florrie, and Ed had liaised with the local printing firm, so that the resultant posters and stand were glossy and professional-looking. 'Oh, jeepers, are you sure that's not going to scare the customers away?' She chuckled as her eyes landed on the life-size image of her Ed had positioned next to the leather-topped desk where a pile of her latest books had been placed. At the opposite end of the desk, a blowsy arrangement of faux flowers spilled out of a rustic jug.

'I think it looks great! I'm Ed, by the way.' With a wide smile crinkling his eyes, Ed strode over to her, his hand outstretched.

'Hiya, Ed, I'm Jenna.' As previously, the hand was ignored in favour of a hug. 'I'll bet my ugly mug's been giving you lot nightmares.' She giggled once she'd released Ed from her embrace.

'Not at all, we're really pleased with it.' Ed smiled. 'And your reading's generated a load of excitement. We're all very much looking forward to this evening. We've got more of your books over here next to the till.' He gestured to a table they'd positioned in the corner as a makeshift counter. They'd decided to invest in a separate till for the reading room after one of Jack's readings, hoping to maximise sales and ease the lengthy queueing process after such events.

'Ey up, you've done a grand job in here.' They all turned on hearing Jack's gravelly North Yorkshire tones.

Jenna's face lit up. 'Jack!' Florrie and Ed looked on as the author rushed over to him, hugging him tightly and delivering a noisy kiss to his cheek.

'By 'eck, it's grand to see you, lass.' Jack chuckled, oblivious to the pink lipstick kiss that was smudged across his cheek. 'How was the trip down? Not too scary, I hope.'

'Ugh! Fraught doesn't even begin to cover it.' Jenna rolled her eyes. 'We so can't cope with winter weather in this country. The first train was cancelled – too much snow on the line at the station it was coming from apparently. After an hour's wait, the next one turned up, only to break down halfway here. I feel like I've been travelling for flippin' hours. And to make it worse, the station waiting rooms were absolutely freezing, my feet were like blocks of ice. In fact, they're still numb.'

'Please tell me you're not travelling back tonight?' Florrie asked, concerned.

'No, definitely not. I was hoping to stay overnight, get booked into one of the little guesthouses here.'

Florrie pulled a regretful face. 'I don't fancy your chances. It's out of season, they'll all be closed for winter.'

Jenna's face fell. 'No way?'

Florrie's eyes met Ed's, and from the expression she found there she knew they were thinking the same thing. She was just about to offer Jenna the use of their tiny box room for the night when Jack stepped in.

'Don't worry, I've got a spare room at my little cottage down in the cove – you're very welcome to rest your head there for the night rather than tackling the trains.' Jenna's frown was instantly swept away and replaced with a bright smile.

'Jack, pet, you're a star! As long as it's no bother, I'd love to take you up on that offer.'

Just then, Jean came into the room armed with Jenna's cup of tea. A smile lit up her face when she spotted Jack. 'Hello there, son. I'll grab you a cuppa in a tick.' She patted his arm affectionately on her way to Jenna. 'There you go, lovey.'

'Now then, Mother.' Jack smiled back at her. 'There's no need, I can sort myself out.'

'Thanks, Jean.' Jenna looked from Jean to Jack, her eyes twinkling. 'So this renegade's your son, then, is he?'

'He is that,' Jean said proudly.

After discussing the plans for the reading, Jack set his mug down on the desk. 'Right then, Jenna, I reckon we'd best get off. I promised I'd treat you to a bite to eat down at the Jolly and as I'm a man of my word, we'd best get a wriggle on before they think we're not going to show up.'

Florrie exchanged a knowing look with Ed – he'd clearly

picked up on the frisson that had been dancing between Jack and Jenna, too. Now Florrie came to think of it, the author's name had cropped up regularly since Jack had returned from his publisher's summer party. Plus there was the fact she knew Jack had been influential in orchestrating this evening's reading. Why else would an author of Jenna's standing offer to make an appearance at a little place like The Happy Hartes Bookshop? Granted, Jack was nationally revered, too, but his birth mother was the connection to the bookshop. Could there be a budding romance playing out before them? she wondered. With Jack in his mid-fifties, and Jenna in her mid-forties, there was a bit of an age gap, but they seemed to hit it off really well; it would be nice for Jack to have some love in his life. She'd often thought there was an air of loneliness about him. And from the way Jean was observing her son's interaction with Jenna, she evidently felt the same. *Ooh, watch this space!*

TWENTY-FOUR

Once Jenna and Jack had left, the afternoon went by in a blur just as they'd all done since the start of December. Florrie was sure this was in no small part down to Ed's festive window displays which still garnered much interest and tempted people into the bookshop, setting the till ringing happily and keeping them busy. Florrie had let Leah slip off early since the young girl had been barely able to contain her excitement about Jenna's reading and had been chattering away nineteen to the dozen about what she was going to wear for it, how she was going to do her hair. Florrie had struggled to keep up at times. Though she had to admit, Leah's enthusiasm had been infectious, and as soon as five o'clock arrived, Florrie had rushed over and locked the bookshop door, pulling down the blind, uncharacteristic giddiness brewing inside her. She gave the reading room one last check over, releasing a happy sigh – it looked perfect.

Florrie was holding Gerty's lead while Ed locked the bookshop door, when a shiny four-wheel drive caught her eye. It cruised slowly along on the opposite side of the road exuding an air of danger. Her stomach clenched. 'Uh-oh. Don't look now, but have you seen who's driving by over there?'

'Who?' Ed handed her the keys, his expression darkening as he stole a look at the car from beneath his fringe. 'What the heck's he up to swanning around like he's some sort of gangland boss? Doesn't he realise he looks like a right turkey?'

The expression "gangland boss" sent a shiver prickling up Florrie's spine. 'I hope he doesn't think he can swan in for Jenna's reading this evening,' she said, pushing the keys into her backpack. She recalled Leah telling her how she'd also seen him lurking close by on the morning of Jack's reading. She couldn't help but think it was no coincidence he was making his presence felt when the bookshop was hosting an event.

'He won't get a chance with your dad and Jack on the door. They're going to put the bolt across once everyone's in.'

Rather than Jean standing at the entrance to the reading room and taking tickets as had become the norm for the bookshop's author events, they'd decided it would be best to take tickets before anyone set foot in the shop. That way, they could keep an eye on who had a valid reason to come inside, and keep unwelcome individuals out. Namely Dodgy Dick and Wendy who, much to their relief, hadn't bought a ticket.

'Yeah, good point.' Though Ed's words offered some reassurance, Florrie couldn't help but think the slippery businessman had driven by to make his presence felt. To send out a warning, almost. And from the nerves that had started jittering in her stomach, he'd succeeded.

By the time they arrived home, there was barely a chance to wolf down a hastily prepared tea, get changed and head back to the bookshop. They'd opted to take the car for the trip back in order to save time and avoid a cold walk home.

'Talk about a fast turnaround,' said Florrie, as she unlocked the bookshop door for the second time that day. There was no Gerty accompanying them this evening; they thought she'd prefer to avoid the hustle and bustle of so many customers piling in for the reading, and would appreciate the chance for some peace and quiet, snuggling in her bed at Samphire Cottage.

Jenna had arrived with Jack not long after Florrie and Ed. She looked stunning in a pink crushed velvet dress that showed off her generous cleavage to full advantage. She wore her hair in a chin-length French bob that had been fixed in fashionable waves, while her smoky eye make-up emphasised her large eyes and long lashes. Her glowing complexion made her look younger than her forty-four years.

'Ooh, I adore your shoes,' Florrie had exclaimed, her eyes landing on the twenties-style deep-pink Mary Janes, trimmed with diamanté buckles that adorned Jenna's feet. Florrie had a particular fondness for the fashion of that era.

'Thanks, pet. I picked them up on my last trip to London, fell in love with them as soon as I clapped eyes on them. What's even better is they were a steal – I'm a girl for a bargain.'

Florrie loved how refreshingly down to earth Jenna was, despite her meteoric success. The author had the ability to fill a room with her bubbly personality.

It hadn't taken long for people to start queueing outside the bookshop. Happy voices brimming with anticipation on the pavement outside filtered through the glass. Unlike Jack's author events that invariably attracted an even mix of men and women, Jenna's audience was predominantly female, many of them clasping well-thumbed copies of her books.

Lark and Stella arrived early, along with Maggie and Bear, and the four of them took their seats in the reading room. With more snow being forecast, Bear had volunteered to scoop the friends up in the Land Rover and drop them off afterwards, though they all knew it was because his mother hen mode was in full swing with Maggie's due date inching ever closer. Jasmine, who'd been excited about the reading, had been disappointed not to be able to make it owing to a last-minute order for an anniversary cake. 'I'm just so far behind, panic's setting in big time. I'm already going to be working till the early hours as it is – it's being collected first thing. Sorry, flower,' she'd said on the phone earlier. Florrie's heart had gone out to her friend, hearing the stress in her voice. She'd done all she could to reassure her that the ticket wouldn't go to waste on account of the number of names on the waiting list. She knew the extra cash Jazz would earn from the cake would make a difference.

Jenna's eyes flicked to the clock behind the counter. 'Right, folks,' she said, her eyes sparkling, 'shall we get this show on the road?'

'Aye, I reckon we should, Jen, your adoring fans having been waiting long enough.' Jack smiled indulgently at the author. 'You go and get yourself comfy then Charlie and me'll open the floodgates.'

'Righto, thanks, chick.' Jenna beamed back at him as she sashayed towards the reading room, Jack's eyes glued to her.

So it's "Jen" now. Florrie's mouth curved into a smile. She was sure she wasn't the only one to notice the sparks dancing between them. Now she came to think of it, the pair were well-suited, both sharing a self-deprecating sense of humour.

With everyone in their seats, the room thrummed with anticipation. Jenna perched herself on the front of the desk, which was how she said she preferred to do her readings. It lent an intimate, informal air to the event, which suited her friendly personality to a T.

In no time, Jenna had the audience captivated, her warm, Geordie accent the perfect complement to her prose. Jenna's novels were well-loved for how her humour leapt off the pages, but hearing her read aloud, Florrie felt, added a whole new level. She relaxed in her seat beside Ed at the back of the room and chuckled along with the rest of the audience. At one point, her ears twitched at a handful of faint, unfamiliar sounds from the shop but she told herself it was just her dad and Bear who she hadn't seen come into the reading room.

The lights flickered momentarily. 'Oh, hello,' said Jenna.

A second later, a collective gasp went up as a bang rang out from the storefront and the lights went out, including those on the Christmas tree, plunging the bookshop into darkness.

'Uh-oh! Was it something I said?' Jenna chuckled, the audience joining in.

Florrie blinked, waiting for her eyes to adjust. She was half-aware of the background murmuring of voices as she tried to process what was happening. It didn't take long for her to realise it would be impossible for Jenna to continue her reading.

'Ey up,' said Jack. 'I daresay the weather's got summat to do with that.'

'Or someone wasn't enjoying my storytelling and thought it was the best way to get me to shut my trap.' Jenna laughed good-naturedly. 'Honestly, folks, I can take a hint, there's really no need for such drastic measures.' A ripple of laughter ran around the room.

'Sorry about this, folks, but if you all stay where you are, we'll go and investigate, see if we can get the lights back on,' said Ed, giving Florrie's arm a squeeze. 'Really sorry about this, Jenna,' he said as he carefully picked his way out.

'Hey, it's no bother, and it's not as if it's your fault,' she said kindly, as the audience began to put the torches of their mobile phones to good use. It went some way to illuminating the room.

'The streetlights are still on,' came a voice from the audience. Florrie looked back at the window to see the observation was right. Her mind started racing. Surely they hadn't overloaded the system with the extra Christmas lights, had they? It's not as if there were that many. And she doubted it would be the wiring since she recalled Mr H had organised a complete re-wire of the shop and the flat about five years earlier.

She needed to speak to her dad; as a builder he might have an idea what could have caused the blackout.

She found him in the shop talking to Ed and Bear, their faces lit up by the torch on her dad's phone. The three of them wore serious expressions. 'We're the only shop in complete darkness,' Ed said quietly when she reached them.

'What?'

'We're the only building affected by the power cut. Bear and I have been out to take a look – it's just the bookshop.'

'But—' Her mind started racing as she absorbed the implication.

'We found these torches in a drawer in the kitchen, so we're just going to set them up in the reading room, lovey.' Her mum shot her a smile as she bustled by, Leah in tow.

'Okay, thanks.' Florrie gave a grateful smile, glad of their quick thinking.

'I've had a look at the consumer unit but it's difficult to isolate what's caused the loss of power without running round turning everything off and taking all the plugs out of the sockets. I'm not so sure it's the time to be doing that.' Charlie looked troubled. If that's what her dad thought, Florrie was happy to take his advice.

Ed blew out his cheeks, jabbing his fingers into his hair. 'Of all the times this had to happen. It's as if—' His gaze met Florrie's.

'Dodgy Dick,' they said together. Florrie felt her stomach twist.

'What?' Charlie asked, his brows knitting together. 'Are you saying you think that plonker's got summat to do with it?'

Florrie lowered her voice. 'I don't know for certain but...' Ed picked up the story, telling Charlie and Bear how they'd seen Dodgy Dick as they'd left the bookshop earlier that evening, the menacing air his presence had exuded, and the odd things that had been happening at the bookshop.

'I'm not sure that means he could have anything to do with this, though, do you, Dad? Surely it's just down to a fault here in the shop.' Florrie was willing him to agree with her. If Dodgy Dick did have something to do with it, then his campaign of intimidation had been cranked up considerably. She didn't want to think what he'd go on to do next. She caught Ed's eye, and the knots in her stomach tightened.

'Look, I don't think you should go upsetting yourself, speculating about that fella, love.' Her Dad mustered up a smile. 'Whatever the cause, we need to get the evening back on track as soon as possible. I'll pop over to my workshop and grab a generator, then we can rig up some temporary lights here. How does that sound? Won't take long.'

'Sounds brilliant, thanks, Charlie,' said Ed, brightening.

'Oh, thanks, Dad.' Relief lifted like a weight from Florrie's shoulders. She'd forgotten her dad had a generator. At least the book reading could continue.

Her dad and Bear had just headed off to gather the generator and necessary cables when Stella and Lark arrived by her side. 'Is there anything we can do to help, flower?' asked Stella, squeezing Florrie's shoulder. 'Would you like me to go and fetch a torch from my apartment? I daresay Alex has got one we could use, too. The more the better, I guess.'

'And Nate's got a big one,' Lark said.

'Has he now?' Stella jumped in, quick as a flash. 'And here's us thinking you'd got him strictly wedged in the friend zone,' she said dryly, her comment raising a small smile from Florrie who appreciated Stella's attempts at lightening the mood.

'That's not what I meant, Stells, and you know it.' In the half-light Florrie could see a smile twitching over Lark's mouth.

'And not for the first time I reckon the lad deserves a medal for the length of time you've kept him dangling.' Stella chuckled. 'Anyway, back to the matter in hand. Shall I go and grab those torches?'

'And I was going to ask if you'd like me to grab Nate's, before I was rudely interrupted.'

'I think we know Nate's answer to that.' Stella gave a dirty giggle, earning herself a nudge in the ribs from Lark. Florrie couldn't help but laugh.

'That's really kind, lasses, but I don't think it'll be necessary.' Florrie quickly explained about the generator. 'Hopefully, my dad won't be long.'

The three women headed back into the reading room where Paula, Jean and Leah had done a sterling job of setting up torches about the place. Florrie was pleasantly surprised at how cosy it looked. The audience helped, too, using their phone torches. It made for an atmospheric scene. Florrie stopped beside Jenna, turning to face the sea of faces. 'Thanks for your patience, folks. Again, I'd just like to apologise for the unforeseen situation, but I'm very pleased to say we should have some temporary lighting rigged up shortly.'

A small cheer rang out, followed by the odd, 'Woohoo!'

'Tell you what, why don't I try reading by torchlight until then?' said Jenna. 'It'll be just like when I was a little lass, reading under the covers when I was supposed to be asleep. I daresay I'm not the only one who's guilty of that, am I? It'll be all nostalgic and cosy, like.'

The suggestion was met with a noisy cheer and enthusiastic round of applause. Jenna turned to Florrie, catching her eye, the pair exchanging happy smiles.

TWENTY-FIVE

After everyone had left, and only Ed, Florrie and her parents remained, Charlie broke it to them that he and Bear had traced the source of the power failure back to the till in the main room of the bookshop.

'There was someone else here in the bookshop,' Charlie explained. 'I heard them hurry by the kitchen. I followed whoever it was up here but before I caught a proper look at them, the lights went out and I heard them scarper off down to the back of the shop. Sounds like they sent a display flying while they were at it.'

They'd given chase as best they were able given the icy conditions, but the hoody-wearing youth had been too quick for them and had made his escape, melting into the wintry evening. Charlie had been tidying the display of books when Bear noticed the counter was swimming in water, as was the till and the attached card reader. It appeared that the unwelcome guest had given it a thorough dousing, which would account for the power outage.

The revelation sent panic scorching through Florrie, her thoughts rushing to Dodgy Dick.

Paula was distraught at the thought of someone sneaking in with the intent of causing trouble for her daughter. 'We need to let the police know about this, Charlie,' she said. 'It needs stopping before it gets out of hand. It was bad enough them having to deal with the Christmas tree in the doorway but this is another level.'

'I agree,' Charlie said, gravely. 'I'm happy to give 'em a ring, if you like, love?' he asked, looking over at Florrie.

'Thanks, Dad, I'd appreciate that, especially since you witnessed part of it.'

'Aye, good point. Hopefully they'll be able to lift some fingerprints from the back door and maybe the jug, if the intruder wasn't wearing gloves, like. I just feel terrible that whoever it was had managed to sneak in with Jack and me being so vigilant about checking tickets.' Charlie puffed out a frustrated sigh.

'I'm sure whoever it was can't have crept in earlier in the day and hidden themselves in the shop,' said Florrie. 'I would've noticed, as would Leah, and she never mentioned anything.'

'Plus, Gerty would've been barking and growling, you know how protective she is,' Ed said.

'True.' Florrie had to agree with that, Gerty had always been quick to root out anyone she considered unsavoury. The Labrador's reaction to Dodgy Dick when he'd called with Wendy slid into her mind.

'Well, I'd say we pretty much knew everyone who came to Jenna's reading,' Paula said, looking thoughtful. 'And there wasn't a soul who stood out as being shifty to me in that gathering – everyone seemed really nice and normal and thrilled to be there. I just don't get it.'

'Actually,' Charlie said, slowly, scratching his chin, 'I think I might have an idea who it could be – not his name, mind, but I'd definitely recognise him if I saw him again.'

'Well, it could be something to build on.' Ed sounded hopeful.

'Who, Dad?' His words sent fear scurrying up Florrie's spine.

'I'll run it by you, see what you think. I'm not sure if any of you witnessed owt though, but it could jog a memory or two.'

The three of them listened as Charlie told them how he'd recalled a brassy-looking woman making a fuss at the door as they'd taken tickets and let people in. A youth, the hood of his sweatshirt pulled over his head, had loitered beside her. The lad had stood out as not being what he'd considered your average Jenna Johnstone fan.

'I can remember thinking at the time that he had a shifty air about him, seemed reluctant to make eye contact or show his face.'

Charlie went on to say how he hadn't had much time to dwell on it since the brassy-looking woman started to kick off about not being allowed inside. She was insistent that she'd paid for a ticket and that Florrie had supposedly written her name in a book she kept at the counter – 'I think she called herself Sylvia Hicksworthy, but I'm not the best with names, so you might be better checking that with Jack.' He heaved a regretful sigh. 'Anyroad, she was creating a right stink about it, being very forceful, so Jack said he'd go and have a look, see if he could find this book she'd been wittering on about. Next thing I know she'd dropped her handbag on the floor, sending the contents rolling all over the place and blaming me for it, can you believe?'

'Why did she blame you, Charlie, love?' Paula asked.

'I hadn't a clue at the time. All I can remember thinking was that we needed to get rid of her and sharpish.'

'I'm not surprised, Dad, she sounds like a right nightmare.'

'Ugh! And some,' Charlie said. 'I can just remember getting proper irritated because she was barking orders out, telling me to look for stuff she reckoned had rolled into the shop. By this

time, folk behind her were starting to get a bit impatient. I
wasn't half glad when she'd gone, which, now I come to think
about it, she did all of a sudden. I can remember thinking it
strange that she'd created all this drama, demanding her ticket,
ordering me to find stuff and then suddenly she was gone, quick
as a flash. But I was that glad to see the back of her so I could get
on with letting folk in, I didn't stop to give it much thought at
the time.'

'No one can blame you for that, Charlie, it was cold outside,
and folk had been waiting a long time.' Paula gave her
husband's shoulder a reassuring pat.

'Aye, that's what Jack and me were worried about. Anyroad,
turns out Jack couldn't find any mention of a Sylvia Hicksworthy. His theory is that she was just trying her luck at blagging a
free ticket. But after what's happened tonight, I reckon it was
more like a premeditated ruse to distract us.'

'I'm beginning to think you're right.' Ed shot Florrie a
concerned look.

'Actually, I don't recall making a record of that name
anywhere, or seeing it in the list of reserved tickets, for that
matter. I suppose Leah or Jean could have,' Florrie said. 'But no
one was collecting their tickets on the door. We would've told
you and Jack if that had been the case, made sure you had them
ready to hand over.'

'Sounds like she was in on the plan with the little wrong 'un
who tried to sabotage Jenna's reading,' Ed said.

'Seems he made a hasty escape out the back door. We found
it flapping open, same with the one to the backyard.'

Florrie recalled being faintly distracted by a disturbance
from the bookshop just after the lights had gone out, but she'd
assumed it had been something to do with her dad and Bear
who she hadn't seen enter the reading room. It would seem
she'd been wrong.

'Right, we might as well head home,' said Charlie. He'd

returned from the reading room where he'd gone to make a call to the police. 'They said seeing as though it's not a serious incident, they won't be sending anyone out till the morning.'

'Oh, okay.' Florrie couldn't help but feel relieved at hearing this – she was shattered and suddenly desperate to get home.

'Mind, the lass on the phone said not to touch owt just in case it contaminates any evidence. I did tell her we'd done a bit of tidying up here in the shop, but she said not to do anything else, especially in the kitchen.'

'Fair enough, love.' Paula gave a tight smile.

'Might be an idea to have a last check round, make sure nothing else has been damaged or taken, even. Plus, it'd be reassuring to know that all the doors and windows have been secured before we head home. Surely that can't hurt.' Ed had put into words exactly what had been running through Florrie's mind. What had happened already was bad enough, but it didn't bear thinking about how awful it would be if they returned in the morning to find the place had been trashed.

Much as she didn't like to admit it, there was no escaping it: this latest unpleasantness could only be down to Dodgy Dick. No one else had an axe to grind with them.

'Well, I'm just glad no one was hurt.' Her mum's words sent a shard of fear spiking through Florrie, nausea churning in her stomach.

What would have happened if her dad or Bear had tackled the youth? Goosebumps sprang up over her skin at the thought and she quickly shook it from her mind, not wanting to give any headspace to such a horrible scenario.

Their peaceful life had been turned on its head and, if the evening's unpleasantness had been anything to go by, she could only assume things were going to get worse.

TWENTY-SIX

THURSDAY 14TH DECEMBER

'Thank goodness you suggested we buy this second till,' Florrie said the next morning, as she set it up on the counter, its predecessor damaged beyond repair.

Ed gave her a watery smile. She knew from the conversation they'd had over breakfast he was feeling as deflated as she was. 'Yeah, little did we know just how useful it would be.'

Florrie returned his smile. She'd barely slept last night and was feeling bleary-eyed this morning. Her tiredness had added to her building anger that someone had tried to sabotage their special evening. An evening that so many people had been looking forward to. She was just thankful that her dad and Bear had been around to stop anything worse from happening, glad that, with their quick thinking, they'd been able to turn things around. It went without saying that Jenna's professionalism had helped, too.

'I can't help but worry about what's going to happen next.' The thought had been running over and over in her mind on an endless loop. 'I mean, it's not going to stop there, is it?' Her throat tightened and she felt the sting of tears.

'Oh, Florrie, c'mere,' Ed said softly, stopping what he was

doing. In the next moment, he'd enveloped her in a soothing hug, his strong arms wrapped around her. 'I can't tell you how sorry I am it's come to this.'

'It's not your fault, Ed. You're hardly responsible for the actions of that horrible thug of a man.'

'I know, but—'

A sharp rap at the shop door silenced Ed and made Gerty bark and jump up from her bed.

'Who the heck's that at this time of the morning?' Florrie's gaze shot to the clock behind Ed. It was only quarter to eight; way before opening time.

'I don't know.' Ed's tone was threaded with wariness as he followed Gerty to investigate. He peered through the glass, his face breaking out into a smile.

'S'only me.' Relief surged through Florrie as she recognised her dad's voice.

Ed hurriedly drew the bolt back and opened the door. 'Come in, Charlie. This is an early visit, not that it's not good to see you.'

'Morning, Dad.' Florrie dredged up a smile as he stepped into the shop.

'Morning, flower. You okay?' He smiled back, concern evident in his eyes. He was dressed in his work clothes and had a woolly hat pulled low over his head. 'I'll just stop here on the mat with me having my work boots on.'

'S'okay, we haven't vacuumed yet.' They hadn't felt like it last night, agreeing to leave it till morning.

'Best not, love. Your mother'll be after me if she thinks I've paddled mucky footprints all over the carpet.' It was a regular gripe of Paula's.

'Florrie's right, and your boots don't look too bad to me, Charlie,' Ed said, sliding the bolt back across. 'Have you got time for a cuppa?'

''Fraid not. I told the Bradshaws I'd land at eight o'clock to make a start on their guttering that's come down after the snow the other day, and I don't want to keep them waiting. Anyroad, I've been trying to call you but both your mobiles are off, so I thought I'd pop in here en route to the Bradshaws. Had a feeling this is where I'd find you.'

Florrie clapped her hand to her forehead. 'Blast! I'd meant to charge my phone when we got home last night but I forgot, what with everything that'd been going on. The battery must've died with me using the torch. I hadn't realised. Sorry, Dad.' She assumed Ed had kept his phone off as he now did most evenings, and hadn't got round to turning it back on.

'Not to worry. All I wanted to say was, if you want me to rig up a new security system here at the shop, just let me know. I can do it on Sunday when the shop's closed, that way it'll minimise disruption. Jeff, the electrician, said he's happy to give me a hand, so the two of us should make short work of it.'

Florrie wondered if her dad had read her mind. Last night, while she'd struggled to sleep, she'd started thinking they should maybe have the burglar alarm upgraded. She'd intended to mention it to Ed today. She couldn't remember how long ago the current system had been installed but it was an antiquated affair and, at a guess, at least twenty years old.

She looked over at Ed, raising her eyebrows in question. 'If it would make you feel better,' he said to her.

Her thoughts briefly hovered on his response, his choice of words setting a niggle away. Why wouldn't it make them *both* feel better? Why did he single her out? And why didn't he just say he thought it would be a good thing to do anyway? *You're overthinking again, Florrie, give it a rest. Isn't there enough going on without you heading down that route?*

'It would.' She nodded decisively, clearing the doubts from her mind. 'Thanks, Dad, we'd love it if you could rig up a new alarm system.'

He beamed at her, unmistakable relief in his expression.

'Good stuff, your mother'll be glad to hear it. Right then,' he said, rubbing his gloved hands together, 'now that's sorted, I'd best be off.' He turned to leave. 'Oh, and good luck with the bobbies. And don't forget to leave things as they are in the kitchen and around the back door – no wiping around in case you remove any potential fingerprints.'

'Yeah, we've been mindful of that,' said Ed.

'Thanks for offering to upgrade the burglar alarm, Dad.' Florrie hurried over to him and gave him a quick hug, dropping a kiss onto his rosy cheek.

'No worries, sweetheart, happy to help.'

It was after he'd left that Florrie remembered this Sunday was the trip to Danskelfe Castle and the sleigh rides. It had slipped her mind what with the excitement about Jenna Johnstone's reading and the disruption that had followed. She hoped nothing would happen to spoil her surprise for Ed. After all, they were meant to be creating happy Christmas memories, and the events of the previous evening were anything but.

TWENTY-SEVEN

Leah was shocked when Florrie and Ed shared what had happened. 'Oh my God! No way! I had no idea! I was that engrossed in Jenna's awesome reading, I was totally oblivious to anything that was going on in the shop,' she said. Hearing this had gone some way to reassuring Florrie that it had more than likely been the same for the rest of the audience.

'But now you come to mention it, I do recall hearing a bit of a kerfuffle from the direction of the shop beforehand, when people were first coming into the reading room, but I was adding more of Jenna's books to the table at the back and didn't really think any more about it.' A troubled expression clouded her young face. 'And there was that bit of noise when Jenna was doing her reading, too.'

'Well, try not to worry about it. We think it was just some daft lad playing a prank and showing off to his friends, but obviously we're going to do all we can to make sure it doesn't happen again,' Florrie told her. She and Ed had agreed to play down the sinister side of what had happened, not wanting to frighten their young assistant. They were also keen not to broadcast that Dodgy Dick might be behind it, worrying it could be bad for business if word got out, something that would no doubt afford the slippery businessman a degree of satisfaction, which neither Ed nor Florrie were keen to do.

Florrie and Ed had been talking to PC Nixon for the last half hour while the scenes of crime officer was busy dusting for fingerprints around the back door and kitchen. They'd called round from the local station in response to Charlie reporting last night's disturbance. The couple had also filled the police officer in on the incident with the Christmas tree and the envelope filled with pieces of smashed snow globe. Florrie was reluctant to mention Dodgy Dick's visit to the bookshop with Wendy for fear of antagonising him and making the situation worse. The slippery character seemed to revel in his growing reputation amongst the locals as someone to keep on the right side of, and she didn't think he'd take kindly to having his collar felt by the local police force. Florrie was relieved when Ed had agreed with her, albeit reluctantly.

PC Nixon was draining his mug of tea, Gerty's eyes glued to the plate of biscuits before him on the table, when there was a knock at the door of the reading room. The three of them turned to see Leah walk in, her cheeks flushed.

'Jean's just popped in, said she'd look after things for a minute.'

'Oh, right,' said Florrie, curious as to what could be responsible for the agitated expression on their young assistant's face.

Leah tapped on the screen of her mobile phone and held it out to Florrie. 'I was checking the bookshop's social media pages when I spotted we'd been tagged in this.'

With Ed leaning into her, Florrie watched the video footage of people queueing outside the shop the previous night. Though it had been dark, the streetlights and those above the shop's signage had been bright enough for the phone camera to pick out people's faces.

'Thought the woman who was causing all the drama and the lad that was with her might be on there. There's more, too, loads actually.'

'There!' said Ed. 'Pause the video!'

Florrie acted as quickly as she could. 'Where am I looking?'

'That woman with the massive hair. Her. There!'

Florrie squinted at where Ed's finger was pointing, enlarging the image. Sure enough, there was a woman who fitted her dad's description. And standing beside her was a lanky youth, his face clear for all to see as his hoodie had momentarily slipped backwards, revealing his face.

Florrie pressed her hand to her mouth. 'Leah, you're a star! I reckon that's them.'

'It just crossed my mind that there might be a chance they'd be captured in someone's photos, knowing how people are keen to share stuff like this, especially with it being something as popular as a Jenna Johnstone event.'

'Good thinking, young lady,' said PC Nixon. 'Maybe you should consider a change of career and come and join us.' He chuckled and Leah smiled shyly.

'Don't suppose they're familiar to you, PC Nixon?' Ed asked, as Florrie handed the police officer the phone.

PC Nixon's eyebrows twitched as he looked at the screen. 'Oh, they're familiar all right, too familiar for my liking, actually.' He glanced over at Leah. 'Do you mind if I take a look at some more?'

'Not at all. There's this, too.' Leah took her phone and tapped on the screen, handing it back to him.

He regarded further similar footage of the youth and the bouffant-haired woman, shaking his head. 'I'll need you to send me the link to these.' He fished around his pocket, pulling out a small card. 'Here's my number.'

''Course.' Leah nodded.

'Right then, I'll need to speak to Jack and your father, Florrie, but leave it with me and I'll see what we can find out,' PC Nixon said.

'Okay, thank you.'

With the police officers gone, Ed and Florrie asked Jean to join them in the reading room while Leah manned the till.

'Oh, my goodness! All that was going on while Jenna was doing her reading?' Jean said in disbelief when they'd finished updating her on the drama.

'It was.' Ed nodded.

'Credit to your dad, Bear and my Jack for keeping it so well contained.' Jean's brow crumpled. 'Mind, what a dreadful thing to do, causing a power cut like that. But it was very impressive of Jenna not to get fazed by it at all. She just carried on, in her element, reading to everyone.' Her face brightened at the mention of the author. 'She's a lovely lass, that one. Hasn't let her success go to her head, same as my Jack.'

'You're right there, Jean.' Her words raised a smile from Florrie. 'From your reaction, I'm guessing Jack hasn't mentioned anything to you, about what happened last night, I mean?'

'Not a word, lovey, but then again, I suppose he hasn't had the chance. He and Jenna headed straight to The Cellar after the reading, and I haven't seen him today. Though before he left last night, he did mention something about the possibility of taking Jenna back home to Newcastle, what with the trains being what they are.'

'That's fair enough.' Florrie assumed he hadn't wanted to worry his mum with her living alone and going back to an empty house. Her next thought had been that Jack and Jenna had clearly got along well the previous evening. The implications gladdened her heart.

'Well, let's hope the police trace the culprit, and quickly at that. Bernard would turn in his grave if he thought this was going on.'

Florrie tucked her chin deeper into her scarf. She was beginning to wish she hadn't ventured quite so far along the top prom taking Gerty for a walk. The wind, whipping in from a gun-metal-grey sea, frothing with white breakers, was bone-numb-ingly cold and she hadn't passed many other folk daft enough to brave the elements.

She had to do a double-take as she spotted Jack and Jenna walking towards her. Despite the plummeting temperature, the pair were chatting away happily, sauntering along at a leisurely pace, Jenna's infectious laugh whipped away on a sudden icy gust. They didn't seem to notice the pinhead flakes of Alpine snow that the sky had suddenly decided to scatter over them. But what had really piqued Florrie's interest was that they were holding hands. 'Oh, wow!' she said under her breath, her heart lifting at the sight. Jean would be over the moon to see this.

Spotting her, Jenna gave an enthusiastic wave. 'Hiya, Flor-rie, pet.'

'Now then, Florrie,' Jack said in a familiar Yorkshire greet-ing. He was wearing a warm smile.

'Hi there.' Florrie waved back, smiling broadly as Gerty tugged hard on her lead to get to them.

With greetings out of the way and a thorough ear ruffling for Gerty from both authors, Jenna asked, 'How's your day been so far? Jack told me about last night, by the way.' Her words clouded in front of her as her smile fell. 'I'm so sorry someone would think to do such a thing, it's shocking. Mind, it'd take more than a piddly power cut to get me to shut my trap!' The author gave another giggle, making Jack and Florrie laugh, too.

As the wind swirled around them, Florrie went on to explain about the social media footage and the visit from the police officer, as well as filling them in on the other things that had happened in the build-up to last night's act of sabotage. 'Hopefully, they'll be able to trace whoever was responsible and put an end to the trouble we've been having.'

'That Dodgy Dick bloke is getting way too big for his boots, and he's not being too clever about how he goes about his little intimidation campaigns either,' Jack said, his nose a vivid red from the cold. 'Mark my words, he'll get himself caught before long.'

'It won't come soon enough as far as I'm concerned,' said Florrie, just as a seagull started screeching from a nearby rooftop.

Jenna reached out and gave Florrie's arm a sympathetic pat. 'I'm glad we've seen you actually, pet. I have an idea and I'd like your opinion.'

'Ooh, I'm intrigued.' Jenna's words had resurrected Florrie's smile.

'Mind, it's so bloomin' cold here and we're starting to get a covering of snow on us – we're going to end up looking like snowmen! Tell you what, Jack needs to pop in on his mam, so why don't I meet you at the bookshop? We can have a chat about it there?'

'Are you sure you have time? I mean, aren't you heading back today?' Florrie asked. She reckoned it must be getting on for half past two already.

'I've talked Jenna into staying for an extra day.' Jack's grin was classic cat-that-got-the-cream.

'Uh-huh, that's right, Jack had very kindly offered to take me home today – the trains have been cancelled again – but then, as I don't have to be back until Saturday evening, we both thought I might as well hang around here for a bit longer, make the most of it. I have to be honest, I'm quite taken with Micklewick Bay.'

And not just Micklewick Bay, from what I can see.

. . .

'So, this is only a suggestion, and please don't feel you have to agree to it if it'll interfere with your plans, okay? I promise you I won't be offended, pet.' Jenna flashed a smile at Florrie, her hands wrapped around a mug of tea. In the warmth of the reading room, she was sitting opposite the bookshop owner at the very same desk she'd given the reading from the previous night.

Florrie smiled back, thinking she could listen to Jenna's Geordie accent till the cows came home, it had such a happy ring to it. She adjusted her glasses and leant forward, resting her chin on her hand. 'Fire away, I'm all ears.'

'Righto, here goes. How would you feel about me coming back to the bookshop to do a book signing session? It'd be to compensate for last night, with it being cut short, like.'

'Are you serious?' *Oh my days!* This was music to Florrie's ears.

'Uh-huh. I'm deadly serious. There's no way I'm gonna let that brute Dodgy Duck, or whatever the plonker's called—'

Florrie snorted, almost choking on her tea. 'It's Dodgy Dick, but I like Dodgy Duck. It has a wonderfully comedic ring to it, that somehow suits him so much better.' She and Jenna dissolved into a fit of the giggles, Jenna's cackle filling the room.

When their hilarity had finally subsided, Jenna elaborated on her suggestion, saying how she was planning regular visits to Micklewick Bay and that she'd be staying with Jack.

Interesting!

'We could use the opportunity to do a further book signing session. In fact, if it works for you, I could probably squeeze one in just after Christmas, if you fancy? I'll let you know the dates I think I'll be here, and we can take it from there,' Jenna said with a wide smile.

'That would be brilliant, thank you!' Florrie's mind set to

work straight away. It wouldn't matter if the book signing was organised at short notice, Jenna was so popular, she was sure it would be a success.

'Now, this is strictly confidential, cos it's just very early stages – though you can tell Ed, of course,' Jenna said, conspiratorially, her hazel eyes twinkling, 'but Jack and me were actually talking about organising some sort of book festival for the town in the summer, like.'

Florrie gave a gasp of delight. 'Oh, wow!' she whispered. 'That would be fantastic!'

Jenna beamed at Florrie's reaction. 'I'm chuffed to bits you like the idea. We thought we could get a few authors together, do some talks, Q&As, workshops, that sort of thing. We could maybe even hold some of the events here, if you fancy? Really showcase this gorgeous gem of a bookshop.'

A wave of excitement rushed through Florrie. 'This is like a dream. It would be awesome to hold some of the events here. In fact – keep this to yourself, though it's okay for Jack to know – but Ed and I have plans to extend the bookshop and create a tearoom here. Like your book festival idea, it's very early days but we're currently having plans drawn up that involve converting the flat upstairs.'

Jenna's eyes grew wide. 'A tearoom in a bookshop? Could there be anything more perfect?'

TWENTY-EIGHT

FRIDAY 15TH DECEMBER

Leah was helping local taxi driver, Joe Taylor, choose a book for his wife, Ceri, whose birthday it was that day. He'd been the first customer through the door just as the bookshop opened, apologising for rushing in and explaining how he'd forgotten all about the significance of the day until their four-year-old daughter had run into their bedroom bright and early, wishing her mummy a happy birthday. With his wife being an avid reader of cosy mystery books, and a regular at The Happy Hartes Bookshop, he thought he'd be able to redeem himself by stocking up on a few novels by her favourite authors, though he was struggling to remember what books she'd read. After pulling an "oops!" face, Leah had volunteered to help and had accompanied him to the relevant aisle.

Florrie was holding out the card reader to a customer when PC Nixon's square-shouldered frame stepped through the doorway of the bookshop. Her stomach clenched as anxiety took a hold of her. She knew the reason he was here and the reminder wasn't at all welcome, especially when she'd been distracted by what Jenna had told her yesterday. *Talk about life being like a roller coaster!*

The police officer hung back until Florrie's customer had gone, the bell above the door chiming noisily. 'Good morning.' He stepped forward, giving her a friendly smile.

'Good morning, PC Nixon. I'm guessing you're not here to buy a book?' She gave a small laugh, attempting to make light of the situation while the turmoil inside her was escalating.

'Not today.' He smiled kindly.

'Can you just keep an eye on things for a few minutes?' Florrie asked quietly as she passed Leah on the way to the reading room with the police officer.

Leah nodded, throwing Florrie a concerned smile.

Florrie closed the door softly behind them. 'Is there any news?' she asked, her stomach in knots. She wished Ed were here with her, he'd remember everything that was said. She was feeling so nervous, she was sure her brain would struggle to hang on to a single word of what PC Nixon was about to share with her. 'Ed's just had to pop back home for a minute. He shouldn't be too long.' *Actually, he's been more than a minute, he must've been gone well over an hour.* He'd made some excuse about heading back home before the bookshop had opened which she'd thought odd at the time, setting a fresh flurry of worries rushing around her stomach. His lack of communication was frustrating at times. She swallowed the ball of nerves that was clogging her throat. *Park that for now, Florrie, you can wonder what he's been up to after you've heard what PC Nixon has to say.*

'That's okay, if you don't mind me telling you on your own?'

'No, that's fine. Please, have a seat.' She pulled out the wooden chair opposite and dropped into it, hoping her jitteriness wasn't obvious to the police officer, willing the news he was about to deliver to be nothing horrendous.

He sat down, removing his hat and placing it on the table in front of him, smoothing his closely cropped dark hair with his hand. 'Right, well, I can tell you that the couple you pointed out in the video footage and the photos were Dillon Swales and his mother, Patricia. She's sister-in-law to none other than Micklewick Bay's very own Dick Swales, probably better known as Dodgy Dick.'

'Oh, right.' Florrie's shoulders slumped with disappointment. 'Unfortunately, the woman who gave my dad and Jack the run-around wasn't called Patricia Swales. She told them her name was Sylvia Hicksworthy.'

'Ah, well, interestingly, Patricia was a Hicksworthy before she married Dick's brother, Ron, thirty odd years ago. I expect she was using Sylvia instead of her real name, because she knew her little cherub of a son was planning on getting up to no good here. And I suspect she fabricated the story about having her name on a waiting list.'

'That's what we thought.'

'But there's no doubting it's her in the photograph and video footage, my colleagues back at the station have confirmed that. And as for that daft lad of hers, I knew he wasn't the sharpest knife in the drawer, but you'd think if he was planning on getting up to no good, he'd at least have the sense to hide his face.'

'Lucky for us he didn't, though,' said Florrie. 'Or his mum, come to think of it.'

'Aye, he obviously gets his lack of sense from her. Anyroad, useful as it was in pointing us in the right direction, it turns out we didn't actually need the video proof of Dillon Swales's presence in your shop since his fingerprints were found in the kitchen here, on the jug as well as on the handles of the back door and yard door. Thankfully for us – but a fundamental mistake for him – he didn't think to wear gloves.'

'At least we know who did it,' Florrie said, the news offering some relief at least.

'And from my further investigations, it would seem his Uncle Dick has been training him up – not doing a very good job of it by all accounts. But apparently, he's taken Dillon under his wing while the lad's father's in prison. Dillon and his mother live over in Lingthorpe which is probably why you didn't recognise them.' He rested back in his seat. 'As for motive, we reckon it's all part of Dick Swales's bid to buy up as much of the property in town as possible, as cheaply as possible.'

That sounds about right. 'So, what happens now?' Florrie didn't want to ask what Dodgy Dick's brother was in prison for, she'd rather not know.

'Well, there's nothing we can do about Patricia Swales, as, while she might have been a nuisance, she didn't actually break the law, but we've charged Dillon with criminal damage. It's set the wind up him as he was already on conditional bail for burglary, so I doubt he'll be giving you any more trouble.'

When PC Nixon had left, Florrie couldn't decide whether she should be relieved or worried about what he'd imparted. On the one hand, it was a relief to know the culprit had been identified. But on the other, she was more than a little concerned at how Dodgy Dick would take the news that his nephew had been arrested and charged.

It hadn't helped that Ed had seemed preoccupied when he'd returned, only half-listening as she recounted what PC Nixon had said. That, together with getting her head around Dillon Swales, had put her in a prickly frame of mind, which wasn't what she wanted on a Friday, especially when she was meeting her friends for their usual get-together later at the Jolly.

TWENTY-NINE

'Florrie, lovey, is there any chance Jack and I could have a word with you and Ed at some point today?' Jean asked. They were getting the reading room ready for another visit from the local primary school who'd booked a Christmas storytelling session, which was one of Jean's favourite bookshop events and she'd been humming away happily to herself all morning. Later that afternoon, she'd be telling the group of six-year-olds a festive story written by a popular Yorkshire author by the name of Noah Bentley whose first book had been made into an animated film and was to air on Christmas Day. They were anticipating high levels of excitement to arrive with the youngsters, which was something Jean appeared to thrive on. It often made Florrie think how sad it was that Jean had missed out on Jack's child-hood, of being mother to a mischievous little boy. It made her wonder if it was part of the reason being around young children gave her friend so much joy. Jean was a natural with them, her warm nature and kind-heartedness shining through, and they in turn seemed to enjoy being around her.

'If it's not convenient, we could always do it another time.' Jean's question brought Florrie back into the moment.

'Yes, of course.' The serious note in Jean's voice made her stop and turn to look at her friend. 'Is everything okay?' She hoped they wouldn't have anything further to disclose about Dodgy Dick and Dillon's antics from the other night.

'Oh, yes, everything's fine. Sorry, I didn't mean to worry you. It's just there's something we'd like to run by you both, that's all.'

'Oh, right. Okay.' Florrie couldn't even begin to imagine what it could be.

'Would later this afternoon suit? I know your mum's popping in to do a shift. How about while she's here?'

'Yes, of course, I'll let Ed know. Is three o'clock any good? The school children should be long gone by then and it tends to be a quieter time around the school run hour. I'm sure she won't mind hanging back for a bit, she usually does anyway.'

'It's perfect. I'll send Jack a quick text right away. I'll be two ticks.' With that, Jean bustled off to find her phone, her face lit up with a smile and an air of excitement about her which only added to Florrie's curiosity.

'We're dying to know what the mystery's all about.' Ed grinned over at Jean and Jack. He and Florrie were sitting on the opposite side of the large desk in the reading room. 'It's all very cloak and dagger.'

Jack gave a deep chuckle. 'Ah, you can't beat a bit of drama to add a dash of interest to proceedings.' He gave his mum a theatrical wink. 'What d'you think, Mother?'

'Ooh, I couldn't agree more, son.'

Florrie had no idea what they were about to hear, but judging from the wide smiles passing between Jean and Jack she was relieved to see they weren't about to deliver anything dreadful. She took a sip of her tea, noting the sparkle in Jack's eyes. Was Jenna responsible for that? she wondered. *Who are you kidding, of course she is!* Florrie caught Ed's eye, exchanging a smile; he was clearly thinking the same thing.

'Right then, you young 'uns, I reckon we've kept you in suspense for long enough.' Jack beamed at them.

'I reckon we have, son.' Jean was practically jumping up and down with excitement.

'Yes, *please* put us out of our misery, I don't know what to think here!' Florrie chuckled.

'I'll let you tell them, Jack.' Jean gave him a gentle nudge with her elbow. 'You're better at saying stuff like this than I am.'

Jack's face took on a serious expression as he looked from Florrie to Ed. He rested his hands on the desk, threading his fingers together. 'So, recently, my mother and I have been having a chat about things here at the bookshop. We've had quite a few actually.'

'Oh?' said Ed, stealing a confused look at Florrie.

'You have?' she said, wondering where the heck this was going.

'Aye. See, the thing is, my mother took me into her confidence and told me all about your plans for extending the bookshop and creating a tearoom in the flat upstairs – which I have to say I think is a bloomin' brilliant idea.'

Jean interjected, giving an apologetic smile. 'I didn't think you'd mind Jack knowing, but you'll see why I needed to tell him in a minute. He's the soul of discretion, won't breathe a word to anyone. Until you're ready, that is.'

'Of course, that's absolutely fine. I'd spoken to Jenna about it and said it would be okay for her to tell Jack.' Florrie wondered if what they were about to hear was connected to the book festival Jenna had mentioned.

'Yes, 'course.' Ed nodded, equally baffled.

'Anyroad, owing to finances, I gather you might have to tackle the building work in stages.' Jack paused for a moment.

'It's looking that way,' said Ed. 'I've been trying to get a rough idea of costs.'

'We don't want to find ourselves in a difficult position financially, and end up having to sell the bookshop – especially not to the likes of Dodgy Dick.'

'Urgh! I don't blame you.' Jack gave a theatrical shudder. 'Dreadful individual. Makes my skin crawl.'

'Which is exactly what prompted me to speak to Jack,' said Jean. 'I felt sorry for you after you'd told me about it. You'd seemed all fired up about the idea – which, I should add, I think is genius – but the concern on your face when you started talking about not getting yourselves into a financially sticky situation just about broke my heart. And as for the way that man's been hounding you, it's a disgrace. What happened at Jenna's reading just spurred us on to approach you about our... well, I'll hand you back to Jack, let him carry on telling you.'

'Thanks, Mother.' He smiled, turning back to Florrie and Ed. 'So, pushing that slippery weasel aside, the upshot of our conversation was that we have a business proposition for you.'

THIRTY

Florrie sat dumbstruck for what felt like several long minutes as her brain tried to process what they'd just been told. 'A business proposition?' she said, finally finding her voice. Next to her, she sensed Ed sit up straight in his seat.

'Yes, lovey.' Jean beamed at her. 'A proper, official business proposition, drawn up by a solicitor, all done legally.'

'What we're proposing is that we invest in the bookshop – that way, the conversion of the flat could get started as soon as possible. You wouldn't need to scrimp and save, you could get the place looking exactly as you want it from the kick off. I hear you've got a rather wonderful vintage staircase lined up.' There was no hiding Jack's enthusiasm.

'Er, yeah, we do.' Ed ran his fingers through his hair. 'Nate gave us a tip off about it. It's a beauty.'

'An investment from Jack and me would also have another benefit.' Jean focused her attention on Ed. 'I'll apologise in advance for what I'm about to say, lovey, but having two extra investors – who love the bookshop dearly, and only have its, and yours and Florrie's, best interests at heart – would make it more difficult for your parents, or that dreadful Dick Swales, to get their hands on the place. I'll be honest with you, after hearing who was behind the power cut the other night, I just thought, "enough's enough". Us investing in the bookshop should, hopefully, get the message across loud and clear: it's not for sale!' It had been a while since Florrie had seen Jean so fired up.

'We wouldn't ask for a huge percentage of shares in the bookshop, but just enough to make a difference and to allow you to crack on with your conversion plans. You'd be the main shareholders, it's not about us wanting to take control, or tell you how to run the place – you're doing a brilliant job of it as it is and we wouldn't expect you to change anything. We'd just ask for enough so that our involvement would add a couple more layers of protection, if you like. With us on board there'd be two extra people for them to have to wear down,' added Jack.

They really have been giving this some serious thought.

'We'd love nothing more than to contribute to the bookshop's continued success.' Jean smiled.

'See, the thing is, I've got a bit of money left to me from when my adoptive parents died. It's just sitting there in the bank, doing nowt, and I'd rather it was getting put to good use.'

'And I've been squirrelling money away for years and have a decent little nest egg that I've been saving for a rainy day. And I think that rainy day has finally arrived. Nothing would give me greater happiness than to invest in you two wonderful young people.'

'Think you'd better change that to a snowy day, Mother.' Jack chuckled as he nodded towards the window where fluffy snowflakes were swirling frantically outside. Shoppers were now hurrying by, their heads bent against the elements.

Florrie blinked, her mind spinning as she followed Jack's gaze. 'Wow! And I don't mean about the snow.' This all felt slightly surreal. If she'd been asked to guess what Jack and Jean had wanted to talk to them about, there was no way she'd ever have come up with anything like this.

'Yeah, wow!' Ed scratched his head.

Jack and Jean chuckled. 'You don't have to give us your answer now. Take your time to think it through, have a good chat about it over the weekend,' said Jean.

'We can talk figures when you've had a chance to consider it fully,' added Jack.

'I'll be at Clifftop Cottage on Monday morning, helping Maggie with the bears, but I'll be free in the afternoon, if that's not too soon,' said Jean.

'That's amazingly generous of you both,' Florrie said. 'Thank you doesn't even cover it.'

'It's... it's... mind blowing,' said Ed, bemused.

Jean and Jack's offer occupied all of Florrie's thoughts for the whole afternoon. She and Ed had saved discussing the unexpected proposition until they were safely back at Samphire Cottage that evening, not wanting to risk anyone overhearing their conversation. Gossip had a knack of whipping round the town faster than lightning and they didn't want word getting out before they'd reached a decision. She had a brief discussion with Paula as her mum made a pot of tea. Florrie had joined her in the bookshop kitchen, quietly closing the door. Speaking barely above a whisper she gave an abridged version of the conversation, Paula listening intently.

'You know your dad and me are always happy to help you out financially, lovey. You only had to ask.'

'It's very kind of you, Mum, and I know you would, but I wouldn't feel comfortable about it.' Though Paula and Charlie were always keen to make sure their daughter had no financial worries, Florrie persistently refused their offers of money. She was proud of her independence, and besides, it didn't feel right taking from the pot of money they'd been saving towards their retirement. They'd often spoken of their plans to do a spot of travelling, and after Paula's brush with cancer, Florrie was eager for them to fulfil their dreams and make the most of being able to relax and take things easy together. 'And anyway, it's not about the money, it's more about the strong message it'll send out, having Jack and Jean as investors in the bookshop. It wouldn't be the same if it was Dad and you – no offence. And besides, Dad's offered to do the work cheaply for us, which is more than I could ask for.'

'Aye, when you put it like that, I suppose you're right, sweetheart. And it does sound like a brilliant idea – joining forces, as it were, with Jean and Jack. It's very fitting, what with Jean's connection to the bookshop and her being such a good friend of Mr and Mrs H. But don't forget to shout up if you need us.'

Florrie smiled affectionately. 'I won't, Mum. You and Dad are the best.' She dropped a kiss to her mother's soft cheek and gave her a squeeze. 'Love you.'

Florrie was relieved that Bear was giving her a lift down to the Jolly that evening along with the others this side of town. Though it had stopped snowing, the town was now covered in a couple of inches of snow which would make walking down Skitey Bank something of a challenge; Jasmine would be sure to end up in a heap on the floor, especially if she was wearing the boots she had on last time. It had been bad enough walking home from the bookshop, never mind how bone-numbingly cold it had become, and it would be even worse later tonight. Maggie had texted earlier, saying she and Bear would collect everyone in the Land Rover at around quarter past seven, which gave Florrie and Ed a bit of extra time to chat about Jean and Jack's proposition.

And, from their initial discussion, it would appear they both seemed keen to accept the offer.

'I just have this really strong feeling that your grandparents would be over the moon to think that Jean and Jack were involved with the bookshop and helping secure its future,' said Florrie. 'They have a connection that goes back such a long way.'

'True.' Ed nodded. 'And when you think about it, the bookshop played a big part in bringing Jean and Jack back together after all those years apart, which somehow would make their involvement extra special.'

'Ahh, it so does.' Florrie gave a happy sigh, recalling the day Jack had learnt Jean was the mother he'd come to Micklewick Bay in search of. 'I think Jean and Jack investing in the bookshop would be brilliant, especially as they say they're happy for us to keep running it as we are.'

'I agree. It would be a wise move from a business perspective, too. Actually,' he chuckled, 'I can just imagine my grandfather looking down now, feeling thoroughly pleased at how things have panned out.'

'Oh, you're not wrong there,' Florrie said. 'He loved nothing better than a good old meddle, and we're prime examples of that!'

At that moment, a photo of Mr H and Mrs H, Gerty sitting between them, fell forward on the old pine dresser, making Ed and Florrie start. Gerty jumped up from her bed, headed over to the dresser and whimpered.

'Oh my days! That frightened the life out of me.' Florrie pressed her hand to her chest, her heart beating rapidly beneath her fingers.

Ed got to his feet and picked up the photo. 'Sending us messages from beyond the grave, are you, Grandad?' He smiled fondly at the image before setting it down in its usual place. 'If I didn't know better, I'd say that was a sign, wouldn't you, Gerty-Girl?' The Labrador wagged her tail as he gave her a quick scratch between the ears. He turned to Florrie, his eyes shining. 'I reckon that was Grandad telling us to go for it.'

Florrie joined him by the dresser. She rested her hands on his broad chest. 'You know what? I think you could be right.' She smiled up at him, the look in his eyes making her heart skip a beat. In the next moment, his lips met hers, soft and warm as she let herself melt into his kiss.

'Two years ago, I couldn't even begin to imagine that any of this would happen. It's crazy,' Florrie said, once they'd pulled apart.

'It is.' He nuzzled her nose, his floppy fringe tickling her cheek. 'But the best kind of crazy.'

She fell serious for a moment, Ed's father and Dodgy Dick invading her happy thoughts.

Though she was reluctant to spoil the moment, the business proposition from Jean and Jack meant she felt compelled to broach the subject of his reluctance to speak to his father. She was mindful that it should be done gently, though, no wading in and asking head on. 'What about your mum and dad? How do you think they'd react if we accepted Jean and Jack's offer?' she asked tentatively.

She felt his arms tense around her as a cloud passed over his face, snuffing out his smile. 'I've got a feeling it wouldn't go down well at all.'

'Oh?' She waited, watching his expression, her breath caught in her throat. It was the perfect opportunity for him to elaborate, to share what his father had said in that dratted phone call. But nothing was forthcoming. It irked her that there was something about Jean he wasn't telling her. It couldn't be anything bad, she reasoned. But it rankled that Peter Harte was potentially bad-mouthing such a thoroughly decent person as Jean.

'Right,' he said, releasing her from his embrace and stepping away, 'I'd best go and check on the fire, see if it's got going yet.'

Florrie watched him disappear into the hallway. Not for the first time she found herself wishing he was better at sharing things instead of bottling them up. Her emotions felt like they'd been tipped in a jar and given a thorough shaking with all that had happened recently, and his habit of clamming up didn't help. If she was honest, it was draining. And she had a horrible feeling that something was brewing – and that *something* was going to come to a head soon.

THIRTY-ONE

SATURDAY 16TH DECEMBER

'Did you find what you were looking for when you came back here the other day?' Florrie asked, taking a bite out of the chunky slice of toast she slathered with marmalade. She was sitting opposite Ed at the small, scrubbed pine table in the kitchen. The cosiness of the little room belied the below freezing temperatures outside where night was keeping daylight at bay. Even with all that had been happening, what with PC Nixon's visit and Jean and Jack's business proposal, whenever there'd been a gap in her thoughts, she'd found herself being pulled back to how he'd sloped back here on Thursday. That he'd offered no explanation had only heightened her suspicions; he could've made some excuse, said he'd forgotten something, but he hadn't even bothered to do that. She had to keep reminding herself that Ed wouldn't be considering Jean and Jack's offer if he were having second thoughts about the bookshop, but it wasn't enough, and a lingering doubt remained.

'Huh?' Ed flashed her a look she couldn't quite fathom.

'Thursday morning, when PC Nixon called round, you'd nipped back here. I thought you must've been looking for something.' *Rummaging around the attic again, no doubt.*

'Oh, that.' He smiled, making eye contact for the briefest of moments. 'I, er... I've been looking for a little painting I made years ago. Came to mind last week, thought it'd make a good Christmas gift for Maggie and Bear. It's of a cottage that reminds me of theirs. Been struggling to lay my hands on it.'

'Okay.' This was the first Florrie had heard of such a painting. 'The men aren't usually involved in the gifts, it's just us lasses that buy for each other.' Surely he could remember that from last year. 'Which is why we've clubbed together and bought Jazz the tickets for—' She clamped her hand over her mouth. 'Oh, um, this thing we thought she'd like.' *Yikes! That was close!*

Ed gave her a puzzled look. 'Tickets for what thing you thought she'd like?'

'S'just this *thing*, that's all. Wouldn't interest you.' She turned her attention to brushing toast crumbs off her dressing gown, hoping he wouldn't pursue it.

'Surely you can think of a better way of describing it than a "thing"? I hope, for Jazz's sake, it's more exciting than it sounds.' He gave a deep chuckle before adopting a faux cheery voice. 'Merry Christmas, Jazz, here's a ticket for a "thing" you like. Enjoy!'

Though he was laughing it off, Florrie could tell he wasn't convinced by her explanation. At least he would get a taste of how he regularly made her feel, not that it was what she'd intended. 'Can't say. Sorry. Don't ask anything else, cos I won't tell you, even under pain of death.' She gave a wide smile. She only had one day left before she could let him know about the tickets for the sleigh ride at Danskelfe Castle and she'd nearly let it slip. She'd got it all planned how she was going to tell him, and she didn't want to risk spoiling it at the last minute.

'How about torture by tickling your feet?' Ed raised a questioning eyebrow. 'Would that get a straight answer out of you?'

'Don't you dare!' She chuckled, tucking her slipper-clad feet under her chair and well out of his reach, the awkwardness of moments earlier floating away. *Time to move on to a different subject!* She reached for the teapot, topping up their tea. 'I'm still getting my head around Jean and Jack's offer. I keep thinking it must be a dream. I mean, it's been a bonkers week, what with everything that's happened. Talk about being one of wild contrasts.'

'You're not wrong there.' Ed picked up his knife and started buttering another slice of toast. 'At least we've got tomorrow to devote to properly thinking their proposal through.'

The words, 'Not quite all of tomorrow,' were just about to leave her mouth but she pulled herself back in time. They would have to leave a good hour before the sleigh ride, probably sooner if the roads were dicey with the snow. 'I don't think I'll be able to think about much else today, actually.'

'I reckon you will. With it being the Christmas market, we'll be rushed off our feet if last year's was anything to go by,' Ed reminded her.

Each year, on the third Saturday in December, the town held its Christmas market. It was always a popular affair, filling the square with a mixture of festive aromas from roasting chestnuts to mulled wine. The traditional sweet stall was a particular favourite of Florrie's, the smell of candy infusing the air around it. Adding to the air of nostalgia were the musicians who played at the Jolly of a Friday evening. They pitched up at the entrance to the station, their cheerful, lilting tunes blasting forth. The stallholders did a roaring trade, as did the local shops, reaping the rewards of the extra business the market brought in. The event was topped off by carol singing around the large Christmas tree at the head of the square, accompanied by the local brass band and the Micklewick Bay choir. Florrie only hoped a certain dodgy businessman didn't seize upon the moment to cause more mayhem, especially since she and Ed had decided to give the carol singing a miss. They were going to use the time to decorate their home for Christmas since they hadn't had the chance to do it before now. Florrie had never been so late getting her home decked for the festive season!

Florrie told her friends of her concerns over Dillon Swales and his uncle when they'd had their catch-up at the Jolly the previous evening. They'd all offered much-needed words of reassurance, just as she'd hoped they would.

'You might find things quieten down now, flower,' Stella had said. 'Especially if Dodgy Dick thinks the police are watching him and his grubby little sidekicks.'

'I'm sure Stells is right. Just don't let it dominate Christmas and your exciting plans for Ed and The Happy Christmas Memory Project. Focus on having a wonderful time instead.' Lark had smiled kindly at her.

'I always say there's no point fretting over something that hasn't happened yet,' Jasmine had said.

'Do you, Jazz?' Maggie had asked, scrunching her nose up.

'No.'

'Didn't think so.'

'Just thought it sounded good.' Jasmine had given a mischievous smile, making them all laugh, which was just what Florrie had needed.

'Anyroad, what's the goss with Jack and Jenna? I heard they'd been seen snogging at the end of the pier.' Jasmine had skilfully changed the subject, lightening Florrie's mood in the process.

Though she'd kept it to herself, Florrie had considered inviting Jenna to join them for their get-together that evening, knowing the others would be fine with it – as Alex's sister Zara did whenever she was in town – but had thought better of it. With Jenna heading back up north the following day, she'd no doubt be keen to spend as much time as possible with Jack.

'Doesn't surprise me, the sparks flying between them at her book reading the other night were pretty obvious.' Stella had arched a knowing eyebrow. 'Even when the lights went out.'

'More so when the lights went out!' Maggie had added with a chuckle.

Their good-natured banter had gone some way to easing Florrie's disquiet over Dodgy Dick, and she'd managed to put him to the back of her mind. Until his reappearance that afternoon.

She'd been taking Gerty for a walk when she became aware of a large car crawling along on the road beside her. She'd been startled to see it was the one that belonged to Dodgy Dick, the blacked-out windows magnifying his menacing air. She'd eventually shaken him off by ducking into a narrow snicket that led back into town, her feet losing purchase several times on the icy path, causing her to slip over. By the time she got back to the bookshop she was trembling, panic squeezing in her chest.

This was getting out of hand. And it made her all the more determined to accept Jean and Jack's offer.

THIRTY-TWO

SUNDAY 17TH DECEMBER

Florrie opened her eyes, the remnants of sleep slipping away. In the next moment a feeling of excitement rushed through her. The day of the sleigh ride at Danskelfe Castle had arrived! Beside her, Ed was breathing deeply, cosy in the embrace of slumber, oblivious to the surprise that awaited him. She squinted at the alarm clock beside her until the numbers came into focus. It was seven thirty. Much as the bed was blissfully comfy, Florrie was already too wide awake for sleep to reclaim her. Plus, she was eager to get everything in place for when she could share her surprise with Ed. All she'd told him so far was that he needed to keep the day clear and that he shouldn't question it – just as she'd done with Jasmine.

She eased herself out of bed, being careful not to disturb him, wriggled her feet into her slippers and reached for her dressing gown.

By the time Ed had landed downstairs in his pyjamas almost half an hour later, Florrie had the table set and Christmas carols playing in the background. The mouth-watering aroma of bacon was floating around the kitchen, Gerty drooling from her vantage point in her bed.

'Mmm. Something smells good.' He ran his fingers through his sleep-ruffled hair before making his way over to the oven where Florrie was tending a skillet full of sizzling bacon rashers. He wrapped his arms around her, delivering a kiss to the back of her neck, making her knees go weak.

'Thought I'd treat us to a couple of bacon butties with a side order of scrambled eggs.'

'Mmm. Perfect.' He kissed her again, sending delicious electric pulses firing through her. 'Need a hand with anything?'

'No, thanks, everything's under control. You just park yourself at the table and I'll bring this over to you in two ticks. Oh, and there's tea in the pot, by the way. Should be the perfect temperature.'

'Sounds good. Morning, Gerty-Girl,' he said, pulling out his usual seat at the table and smiling at the Labrador. 'Sleep well, lass?'

Gerty trotted over to him, pushing her head into his lap, her solid tail swishing across the floor and knocking the table leg.

'Gerty, you know the rules when food's around.' Florrie gave the Labrador a mock stern look, pointing in the direction of her bed. Gerty's ears flattened, her expression saying, 'Do you really mean that? Surely there's a bacon and scrambled egg butty for me?'

Florrie, holding back a giggle and attempting to keep her voice stern, said, 'Gerty, bed.' Gerty looked up at Ed, as if expecting him to jump in on her behalf, before plodding her way slowly back to her squishy sheepskin bed where she flumped down with a *harumph* that was loaded with disappointment.

'Full marks for trying, Gerty-Girl.' Ed chuckled as he poured tea into his mug.

· · ·

'That was delicious.' Ed patted his stomach having cleared his plate of every scrap of food. 'Just what you need on a cold December morning.'

'Glad you enjoyed it.' Florrie smiled, reaching for his plate, savouring the flavour of crispy bacon mixed with tomato ketchup that lingered in her mouth. She was raring to move on to the next stage of her plans.

'I'll see to that, you stay where you are, grab yourself another cuppa.' Ed rested his hand on Florrie's, the warmth of his touch seeping into her skin and sending a shiver of delight through her.

'Actually, I just need to get something.' She slipped into the living room, returning moments later with a neatly wrapped parcel, decorated with festive bows and ribbons that she'd secreted at the back of the Christmas tree.

'Right then, come and sit back down, I've got a little something for you and it involves The Happy Christmas Memory Project.'

'Oh?' Ed put the plate he'd been rinsing into the washing-up bowl, his eyebrows raised in surprise.

'There you go, you can open this early.' Florrie waited for him to sit back down then pushed the parcel across to him, her heart dancing happily.

'Okay,' he replied as he tugged at the ribbon. 'Thank you. Though it does seem a shame when you've wrapped it so beautifully.'

'I enjoy wrapping presents,' she said, her heart thumping with anticipation.

He released a roar of laughter as he lifted out a woollen jumper decorated with a cheerful-looking snowman complete with a robin perched on his floppy hat. 'I love it!'

Florrie couldn't contain her giggles. 'Thought you might.'

'It's my first ever Christmas jumper and I couldn't have

chosen better myself.' He leant across the table and kissed her, despite them both laughing.

'It'll come in very handy for this.' She passed him an envelope she'd decorated with festive-themed stickers they stocked at the bookshop.

'There's something else?'

She nodded, a mysterious glint in her eyes. 'There is.'

Ed sat in stunned silence as his eyes landed on the contents of the envelope. Knowing his dyslexia would be holding things up for him, she jumped in. 'I've booked us a sleigh ride at Danskelfe Castle. It's for quarter past three today and we're going with our posse of pals, including Chloe and Zak. And we're all wearing Christmas jumpers, hence the one you've just unwrapped.'

She studied Ed's changing expressions, his smile fading. He blinked quickly. 'I... um...' His voice was thick with emotion as a tear rolled down his cheek.

'Oh, Ed.' She reached across the table, taking his hand. 'Why are you crying?'

He sniffed before clearing his throat. 'I'm just blown away.' Another tear slid down to his chin, quickly followed by a third. 'That you've done this for me... I'm... I mean... Ugh!' His gaze met hers, his lashes damp. 'What... what I'm trying to say is, you're one amazing woman, Florrie. You constantly surprise me with your kindness.'

Gerty rushed over, nudging at him, whimpering at his distress. He reached down, smoothing his hand over her glossy black head.

'Give over.' Florrie felt the warmth of a blush in her cheeks, the feel of his fingers as they squeezed hers. 'It's nothing.' She gave a shrug. 'It was Stella that mentioned the sleigh rides, which got me thinking it would be fab if we all went together – happy Christmas memories for everyone.' She went on to explain about what had been arranged for Jasmine and the kids.

'I rest my case – you're the most thoughtful, kind-hearted person I've ever encountered.'

'Hmm. I'm not so sure you'll still think that when I tell you, you're on washing-up duty.' She laughed, uncomfortable to have such praise lavished upon her.

Ed feigned a look of outrage. 'In that case, I take it all back. You're a hard taskmaster!'

THIRTY-THREE

The tooting of a horn at bang on twelve forty-five p.m. alerted Florrie and Ed to the arrival of Maggie and Bear. They hurried out of the warmth of Samphire Cottage and into the breath-taking cold of the street, diving into the Land Rover as quickly as they could. Zak and Chloe were up front with Bear, while Maggie and Jasmine were in the back. They were met with a slew of hellos and excited chatter as Zak and Chloe spoke on top of one another.

'Florrie! Florrie! Where are we going?' asked Zak, his voice giddy as he turned to face her. 'Mum says you haven't told her.'

'Yeah, Mummy says it's a secret surprise.' Chloe beamed.

'Please tell us! It's *torturing* me!' Zak's voice had cranked up several volumes.

Jasmine stuck her fingers in her ears and waggled them theatrically. 'Er, Zak, lovey, Florrie's not in Lingthorpe, she's right behind you, so there's no need to bellow, especially when my lugs are this close to your mouth.'

'Soz, Mum.' He laughed, his impish grin looking anything but. 'Florrie, please can you tell us where we're going?' He reminded Florrie so much of Jasmine at that age, her heart squeezed with affection for him.

'Are we going sledging again, Florrie?' asked Chloe, blinking sweetly. 'That was the best time!'

'Yeah, it was so mint!' Zak started bouncing up and down in his seat.

'I think you'll like what we're going to do even more.' Ed smiled at the young lad which resulted in whoops of joy from him and his sister.

'Please put them out of their misery, and before my eardrums burst.' Jasmine looked at Florrie pleadingly but laughing all the same.

'Okay,' she said, as both children fell silent, eyes wide with anticipation. Florrie didn't think they could get any more adorable. 'We're heading over to Danskelfe Castle on the moors, where we're booked in for a sleigh ride in the grounds, followed by mince pies, Christmas cake and shortbread.'

'*No way*?' Zak's mouth fell open and Florrie nodded.

The shrieks of joy that followed were deafening.

Jasmine shot Florrie a confused look, a hint of discomfort hovering in her expression.

Florrie leant into her. 'Early Christmas presents. Your ticket is from all the lasses and me, the kids' tickets are from Ed and me.'

Relief brightened Jasmine's features. 'Oh, thank you all so much,' she said as the explanation set in.

The journey across the moors was an upbeat one, with the children instigating a lively sing-along of festive songs. The towns soon gave way to sprawling, snow-covered moorland, huge drifts piled up on the side of the roads where the ploughs had pushed through. Zak and Chloe were fascinated by the sheep that roamed the moors freely, clumps of frozen snow hanging from their dense fleeces, and the great number of rabbits that hopped about, occasionally darting out in front of the Land Rover, Bear having to touch his brakes.

They drove on, passing through achingly beautiful villages filled with characterful thatched cottages all dressed for Christmas. Before they knew it, Danskelfe Castle – home to generations of the titled Hammondely family – complete with flag fluttering above one of its turrets, came into view from its position built into a great crag overlooking the sweeping dale of Danskelfe from which it took its name. Ed turned to Florrie, and they exchanged giddy smiles.

Nate's pickup appeared behind them as they followed the signs for the castle, which directed them down a lane that was lined with Christmas trees, their lights twinkling in what was left of the fading daylight. Soon the castle's great walls loomed before them. It made for a brooding and imposing sight. Bear drove carefully through an impressive stone archway, decorated with thousands of tiny lights, Zak and Chloe peering out of the Land Rover's windows in awe. With the vehicles parked up, the party followed the signs that led into a cobbled courtyard.

Florrie's gaze swept all around her, taking in the Hammondely coat of arms above the castle's broad oak door. Beside it stood a tall Christmas tree generously trimmed with warm white lights and oversized baubles, its branches swaying in the breeze that was creeping its way around the ancient walls. Standing in the centre of the courtyard was the "sleigh" which was even more spectacular than Florrie had expected from the images on the castle's website. It consisted of a carriage, its exterior clad to emulate the stereotypical image of a "Father Christmas" sleigh, painted a deep red and trimmed in gold. Florrie was thankful to see it had a sturdy roof, festooned with a plethora of fairy lights, that would at least go some way to protect them from the elements. Tethered to it, three majestic-looking white horses waited patiently, their manes and harnesses given a festive finish.

With everyone in their seats, two liveried drivers gave the orders and the horses set off at quite a pace, their hooves clattering through the courtyard and thundering over the now permanently fixed wooden drawbridge. They followed a track, cleared of snow, leading out into the castle's extensive grounds, Zak and Chloe wearing face-splitting smiles and cheering with the joy of it all. The scenery couldn't have been more stunning if it tried. In the distance the dense coniferous wood of the Danskelfe Estate exuded a magical air, with its generous covering of snow. The views over the sweeping Danskelfe Dale were breathtaking, great swathes of moorland giving way to farmland that lined the dale, peppered with farmsteads, their lights already twinkling.

'Oh, wow! Look!' Everyone turned to where Zak was pointing to see a large stag break cover from a cluster of trees. A gasp ran around the group of friends as they watched it race over the open land where it leapt effortlessly over a drystone wall and disappeared into a small copse of rowan trees.

'So beautiful,' Lark said dreamily.

'They're such magnificent creatures,' said Ed.

'I can't believe we've seen a real-life stag,' said Zak. 'It was ginormous!'

'Do you think it was Rudolph, Mummy?' asked Chloe, melting Florrie's heart and making Zak snort at his sister.

Jasmine shot him a reproving look and said, 'Maybe his cousin, but Rudolph and his pals who pull Santa's sleigh are reindeer, lovey.'

Florrie felt a rush of exhilaration as the sleigh powered on, not caring that the wind was biting cruelly at any exposed skin, though she was glad of the fleece blankets they'd found folded up on each seat. She pulled hers up to her chin, snuggling closer to Ed. He wrapped his arm around her, giving her a squeeze. 'This is amazing,' he said, his eyes shining.

'I'm so happy you're enjoying it.' She smiled up at him. *Another successful mission for The Happy Christmas Memory Project.*

'You all right, Mags?'

Florrie turned to see Stella regarding their friend closely. A spike of alarm shot through her. *Uh-oh!* Maggie and Bear's baby was due any day and, much as she was mindful of this, Maggie had still been keen to join them if Baby Marsay hadn't already arrived.

Maggie nodded. 'Just feeling a bit travel sick. I'll be fine in a minute.'

'You sure, missus? You haven't half gone pale.' There was no escaping the concern in Bear's voice.

'I'm okay, don't fuss.'

The friends exchanged concerned looks; it was unlike Maggie to be snappy with her husband.

The sleigh ploughed on, passing through a long wrought-iron archway decorated with branches of fir tree and smothered in yet more fairy lights, generating further gasps of delight from the group. Not long after, they passed a miniature wooden lodge with a thatched roof and a sign that said, "Santa's helpers", causing Chloe to give a shriek of delight. As they rounded the corner, heading back in the direction of the castle, they encountered yet another wooden lodge, surrounded by small, decorated Christmas trees, this one bearing the sign, "The House of Christmas Magic". The sleigh slowed down, allowing the group to watch as the door opened, revealing a fairy dressed in a shimmering gold gown.

Chloe was beside herself with excitement, waving back frantically and jumping up and down, her eyes wide with delight. 'Did you see that, Mummy? Did you see? It was a fairy!'

The light had faded considerably as they drew closer to the castle, which looked magical in its festive finery.

Once parked up in the courtyard, they clambered out of the sleigh and helped themselves to the mulled wine – a non-alcoholic version of which was available for those who preferred it – or orange juice, for the younger guests, and availed themselves of the warm mince pies, Christmas cake and chunky slices of shortbread that were being offered around on trays by the castle staff.

'How did you enjoy that?' A cut-glass accent made Florrie turn to see a tall, coltish-looking woman, dressed in classic country clothing smiling at her. A wide-brimmed leather hat sat on top of her chestnut hair that was pulled back into a low ponytail.

'It was wonderful,' Florrie said politely, wondering if the woman had something to do with the Hammondelys. She'd been chatting to Maggie, eager to make sure her friend was feeling better when she'd heard the voice behind her.

'Oh, I'm so delighted to hear that. I'm Caro, by the way, Caro Hammondely.' She held out her hand.

'Pleased to meet you,' Florrie said. Caro – or *Lady* Caroline Hammondely – exuded such an air of confidence, Florrie found herself feeling slightly in awe of her. She looked on as Caro introduced herself to everyone else, keen to know that the sleigh ride had lived up to their expectations.

'It's our first year offering sleigh rides, and we're thrilled with how popular they've been. Since I've become involved in the running of the place, I've been eager to try out lots of new, exciting ventures to tempt people to visit us. Make the old gal earn her keep, as it were.' She nodded towards the castle.

Despite being ultra confident, Caro had a warm and friendly manner that Florrie couldn't help but find appealing.

'Oh, golly gosh! I've just realised! I knew I'd seen you somewhere before. I recognise you from your photo on your website.

You're Maggie of the Micklewick Bear Company who made the adorable teddy bears for our lodges. They're absolutely *divine* and I'm about to place an order for some more for the new lodges we're having built.'

Florrie turned to Maggie, expecting to see her beaming happily at the praise for her bears. Instead, she was shocked to find her friend's face distorted by a grimace. 'Mags, are you all right?' she asked, rushing over to her.

Before Maggie could answer, Zak said, 'Er, Mum, I think Maggie's just peed herself.' They all looked to see a dark stain spreading over Maggie's red maternity trousers.

'Oh, gosh!' said Lady Caro, looking momentarily shocked.

'I think Baby Marsay's on his or her way.' Maggie gasped, forcing a smile at Bear.

'What? Now, this minute?' Bear dragged his hand down his face. 'Oh, flippin' 'eck, Mags.'

'Darling, what can we do to help?' asked Caro, taking Maggie's arm.

'We need to get her to hospital,' said Jasmine.

'Of course. Where's your car?'

'It's in the car park,' said Stella, cool and calm as ever. 'Is there any way we can bring it closer to Maggie, save her struggling to it?'

'Yes, absolutely, just drive right up here.'

'But how's everyone going to get home?' Maggie asked. 'I can't expect you all to traipse over to Middleton-le-Moors with us, especially the kids. Who knows how long we could be there?'

'Don't go worrying about us, Mags, we can get a taxi or something,' said Florrie. 'You just focus on yourself and Baby Marsay.'

'Did you all travel here together?' Lady Caro asked.

'Alex and I travelled with Nate and Lark here,' said Stella, 'but the others all got here in Bear's Landie.'

'I see.' Lady Caro looked thoughtful for a moment. 'Do any of you have all vehicle insurance?'

'I do,' said Ed.

'Perfect. You can take the others back in Bear's Landie and I'll whizz Maggie and Bear over to Middleton hospital in mine. It's not far from here, so we'll have you there in a jiffy, Maggie. I assume you can call someone to collect you when necessary?'

'Yes, but—'

'No buts, darling.' Lady Caro glanced up at the sky as snowflakes started gently tumbling down. 'We need to get you and your baby safely to hospital before the snow sets in. The weather's notoriously capricious out here and can change in a heartbeat. We need to leave now, if the forecast is anything to go by. I'll just grab my keys.'

As soon as Ed had retrieved Maggie's hospital bag from Bear's Land Rover – she'd had the foresight to bring it with her, just in case – Lady Caro had bundled the expectant mum and her husband into her new Land Rover Defender, the others waving them off, cries of good luck trailing after them.

Florrie watched the vehicle disappear down the lane, willing with all her might that everything would go well for Maggie and Bear, and that Lady Caro would get them to hospital before Baby Marsay made his or her appearance.

THIRTY-FOUR

'Well, that was what I'd call a truly unforgettable day.' Ed gave a contented sigh, stretching his legs out in front of him as Florrie drew the living room curtains – a vintage find from Lark's shop. He'd swapped his jeans and Christmas jumper for his pyjama bottoms and long-sleeved T-shirt. Florrie had changed into her favourite brushed cotton checked PJs, ready for a couple of hours' relaxation in front of the television. Gerty was in her usual place, toasting herself in front of the fire.

'You're not wrong,' Florrie said, flopping down beside him.

'I wonder how Maggie's getting along, Bear too. Poor bloke looked terrified,' he said with a chuckle.

'They've waited so long for this baby, he'll want everything to be perfect for Mags.' She hadn't been able to get her friend out of her thoughts since they'd got home, willing everything to be okay for her. She'd called Bear's parents, Chrissie and Dom, before they'd left Danskelfe Castle, while there was decent phone signal, bringing them up to speed with the situation, explaining that Bear was without a vehicle. Much as she and Ed would be happy to go and collect him, Florrie felt sure it was something Bear's mum and dad would much rather do; they'd been beside themselves with excitement at the prospect of becoming grandparents, so they wouldn't want to waste a moment getting to the hospital.

'Thank you again for such an awesome experience.' Ed draped his arm around Florrie, pulling her close to him. 'I loved every minute, especially seeing how excited Zak and Chloe got about it all – the wonder and sheer joy on their faces was price-less. It was a thoughtful thing to do, and not just for me.'

'I'm glad you enjoyed it. I guessed it would be fun, but it way outdid my expectations. And how lovely was Lady Caro?'

'Yeah, she was cool, actually. Had us all whipped into shape before we had a chance to catch our breath.' He and Florrie laughed at that.

'And tomorrow's going to be another exciting day but for a different reason.' She felt a flutter of butterflies at the thought.

'It is indeed.' He tipped her face towards his and kissed her, making her heart dance.

That morning, they'd had a good chat about Jean and Jack's offer, weighing up all the pros and cons, thinking not only with their hearts, but also their heads. The outcome of which had been a resounding yes from both of them. They'd agreed to contact mother and son first thing, telling them of their decision and suggesting they toast their new business partnership with a glass of something fizzy.

Florrie couldn't wait to share her news with her friends, though she was less enthusiastic about Ed telling his parents. She knew it wasn't going to be received well by them.

At just gone midnight, Florrie was awoken by the trilling of her mobile phone, setting her heart pounding. Ed stirred beside her. 'What's up?' he asked, sleepily.

'Um, I'm not sure.' She reached for her phone to see Bear's number illuminating the screen. 'Oh, it's Bear.' She pushed herself up, panic replaced by expectation, hoping everything was going smoothly for the Marsays.

'Oh, right.' Ed snapped awake and flicked the bedside light on, watching her intently.

'Hi, Bear. How's Maggie?' Florrie put her phone on loud-speaker. 'Ed's here, too.'

'Hi, guys. Mags is amazing! And so is our baby girl!' His voice boomed out into the room, brimming with happiness. 'Can you believe it? We've got a little daughter! I'm a dad.' His voice quavered and a sob escaped as he gave in to happy tears. 'I'm actually a dad.'

'Oh congratulations, Bear.' She turned to Ed, beaming.

'Yeah, congratulations, Bear, that's awesome news.' Ed beamed back at her.

'Cheers, mate.' Bear sniffed noisily down the phone. 'Honestly, she's the most gorgeous little girl I've ever clapped eyes on. She looks just like her beautiful mum, has her big eyes and a headful of dark curls and the most perfect little rosebud mouth. She was just gazing up at me as if she knew who I was. And she's tiny. So tiny, I hardly dare hold her.'

Florrie giggled at the thought of giant Bear and his huge, shovel-like hands cradling his newborn daughter. 'Well, we're over the moon for you both.'

'Aye, well, Maggie was a total star. She coped so well, I'm in complete awe of her, she's amazing.'

'She is that. Oh, and what about a name? Has your gorgeous little girl got a name yet?' Maggie, not wanting to tempt fate after suffering so many miscarriages, had kept their choice of baby names a secret, even from her best friend.

'Lucia, after Maggie's Italian nonna, but we're going to use Lucy for every day.'

'That's a beautiful choice, Bear,' Ed said warmly.

'It is.' Florrie looked over at Ed and grinned. 'Now you go and kiss that wife of yours and give baby Lucy a cuddle from me. And try to get some rest.' It was good to hear the happiness in his voice after the terrible time they'd had in the summer thanks to Maggie's troublesome cousin, Robyn. Those days were long behind them, thank goodness.

'Do you need picking up, mate?' asked Ed. 'I'd be happy to come and get you.'

'Kind of you to offer, but my mum and dad are here. I'm heading back with them soon. Mags and Lucy should be good to bring home tomorrow.' His tears had subsided, and they could hear the smile in his voice. It was infectious.

'Well, shout up if there's anything we can do,' Ed added.

With the phone call ended, Florrie snuggled back into Ed, happiness coursing through her as her mind started going over their day. It had far exceeded her expectations and created another special memory for The Happy Christmas Memory Project. And what a way to end it, with the arrival of little Lucia Marsay.

She drifted off to sleep, her mind wandering down the path towards a time when Ed might be making the sort of phone call Bear had just made. The thought sent a warm glow spreading through her.

THIRTY-FIVE

MONDAY 18TH DECEMBER

Florrie called Jean early that morning to share the happy news of Baby Marsay's arrival. It crossed her mind that Jean was supposed to be working for Maggie at Clifftop Cottage until lunch time that day and she doubted it would have been at the forefront of Bear's mind to let her know Maggie wouldn't be there, since he'd be so wrapped up in the urgency of his little girl's arrival. She was sure the two women would have planned for what to do when the situation arose, but, in any event, Florrie felt it would be a good idea to give her prior warning. She didn't know if Jean had a key to Clifftop Cottage and didn't want her to have a wasted journey if no one was home to let her in, and neither did she want to trouble Maggie and Bear about it.

Jean had been delighted to hear Maggie and Bear's news, though Florrie hadn't shared Baby Marsay's name, not wanting to deprive the new parents of that pleasure themselves.

Of course, there was another reason for Florrie's call. She also wanted to check when would be a good time for her and Ed to have a chat with Jean and Jack; they'd agreed it would be better to tell them when they were all together. Florrie had detected an air of excitement about Jean when she'd suggested the four of them meet at The Cellar early doors after the bookshop had closed.

'Ooh, The Cellar, I do like it there. I'm looking forward to it already,' Jean had said.

With the call out of the way, Florrie and Gerty had jumped in the car and followed Ed to Clifftop Cottage in Bear's Land Rover. The plan was for him to leave the Landie there, post the keys through the letter box if no one was home, and have a lift back into town with Florrie.

When they arrived, Clifftop Cottage was shrouded in darkness, the curtains drawn tightly at the windows, the wind, laced with the threat of more snow, battering the walls relentlessly. Uncertain if Bear was catching up on his sleep or still at the hospital, they did what they needed to do as quietly as possible and headed to the bookshop, both glad to be back in the warmth of the car.

There they met Florrie's dad who demonstrated how to use the new alarm he and the electrician, Jeff, had rigged up for them the previous day. Having the up-to-date system had afforded Florrie a sense of relief she hadn't anticipated, and she was further pleased to find that it was a more straightforward affair than the old one.

'If we're going to The Cellar tonight and we'll both be having a glass or two of fizz, it would make sense if we didn't have the car here. I think I might drop it off at the cottage and walk back,' Ed said casually, jangling the keys in his hand as Florrie was tidying the shelves in the autobiography section.

'Oh, okay.' She looked up at him. Much as she hadn't been expecting that, she could see his logic.

'Won't be long,' he said, as he headed out of the door a few minutes later.

It was when he still hadn't returned an hour later that Florrie started to think something was amiss.

THIRTY-SIX

'He said what?' Still in her coat from taking Gerty for a walk, Florrie stood looking at Leah, trying to make sense of what she'd just heard.

'He said, he had to go, and that he was sorry, but he'd be in touch. He was in a right rush, looked really flustered.' Leah had followed Florrie down to the kitchen where they hung their coats, not wanting to relay this in front of the browsing customers. The young girl squirmed uncomfortably. 'He had a backpack with him, which looked stuffed.'

Florrie took a few moments to mull over the significance of the backpack, a feeling of unease creeping over her.

'And how long ago was this?'

'I'd say about five minutes after you'd gone out with Gerty,' she said, biting her bottom lip.

Florrie glanced at her watch, her thoughts turning over. That was at least half an hour ago. 'And he didn't say where he was going?'

'No.' Leah shook her head.

'Did he say when he'd be back?'

'No, sorry.' Leah fiddled with her fingers. The poor girl looked decidedly awkward.

'There's no need for you to apologise, flower.' Florrie reached out and squeezed Leah's shoulder. 'I'm just surprised – it's all a bit out of the blue and unexpected. I daresay he'll be back soon.' She spoke with more conviction than she felt.

Florrie waited for Leah to head to the front of the shop before she tried Ed's mobile, but, frustratingly, it just rang out before the voicemail kicked in. She tapped her phone against her chin, not welcoming the feeling of disquiet that was beginning to creep over her as she recalled the last time he'd taken off and left her like this.

By the time quarter to five arrived and there was still no sign of Ed, Florrie was thoroughly agitated. She'd spent the afternoon swinging between feeling annoyed and being concerned. And whenever the bell went above the shop door, her heart leapt, hoping Ed would walk through it, all smiles. But each time she was disappointed.

She tried his phone numerous times, but it always ended up going to voicemail. *Ed Harte, what the heck are you playing at?* Her mind went to the attic at the cottage, wondering what he'd been searching for. She couldn't shake the feeling it had something to do with that. Her pulse started to race, panic prickling over her skin. How she hated feeling this way. Is this what life with him was going to be like? she wondered. Periods of calm, followed by more of his unsettling flaky behaviour? *Stop jumping to conclusions! He hasn't been gone long at all! Give him a chance.*

And now she found herself in the uncomfortable position of having to call Jean and tell her they couldn't make it to The Cellar. It was something she didn't relish. She hardly knew what to say, dreading hearing the disappointment in her friend's

voice. She didn't want Jean to think they were messing her and
Jack about.

She was relieved and, not to mention, thankful when Jean
took it well.

'Don't worry, lovey, we can meet up when Ed gets back.
And try not to dwell on it. I'm sure it's not like last time when
he wanted to get away from everything. I expect he's gone to
source a Christmas present for you or has maybe even got wind
of something fabulous for the new tearoom,' she said kindly.

But Florrie wasn't so sure.

Arriving back at Samphire Cottage, Florrie soon found the
reason Ed hadn't been answering his phone: he'd left it on the
kitchen table, along with a dog-eared brown envelope. Its
address had been crossed out, rendering it illegible.

She ran upstairs to the attic where her worries were
confirmed. Papers had been pulled out of boxes and strewn all
over the floor. She felt tears sting her eyes. Her suspicions had
been right. He'd got cold feet.

Back downstairs, Florrie sat at the kitchen table, her head in
her hands, her mind spinning with confusion. She felt too
annoyed to cry. After the wonderful day they'd had yesterday,
how could he do this to her? Never mind that! After this last
eighteen months with them growing closer every day, how could
he just make some sort of rash decision to up and off like this?
Did their relationship mean so little? And it was one thing
treating her this way, but leaving without having the good
manners to speak to Jean and Jack was another. The last time
he'd done this, he'd come back, his tail between his legs, full of
apologies, and she'd told him she couldn't go through it again,
the uncertainty, the insecurity. She thought from what he'd said
afterwards that he understood. He'd promised her he wouldn't
do it again, promised her that if he ever had any doubts or

worries about being involved in the bookshop, he'd talk to her about it first. Agreed to be honest and upfront.

'Pft!' Florrie snorted. 'Once a flaky loser, always a flaky loser.'

She wouldn't give him the chance to do it again. Though it didn't stop her from making a mental note to check through the papers he'd so recklessly cast around the floor. Despite her anger, she was curious to find out if it would offer any clues as to his hasty departure.

THIRTY-SEVEN

TUESDAY 19TH DECEMBER

Florrie functioned on autopilot since Ed did a runner. Not wanting to worry her parents, she'd kept his sudden disappearance to herself, and had asked Leah to do the same. Florrie hadn't shared her concerns with her young assistant, and had just said he'd gone to see a friend he hadn't seen for a while and who wasn't going to be in the country for much longer, by way of explanation. She didn't want to risk Dodgy Dick finding out she was alone. She hoped her excuse hadn't sounded as lame to Leah as it had to her own ears.

Jean Davenport had knocked at the shop door before opening time and before Leah was yet to arrive. She'd swept Florrie into a warm hug, offering her words of comfort as the young woman had sobbed on her shoulder, Jean reiterating what she'd said the previous day. 'Honestly, lovey, anyone can see from the way he looks at you, he's besotted.'

'If that's the case, why hasn't he rung, Jean?' She'd dabbed at her eyes with the paper tissue Jean had handed her. 'I know he's forgotten his mobile, but there are other phones. He could've called me from one of those, set my mind at rest.'

Jean hadn't been able to argue; his lack of contact did look bad. 'I still think you're jumping to conclusions, Florrie, love. He was so fired up about having a tearoom here, and you saw what he was like about the staircase. Mark my words, he'll have a valid excuse for dashing off so suddenly – mind, I have to agree, he could've handled it better. He's definitely got more than a drop of his grandad's spontaneous nature about him. Dinah used to go mad about Bernard sometimes.'

Though Jean's words had offered a tiny glimmer of hope, Florrie still couldn't excuse the way he'd made her feel. It was as if she'd had her heart ripped out and given a thorough stomping on. Again.

The only highlight of Tuesday morning was when she received a text from Maggie telling her she was home and settling into her new routine with baby Lucy. It came with an invitation for her and the rest of their friendship group to call in and meet the new arrival the following day after the bookshop had closed. Much as she valued her friends' opinion on, well... everything, Florrie made a conscious decision not to mention Ed's disappearance to them. This was Maggie and Bear's time – and baby Lucy's – for celebrating the arrival of a much-longed-for baby. There was no way she was going to wade in and spoil it with her moaning and negativity.

'We've had a really weird phone call,' Leah said, joining Florrie in the kitchen.

'In what way was it weird?' Florrie's thoughts went straight to Ed, wondering if he'd try to contact her on the bookshop's landline. If he'd left his phone at home, it was more than likely he wouldn't remember her mobile number. In truth, she wouldn't know his off the top of her head, or anyone else's for that matter. And they'd had the landline at Samphire Cottage disconnected recently since they used it so infrequently, so he couldn't call on that number.

'Well, whoever it was that called sounded like they had their head in a metal bucket and were gargling under water.'

'Oh.' Florrie tried to imagine what that might sound like. 'That would've made for an interesting conversation.'

'They hung up before I could get any sense out of them.'

It had fleetingly crossed Florrie's mind that it might be Dodgy Dick or one of his lackeys in another attempt at spooking them by making creepy phone calls; there had been a couple yesterday and a handful on Saturday. Florrie had been too busy, her head too full of thoughts of Jean and Jack's offer and then the sleigh ride to pay much attention to them.

That evening, after Florrie had pushed away her half-eaten bowl of soup – her appetite had disappeared along with Ed – she headed up to the attic, hoping to find any clues as to what he'd been up to, what had made him flee so suddenly. Her heart sank at seeing the chaos again. *Why would he leave so hastily and with all his stuff in such a mess?* Feeling guilty at going through his paperwork, she tidied it all into a neat pile and set it beside the shelf where he kept some of his boxes. What she'd found hadn't revealed anything anyway, and had mostly been bumph about art exhibitions and old posters advertising them. Feeling utterly despondent, she headed back downstairs.

Just as she had the night before, Florrie had lain awake for hours, her head going over everything up to the point Ed had left. Each time, she came back to the same thing: the bookshop and his father's phone call. She'd convinced herself that, as keen as he'd originally been about Jean and Jack's offer, it had made him focus his mind on what he really wanted for his future. Made him realise, when it came down to it, he didn't see the bookshop in those plans. He was going to hand his share to his parents, or sell it to Dodgy Dick, and she'd have no choice but to do the same. There was no other explanation for it. And it made her sick with worry.

THIRTY-EIGHT
WEDNESDAY 20TH DECEMBER

Stella managed an early finish thanks to the defence barrister in the armed robbery trial she was prosecuting having suddenly taken ill. She'd sent round a quick text to the group of friends, offering them all a lift to Clifftop Cottage. Having recently switched her sporty Mercedes for a sleek Range Rover Evoque in a stylish shade of metallic grey she now had room for everyone.

'Were you being so savage in court, you frightened the life out of your opponent and made him ill?' Jasmine asked, when they were driving down Skitey Bank, making them all giggle. Her mum, now fully recovered from her stomach bug, had said she'd sit with Zak and Chloe while Jasmine popped out.

'Not at all. Aiken Ferdinand is very experienced, fights his corner. He'd been complaining of feeling rough in the robing room first thing. Thought he'd eaten something dodgy the night before. Poor Ferdy actually looked green when we were in court, so I'm amazed he managed to keep going as long as he did. The judge adjourned till tomorrow in the hope he'll be feeling better, but from the way he was looking I very much doubt it.'

Bear met them at the door of Clifftop Cottage, his huge shoulders filling the space, a beaming smile on his face.

'Hello, Daddy Bear,' said Lark, standing on her tiptoes to kiss his whiskery cheek.

'"Daddy Bear", I like that,' he said, his beam growing wider. 'Come in, lasses, Mags is dying to see you all.'

In the cosy kitchen, they found Maggie sitting on a cluster of plumped-up cushions in a rocking chair by the Aga, a little bundle snuggled up in her arms, their Labrador Daphne lying protectively at her feet. The warmth of the room stood in stark contrast to the bitterly cold temperatures that raged outside.

'Mags, congratulations! You look gorgeous,' said Florrie, taking in the picture of contentment before her. It was true – Maggie looked positively radiant, her cheeks flushed pink, her hair glossy. Florrie's heart filled with happiness for her friend, who'd been desperate for this day to arrive for so long.

A flurry of congratulations followed as Bear filled the kettle in readiness for an enthusiastic round of tea drinking and Maggie filled them in on what had happened after they'd made their hasty exit from Danskelfe Castle.

'Lady Caro was amazing and ever so calm. She just took control and got us there safely, saying to call her if we needed anything. She gave Bear her private phone number,' Maggie said in amazement.

'Quite a way to end the sleigh ride, Mags.' Jasmine giggled. 'Which, I might add, was a fantastic experience. I won't go on about how you all shouldn't have spent so much on the kids and me – which you did, by the way – but seeing the expressions on their faces was priceless. They haven't stopped talking about it. So, thank you all.'

'It gave us so much pleasure to see them enjoying them-selves too, Jazz. They're adorable children.' Lark gave one of her gentle smiles. 'And it was definitely something amazing to add to The Happy Christmas Memory Project. I'll bet Ed's still talking about it, too.'

All eyes turned to Florrie. She mustered up her best smile and said, 'He loved it. It's thanks to Stella for mentioning it, and it looks as though going over those bumps helped with this little one's arrival.' *Time to divert attention away from Ed and The Happy Christmas Memory Project.*

Which worked perfectly. While Maggie set to opening the pile of gifts they'd brought, each of the friends took a turn in holding baby Lucy, even Stella who'd sworn she was never going to have children, declaring herself allergic to them. 'Seems you're a natural, Stells,' Jasmine said, a knowing look in her eye as their friend got to her feet, rocking the little bundle in her arms, gazing down at her in wonder.

'You'll be next, flower,' said Maggie, waggling her eyebrows, when it was Florrie's turn for a cuddle.

'I'm not so sure about that,' Florrie replied, more lightly than she was feeling. A pang of loss squeezed in her chest and she pushed away the image of Ed that had loomed in her mind. She couldn't imagine that featuring in her life plan any time soon. Her heart twisted at the thought.

It was when she was driving home that she peeled off her brave face, let her act drop and allowed the tears to flow. And flow they did, leaving her all puffy eyed and snotty nosed. The hurt Florrie felt at Ed's unexpected departure went way deeper than the first time. It was going to take an age to get over him, if she ever could. She honestly had no idea how she'd managed to get through these last few days without breaking down and ending up a sobbing, crumpled heap on the floor. It was prob- ably why tears had started tumbling down her cheeks as soon as she was alone and well clear of Maggie's. As for getting a good night's sleep, there was no chance of that any time soon. She knew as soon as her head hit the pillow, her mind would start running over every possible reason Ed could have had to leave her again, just as it had done the last couple of nights, tormenting her way into the early hours and leaving her exhausted. She had no idea how she was going to tell her parents – they'd be devastated, too. As for poor old Gerty... Ugh!

THIRTY-NINE

As soon as Florrie arrived back at Samphire Cottage after visiting Maggie, she knew something was different. The usually still and silent air that met her whenever she returned home had been disturbed. Her heart started ricocheting around her chest. There was someone in her house.

Swallowing nervously, her thoughts went to Dodgy Dick and his nephew Dillon. She froze, her breathing becoming short. Where was Gerty? She usually hurtled down the hall to greet her even if she'd only been out for ten minutes. Florrie took a couple of tentative steps forward when the Labrador in question came bounding giddily towards her, her tail wagging so hard it was making her bottom wiggle. Relief rushed through Florrie – if there was anyone unsavoury in the house, Gerty wouldn't be behaving like this. It was probably her mum or her dad. They had a key after all, and her mum regularly dropped a casserole off for them. She bent to give Gerty a pat. 'Hello there, flower. What've you been up to?' Before she had a chance to straighten herself, a shadow fell over the hall carpet.

Florrie glanced up, her pulse racing, her mind swirling. 'Ed!' She was bombarded by myriad emotions: anger, relief, happiness, frustration. She didn't know which one to give vent to first, though she had a feeling anger would come out on top. She bit down on the tears that threatened.

'Hiya, Florrie.' He gave her a sheepish smile. 'Sorry I had to dash off the way I did, but I didn't have much choice and didn't have time to explain. Forgot my phone, too.'

'And you didn't think to call from a phone box or wherever it was you were staying?' She jolly well wasn't going to make this easy for him. She pulled off her hat and unwound her scarf, hanging them on the coat peg by the door. She could hardly bear to look at him.

'I tried actually – not your mobile number, I couldn't remember that – but I found the bookshop's number and rang that. Couldn't get through properly, though.'

What Leah had said filtered into her mind. Maybe the strange calls she'd told her about had been Ed.

'That aside, I just can't make any sense of why you took off the way you did, with no warning at all. What was I supposed to think?' Anger was making her breathing short.

Ed's face fell as he appeared to realise what she meant. 'Oh, no... you didn't think I'd gone?' He took a step forward but the stony look she shot him stopped him in his tracks. 'I didn't... I mean, I thought you knew how I felt.'

Was he for *real*? She threw her arms up in disbelief, her chest heaving. 'What the heck else was I supposed to think? You took off with no prior warning, just like last time.' She felt her bottom lip quiver, hurt rushing in, pushing anger out of the way.

He clasped his hand to his forehead. 'Florrie, I'm so sorry. How *stupid* of me, I should've thought. Is that why you've been crying? I was so wrapped up in what I needed to do, I didn't think how it might look. But I promise you, it's not what you're thinking.' His expression was so earnest, his eyes so pleading, she felt sure he must be telling the truth. At least, she hoped he was.

Before she'd had a chance to formulate an answer, he was standing in front of her, his hands on her shoulders, his eyes seeking hers.

'Come into the kitchen, let me explain. I'll make us a pot of tea. I've got something interesting to tell you. Well, a couple of things actually.'

When she didn't reply straight away, he said, 'Please, Florrie, you'll understand when you hear it. And I'm so sorry I've made you cry.'

Sitting opposite him at the kitchen table, Florrie listened quietly, her mug of tea growing cold before her, as Ed launched into his explanation. She noted he spoke slowly and carefully, being sure to choose the right words, anticipation reverberating through her.

He told her how her gentle suggestion that it might be better if he found out the reason behind his father's angry call had taken root in his mind, growing and gathering momentum until he could no longer ignore it. Overwhelmed by the urge to get it over and done with, he used the excuse of taking the car back to Samphire Cottage, where he could call his father and speak to him in private, without the risk of anyone overhearing.

What he hadn't expected was for his dad to tell him he'd just checked into a hotel in London, with the intention of calling his son to arrange a meeting. Ed's father was eager to speak to him face to face but didn't want to travel up to North Yorkshire, declaring there was someone he'd rather not run into.

'He must've been pretty desperate to speak to you for him to travel all this way,' Florrie said, panic setting in. She braced herself for what she was about to hear.

'Which is why I was in such a rush to leave as he was only

there until the following day – yesterday – and I didn't want to risk the trains being cancelled.'

'And was he okay with you?' Florrie hoped Ed hadn't been met with his father's usual rage and hot-headed style of communication.

'He got pretty het up at times, but he managed to punctuate it with some moments of calm, which meant he could explain what had been bothering him.'

She nodded, relieved to hear father and son appeared to have made progress.

But what Ed had gone on to tell her had stunned her and given her a different perspective on a situation. One she'd held Peter Harte in contempt for, for so many years.

It transpired that the reason for Peter's original fallout with his parents all those years ago hadn't purely been about money – though there was no getting away from the fact it had gone some way towards it. It was Ed's mother who had been reluctant to get involved in the bookshop, not that Peter had taken much persuading, with Dawn being the driving force behind their nomadic lifestyle. Peter had become angry with his parents when he overheard them talking about their involvement with Jean and her unborn baby. It horrified him that they'd orchestrated an illegal adoption. He'd accused them of being deceitful, of taking the law into their own hands. Who did they think they were? he'd asked, accusing them of being no better than criminals. He'd been so blinded by his outrage, he couldn't see the situation from their perspective: how they'd helped two lots of people and saved a whole load of heartache. If she'd kept her baby, Jean, as an unmarried mother at a time when it was frowned upon, would have been cast out by her family, while the family her baby went to would have more than likely ended up childless. In Bernard and Dinah Harte's eyes, that the infant had grown up in a loving family meant they'd done good, not harm. But Peter hadn't seen it that way and had washed his hands of his parents.

'From what I can gather, there was no way either of them would back down, and by the time the rot had set in, there was no going back. My father wanted nothing more to do with my grandparents and the animosity just deepened and festered over the years.'

'Goodness, I don't really know what to say.' It didn't come as a surprise to her that Mr and Mrs H hadn't mentioned the reason for the fallout with their son, since she hadn't known about the secret adoption until Mr H had passed away. And in fairness to them, they'd never bad-mouthed their son and daughter-in-law. All they'd done was express their sadness at not being in contact with them, and as a consequence Ed.

'I appreciate it's a lot to take in.'

Florrie nodded. 'But to go for so long and not make any attempt at moving forward seems a bit of a drastic reaction.'

'I agree, but I think it's got a fair bit to do with my mother not wanting to be tied to the bookshop – my dad said she always thought my grandparents were being controlling by hoping they'd take over the business. She's always been the one who's been keen to explore the world, has a spirit of adventure. But in fairness, my dad hardly dug his heels in and protested. I know he's no saint.'

You're telling me he's not.

The look Ed shot her made Florrie wonder if he could read her mind. 'And there's no getting away from the fact they were both crappy parents. He can't ever excuse that. Seeing how Jasmine is with Zak and Chloe, and how your parents are with you, just highlights how shocking they were.'

Not knowing how to answer that without sounding like she was being rude about his parents, Florrie gave him a small smile.

'I told him about what's been happening with the bookshop

and Dodgy Dick, and he said the creep isn't acting under their instruction.'

'What?' She wasn't so sure she could believe that.

'Apparently Dodgy Dick contacted them, saying he had a client who was interested in the bookshop and he wanted to buy it on their behalf, wouldn't listen when they told him they were no longer pursuing it.'

'Oh, yeah.' Florrie couldn't hide the cynicism from her voice.

'I know, that's what I thought.' Ed went on to say how Dodgy Dick had started to get more intimidating with every phone call, until he finally got the message they weren't interested. That seemed to tie in with when things started to happen at the shop: Dodgy Dick and Wendy's visit, the Christmas tree, the snow globe, and the power cut. 'My dad says he knew the slimeball would do all he could to get the property for peanuts and use his bullying tactics to do so.'

Florrie inhaled slowly. This, together with what Ed had told her about the reason behind the fallout between his father and grandfather, was a lot to take on board. 'I wonder if the "client" Dodgy Dick mentioned to your dad was Wendy. She seemed pretty keen for it to become a beauty parlour.'

Ed nodded. 'I suspect she was.'

Their eyes met. The sorrow she saw lingering in Ed's caused an ache in her heart. This couldn't have been easy for him, facing his dad, hearing about the life-long fallout that could so easily have been resolved instead of simmering and growing increasingly toxic as the years went by.

Ed sat back in his seat and released a long sigh. 'And there's more.'

'*More*?'

Ed nodded. 'It's the real reason my father flew halfway around the world to speak to me. Somehow – my dad wouldn't say how, didn't want to cause ructions for his contact who'd told

him in confidence – he found out about Jack's proposed autobiography, and that's what's sent him into such a tailspin.'

'Okay.' Florrie took a moment to process Ed's words. She
wasn't sure how word of Jack's autobiography could have spread
so quickly. From her understanding the author was only in early
talks with his agent and publishers. But then again, she
reasoned, things did have a habit of sneaking out, in no small
way thanks to social media.

'He's worried my grandparents' involvement with Jack's illegal
adoption is going to cause a "worldwide scandal". He and my
mother aren't just annoyed about it, they're deeply embarrassed
about it, too. They're worried the Harte name will be "irreparably
tarnished", as he said, and that they're going to be tarred with the
same brush, be vilified and chased out of their village. It's why he
called, full of hell, in the early hours – he'd just found out.'

'Wow! I'd never have guessed that as the reason in a million
years.'

'Me neither.'

'I can imagine it would generate a lot of interest in the UK,
particularly Yorkshire, but a "worldwide scandal" seems a little
dramatic.' She felt the prod of a memory. 'Ah, explains why I
heard your father mention Jean Davenport's name in the call.'

Ed nodded. 'Yeah, he was being unkind about her which is
the reason I didn't want to continue the conversation with him.
I have no time for nastiness like that.'

Florrie smiled. It warmed her heart that Ed was a thoroughly decent person and refused to get dragged into spiteful
gossip.

'Anyway, the upshot is that my parents want me to speak to
Jack, ask if he'd consider not identifying my grandparents as the
people who set up his adoption. They're okay with the bookshop being mentioned as some sort of link, though.' He
scrunched up his nose. 'Said he'd sue if his request was ignored,

but I'm going to keep quiet about that when I first broach the matter with Jack.'

'Yikes! Can't say I blame you. But knowing Jack, I can't see that being a problem.'

Ed nodded. 'That's what I thought.' He tapped his hands against the table, making Gerty jump. 'Anyroad, this tea's gone cold. How about I make a fresh pot? Then I can tell you the rest of the stuff we spoke about.'

'Oh, blimey, there's more?'

'There is, but nothing quite as shocking.' He flashed her a smile.

With fresh tea poured, Ed continued sharing the details of the meeting with his father.

After Peter had got his grievances and concerns off his chest, Ed had told him about Jean and Jack's business proposal. 'I actually told a white lie, said we'd already accepted it and that the wheels were in motion, just in case he tried to talk me out of it.'

'Really? You told him? What did he say?' Florrie braced herself to hear that normal hostilities had been resumed.

'Well, this is what surprised me the most. He didn't put up a fight, just seemed to accept it. Said if that's what we thought was best, then that's what we should do, especially if it got Dodgy Dick off our backs. He seemed genuinely wary of the bloke.'

Florrie was finding it difficult to absorb this latest revelation. Had she heard right? 'I wonder what his reason could be for such a dramatic about-turn?'

'I think I know the answer to that.' His face took on a serious expression. 'He had a health scare. Seems he has a problem with his heart – I couldn't get any further details. I got the impression he didn't like to talk about it.'

Sounds familiar! 'I'm sorry to hear he's been unwell.'

Learning of his father's illness couldn't have been easy for Ed, especially on top of everything else.

'From what I could gather from the little information he gave me, him getting himself so worked up the way he does hasn't been helping his blood pressure nor his heart condition. It's been quite the wakeup call by all accounts.'

'I can imagine.' Peter's irate phone calls sprang to mind, his voice screaming down the phone. It was a relief to think Ed wouldn't be on the receiving end of those anymore.

He reached across the table and took Florrie's hands in his. 'I want you to know, I'm really sorry about leaving the way I did. It was thoughtless of me, I just acted in the heat of the moment. I panicked when I'd heard my dad hadn't been well and booked the next available train to York then London. I'd intended to explain everything when I got there.'

'I can understand that, because I'd be exactly the same, but maybe if you'd given Leah a few more details, it would've stopped me worrying about why you'd hared off the way you had.' She wasn't going to give him a hard time about that; she'd down everything if she'd had such news about either of her parents, too. Wild horses wouldn't keep her from going to them.

'Message understood.' The smile he gave was all it took to extinguish any lingering anger she had. 'Am I forgiven?'

'Forgiven.' She smiled, the look in his eyes making her soften further. 'But you've got to promise me you won't go rushing off like that without a proper explanation, leaving me thinking all sorts.'

'I promise.'

He leant towards her, cupping her head in his hand, and kissed her, sending any residual doubts scattering. 'I love you, Florrie Appleton.'

Hearing those words sent happiness surging through her. 'I love you, too, Ed Harte.'

He flopped back, a smile spreading over his face. 'Why

don't we text Jean and Jack, see if they want to meet up at The Cellar tomorrow night? We can tell them we'd love to have them on board at The Happy Hartes Bookshop, seal the deal with a glass of fizz. The sooner we set things in motion, the better. Hopefully they won't change their mind when they hear about my dad's demands.'

'I'm sure they won't. If you remember, Jack actually asked if we'd be okay with him including us and the bookshop in his autobiography. He's respectful of people's wishes and I'm sure he'll understand.'

'Yeah, you're right.'

And just like that, her world was back on track.

FORTY

CHRISTMAS EVE

'Any idea of what you'd like to do today, or are you just fancying a chill in advance of the big day tomorrow?' asked Ed. They were sitting at the kitchen table in their pyjamas, munching on buttery oven bottom muffins, a large teapot of freshly made tea sitting between them.

'Hmm.' Florrie scooped a dollop of marmalade from the jar. 'I've got something else to add to The Happy Christmas Memory Project.' She gave him a mysterious smile.

'Something else? Haven't you done enough? The project is groaning with happy memories.'

'Another one isn't going to hurt.' She grinned as she bit down on her muffin, making Ed laugh.

'Fair enough. And are you going to give me any clues?'

'Nope. Only that you need to dress up warm, maybe put that Christmas jumper to good use again. Oh, and you'll have to stay out of the kitchen for an hour.'

'Oh, right.' Ed's eyebrows drew together in bafflement.

'All will be revealed when the time's right. You just need to be ready to go out at about one o'clock.'

'The plot thickens,' he said with a smile.

. . .

Bang on the dot of one o'clock, Florrie and Ed left the house, taking Gerty with them. Ed followed as Florrie headed towards the car, zapping it with the key fob. It was another beautiful wintry day with clear blue skies above. There'd been a light dusting of snow overnight, but nothing that would hinder Florrie's plans. She'd already been out earlier and had cleared the car's windscreen, giving it a thorough spraying of de-icer for good measure.

'Can you tell me where we're heading yet?' Ed asked, as she turned the engine on and set the air vents on full blast.

'Patience.' She grinned at him as she flicked the indicator and put the car into gear. A thrill rushed through her as she anticipated Ed's reaction to her latest plan in The Happy Christmas Memory Project.

Soon they were heading down the steep incline of Skitey Bank. Though the gritters had been out earlier, Florrie still drove cautiously; she didn't want to risk losing control of the car and have them careering down to the bottom prom, as some unfortunate driver had done the previous winter, ending up crashing into the wooden railings.

'We're going for a walk on the beach?' Ed said, when she pulled up in the seafront car park. Gerty peered gleefully out of the rear window, the prospect of a run along the sand making her shiver with anticipation. Most of the snow had gone there, with just traces by the edges of the wall and around the kiosks, the salty sea air making short work of it.

'Not just yet.' She stilled the engine and gave him a smile, her eyes glittering. 'But we need to get out here.'

'Okay.' Ed laughed.

'Right, it's this way.' Florrie hooked the backpack she'd taken to the car earlier over her shoulders. 'It's not far.' She slipped her gloved hand into Ed's and cast him a smile.

'I'm intrigued,' he said, grinning down at her.

A short walk later, she stopped outside a chalet painted a tasteful shade of duck-egg blue. A festive wreath hung from its door, the inclusion of seashells giving it a seaside twist. 'This is us,' she said, pushing the key into the lock and opening the door, while Gerty had a good sniff around the ground.

Inside they were greeted by an achingly cosy sight. The chalet's compact exterior belied the spacious room within. The walls were clad with white painted matchboard while the floor was covered with a rustic sisal carpet, in keeping with the location. At the back of the room was a set of built-in bunkbeds; to the right was a compact fitted kitchen painted a smoky shade of blue, as was the dining table and its two chairs. To the left was a lounge area with two small armchairs that flanked a wood-burning stove. The accessories had a tasteful seaside theme, with the soft furnishings in variations of blue and white, while watercolour paintings of Micklewick Bay beach and Old Micklewick adorned the walls. But best of all, the beach hut had been decorated for the festive season, and a small Christmas tree stood by the door, while twinkling fairy lights were draped around the walls, and a reed diffuser infused the air with the aroma of cinnamon and ginger.

'Oh, wow! This is amazing,' said Ed, looking around him in awe.

'I know. It belongs to Stella's mum. She said we could use it for today.' She went to plug in the electric heater Alice had told her about. She'd advised her to put it to use while the stove got going.

'She did?' Ed asked, looking puzzled.

Florrie slid the backpack off her shoulders and set it on the small kitchen countertop. She reached inside and pulled out a tub. Turning to him, she said, 'I've made us a picnic, a Christmas one. I thought it'd be fun.'

Ed's smile widened. 'A Christmas picnic? I can honestly say I've never had one of those before!'

'I'd originally planned for us to just have it in the car looking out to sea – I'd told the girls about it. Anyroad, Stells had mentioned it to her mum, who said we could have the use of this place, make more of an occasion of it. I don't know about you, but I think it's loads better than sitting in our little banger.' She laughed, thrilled it had gone down so well. She'd had a moment's doubt the night before, suddenly thinking it was a daft idea. But she'd reminded herself of the Christmas picnic her parents had surprised her with when she was a young girl and they'd driven to the moors and picnicked in the car as snow had fallen around them. It was one of her favourite Christmas memories.

'It's amazing. And very generous of Stella's mum.' Ed released Gerty from her lead and the Labrador trotted off, sniffing busily around the room. Ed headed over to Florrie, slipping his arms around her waist. 'And so thoughtful of you, Florrie. I really don't expect you to go to all this effort for me.'

She turned to him, reaching up and wrapping her arms around his neck. 'It's no effort at all, it's fun. I've loved thinking of things for The Happy Christmas Memories Project.' She pressed a kiss to his lips, still chilly from their short walk to the chalet.

'Well, I want you to know, I appreciate everything you're doing. I feel thoroughly spoilt.' He squeezed her tight. 'Is there anything I can do to help?' he asked, releasing her from his embrace.

'You could chuck this cloth over the table so I can set the food out, then you could maybe light the stove. I don't know what you reckon, but I thought it might be nice to keep the door open and set the chairs next to it. That way we can eat while looking out at the view. But if you think it'd be too cold, I'm happy to eat at the table.'

'I love the idea of looking out to sea, and we'll still be sheltered from the breeze.'

'Oh, and we need to pull a cracker each first, that's very important.'

'There are Christmas crackers, too?'

'Of course!'

'You've thought of everything.'

'I'll have you know, no Christmas picnic is complete without Christmas crackers,' she said with a faux serious face.

'Can't argue with that.' He grinned as he took the end of the cracker she was holding out to him, pulling it with a snap.

'And the rule is you keep your Christmas hat on till we're back home.'

'Happy to oblige.' Chuckling, Ed fixed his paper crown on his head.

'Suits you.' Florrie grinned at the ridiculously cheerful smile he was wearing.

With the picnic devoured – amongst other foodie treats, it consisted of turkey and stuffing sandwiches in fluffy white bread buns with a generous smear of cranberry sauce, pigs-in-blankets, mince pies and gooey mini chocolate Yule logs, washed down with a flask of tea – they sat back in their chairs, looking out at the dark-grey sea. White horses were breaking as waves charged to the shore, crashing noisily. Seagulls screeched overhead. One particularly vocal herring gull stood on the railings and cawed for all it was worth.

Florrie blew on her mug of tea, her thoughts meandering to the other night at The Cellar with Jean and Jack. They'd been in raptures at hearing the young couple had accepted their offer. 'It's a whole new chapter for The Happy Hartes Bookshop,' Jack had said as they'd clinked their glasses of fizz. 'Pun very much intended.'

Ed and Florrie had been inordinately relieved to find that Jack was understanding regarding Peter Harte's request to retain Mr and Mrs H's anonymity in their role in his adoption. 'I appreciate it's a highly sensitive topic and I'm very mindful of folks' feelings. Please reassure your parents I won't tell a soul.'

In turn, Florrie and Ed had agreed never to reveal to them the reason behind Mr and Mrs H's estrangement from their son, knowing how it would devastate Jean. She'd no doubt blame herself, which they didn't want. It wasn't fair to inflict such pain on a warm, kind-hearted person like Jean. She'd been through enough already.

'There's another reason I went to London that I haven't told you about.' Ed's words sliced through Florrie's thoughts, jarring with the happiness that only moments ago had her in its clutches.

Uh-oh. 'There is?' *Please make the reason be something good.* Her pulse started pumping hard around her body.

FORTY-ONE

Ed got to his feet and reached into his coat pocket, pulling out something indiscernible. 'I'd intended to save this for tomorrow, but I think now would be the perfect time.'

'Save what? Ed, why are you talking in riddles?' Florrie's mind was swirling again.

'I needed to get it fixed as soon as possible. I'd been looking for it for ages, thought I was never going to find it – it's what I'd been searching for in the attic. Anyroad, when I found it, I saw it had split. I've a friend who said he could fix it for me quickly, while everywhere else I'd asked said they couldn't do it in time. Only trouble was, he was in London and only there till Wednesday – he was flying out to spend Christmas with his girlfriend in Bruges. It all added to the urgency for me to get to London.'

'Oh right, I see – I think.' Florrie didn't see at all. She hadn't a clue where he was going with all of this gabbling. In fact, she'd go as far as to say she'd never seen him looking so antsy. 'Are you okay?'

'Never been better.' He flashed one of his smiles, raked his fingers through his hair and started shuffling from foot to foot, rubbing his hand nervously across his mouth.

Could've fooled me. She studied his face intently, growing more confused by the second. He took a long pause and swallowed audibly before throwing her an uncertain smile. *What the heck happened to him down in London that has made him behave so oddly?*

Ed reached for her hand and gently pulled her up from her seat. He took a deep breath. 'Okay,' he said to himself. 'Time to do it.'

Time to do what? And why is he suddenly looking so... so... weird? 'Ed, what's going on?'

He paused, ceased his fidgeting and drew in another breath, then turned his full navy-blue gaze onto Florrie, which made her stomach roll over unexpectedly.

'Florrie.' Another pause. 'You're nothing short of amazing. In fact, you're without doubt the most amazing person I've ever met. You've got the biggest heart – The Happy Christmas Memory Project is evidence of that. Who else would think of doing something so thoughtful and completely wonderful? I could go on and list a million other reasons to explain why I think you're so special, but we'd be here all day.' He gave a little laugh. 'So, what I really want to say is that I love you with all my heart. And...'

Florrie looked on, her mouth falling open as he got down on one knee, her thoughts scrambling together, trying to work out if she was hallucinating, or if he was falling. But neither would seem to be the case. She tried to speak, but found herself unable to form a single word. All she could do was look down at Ed's earnest face looking back at her.

Gerty pulled her eyes away from the remains of the picnic and threw Ed a cursory glance before turning her attention back to the food.

'Florrie Appleton, would you do me the honour of

becoming Florrie Harte – or Florrie Appleton-Harte, if that's what you'd prefer?' He opened his hand, a small, battered leather box sitting in his palm. He carefully lifted the lid to reveal an exquisite antique ring glinting up at them. The princess cut emerald flanked by two half-carat diamonds looked instantly familiar to Florrie: Mrs H's engagement ring.

'Oh!' She gasped, pressing her hand to her mouth. She hadn't been expecting any of this!

'Will you marry me, Florrie?' Ed asked hopefully.

'Yes!' She nodded, her eyes blurring with tears as her heart soared with a happiness she'd never thought possible. 'Yes! Yes! Yes! I'd love nothing more than to marry you, Ed.'

'Woohoo!' he cried at the top of his voice, making Florrie laugh. In the next moment, beaming broadly, he slid the ring onto her finger. 'I guessed it would be a bit loose on you and would need adjusting, which we can get done at the jewellers in town, but I didn't want to propose to you with a ring that had a split in the band.'

'I wouldn't have minded,' she said, gazing down at her hand as Ed pulled himself upright.

'Yes, but I would. It wouldn't have felt right.' He gave a gentle smile. 'It's my grandma's engagement ring, but if you'd rather have something new or—'

'I love it, Ed. I can remember your grandma wearing it and I always thought it was beautiful. Lark would say it's full of happy energy from all the years your grandparents were together. For so many reasons, it's the most perfect ring.' She could barely tear her eyes away from it. *So this is what he'd been looking for when he was spending all that time in the attic!* It couldn't be any further from the reason her fears had led her to believe.

He cupped her face in his hands. 'I don't know about you, future Mrs Harte, but I think this rounds up The Happy Christmas Memory Project rather nicely.'

'I think it rounds it up perfectly. In fact, I'd say it's the most perfect Christmas memory of them all.'

'I had to play a part in making some, I couldn't leave you to do all the work,' Ed joked, before kissing her deeply, her stomach performing a series of somersaults.

'I only wish my grandfather could have been around to see this day.' He heaved a wistful sigh when they finally came up for air, wrapping her in his arms and holding her close.

'Oh, I don't doubt for a second that Mr H – AKA *Cupid* Harte – is looking down at us wearing the *biggest* smile and congratulating himself rather smugly.' Florrie wished they could stay in this moment forever, wished she could bottle the joy in her heart, be able to lift the lid and savour every delicious emotion all over again.

'Yeah, I think you could be right.'

EPILOGUE

WEDNESDAY 27TH DECEMBER

'Come in!' Stella threw open the door to her apartment. She was looking stunning as ever in a velvet knee-length shift dress in a rich shade of midnight blue, the fabric rustling as she moved. Her blonde hair was sculpted into a neat French pleat and her make-up had been expertly applied, complete with a flattering smoky eye. 'Everyone's here, even Jazz!' She gave Ed a quick peck on the cheek before pulling Florrie into a hug that smelt of her friend's crisp floral signature perfume.

Stella usually hosted what she referred to as a cocktail party in the week between Christmas and New Year, opting for a day she knew all of the friendship group would be available. This was the first such party in her fancy new apartment with stunning views out to sea, stretching right along to Thorncliffe.

Stella hung up their coats while Florrie and Ed kicked off their boots – there'd been more snow that day so they'd opted for their wellies in case it continued. They followed their statuesque friend down the hall and into the open-plan living room, where a large contemporary electric fire flickered with surprisingly realistic faux flames and subtle music murmured away in the background. The dining table was laden with artfully arranged nibbles, while a large Christmas tree occupied the space between the two glass doors that led out onto the balcony. It was draped in cool white lights and studded with baubles in various shades of grey, with the odd one in silver tones punctuating the mix and giving the colour palette a lift. The tasteful décor of the space reflected Stella's personality perfectly: minimalist with an undertone of warmth.

Florrie and Ed were greeted by a cheerful chorus of hellos and wide smiles, making them feel instantly welcome.

Florrie's gaze travelled around the room, excitement racing inside her, so desperate was she to share their news. Lark and Nate were looking cosy together on one of the large, L-shaped sofas – *they're so meant to be together* – Jasmine sitting on the sofa opposite next to Alex's twin sister Zara who'd become a regular visitor and had plans to move to the town. Bear was chatting to Alex who stood at the kitchen peninsular where an assortment of bottles and glasses were set out, mixing drinks for Jean and Jack who'd arrived only minutes before Florrie and Ed.

'S'good to see you survived Christmas,' said Maggie, heading over to Florrie, smiling warmly. She was looking voluptuous in a deep-red maxi dress with its plunging neckline, her dark curls framing her face. 'You're looking gorgeous, flower.'

'Thanks, and so are you. In fact, you look amazing.' Florrie felt positively dowdy in her simply cut aubergine knee-length dress – though Ed had told her she looked beautiful when she'd done a twirl for him at home just before they headed out.

'Oh, and please excuse the baby sick on my shoulder. It was a parting gift from Lucy as we dropped her off with the in-laws. I didn't have time to change – or anything half-decent to change into, for that matter, while my boobs are the size of over-inflated watermelons. Nowt fits at the minute.' Maggie chuckled as she swept Florrie into a hug that oozed warmth and happiness with a hint of newborn baby thrown in.

'TMI, Mags,' said Stella, feigning an expression of disapproval. 'Anyway,' she said, addressing Florrie and Ed, 'Alex is chief cocktail maker, so if you let him know what you fancy, he'll impress you with some fancy drink-mixing moves.'

Alex obliged by pulling a mock-cool pose and throwing a cocktail shaker up into the air. Everyone burst out laughing when he reached to catch it but missed and the metal container hit the kitchen floor with an almighty clatter.

'I should point out, when I said *impressive*, that's not what I had in mind,' Stella deadpanned as Alex chuckled.

'And how was your first Christmas as parents?' Florrie asked, looking between Maggie and Bear.

'The best ever,' said Bear, beaming broadly. 'Little Lucy's an angel – the most perfect baby.'

'I'll second that but add exhausting,' said Maggie, picking up her glass of virgin mojito. 'But I wouldn't change it for the world.'

'We've been dying to know how the Boxing Day Dip went,' said Jasmine, sipping a long vivid blue drink through a straw once greetings had been exchanged.

'Ooh, yes, Nate and I saw the pictures on the town's social media pages. You both looked fab in your pantomime dame costumes.' Lark chuckled.

'Aye, you did that,' agreed Nate. 'We'll show you later on.'

'Ugh!' Ed gave an exaggerated shiver. 'I've never been so cold in my life! I swear I still haven't fully defrosted.'

'I take it your name's top of the list for next year's dip.' Jack gave a throaty chuckle.

Ed looked horrified. 'No way! Never again!' He gave Florrie such a pointed look he had everyone laughing.

She returned it with a wide grin, 'You know you don't mean tha—'

'Hang on just a minute,' said Stella, eyeballing Florrie and slicing off her words. 'What's that I see, madam?'

All eyes turned to Florrie as Stella reached for her left hand. Florrie's heart leapt, her face growing warm with the joy of being able to share her news. She caught Ed's eye, his happy smile setting her insides alight. 'It's an engagement ring. Ed proposed.'

'Oh, wow! And it's absolutely gorgeous,' said Stella.

'And I can't tell you how relieved I was when Florrie said yes,' Ed said, struggling to make himself heard through the resultant cheers and whoops that were bouncing around the room. The women rushed over to Florrie, taking it in turns to deliver heartfelt hugs and kisses, while words of congratulations rang out. Florrie had no idea it was possible to feel this much happiness.

'Huge congrats, lovey, Bernard would be over the moon to know his greatest wish had come true.' Jean Davenport pressed a kiss to Florrie's cheek, her face damp with tears of joy.

'Thank you, Jean.' Florrie smiled, emotion making her throat tight.

On top of this joyful news, Florrie and Ed had finally managed to get the message across to Dodgy Dick that they wouldn't be selling the bookshop to him, or anyone else for that matter.

They'd been walking Gerty along the top prom earlier that day when his four-wheel drive slowed down, creeping along and keeping pace beside them. The blacked-out window slowly inched down, sending a shiver of goosebumps over Florrie's skin.

'I hope you two have been giving my offer plenty of thought. I'm a patient man, but I don't need to remind you that this year's drawing to a close and time's running out.' Dodgy Dick's smirk that followed made Florrie's blood boil.

Ed turned to him. 'Actually, Dick, we don't need to wait

until the New Year to tell you our decision, we can do it right now.'

Dodgy Dick puffed himself up. 'I'm pleased to hear it. I'll see to it that the documents are drawn up quick sharp.'

'That won't be necessary,' Florrie said, a strange mix of pleasure at delivering the news and fear at how it would be received making her heart pump fast.

'What d'you mean?' The businessman's smile momentarily faltered.

'We're not selling. In fact, we've only recently gone into partnership with some well-heeled investors. And I can tell you for a fact, selling their shares, or agreeing to us selling the business is the last thing they're interested in. Like Florrie told you on your recent visit, we've got big plans for the bookshop's future, and our new investors are keen to support it in any way they can.'

Dodgy Dick's face fell. He brought the car to a halt. 'What?'

'We never wanted it anyway.' Wendy's voice spilled out of the window. She pushed her husband back, glaring out at them. 'We've found somewhere far superior to your shabby little building. So you can stick it where the sun don't shine as far as we're concerned.'

'Why, thank you,' said Ed.

'We're pleased you've found somewhere more suitable.' Florrie so desperately wanted it to be true.

'Oh, and I don't suppose you know who could be sending us bits of smashed up snow globes or yanking down Christmas tree above the bookshop door, do you? The police are onto it, but we've been asking around, too. Interestingly, the same names have been cropping up. It's looking like there's a family connection with the little cherub who threw water over our till.'

Stella's words of warning about not getting on the wrong side of Dodgy Dick surfaced in Florrie's mind, sending a pulse of alarm rushing through her. She willed Ed not to say anything further.

'I know nowt about what's been going on at your poxy little bookshop. And I wouldn't be seen dead going in there now. I'll thank you not to trouble me about it anymore.' With that, the window rolled up and Dodgy Dick went to race off with a dramatic wheelspin, but the car stalled with a noisy splutter instead.

Florrie and Ed walked away, snorting with laughter.

'What a turkey,' said Ed. 'I reckon he got the message.'

'Let's hope so,' said Florrie.

'Look at that sky,' said Ed, his words floating out in a cloud of condensation. They were making their way home, hand in hand, after Stella's cocktail party and had paused a moment on the top prom. Frost was sparkling on the ground, the chilly air pinching at their skin.

'It's beautiful.' Florrie tipped her head back, taking in the vast expanse of inky-black studded with millions of twinkling stars that stretched out above them. The iridescent glow of the pale moon shimmered on the sea below. It made for a magical sight. It was only then did she realise they were standing beside Mr and Mrs H's bench. 'Oh, look where we are.'

'I know, it's why I stopped here. I just needed a moment with my grandfather.' Ed smiled down at her before tilting his face heavenwards. 'I know you and I didn't have much time together, Grandad, but I loved every single one of the minutes we shared.' His chest heaved as he sucked in a deep breath. 'And thank you with all my heart for leading me to Florrie. I'll be forever grateful.'

'Oh, Ed.' Florrie leant into him, resting her head on his shoulder, following his line of sight. 'Thank you, for bringing Ed to Micklewick Bay, Mr H.' Her voice was thick with emotion. 'I know I wasn't best pleased at first, but now I'm ever so glad you did.'

Just then, a cloud floated across the sky and large featherlike snowflakes started swirling down.

'I reckon he heard us,' she said, blinking back tears.

'I reckon he did,' Ed said softly, their eyes meeting as he kissed her tenderly.

A LETTER FROM THE AUTHOR

Huge thanks for choosing to pick up *Christmas at the Little Bookshop by the Sea*. I hope you were hooked on the latest instalment of Florrie and Ed's adventure. If you'd like to hear about my new releases with Storm Publishing, you can sign up here:

www.stormpublishing.co/eliza-j-scott

If you'd like to join other readers in hearing all about my new releases and bonus content, you can sign up for my newsletter!

www.elizajscott.com

If you enjoyed this book and could spare a few moments to leave a review, that would be hugely appreciated. It doesn't have to be long, just a few words would do, but for us authors it can make all the difference in encouraging a reader to discover our books for the first time. Thank you so much. If you click on the link below it will take you right there.

It wish I could say that writing a Christmas visit to The Happy Hartes Bookshop was my idea, but it hadn't even crossed my mind – I've no idea why, I *love* writing festive books! Instead, credit for this festive instalment must go to my lovely editor, Kate Gilby Smith, who suggested it in our very early talks about the series. Thank you, Kate! Since then, and during the writing of *Finding Love in Micklewick Bay*, it had been bubbling away at the back of my mind, and I was thrilled when I was finally able to give it my full attention and put pen to paper.

I do hope you enjoyed your festive trip to Micklewick Bay, catching up with Florrie and Ed – and the rest of the gang. I was thrilled when the idea of Jean and Jack's involvement with the bookshop came to me (I'm so excited to find out how their plans for the bookshop's future pan out!), not to mention Jack finally finding love with Jenna – as usual, inspiration for both of these plotlines struck during a spot of weeding in the garden! And it felt good to tie up the loose ends with Ed's father, Peter, and finally get to understand what has made him so cantankerous after all these years – not that it excuses his behaviour, by any means!

I really enjoyed researching another book in the *Micklewick Bay* series, and having the opportunity to head back to the beautiful towns and villages that line the North Yorkshire Coast – as I mentioned in book one, my fictional town of Micklewick Bay is actually an amalgamation of these places. Starting with the Victorian seaside town of Saltburn-by-the-Sea, with its grand houses that boast panoramic views of the beach and the sea, not forgetting the magnificent Huntcliff. It's thanks to this lovely town that Micklewick Bay has its pier and funicular, and if any of you are familiar with Saltburn, you've probably guessed Huntcliff is the inspiration for my Thorncliffe. The quaint little fishing villages of Staithes, Runswick Bay and Robin Hood's Bay are the places I had in mind when writing about Old Micklewick, with their characterful houses that just ooze charm. I've spent many happy hours wandering their cobbled streets, ice cream in hand, keeping a watchful eye for those pesky seagulls – my daughter recently lost her lunch to one! The bustling harbour town of Whitby must also get a mention, not least because of its delicious fish and chips – many portions of which were consumed in the name of research!

www.elizajscott.com

Bluesky: @elizajscott.bsky.social

[f] facebook.com/elizajscottauthor

[X] x.com/ElizaJScott1

[O] instagram.com/elizajscott

[BB] bookbub.com/authors/eliza-j-scott

ACKNOWLEDGMENTS

Here's where I get to say thank you to everyone who's helped get *Christmas at the Little Bookshop by the Sea* ready for publication. I'm going to start by saying a massive, heartfelt thank you to my wonderful editor, Kate Gilby Smith, for her unwavering support and enthusiasm. Kate is an utter joy to work with, her edits are kind and insightful, and her positivity is infectious – a conversation with Kate, whether it be by email, phone or on screen, always leaves me with a happy smile on my face! As I mentioned earlier, it was Kate who came up with the idea for *Christmas at the Little Bookshop by the Sea*, so I owe her an enormous thank you for that, too!

Next up, I owe a great big thank you to Storm's fab Editorial Operations Director, Alex Holmes, whose formatting skills are second to none! Thank you for getting all of my books ship-shape and ready for publication day, Alex. Your patience is much appreciated (apologies for all my tweaking!).

In fact, I'm grateful to the whole amazing team at Storm, including head of digital marketing, Elke Desanghere and publicity manager, Anna McKerrow for their work in promoting the Micklewick series. Big thanks for securing the Little Bookshop BookBub, Elke!

Thanks are also owed to eagle-eyed copyeditor Shirly Khan and proofreader Amanda Rutter for their part in the editing process and giving this book the polish it needs in readiness for publication day.

Once again, thank you so much to Melanie Crawley for her

wonderful narration of the Micklewick Bay audiobooks. As soon as I heard Melanie's voice, I knew she was perfect for the series! I could listen to her all day!

As always, a great big thank you goes out to the awesome Rachel Gilbey of Rachel's Random Resources for organising another fabulous blog tour. I've lost count of how many blog tours Rachel has arranged for my books, but I'm always impressed by her amazing organisational skills. Thank you, Rachel!

Which leads me nicely on to the next shout out, which goes to the wonderful band of bloggers who've taken part in the *Christmas at the Little Bookshop by the Sea* blog tour. I'm truly grateful to them for giving up their time so generously to read and review my books as well as featuring them on their blogs or Instagram – especially so close to Christmas when other things will be demanding their attention! Sending out much love, and an enormous thank you all!

Now it's time for me to say a mahoosive thank you to my fabulous author friends Jessica Redland and Sharon Booth, whose unwavering kindness and support means more than I can ever say. I always look forward to our catch-ups – I promise it has absolutely nothing to do with the fact that scones and cake usually feature! Jessica and Sharon are both genuinely warm-hearted and utterly wonderful, and I'd be just as happy to meet up with them if no cakes or scones were involved at all!

It goes without saying that I owe an enormous thank you to my family, who uncomplainingly (well, *most of the time!*) put up with me disappearing into my little writing room and staying there for hours on end (maybe they like the peace and quiet!). Thank you also for the endless supply of writing fuel in the form of tea and ginger biscuits. You're stars!

Next up, I owe a warm thank you to the beautiful places I've named above for providing me with so much inspiration, not forgetting the residents for their friendly welcome.

My final thanks go to you, the reader, for taking the trouble to pick up my book and read it. Thank you so much for being a part of this journey with me; I really am truly humbled and grateful. I hope you'll stay in touch and follow the further adventures of the friends in Micklewick Bay.

Wishing you all the merriest of Christmases and every good wish for the New Year.

Much love,

Eliza xxx

Printed in Great Britain
by Amazon